THE Gentile

AND THE Jew

A DIVINE ROMANCE

THE

Gentile
AND THE Jew

Marilyn Denny Thomas

Pleasant Word

Edited by Edie Veach

Front cover art by Pamela Suran

The characters in this book are fictitious; however, historical information and figures are included. The endnotes provide annotation and source information for further study of non-fictitious elements.

Printed in the United States of America

ISBN 1-4141-0580-0
Library of Congress Catalog Card Number: 2005908603

Dedication

This book is lovingly dedicated to my beloved husband,
Ricky Thomas,
who exemplifies the very best of
Mike, Isaac, Tom, Abraham, Solomon, Jordan, and Aron,
all wrapped up in one.

Acknowledgments

I would like to thank all those who encouraged me in writing this simple love story, especially my husband, Ricky Thomas, and my daughters, Joelle Thomas and Jodi Fucili. Much of Carrie Jernigan's character comes from the combined hearts of both my daughters and my two lovely granddaughters, Anna Brown and Blair Taylor.

Many thanks go to dear friends who read the early pages and encouraged me to keep on writing and telling the story, particularly Ruth Wallace, Ann McMahon, Patty Juster, Rudene Kennedy, Beverlie Brewer, and my faithful friend, Della Futrell.

Special thanks goes to Ann Dalton, a new friend and talented author of children's books, who believed in me and proved it.

I would like to thank my editor, Edie Veach, who poured into this work so much more than I ever expected from an editor. She is a true jewel with whom I hope to work on many future projects.

Lastly, very special thanks for inspiration go to my firstborn grandchild, Anna Brown, who left home for college as this manuscript went to press.

Prologue

The boy was freezing. Just a little fellow no more than six or seven years old, he had run outside to help Papa bring in some of the firewood he had chopped earlier in the day. They had hauled the heavy logs from the forest just outside Bucharest with a borrowed horse and cart. Waiting patiently for Papa to load his thin arms with a log or two, he suddenly heard the roar of a diesel truck as it rounded the corner and came barreling down the narrow street, screeching to a stop just in front of their small home. Within a matter of minutes, the Fascist legionnaires had rounded up as many of the Jewish men in the neighborhood as they could find, herding them like animals into the back of the huge vehicle, packing them in with those already loaded. While the boy stared in disbelief, clutching the splintery log against his chest, Papa became one of the herd.

The evil-looking black truck roared off down the street, leaving him with only one thought: *I have to go with Papa.*

He was able to keep up with the screeching truck but only because it made stops all along the narrow cobblestone street. The frightening, uniformed men shouted and screamed as they pushed and shoved the Jews toward the back of the truck. He watched from a safe distance as the horrible men, who looked something like soldiers, slammed the butts of their guns into the faces of their stunned victims, knocking them to the ground, only to then order them to get up and climb into the truck. On and on the monster truck drove through the streets, screeching and halting and then roaring off again. Its terrified cargo stared in stunned silence at the homes and family that might never be seen again.

At the edge of the city, the boy ran faster and faster, desperately trying not to lose sight of the vehicle that held Papa in its evil clutches. He was close to losing the race when the truck suddenly stopped just inside the sparse forest where he and Papa had gone to cut wood that very morning. He hid behind a big tree; his heart pounded in his ears; his whole body shook like the leaves must have when they had fallen but were now lying still beneath the snow.

The uniformed men shouted again—yelling and screaming, shoving the men out of the back of the truck onto the frozen ground. Many were not even wearing coats. Having been rounded up so quickly, they hadn't had time to prepare for the cold. But, it didn't matter. Within a matter of minutes, none of the one hundred and twenty-seven Jews were wearing their coats, or anything else. They were stark naked, standing in long rows among the leafless trees.

The little boy stared. He had never seen Papa or Grandpapa naked. Something inside him said it just wasn't right to see people without their clothes, especially all together with so many other naked people. He closed his eyes for just a second, trying hard to be polite, yet still desperate to spot his Papa and run to him.

And that's when it happened.

In the frozen forest, empty but for the terrified herd of innocent human beings and their unknown enemy, the ear-shattering noise of the machine guns echoed so long the boy thought it would never stop. Both hands covered his ears, and his eyes were tightly shut. By the time the horrendous noise subsided, the black truck thundered down the road back into Bucharest.

The little boy slowly opened his eyes. There on the forest floor before him, looking to the six-year-old as if they were skinny trees just toppled by the wood cutters and laid in long neat rows, were one hundred and twenty-seven naked bodies. Their bright red blood poured through the cold white snow onto the frozen ground. He watched the blood spread quickly across the forest floor, the soil too frozen to receive the innocent sacrifice, seeming as if the earth itself was refusing to be a part of the evil that had been done there that day.

He walked slowly, desperate to find Papa. Surely he was still alive. Only an hour earlier, he and Papa had stacked wood in the backyard while Mama and his grandmother were at the market trading eggs for flour and fresh vegetables. Of course Papa was alive. Why shouldn't he be? Who would want to hurt his gentle Papa?

But the little fellow was terrified. What if he had to look into the faces of all those bodies before he could find Papa? He felt dizzy. He could feel the

Prologue

sour vomit rising to his throat. But, strangely enough, he couldn't scream for someone to come and help him. He couldn't even cry for Papa. So he kept walking toward the bodies. He was almost there, close to the first body. Then he saw the eyes. Suddenly, he turned and ran. And ran. And ran.

Chapter One

An early winter storm charged into Chapel Hill during the night and now rivers of icy sleet were pelting the skylights as Carrie glanced up from her curled-up position on the comfortable old sofa her mother had given her. Pushing her long brown hair back from her face, she snuggled deeper into the cozy cushions and rested her eyes on the printed page. Content to be home with a good book on her only day off, she forced herself to pace her reading in hopes the book would last until dinnertime at least, but after a few paragraphs, her thoughts began to wander. She suddenly realized she had lost track of the once interesting story. Memories invaded her mind in waves like battalions of soldiers on a battlefield, mercilessly lancing the open wounds in the broken heart she was trying desperately to ignore.

Only a few weeks ago, Carrie had been hopelessly in love—in love with life and in love with a good-looking guy who seemed absolutely perfect. She had been content with the ordinariness of her life throughout her twenty-three years. Her parents had worked hard to send their three children to college where each one had worked a few days a week to supplement tuition and lodging. Now that she was in graduate school, Carrie continued to work in the little Corner Cafe where Charlie, the owner, treated her as if she were his own daughter. She didn't mind working. In fact, she enjoyed the hours spent waiting tables in the little cafe in the quaint university town that often reminded her of the miniature village her mother placed under the Christmas tree every year.

The Gentile and the Jew: A Divine Romance

Tree-lined streets wound up and down rolling hills while beautiful old homes cuddled the wide southern sidewalks. In early spring, colorful azaleas and dogwoods flanked lovely wrought-iron gates and white picket fences, painting the little village like a Thomas Kincade canvas, inviting visitors to come and drink in the beauty that swelled around each curve of the shady streets. By the first of June, delicate white gardenias released their powerful fragrance throughout the town, followed by rainbows of annuals and perennials, guarded in late July by the bright pink explosion of hundreds of crepe myrtle trees.

Autumn in Chapel Hill was Carrie's favorite season. The colors of spring and summer couldn't surpass the brilliant yellow maples and red dogwoods protecting the golden chrysanthemums that grew abundantly in nearly every yard in town. Even winter boasted its own stream of color as holly berries, nandinas, sasanquas and camellias mingled with an amazing assortment of evergreens, each releasing its own delightful aroma into the cold, winter air. With its ancient oaks and historic buildings, the university campus flowed into the picturesque little town, and like a beehive and its honey, the town and campus became one.

Carrie was good at what she did—waiting tables, talking to the streams of interesting people who wandered into the Corner Cafe each day, even helping Charlie with the books from time to time. She was a good student as well, possessing an innate love of learning and her parents' philosophy that it takes a lot of hard work and pure common sense to accomplish anything in life.

Although life had seemed lovely and kind and gracious to Carrie, it quickly and without provocation turned on her. She found herself experiencing an unexpected free-fall—that sense of falling that you get when you're having a nightmare and can't wake up. Suddenly, she hit bottom and found a horde of dreadful enemies awaiting her—among them were loneliness, despair, and the worst demon of them all, depression. Most psychologists would likely say that many slide into depression, slowly becoming more despondent each day, but Carrie had taken a quick fall, hitting rock bottom with a loud thump, feeling as if her little storybook world had disintegrated before her very eyes. And now the merciless memories continued their assault as the winter storm kept its charge outside her apartment window.

Carrie remembered when she first noticed the tall, attractive guy with the darkest eyes she had ever seen. She recalled the times he sat down in his usual spot in the back booth by the porthole-shaped window in the Corner Cafe. He often came in with his best friend. They talked guy talk, laughing and eating with equal gusto. Then there were days when he seemed to meditate in the booth by himself, a book open on the table beside his sandwich, his eyes roaming from the book to the window and back again. On those days, she noticed his food seemed to take third place to the book and the world outside the little round window.

I have some good memories, too, she thought, tears filling her eyes as she stared blankly at the book.

"Dit dit dit DA! Dit dit dit DA!"

Carrie's cell phone ringing to the tune of Beethoven's 5th shocked her out of her reverie. She tumbled onto the floor and jumped up to search for the tiny persistent contraption that never seemed to be where she thought she had left it.

"Dit dit dit DA! Dit dit dit DA! Dit dit dit DA!"

By the time Carrie found the phone deep in the pocket of the coat she had thrown across the wing chair, the aggravating thing stopped ringing. She hit *Caller ID*, and the knot in her stomach jerked in pain as the familiar number glared up at her like a blinking neon sign.

Oh, no—not again! I can't talk to him now! I just can't!

She hit the off button and dropped the little phone back into the pocket of her coat. The indention she made on the sofa beckoned her back to her cozy nest, but even though the last pages of the mystery novel were awaiting her return, Carrie had lost interest. She flopped down on the couch, tossed the book on the floor and pulled the green chenille throw around her shoulders as hot tears began to seep into the soft down pillow.

"Hey, Jordan, wait up!" Mike yelled across the parking lot.

"Don't have time, man," Jordan yelled back as he jumped on his Harley and shifted gears. "Got an appointment with my advisor in five minutes. Can't be late! See you at the cafe at three!"

Jordan had been Mike's best friend since high school, soon after the Kramers had moved from Long Island to Wilmington, North Carolina. During the first week of the tenth grade, the two boys were assigned to the same table in earth science lab and positioned as partners on the track team. They often joked that they had been thrown together against their wills, but they had quickly developed a close friendship that had lasted through three years of high school and four years at the University of North Carolina at Chapel Hill.

They were now completing their second year of graduate school. Jordan was earning a Master's in Political Science, preparing to enter law school next fall. Mike was working on a Master's in Journalism, not quite sure what he wanted to do after he received his degree, but definitely planning on pursuing faraway places and exciting adventures. He wasn't about to spend his life cooped up in some windowless office in his father's business, or anyone's business for that matter. It wasn't that he was proud, aspiring to be famous or powerful. Mike just wanted to do something unique and exciting with his life, something that would make a difference in the world. He knew Carrie felt the same way, and they talked about the possibilities for hours on end as they meandered down the sidewalks of the charming university village.

Monday morning arrived all too quickly. Carrie's swollen eyes gradually opened to the bright morning light flooding through her bedroom window. As she had done hundreds of times since she was a little girl, she reached her hand into the bright sun rays pouring across her bed. Carrie could almost feel the light as she slowly turned her hand from side to side, fascinated by the thousands of tiny particles that couldn't be seen any other time dancing merrily in the morning sunlight. This particular blue Monday morning, the shaft of light was especially welcome in her dark and dreary world.

She rolled over, squinting her eyes to see the clock face, suddenly remembering that exams were over and the Christmas holidays had begun. *No classes! What a relief!* Even though she had to work longer hours in the cafe, Carrie felt spared not to have to see Mike in class everyday. Her plan was to stay in town five more days and then join her family in Banner Elk for the Christmas holidays. The Jernigans had never celebrated Christmas away from home but since the family had grown so large, they had decided to rent a big log cabin in the picturesque mountain town and gather there for Christmas this year. Although Carrie's heart was aching, she looked forward to being with her family, thankful she didn't have to face friends and neighbors at home just now.

An hour later, she was hard at work in the busy restaurant.

"Carrie! Could you get the table by the front window?" Charlie breezed by with a tray in each hand. He could have retired years ago and lived very well, but he would have died of boredom. The Corner Cafe was a world of his own creation, and he loved every inch of it, no matter the headaches a self-run business naturally brings.

"Sure, Charlie." Carrie set off with order pad in hand to the sunny booth facing Franklin Street. Checking her customers along the way to see if they needed anything, she didn't notice who was sitting in the booth until she raised her head to ask for the drink order. Her eyes caught Jordan's, and for an instant, she was too surprised to say anything.

"Jordan! I didn't expect to see you here," Carrie almost stuttered.

Chapter One

"Hello, Carrie. Good to see you," Jordan murmured, trying to speak quietly so that the couple in the next booth couldn't hear what he said.

"You, too, Jordan," Carrie said quietly. "I've missed you."

"How long are you going to be in town?"

"Just a few more days. I'm going to be with my family in the mountains for Christmas. Will you be going home for the holidays?"

"Oh, yeah, you know my Mom. She would have fits if I didn't come home for Christmas. When I'm seventy and she's ninety-five, I'll be right there with Mom, singing "Jingle Bells" and holding Dad's shaky hand while he carves the turkey."

Jordan's description of future holidays brought a big grin to his countenance and even Carrie smiled as she pictured him at seventy, holding his Dad's trembling hand. Jordan was truly a great guy and such a clown. She couldn't help but think how much she would miss him now that she and Mike had broken up.

"Carrie! Order up!" shouted Charlie.

"Uh, oh! I forgot what I was doing. I know you want sweet iced tea even in the dead of winter. Be right back." She was gone before he could tell her that Mike was meeting him in the cafe in just a few minutes.

Too late, Jordan thought. He watched Carrie hurry away, wondering what could have possibly caused his crazy friend to lose this prize-winning girl. He would award her a blue ribbon any day. In his opinion, Mike had made one mistake after another with the girl he claimed to love.

Seconds later, the bells on the cafe door jingled as Mike strode in with a gust of cold air. He caught sight of Jordan immediately and quickly slid in the booth, clapping his friend on the shoulder.

"Hey, man! How did it go with your advisor?"

"Okay, I guess. He says I should have no problem getting some pretty good scholarships and grants, but I won't know for sure until the first of the summer."

"I knew it would work out. You just don't know how smart you are, my friend," said Mike, pumping his right arm into the air.

Jordan grinned and then suddenly remembered Carrie was in the cafe working his booth. Not knowing how to approach the subject, he blurted out, "Mike, Carrie's here."

"Whoa. I thought she had already gone home for the holidays." Mike was thoughtful a moment, looking around for Carrie. "I'd better just slip out before she sees me and meet you for dinner at the Rat."

The Gentile and the Jew: A Divine Romance

"Too late. She's coming back with my tea, and she hasn't seen you yet." Jordan looked worried. "Mike, I know you don't want to talk about it, but what really happened with you guys?"

"We just have some differences that need to be ironed out. That's all." Mike ignored his friend's concern as he had for weeks. The wall he had erected around himself was too high even for his best friend to scale.

Carrie looked up just in time to catch her breath before she got to the booth. Confusion invaded her mind like an army of hornets. She didn't know whether to run to the fray or away from it while the glass of tea shook so hard it spilled over her hand and onto the floor. When she regained her senses, she was angry at Jordan for not telling her that Mike was coming, but her top priority was to gain control of her emotions by the time she got to the booth. She didn't want to face Mike—not now, maybe not ever.

"Hi, Mike. How are you?" Her voice was not quite steady.

"Hey, Carrie. I'm okay. How about you?"

"I'm fine. What can I get you?" she asked, pretending she didn't know his usual choice of beverage.

"Coffee with sugar. Don't you remember?" Mike was hoping she would look at him so he could see her eyes and, hopefully, tell how she really felt.

But Carrie couldn't look at him. Instead, she gazed at the pad in her hand and asked for their food order so she wouldn't have to come back any more than necessary. Then she was gone.

Mike struggled to keep his mind on what Jordan was saying, but he caught himself following Carrie with his eyes as she waited on customers and picked up orders. He had always loved to just sit back and look at her, especially when she didn't know it. He was glad she didn't look like one of those Stepford cheerleaders or big wheel sorority girls. Yes, she was different, but he couldn't have explained it, even now as he watched her wait on tables—her long brown hair pulled up in a clip for work and her blue-green eyes smiling at anybody and everybody. What he wouldn't give to hold her in his arms once more, but he didn't know how to repair the breach. What's more, he didn't really understand why she was so angry with him anyway. He couldn't help it if his parents were stuffy and religious.

"Carrie!" called Charlie, nearly bumping her with a large tray piled with plates of food. "Order up!"

Carrie quickly grabbed his arm. "Charlie, could you please take that order for me? It's for the booth by the front window."

One glance in that direction told Charlie all he needed to know. "Sure, honey. Don't worry. I'll take care of it."

Chapter One

"Thanks, Charlie. You're the best."

"And don't I know it!" he answered with a big grin.

Never in a million years would Carrie have guessed that religion could have separated her from Mike. In the few months they had been going together, falling deeper in love every day, the young couple had often skimmed the subject of religion, but along with other topics too numerous to mention, it was placed on a shelf for a more appropriate time. They naively thought they'd get around to it some day.

Carrie had been born into a large Southern Baptist family in a small town in eastern North Carolina, growing up surrounded by mostly Protestant friends and teachers. Although she knew very little about Judaism, her Baptist upbringing and training had given her a great respect for the Jewish people, her church leaders often speaking of their Judeo-Christian beliefs. But Carrie didn't know any Jewish people and neither did her family and friends. In fact, she couldn't remember ever having met a Jew before her college years, and even then, Mike was the first Jewish person she had ever known personally.

A couple of weeks after she and Mike started seeing each other, Carrie made a two-hour visit to the University library, curious as to why Jews seemed to be so scarce in eastern North Carolina. Much to her surprise, she discovered a long Jewish history in the State's coastal plain. She read that in the eighteenth and nineteenth centuries, Jewish peddlers had traveled from farm to farm throughout the South, selling their wares to homemakers living far from cities and stores. When the small settlements grew into villages, then into towns during the late 1800's and early 1900's, many of these Jewish salesmen settled down to raise their families and open dry goods stores. In later years, many of the small stores developed into department stores. If the stores were successful, they developed into department store chains.

Toward the end of the twentieth century, Jewish population in the smaller southern towns began to decrease when the new generation began to move to the larger cities because of the decline of business in Small Town USA. Obviously, the ease of travel lured shoppers to the big cities, but in eastern North Carolina, the demise of the tobacco markets was a major catalyst, causing many downtown areas to become ghost towns. But Carrie's life in rural North Carolina had never brought her in contact with even the smallest Jewish communities in the region.

University life changed all that. Young men and women from all races and faiths flocked to the beautiful old campus at the beginning of each semester, their lives intermingling with teenagers just like themselves who came from very different backgrounds. Every persuasion of religion in the book was

The Gentile and the Jew: A Divine Romance

represented in the little village as is true of university towns the world over, creating a unique small town experience. Carrie accepted this phenomenon just as easily as she accepted the Chinese take-out and the Mexican Cantina. It was exciting to brush past people of different races and cultures each day and listen to the interesting accents spoken in her college classes. She believed this incredible exposure would be the beginning of a life of adventure and purpose. What's more, she only had to travel two hours from home to experience this incredible cultural exchange.

As for Mike, he had often admired the striking waitress in the Corner Cafe, her long brown hair swinging as she walked from table to table smiling sweetly at her customers, her blue-green eyes gazing into his on the days she worked the back booth. She was always too busy to say anything other than, "Hi, how are you today?" So the two had not officially met until they found themselves seated next to each other in a Journalism class. Mike couldn't keep his eyes off her, and although he was very much an extrovert, it took him three days to gather enough courage to introduce himself. Carrie was too shy to speak first so she was greatly relieved the day he stuck out his hand and said, "Hi, I'm Mike."

They walked out of class together that day and continued seeing each other for the following three months, falling deeply in love throughout the cool autumn days. By the time their discussions gradually turned to religion and Mike found out Carrie was Christian and Carrie discovered Mike was Jewish, the two young people were too emotionally bound to see a problem. It wasn't that they weren't concerned at all about their differences—they were, but the old cliché, *Love is blind,* is often painfully true, especially when the issues are as old as time. Mike assured Carrie their religious backgrounds didn't matter. They agreed on the basics after all. Even Mike believed there should be some set of absolutes. All was well....

Then came Thanksgiving. The love struck couple felt it was time to meet their respective families, and since their hometowns were just an hour or so apart, they decided to visit both sets of parents, driving down to Carrie's family home that morning to have an early lunch. They would then continue down to Wilmington to join Mike's family for a late dinner and a long weekend.

The day started out perfectly. Mike picked Carrie up at her apartment at eight-thirty, giving them ample time to enjoy the two-hour drive to Duplin County. Late autumn in eastern North Carolina isn't as colorful as New England or the Appalachians, but it's still beautiful, the air just cool enough for a sweater and a fire in the fireplace, but not too cold to enjoy the outdoors. While Mike drove along Interstate 40 and the last of the golden leaves swirled

Chapter One

across the highway, they talked of all the exciting places they wanted to travel some day, holding hands and risking a kiss now and then as they enjoyed the sunny autumn day.

The large Jernigan family was eager to greet Mike and Carrie with open arms, children spilling out of the two-story farmhouse like bees from a hive. Carrie had an older brother, John, and an older sister, Michele, each of whom was married with two and three children respectively. Mike had met John briefly when he stopped by the campus to see Carrie during a business trip, but he had never met Michele or Carrie's parents. The grandparents were there, too, peering out the window as Mike pulled the car onto the asphalt driveway.

Quickly easing out of the Mazda, he ran around to open the door for Carrie. Mike held her arm protectively as they walked to the house, the Jernigan clan quickly descending upon them, everyone talking excitedly at the same time while each one tried to be the first to hug Carrie and to greet Mike. He was a little overwhelmed by the big family greeting, but being the sanguine fellow he was, he handled it very well. Carrie hugged everyone and teased each child as little hands reached out to hold hers, trying to pull her into the back yard to play games.

"Whoa, whoa, bitsey ones!" Carrie shouted to the children. "Let me at least get in the house and see everyone first. We'll play some more after the feast. I'll have more energy then."

Mike smiled as he watched Carrie with the excited children. He loved kids, too, but he had no plans for them in his life anytime soon. There was too much to see and do right now. Besides, he and Carrie were young and had plenty of time to think about children in the far distant future. Why was he was thinking about children when they hadn't even discussed marriage? *I'm getting ahead of myself*, he thought. But, if there was one thing Mike was sure of, it was that he loved Carrie Jernigan with all his heart, and thoughts of proposing to her were inching their way into his consciousness day by day.

Carrie's mother and father walked into the foyer and greeted the couple with welcoming hugs. Her Dad, Tom Jernigan, smiled at Mike as he shook his hand and then led him into the living room where the grandparents waited with beaming faces. Mike felt like royalty as Papa and Nana ended the explosion of hugs with their big double one and led him to the couch by the fireplace.

Never had a day begun and continued to be more perfect. Mike met John's wife, Claire, and their three children, Matthew, Nick, and Abigail; Michele's husband, Ron, and their two children, Blair and little Luke. Mike told Jordan later that he felt like a little ball being bounced in and out of a crowd of

The Gentile and the Jew: A Divine Romance

chattering smiley faces. But he could tell that this lovey-dovey stuff was not just for his benefit—it was real.

Catherine Jernigan and the girls were in and out of the kitchen and dining room as Nana supervised the placing of mouthwatering dishes on the long table set with her mother's white Irish lace tablecloth, silverware, and the good china. Carrie felt her place was in the living room with Mike for his first visit in her home, so she sat beside him on the couch and enjoyed the lively bantering between the men in her family.

Mike fits in very well, she thought, nearly bursting with happiness.

What a friendly family, thought Mike. His family was never as demonstrative as this. It was a little overwhelming, but...yeah, he could get used to it.

A few minutes later, Carrie's Dad caught his wife's eye and stood up to call everyone to the dining room for Thanksgiving Dinner.

"We added smaller tables to the dining room table since our family is overflowing these days," said Tom Jernigan with a chuckle, smiling down at the cluster of little people at his side. "Why don't we all hold hands now and say the blessing, and then everyone can find their places and help yourselves to Nana's and Catherine's famous cooking?"

Adults and children alike stretched out their arms to reach the closest relative's hand, creating a big family circle to give thanks to God for all their blessings. Tom Jernigan prayed, "Thank you, Father, for all the many blessings you have bestowed on our family this year, for a prosperous year. We thank you for warm houses to live in and for the food on our tables. We acknowledge that all our blessings come from You, and we are eternally grateful for all You are and all that You do for us. Thank you for sending Mike our way and bless his time here with us. We pray in the Name of Your Son, Jesus Christ. Amen."

The entire family loudly echoed Tom's "amen" and then rushed to find their places at the long table filled with everything from turkey and dressing to collards, rutabagas, butter beans, corn, cranberry sauce and chocolate pie.

But Mike didn't move. He suddenly felt extremely uncomfortable, almost miserable. He knew Carrie and her family were Christian, but for some reason he had never taken time to think about what being a Christian really meant. Christianity was a world religion, but Jesus was another matter altogether. *Who was this Jesus anyway? God's son? Could God have a son?* From the untold hours he had spent in Hebrew school growing up, he remembered one particular scripture that was quoted over and over again, *"Hear, O Israel, the Lord your God is one God, the Lord is one."* How then could God have a son when God was God and God was one? It didn't even make sense.

22

Chapter One

Throughout his adolescence, Mike had listened to his father and uncles (one who was a rabbi) debate questions like this hundreds of times, but he had never paid much attention to them, thinking all those religious arguments were a ridiculous waste of time. It would all work out and add up in the end, and there was no need to argue about such things. He had decided early on that he wasn't about to get too involved in his family's Judaism, or any other religion for that matter. Why should he? Religion had never done much for any of his ancestors as far as he could tell, no matter what his mother said.

"Tolerance and acceptance," his religion professors said. "Each human being worships a higher power in his own way, and no way is any more acceptable than the other."

Christ..., Mike pondered. *I think that's the Greek word for Messiah. Hm. Here I am about to complete a master's degree, and I don't know this stuff.* He thought Christians believed Jesus is a prophet or a holy person. He didn't realize they believed he's the Messiah. *Israel's Messiah? How could that be?*

Leaning close to his ear, Carrie whispered, "Mike, are you all right?"

Jolted from his contemplation, Mike whispered back in a rather shaky voice, "I'm fine." But he knew he wasn't fine. He wasn't fine at all. He was suddenly an oddball in this very nice, loving family, and he had no idea why he felt that way.

During the drive to his parents' home later that afternoon, Carrie again noticed how quiet and thoughtful Mike had become. He was usually the talker of the twosome.

"It isn't like you to be so solemn," Carrie said. "Can't you tell me what's bothering you?"

"I'm sorry. I guess I'm just a little overwhelmed by your big family. They're really great, but it takes a little getting used to." Out of the corner of his eye, he saw her face fall. "Hey now, don't worry! I liked them. I really did. I just hope you'll like my family as well, although they're...well...different."

"Of course I'll like them. But, what do you mean by *different*?" Carrie asked.

"I don't know. Just different." Mike grew unusually quiet again.

She wondered just how different Mike's family could possibly be. Most people in North Carolina were basically the same. Everyone in the entire South for that matter. Various temperaments and personalities, yes, but not foundationally different.

Oh, well, I'm sure it's just because my family is so big, she concluded.

But as Mike turned the car through the stone columns into the winding driveway leading up to the Kramer home, Carrie's eyes widened and her mouth fell open. Except for the basics, such as how many siblings each had and the names of brothers, sisters, mothers and fathers, Mike and Carrie hadn't talked about their families very often, preferring to spend their hours discussing politics, current events, travel and their exciting dreams for the future. But now, as her eyes drank in the affluence of the estate, Carrie realized that she had definitely not grasped the full extent of the Kramers' economic status. This was *different*.

The paved driveway curved way back off the wide avenue, leading to a large, rambling, gray cedar and stone house built in the French Country style. The lawn was neatly manicured, and huge stone pots of yellow chrysanthemums welcomed them at the intricately carved mahogany door. Mike grasped her hand and held it tightly as he reached for the antique lion's head door knocker.

He's more nervous than I am, she mused, glancing at Mike out of the corner of her eye. He was looking around as if he wasn't sure he was at the right place. *What's wrong with him*, she wondered?

Soon after the resounding knock, Mike's father opened the heavy door, his wife, Rachel, standing by his side. The resemblance between father and son was striking, the same broad smile spreading over Mr. Kramer's features as he reached out to take Carrie's hand.

"Come in, Carrie. We're so glad you could join us."

He's still a very handsome man with his dark hair and eyes, she thought. *I'm probably seeing Mike in about twenty-five years.* Carrie shook Mr. Kramer's hand and thanked him for inviting her to their home for the weekend.

Turning to Mike's mother, she tried hard not to stare. Rachel Kramer was undoubtedly the most beautiful woman Carrie had ever seen. She couldn't remember ever having seen such stunning green eyes set off by smooth, radiant skin and rich auburn hair all pulled back in a pearl clip at the base of her neck. She was wearing tailored black slacks and a white silk blouse open at the neck, revealing an emerald Star of David pendant that set off her sparkling green eyes even more. She was very gracious, but more reserved than her husband, Isaac.

She might be a little more difficult to warm up to, thought Carrie, as she took Rachel's lovely manicured hand.

"Welcome to our home, Carrie," said Rachel Kramer.

"Thank you, Mrs. Kramer," Carrie responded, feeling warmly welcomed even though the hugs and laughter of her big family were conspicuously missing.

"Come on in," said Isaac Kramer, moving aside to allow them entrance into the large, polished slate foyer. "You look lovely, my dear. Mike's a smart fellow just like his ol' Dad." Carrie didn't miss the warm look Mr. Kramer gave his beautiful wife.

As she blushed profusely, Isaac Kramer smiled and took Carrie's arm, leading her into the living room where Mike's sister, Sarah, and her new husband, David Klein, were waiting. While the introductions were being made, Carrie suddenly realized that Mike hadn't followed them into the living room. She turned around just in time to see him reach down and clasp a tiny little girl in his arms, lifting her up to his face to rub noses and softly say, "Annie, what big eyes you have!"

"The better to see you with, my Mikey," peeped the tiny child.

She seemed no more than three years old and was obviously very special to Mike. But Carrie couldn't remember him having mentioned a little girl in his family. Surely, she would have remembered if he had.

Mike thought of Carrie just in time to catch her eye as she stared at Annie, still tightly wrapped in his arms. The smile he gave her was a little sheepish, but she smiled back with a questioning look in her eyes and turned to answer the question Mr. Kramer was asking, "Where are you from, Carrie?"

"Duplin County, Mr. Kramer, about sixty miles northeast of Wilmington."

That's strange, Carrie wondered. *Surely Mike told his parents where my family lives. Oh well, maybe Mr. Kramer's memory is slipping.*

Mike came over to sit beside Carrie with Annie still in his arms, but just before he plopped into the plush sofa, Mrs. Kramer took the little girl from his arms and announced, "Time for bed, my darling. Say 'goodnight' to everyone."

"Night, everybody. Don't go away, Mikey. Be here when I wake up?"

"Yes, Annie," Mike gently replied. "I'll be right here. Sweet dreams, honey."

"Sweet dreams, Mikey. Sweet dreams, Carrie," Annie said, looking at Carrie with big brown eyes edged in the longest eyelashes she had ever seen. "Night, Sarah. Night, David."

"Love you, Annie. See you tomorrow," said Sarah.

What a precious child, Carrie thought. *But, who could she be?*

As Mike's mother left the room with Annie, Carrie felt Isaac Kramer's eyes watching her, and as if he read her mind, he said, "Rachel and I were lonely in this big house when Mike and Sarah went away to college, so we decided to adopt a child. Annie has been with us since she was a newborn baby, and she's filled our home with joy and laughter. She especially adores Mike and counts the days until he comes home."

The Gentile and the Jew: A Divine Romance

"How wonderful," Carrie responded. "She seems to be such a sweet little girl. Maybe I can get to know her better tomorrow."

"That's very kind of you, Carrie," said Isaac. "I'm sure she would like that."

"Well, Dad, how are you?" Mike asked, changing the subject a little too quickly, Carrie thought.

"I'm fine, thank you, son. The business is doing well, and Annie keeps your mother and me on our toes. How about you? One more semester to go, eh?"

Mike could tell where his Dad was going with that sentence—straight to the old argument about joining the Kramer Company when he completed his master's. "Let's not get into that now, Dad. You know how I feel."

Carrie thought she glimpsed hurt in Mr. Kramer's eyes as his son abruptly cut him off. Mike had told her he and his Dad disagreed on what he would do after graduation, but she hadn't expected him to be so short with his father. Isaac Kramer seemed like a nice guy to her.

Quickly turning to Sarah and David, Mike asked, "How was the honeymoon, you two? I know it's been a while, but I haven't seen you since the wedding."

"Wonderful," they chorused.

"The Caymans are perfect in September, Mike, and we couldn't have asked for better weather," said Sarah. "The beaches are fantastic. The water is incredibly blue and clear like transparent aquamarine, far out into the sea, and the sand is white and soft under your feet. We really had a great time."

Gazing at her new husband with adoring eyes, Sarah reached for his hand. She had completed her Master's in Education last spring and had spent the remainder of the year working on wedding plans and helping David supervise the building of their first house. He had graduated from law school two years earlier and now worked in his father-in-law's company, being groomed to be the top legal advisor in a few years.

Because David's family was much more extensive than Sarah's, the bride and groom had decided to have their wedding in eastern Connecticut in the community synagogue where David's father served as rabbi. Mike had asked Carrie to go with him to the wedding, but since it was in the middle of the semester, she had decided it wouldn't be wise to miss two days of classes and work, too, so she stayed behind, waiting to meet Mike's family at Thanksgiving. She had pried him with questions about all the details of the elaborate ceremony and reception when he returned from the wedding, but he had said very little. Attributing his lack of response to a "man thing," she hadn't thought much about it. Today, reclining on elegant antique furniture in his beautiful family

Chapter One

home on what could easily be called an estate, and meeting a little sister Mike had failed to mention in their three months together made Carrie begin to wonder if there was anything else he hadn't told her.

Exhausted from traveling and the activities of Thanksgiving Day, Carrie woke up late on Friday morning to find herself cuddled under a warm down comforter in a high four-poster bed covered by a tailored canopy that matched the blue toile spread. She stretched her arms wide and snuggled back under the plush covers, turning on her side to study the elegant surroundings. By the wall across from the bed stood an antique walnut highboy, obviously the dominant piece of furniture in the room yet not overpowering. In the corner next to the elaborately draped windows which coordinated with the toile bed covering, an off-white chaise lounge was placed at just the right angle for guests to see out the window into the gardens below while receiving light to read at the same time. Original Impressionists' paintings of all sizes, framed mostly in gold leaf, filled the walls along with lightly ornate lighting fixtures. Along the wall parallel the bed stood a black, hand-painted Chinese secretary furnished with an ivory and silver pen set and stationery engraved with an elaborately scrolled *K*.

The room was elegant beyond anything Carrie could have imagined. But as she lay perfectly still, she suddenly recognized the most unfamiliar yet powerful effect of the room. It was totally quiet. Her family home was never quiet. If anyone desired privacy at any hour, day or night, he would just have to hide somewhere or wear earplugs. Carrie concluded that the silence in the beautifully decorated guest room not only enhanced its elegance but was a unique component of the room's design.

She lay back on the down-filled pillows one more time, her mind meandering through the memories of yesterday, finally coming to rest on a mental picture of the little girl, Annie. Again she wondered why Mike had never mentioned having a little sister. He obviously thought the world of her.

Carrie dressed quickly and walked over to the window for a quick glance down into the courtyard before she hurried downstairs to join Mike and his family for breakfast. She couldn't help but smile when she caught sight of Mike and Annie playing hide-and-go-seek in the garden below.

They do adore each other, she thought, watching Mike counting to ten, his hands covering his eyes. *I guess I'm a little jealous, but I'll just have to get over it and learn to love Annie, too.* She was surprised to discover she was jealous of a three-year-old.

The day turned out to be lots of fun. Carrie did get to know Annie and realized very quickly that she couldn't help but love the delightful little girl.

The Gentile and the Jew: A Divine Romance

After a ballgame with Mike, the merry little soul took Carrie on a guided tour of her mother's lovely late autumn gardens until noon when Rachel called them in for a light lunch in the warm yellow sun room. Mike's Dad had left for his office around eight so he could get enough work done to be back home with the family well before dinner. When Rachel Kramer announced that it was Annie's nap time, the young couple went with David and Sarah to see the house they were building in one of Wilmington's new developments off North Market Street.

"We're so happy to finally meet you, Carrie," Sarah said, turning toward the back seat of the black BMW.

"Me, too, Sarah," Carrie responded. "I'm sorry I missed your wedding. I was really looking forward to it, but there was just no way I could make it with classes and work."

"That's all right," replied Sarah. "We understood your situation. At one point in the planning, we thought about having a November wedding when everyone would have had more time off from school and work, but then we would have missed Thanksgiving, and we wouldn't have missed this holiday with all you guys for anything. You're just supposed to be home at Thanksgiving."

"Yes," David joined in, "Thanksgiving in the South is very special, don't you think? I guess we New Englanders should be the ones to go all out for Thanksgiving, ours being the land of the Pilgrims and Indians, but there's just something about Thanksgiving in the South."

"I agree," said Carrie. "It's always been my favorite holiday—other than Christmas, that is."

She had been gazing out the window at the lovely new homes as they talked, but the sudden silence that followed her statement drew her eyes back to David and Sarah just in time to espy the curious look they were giving each other.

Now, what in the world does that mean, Carrie wondered, turning to study Mike's reaction to the situation. But his head was turned to his side window, and she couldn't see the concerned expression on his face. He was quiet again, very quiet, more quiet than she had ever known him to be. This was the guy who usually dominated conversations, even with Jordan, the clown. *What's with him all of a sudden?*

Carrie enjoyed the guided tour of David and Sarah's beautiful new home more than they would have guessed beforehand. Having considered a career in Interior Design as well as Journalism, she loved architecture in general. But there was just something about a house, any house, and the thought of turning walls and floors and windows and doors into a home excited her to no end. She wanted to see and talk about every detail of the new house, so suffice it to say, the tour took much longer than originally planned. Sarah and David were surprised and delighted by her interest.

Sarah and Carrie had returned to the kitchen for the second time when David shouted from the living room where he and Mike were discussing the pros and cons of gas logs versus a wood-burning fireplace. "Sarah, you girls come on! It's almost Shabbat, and we have to get back to your parents' house well before sundown."

Almost what? Shabbat? What's shabbat? Carrie hadn't a clue what David was talking about. She was wondering if she should ask what he meant when she turned and caught Sarah staring at her.

Seeing the confusion on Carrie's face, Sarah was about to ask what was wrong when she suddenly recalled what Carrie had said during the drive to the new house—*Christmas was her favorite holiday*. Of course, Sarah began to put two and two together. She didn't want to embarrass Carrie, but she knew it would be better in the long run if she said something now, so she quietly asked, "Carrie, I hope you don't mind me asking, but...you're not Jewish, are you?"

"No...no, I'm not. I'm Christian, and I'll have to admit that I don't know much about Judaism, but knowing Mike's liberal opinions toward religion in general, I just assumed his family felt the same way. I'm sorry I must seem so ignorant, but I guess I really am. I didn't realize being Jewish made your everyday lives any different than mine."

"No, no! It's okay, Carrie. Don't worry. Mike should have told you what to expect." Sarah's questioning look faded as her face filled with sympathy.

Why does she look as if she feels sorry for me? Carrie wondered. *I'm a quick-study. I'll just bone up on all this stuff, and then I'll fit right in.*

The ride back to the Kramer home was filled with polite conversation laced with moments of uncomfortable silence. To make matters worse, for the first time in their short but intense three-month relationship, Mike seemed a thousand miles away.

As David drove the BMW onto the long, curving driveway, Carrie once again turned her attention to the beautifully landscaped grounds of the Kramer home. *This is a different world than I'm accustomed to*, she mused. Once again, she recalled Mike's words as they were driving to his parents' home the day before. *Different*. He did say his family was different, but he hadn't explained. She thought at the time that he wasn't really sure himself *how* they were different, but now it seemed that he just didn't want to talk to her about it.

This isn't fair, Carrie thought angrily. Not only was it unfair, it was embarrassing. Why hadn't he told her what to expect? She just couldn't understand Mike putting her in such an uncomfortable position. She glared at him bitterly, soon turning her head to hide the stinging tears quickly filling her eyes.

The weekend went downhill from there.

Being observant Jews, the Kramer family prepared for Shabbat with a reverence Carrie had never experienced other than in church. The entire house had been cleaned under Rachel's oversight earlier in the day, and now unfamiliar but delightfully fragrant aromas were coming from the kitchen as the two young couples entered the lovely house through the back door.

Leah, the maid who had been with the Kramer family for nearly twenty-five years, greeted them excitedly, waving a long spatula in the air. "You children better hurry up and get ready! Your Mama's been looking out the window for an hour, and she's ready to light the candles. You know better than to be late for Shabbat!"

"Don't worry, Leah, we'll hurry." Sarah rushed by, giving her dear old friend a quick hug and a kiss on the cheek.

The two couples ran upstairs to freshen up and then hurried back down to find Rachel and Isaac Kramer waiting impatiently at the beautifully decorated dining room table.

"Shabbat Shalom!" Mike's father greeted the young people.

"Shabbat Shalom!" everyone chorused—except Carrie.

The older Kramers' expressions were not exactly amiable, she thought, quickly taking her place beside Mike. She only had a few seconds to wonder about the two candles on the table in front of Rachel and the lovely lace scarf on her head when Mike's mother began to pray in Hebrew, the ancient language of the Jewish people,

"Baruch atah Adonai, Eloheynu Melech haolam,
asher kid'shanu b'mitzvotav v'tzivanu l'hadlik ner shel Shabbat."

Rachel Kramer sang the haunting blessing that had welcomed the Sabbath through the voices of Jewish mothers throughout the ages. Proclaiming the blessing again in English, she waved her hands over the candles, welcoming the Sabbath into their home.

"Blessed are You, Adonai our God, Ruler of the Universe,
Who hallows us with Mitzvot,
and commands us to kindle the lights of Shabbat."

Chapter One

As the family responded, "Amein," Carrie's eyes filled with tears. *How beautiful*, she thought. *It's as if the Sabbath were a special person being welcomed into this home. No...not a person...it's as if the Sabbath were God Himself.*

Rachel gracefully sat down and Isaac rose to bless the bread and the wine.

"Baruch atah Adonai, Eloheynu Melech haolam,
hamotzi lechem min haaretz.
Blessed are You, Adonai our God, Ruler of the Universe,
Who causes bread to come forth from the earth.
Baruch atah Adonai, Eloheynu Melech haolam, borei p'ri hagafen.
We praise You, O Lord, our God,
Ruler of the Universe, for the fruit of the vine."

Isaac thanked God, giving Him honor that He provided for us by giving us the bread of the earth and the fruit of the vine. Isaac's deep, resonant voice seemed to reach heaven and earth as the sound filled every recess of the large house. Carrie didn't fully understand why she was so moved, but she knew she was privileged to experience a ceremony that was thousands of years old, one that gave God preeminence in the everyday lives of the Jewish people. Although it would be a long time before she could have explained it to anyone, she sensed that in some mysterious way, these blessings were part of her own faith as well.

Antique china and silver serving dishes filled with roasted chicken, potato latkes, green beans, *challah* and the most delicious soup Carrie had ever tasted were passed around the lovely table until everyone had filled their plates. She had been so touched by the blessings that she hadn't noticed Rachel Kramer's stunning green eyes darting back and forth between Carrie and Mike all during the passing of the food. But Sarah had noticed and was perplexed at how to save Carrie from the inevitable. As much as she loved her brother, she was disappointed and even a little angry at him for not preparing Carrie for her introduction to his family.

"I just don't understand Mike," Sarah had said to David during their brief moments upstairs before dinner. "He's never been interested in religion, but what was he thinking to leave Carrie in the dark about our traditions? More importantly, why didn't he explain to her that Mom and Dad expect him to marry a Jewish girl? He hasn't even told them Carrie is a Christian! I could just hit him over the head and yell, 'Wake up, Mike!'"

The Gentile and the Jew: A Divine Romance

"The food is delicious, Mrs. Kramer," Carrie exclaimed happily, blissfully ignorant of all the uptight nerves at the table. The Shabbat blessings had touched her heart and lifted her spirit so much she was actually beginning to forget her concerns and enjoy being with Mike's family once again.

"I've never had this wonderful soup before. What's it called?" Carrie asked.

You could have cut the instant silence with a butter knife. Sarah stared at her mother while Rachel Kramer stared at Carrie and Mike stared at his plate. David reached over to hold Sarah's hand, and Isaac Kramer drew himself up to his full height, awaiting Rachel's inevitable question.

"It's Matzo Ball Soup, of course. You're not Jewish, Carrie?" Rachel's question sounded more like a statement—or a court sentence to be more precise.

"No..., I'm a Christian. Didn't Mike tell you?"

With that question, the silence seemed to become so thick it paralyzed everyone at the table, especially Mike who continued to stare down at his plate, moving his food around with his fork as if nothing was going on. The whole room seemed suspended in time until a forgotten little voice asked the next dreaded question, "What's a Christian, Carrie?"

"We'll talk about that later, Annie," Rachel quickly cut in. "Let's just eat our dinner now."

Saved by the Annie Bell, Mike murmured to himself as he lifted his fork and began to go through the motions of eating the delicious food that suddenly tasted extremely bland in his dry mouth. The only noise in the elegant dining room for the next fifteen minutes was the sound of clinking silverware and Annie's happy little voice as she summarized her morning ball game with Mike and Carrie. She didn't seem to notice that no one else at the table uttered another word or even dared look at anyone but her.

Waking up in the lovely guest room early Saturday morning, Carrie couldn't help but recall how serenely happy she had been only yesterday as she had lounged in the big canopied bed dreaming of her future with Mike.

What a contrast, she thought. *How can life change so fast?*

Since the events of the previous evening, Carrie felt she was living in a dream that was rapidly becoming a nightmare. Her delight in the Shabbat blessings had suddenly been quenched by Rachel Kramer's stiff statement and the entire family's silent reaction to Annie's question that quickly followed. After that, the evening seemed a blur.

Carrie was heartbroken, realizing that Mike must have suspected his parents' negative reaction to having a prospective daughter-in-law in their home who wasn't Jewish. She had waited for him at the top of the stairs that night, longing for the comfort his loving arms and deep kiss would bring, but he had hardly looked at her as he told her goodnight and turned toward his bedroom, leaving her feeling like the ugly duckling in a pond full of elegant swans.

If Mike really loved me, he wouldn't have put me in this horrible position, she thought, turning over to stare out the window at the cloudy sky. To make matters worse, he seemed to be deliberately ignoring her. Feeling terribly alone and heartbroken, she buried her face in the pillow as the pent-up tears began to flow.

Carrie made it through Saturday by telling everyone she had a horrible headache which, of course, she did. Just a few hours earlier, she would have been thrilled to go to synagogue with the family and learn more about the Jewish faith now so connected with her own. She would have enjoyed meeting the Kramers' friends in the Jewish community, proud to be a prospective part of Mike's family. But now, she couldn't shake the rejection she felt from his parents, particularly his mother and even from Mike himself. She knew she might be overreacting, but he actually seemed embarrassed by her presence since last night's charade. Carrie had hoped for an opportunity to talk with Sarah, but the newly married couple had said their good-byes after dinner last night and had gone back to their apartment.

Sarah had given Carrie a gentle hug and sympathetic smile, whispering, "I'm so sorry, Carrie. I hope we get to see you again."

Big chance, thought Carrie, bitterly.

She could barely remember the miserably silent drive back to Chapel Hill after sundown on Saturday evening. The blackness of the nightmare deepened as the cold November evening drew to a close. By the time Mike parked in front of Carrie's apartment house, she was literally nauseous and on the verge of uncontrollable tears.

He put the gear in park and turned to say, "Carrie, I...," but before he could finish his sentence, she jumped out of the car and ran up the steps and into the house. Mike sat still for a few minutes, watching the colorful fall leaves swirling in the light of the old-fashioned street lights in front of the car. Then, as if in slow motion, he pushed the gear shift forward and quietly drove away.

Early Sunday morning, Rachel Kramer sat at her kitchen table drinking a cup of hot tea, staring out the large window that overlooked the gardens in the back yard. An unusually cold November wind was ripping the last of the red and gold leaves from the maples and dogwoods edging the deep lawn, but Rachel didn't see them through her watery eyes. She was in another place and time, watching her beloved mother and father as they stood arm-in-arm to bless Rachel and Isaac on their wedding day.

The young couple stood under the *chuppa* before the rabbi as the final blessings were given. Isaac then crushed the symbolic wine glass with his foot, the traditional act of remembrance recalling the destruction of the Temple, even in the midst of great joy and celebration. They were turning around to be introduced to family and friends as Mr. and Mrs. Isaac Kramer when Rachel's mother reached out to envelope her only daughter in her loving arms. In later years, when memories of that moment flooded her mind, it always seemed to Rachel that her mother was moving toward her in slow motion when her father suddenly reached out his hand to bless his newly wedded daughter. Just before his hand touched her head, time and movement seemed to stop dead still as Rachel's eyes locked on the numbers carved into her father's wrist. She had seen those numbers many times during her twenty-three years and had long ago understood, as well as one born and raised in freedom could possibly understand, the horrors the numbers implied. But that day, her wedding day, the numbers stood out in stark contrast to the joy and happiness surrounding Rachel and her handsome new husband.

Jacob and Golda Liebowitz had told their only child very little about their lives in Eastern Europe before and during the Holocaust. Like most survivors, they believed the less said about the unthinkable the better. They had to live. They had to survive. And survival meant they had to file the unbearable memories of the past in a place where the pain could be borne—hidden away as if it had never happened.

But, it did happen. The memory was real, and Rachel saw the reality of the pain in their eyes at times when her parents were completely unaware—each year at the Passover Seder when there were only three seated at the family table; when Rachel was six years old asking why she had no grandparents or aunts and uncles like the other little girls at school; and always, always, every December, when her parents couldn't help but remember the day they left their family and friends of a lifetime in Romania to begin a terror-ridden journey that finally led them to the ship that would take them to freedom in America. But in the meantime, having hidden from the Gestapo for more than a year, their greatest fear became a reality—their hiding place was betrayed by a friend of the family who had offered them refuge. Within hours, armed SS officers stormed into the old barn with barking blood hounds, cornering the young couple like frightened animals. It was a nightmare from which they would never fully awake. Not in this lifetime, anyway.

Chapter One

Our lives seldom change so dramatically in a split second of time as Rachel's had on her wedding day. As the numbers on her father's wrist flashed before her eyes, she had made a lifelong vow. Never would she let her family forget the suffering her parents and their generation had endured. She would find out all she could about the Holocaust and, hopefully, more about her own parents' experiences if she could do that without increasing their pain. She would even write it all down so that no one would forget, generation after generation. She would honor her father and mother, and she would raise her children to honor them and the family she never knew. Lastly, Rachel vowed that the family she and Isaac were about to begin would always embrace their Jewish heritage and religion with all their hearts, even if that meant forbidding intermarriage.

The sound of the wind whistling in the tall pine trees drew Rachel back to the present long enough to realize she was shivering cold. Pulling the soft yellow cardigan tighter about her shoulders, she walked over to the stove to make herself another cup of tea.

What a strange weekend, she thought, carrying her cup back to the breakfast room to take up her silent watch at the large Palladian window. The longleaf pines were bending dangerously at the force of the savage wind, and Rachel felt as if that same chilling gale was running up her spine, rattling the cup and saucer she held tightly in both hands.

The winds of change are blowing, and I'm afraid, she admitted to herself. She and Isaac had tried hard to keep Torah and to teach their children well. But Rachel sadly realized the world was changing drastically, and even though the United States had been a welcome refuge of freedom for the Jewish people, the prosperous nation had also become the place of greatest assimilation with each generation losing a little more of its Jewish ethnic and religious identity as the years went by. She didn't want that young woman to be hurt, but she just could not approve of Mike marrying a Gentile. Yes, it would be better for both of them if the relationship was severed now before they became too serious.

Hot tears blurred her vision as the wind continued to pound the trees outside the window, leaving the stripped hardwoods looking as cold and vulnerable as she felt. Isaac found her still standing there, her hands clutching her shoulders, oblivious to the blue china tea cup lying shattered on the cold stone floor at her feet.

Chapter Two

Mike and Jordan slowly strolled from window to window in University Mall, unsuccessfully shopping for Christmas presents for Jordan's family only an hour until the last home game before the holidays. Mike usually enjoyed helping his friend shop for his parents and sisters, but this year Jordan didn't seem to care for any of his suggestions.

"What about this?" Mike asked. "I think your Mom would really like this sweater, don't you?"

"Hm..., I dunno. It's sort of blah, don't you think?" Jordan replied.

"No, man, it's not blah. It's classy—elegant. When are you going to acquire some style, my friend?" Mike laughingly asked.

"You're the one with style, Mike," Jordan replied in an unusually sarcastic tone.

"What's wrong with you?" Mike innocently asked. "I've never known you to play Scrooge, man. I thought you were the original jolly ol' elf himself!" Mike laughed, throwing his arm around his best friend's shoulder.

Jordan didn't respond.

Quickly glancing at his watch, Mike announced, "Hey, man! It's almost time for the game. We'd better run across the parking lot to catch the shuttle."

Nothing more was said as they hurried to the Blue Line Bus loading at the other end of the Mall. Jumping onto the already full bus, the two friends moved toward the back and grabbed a pole to hold onto as the driver closed the door and drove away from the curb. The bus was packed with older alumni dressed in Carolina blue sweaters and sweatshirts, many already listening to the pre-game show on their Walkman's. The driver was overly ready to get home on this frigid night. The sides of the roads were banked with snow dunes pushed up by plows earlier in the day, so he drove a little faster than safety allowed, thankfully arriving at their destination just in time for the tip-off. By then, Jordan had determined to confront Mike with questions about his relationship with Carrie, but the conversation wasn't going too well.

"So, what's the deal?" Jordan asked his friend as they hurried up the stairs to their seats in the crowded arena.

"We're going to miss the tip-off, man. Why don't we just can this conversation to a more appropriate time?"

"There's never an appropriate time for you, Mike," Jordan replied. "I know you think it's none of my business and I understand that, but the bottom line is, you've messed up, friend!"

"Forget it, Jordan. Let's watch the game." Mike turned his attention to the activity on the ball court, cheering loudly as the Tar Heels rushed out onto the court.

Carrie wrapped her scarf around her neck and pulled on her gloves as she stepped from the warm cafe onto the cold sidewalk. The weatherman had predicted more snow by nightfall, and the dark gray sky looked as if it might oblige him. Clutching her red wool coat tightly around her slender body, she quickly walked the three blocks to her apartment, careful not to slip on the ice sheets quickly forming on the sidewalk. She had promised her best friend, Emma Tate, that they would order pizza and watch a movie together this evening. Emma had been encouraging Carrie to do something other than work all day and stay home alone every night since her breakup with Mike.

The phone was ringing as Carrie fitted the key in the lock and turned the knob.

"Hello!"

"Carrie, it's me, Emma. Are we still on for our exciting evening?"

"You bet," Carrie answered. "I'll go ahead and order the pizza while you get over here. And, Emma, you'd better bring an overnight bag 'cause it really looks like snow again."

"Okay. Maybe we'll be snowed in by tomorrow, and we can play all day!" Emma exclaimed. "I know we're supposed to be sophisticated grad students now, but who cares. Let's have some fun!"

Chapter Two

"Nah. Wish I could, but the Corner Cafe never closes. Charlie expects me in rain, hail, sleet and snow."

"Yeah, well...be there in fifteen minutes."

Emma is good for me, Carrie mused. Since her relationship with Mike had grown more serious, she and Emma hadn't seen as much of each other as before. But it wasn't solely her relationship with Mike that had kept them apart. Emma was dating someone as well. She and John Owens had been seeing each other since classes started in September, but Carrie hadn't grown to know John as well as she had hoped, mainly because of Mike's attitude. He said he had nothing in common with John who was majoring in philosophy and religion and planning to go on to Fuller Theological Seminary in California for a Master's in Foreign Missions. Inasmuch as Emma had always dreamed of being a missionary, the attractive couple seemed perfectly matched to Carrie, but Mike considered the pair much too religious for his comfort zone. Carrie knew he had other friends in the School of Philosophy and Religion and had no problem socializing with them, so she had finally concluded that his real problem with Emma and John was that their religion was not based on arguments or theories or even theological doctrines. They seemed to simply believe that each of them had some kind of special relationship with God. Mike judged that school of thought as absolutely ridiculous.

"They're just weird," he had said many times in the last few months.

Carrie wasn't sure what she thought. As much as she liked Emma, she did think her friend was a little extreme. Carrie's own Christian upbringing was very precious to her—Sunday School, Vacation Bible School, Summer Youth Camps, prayer at meal times. She knew all these opportunities had given her a good, strong foundation in life. But Emma was different. She didn't just pray before meals and at bedtime. Actually, Carrie had noticed that she seemed to pray most of the time, about anything and everything. And then, too, it was the way she prayed—like she knew God personally and had some special connection with Him. Sometimes when Emma simply prayed before a meal, Carrie had the strangest feeling that God might actually say something back to Emma. And she hated to admit it, but her friend had embarrassed her more than once, especially when she told their college friends about Jesus. Religion should be private, shouldn't it?

Well, Emma may be a little weird, Carrie thought as she went to answer the door, *but she's the best friend I've ever had, and I want to keep her friendship, no matter what Mike thinks. What does it matter now, anyway?*

By the time the pizza and popcorn were devoured and the movie was over, Emma was glad Carrie had asked her to bring her overnight bag and stay the night. At least six inches of snow and ice had fallen since she left her own apartment at the other end of town, and it was still coming down. She stood by the window in Carrie's living room, watching the glistening snow falling on the cold white world outside.

"Father God, You are so amazing! I stand in awe of Your power and creativity!" Emma was talking to God again as Carrie returned from the kitchen with two steaming mugs of hot chocolate.

"Oh, Carrie," Emma exclaimed, "isn't God absolutely awesome? The same creator God Who placed all the planets and stars in perfect alignment; the One Who created everything in perfect order and keeps it by His power—that God... the only God...loves you and me enough to send His only Son to die for us."

"Amazing Love, how can it be, that Thou, my God, would die for me?"[1] Emma sang joyfully as she gazed out the window at the falling snow.

Yep, she's weird, thought Carrie. She didn't respond to Emma's exclamation, having concluded that silence was the best way to handle the strange outbursts her friend sometimes expressed. Her mother had always told her that if you ignore something, it will go away, and so far, her theory had worked pretty well. She handed Emma a big mug of hot cocoa and sat down on the couch with hers, quickly tucking her feet under her and wrapping the green chenille afghan tightly about her legs.

"Just a few more days until I leave town for Christmas," Carrie said. "You, too. I wonder if the snow storm will hinder our travel arrangements?"

"I doubt it. You know our North Carolina weather—snow one day, sunshine the next. This one looks as if it might last, but I'm sure the skies will clear long before you leave town and my flight takes off for Nashville."

"Uh, huh. I'm glad it's snowing. Somehow, it makes me feel that everything's going to be all right. I guess it's because the white snow makes everything seem so clean and new."

"You're thinking of Mike, aren't you?" Emma gently asked.

"Always," said Carrie, staring at nothing.... Oh, I'm sorry. I didn't mean to sound so melancholy."

"What's a friend for if not to be here for you during the difficult times as well as the happy ones?" Emma asked, reaching over to give her friend a quick hug. "Have you talked to Mike yet?"

"No, not really, but he came in the cafe today to meet Jordan. I was so surprised to see him that I'm afraid I acted like I was stupid or something. I think he was a little embarrassed to see me, too."

"I'm so sorry." Emma took a sip of her hot chocolate. "Carrie...I've been thinking about this whole thing the last few weeks, and it just doesn't make sense. Do you think there is any chance you could be misinterpreting Mike's behavior at Thanksgiving? Perhaps he was upset about his mother's reaction to you and just didn't know what to do about it. Or *maybe*, during that uncomfortable dinner, he suddenly realized he should have prepared you, and his family, for your meeting, but then it was too late. Have you thought about that?" asked Emma.

"I've thought of everything. I've dissected the entire weekend a thousand times and analyzed every detail. I do agree with one thing you said, though. Mike *was* sorry that he hadn't prepared me for the visit with his family, but I really don't think he ever intended to tell them that I'm a Christian. Not anytime in the near future, anyway," Carrie's voice trembled, her eyes brimming with tears. She looked over at Emma. "I'm having to face a few flaws in my Prince Charming's character, and number one is that he thinks he can get away with anything. He doesn't like to face the music, so to speak."

Emma sipped her hot chocolate grown cool, glancing at her friend who was dabbing her eyes with a fresh tissue, trying not to start sobbing. The two friends sat in silence as the clock ticked in time to the snowflakes falling gently against the window pane.

"Carrie," Emma asked gently, "have you told your family that Mike is Jewish?"

"Well...no, not really....," Carrie answered quietly. "You see, Mike and I agreed that our differences in religion didn't really matter; that it would all work out somehow. He believes in God, Emma—just not exactly the way we believe. All Christians don't agree on everything either, you know. I wasn't trying to deceive my family. I honestly didn't think we needed to get into all that yet. But, it was a very different situation with his family. Their religious traditions affect everything—especially on the Sabbath, I discovered. Anyway, our visit with my family was wonderful. Mike had a great time, and the subject of religion never came up."

"Not at all?"

"No, not...well, almost not at all. Mike did seem a little pensive during my Dad's blessing before dinner and again during the drive to his parents' home, but he wouldn't tell me what was bothering him. Hmm. Now that I think about it, that's when he first began to seem so distant."

"Sometimes we procrastinate about certain situations we don't want to face; then suddenly, we realize it's too late. We should have done something, but we didn't, and then we feel as if a tidal wave has overcome us, and we can't do anything but hope we survive the wave. Perhaps Mike found himself in that predicament."

The Gentile and the Jew: A Divine Romance

"Maybe...maybe he did," Carrie hesitated. "I guess I can understand that. But Mike is always so sure of himself, and he was so confident that our religious differences didn't matter. To tell you the truth, he actually convinced me we didn't *have* any differences."

"He probably truly believes that, Carrie. From what you've told me, even though Mike's family members are orthodox Jews, he's chosen not to follow that path. That means he hasn't seriously delved into Judaism for himself, and you definitely know he hasn't studied Christianity. Although he tells you he believes in God, it sounds as if he's slid into the world of agnosticism—maybe there's a God and maybe there isn't and even if there is a God, He has nothing to do with me. You know that type of thinking."

"I haven't thought of it that way. I guess I've placed all the blame on Mike for causing all this, but you're right. I have to accept some of the blame as well. I procrastinated, too, not telling my parents about Mike, but it just didn't seem important."

The two friends sat in silence for a few moments, each one lost in her own thoughts and dreams, big white snowflakes splattering silently against the warm windowpanes.

"Emma?"

"Yes?"

"I have to confess something else. I really shouldn't blame Mike for not preparing me to meet his family, either," Carrie said, her lips trembling. "I should have prepared myself. I knew his family is Jewish, and I should have tried to learn about their religion. Here I am, living on a university campus with access to one of the largest libraries in the world. Don't you remember me searching the Net for North Carolina's Jewish history when I first met Mike?"

"Yes, I do, but I'd forgotten," Emma replied.

"Well, I learned a lot of local history, but for some reason, I didn't even think about researching Judaism. In hindsight, I'm sure I thought of the Jews as a people, not as a religious group. Going by my Bible, they believe the same things we do."

"You're right in a way. I think we Christians do a lot of assuming. Of course, a great many Jews don't follow Rabbinical Judaism."

"But, Mike's family does, even though he isn't religious himself. When he was so somber on the drive to his parents' home, he said something I thought was ridiculous at the time. He said his family was different from mine, and I could tell he was concerned about that, but I didn't understand it then. I think I do now. He was raised in a Jewish world, and because that world is perfectly normal to him, he honestly didn't think about it being strange to me until he went to my home and saw firsthand how different we are. Ohhh my, Emma, what do I do now?" Carrie set her mug on the table by the couch and held her head in her hands, rubbing her temples and feeling the onslaught of a bad headache.

"I don't know," she responded truthfully, "but why don't we pray about it together?"

Carrie closed her eyes and welcomed her friend's prayer. For the first time since she had known her, Emma didn't seem quite so weird.

Good-looking and friendly to boot with his bright eyes and sandy blonde hair, Jordan Jackson was popular with students and professors alike. He had a way of telling a story that brought his audience to the floor, laughing until their sides hurt. He was a clown, that's for sure, but he was also a serious student and had big plans for the future. Loads of money and lots of fun—those were Jordan's two main goals in life, and everyone who knew him would have bet millions that he would achieve both in a very short time.

Jordan wasn't shallow, however. He also had a good heart and was a best friend par excellence. Driving home to Wilmington from the Triangle area was usually fun, filled with lively bantering and relaxed conversation with his best friend. But since Mike was going to fly up to Connecticut for the holidays, Jordan was driving alone on Interstate 40, thinking about everything from his friends' broken relationship to how he was going to raise enough grants and scholarships to continue his plans for the future—law school, an exciting career in corporate law, plenty of time for golf and surfing and loads of fun.

Smithfield, Benson, Faison, Warsaw—the exit signs pointed out the small towns that herald the entrance to the coastal plain of North Carolina. Approaching the Kenansville exit at seventy-five miles per hour, Jordan again thought of Carrie and how lucky Mike was to have a girl like her. He started to slow down and turn onto the exit ramp to make a quick stop by Carrie's home to wish her family a merry Christmas, but he quickly remembered she was to meet her family in the mountains for the holidays.

"Wake up, Mike!" Jordan shouted aloud in the empty Volkswagen Golf as the landscape changed from ice and snow to the warmer green pine forest of southeastern North Carolina. Mulling over multiple conversations he had with Mike during the weeks since Thanksgiving, Jordan was convinced his best friend had lost his mind, letting a girl like Carrie slip away like he had. He usually tried to stay out of his pal's personal business, knowing Mike had a mind of his own and definitely wouldn't welcome what he would consider Jordan's interference. This wasn't the first time Mike had refused Jordan's advice regarding his relationship with Carrie. But this time, recalling the hurt on Carrie's face that day in the Corner Cafe, Jordan couldn't help but ask a few questions and try to figure out what Mike had done to cause her such pain. But Mike wasn't ready to talk about it, not even with his closest friend, reducing his answers to Jordan's questions to either of two sentences, "We have religious differences," or, "Can it, Jordan."

This is ridiculous, Jordan thought as he drove along the Interstate. *Mike knew Carrie was a Christian to begin with. If it didn't matter three months ago, why on earth does it matter now?* Jordan didn't understand the whole religion thing anyway, and he could have cared less if Carrie was Christian or Hindu. Come to think of it, he had assumed Mike felt the same way.

In all the years he and Mike had been friends, Jordan had never once thought seriously about his friend being a Jew. Mike had visited in Jordan's home during Christmas holidays or at Easter many times, and there had never been a conflict. Of course, Jordan had to admit that his family celebrated the holidays with Santa Claus, presents, and parties for Christmas; egg hunts and a delicious dinner starring a huge baked ham for Easter. But that recollection proved his point. Mike even ate the ham.

Mike Kramer pulled a red ski mask over his head and wrapped his wool scarf a little tighter about his neck as he began his early morning run in the below freezing weather. *I may not be able to run today*, he thought. He hadn't realized it was quite so cold and icy.

Watching closely for patches of ice, Mike began to jog slowly along his usual path toward the campus sidewalks. Sometimes Jordan joined him for his morning exercise, but he had already headed down to Wilmington for the holidays. Jordan may not have wanted to run with him anyway, considering the attitude he had sported lately. Actually, Mike was glad to be alone this cold morning. He always seemed to be able to think more clearly when he ran, and today he was hoping he might gain some perspective on his relationship with Carrie—rather, his lack of relationship with Carrie.

He jogged past the deserted baseball field and on by the practice field for the soccer team. He was beginning to feel warm despite the bitter cold when all of a sudden, his left foot slipped on a patch of ice he hadn't seen and—Boom! He was falling face forward toward the cold cement, no time to do anything

Chapter Two

except reach out so that his hands and knee slammed the sidewalk a second before his face would have hit full force. But stabbing pain still riveted through his nose and right knee as Mike lay on the frozen cement too stunned to move. After a few seconds that seemed more like hours, he slowly rolled over onto his back.

"Ohhh," he groaned, lying perfectly still on the frozen ground with his hands covering his face, still shocked by the sudden fall and excruciating pain. When he finally relaxed enough to take his hands down, he saw that his gloves were covered in bright red blood.

Mike carefully turned his head and glanced around, hoping there was someone nearby who could look at his face to see if he needed medical help and maybe give him a lift to the university hospital or back to his apartment. But there was no help to be seen on this bitterly cold morning.

Another bad mistake, Mike groaned inwardly. *For a fairly decent guy with a 3.8 GPA, lots of friends, a beautiful girlfriend and an exciting future, I'm making a total mess of everything.*

Jordan's questioned echoed in his mind, "What's going on, man?"

He decided it would be wise to wait a few more minutes before trying to get up and was greatly relieved when he finally pushed himself to a standing position and realized none of his limbs were broken. He was already sore, and each limping step sent searing pain through his right knee. Mike wasn't sure if his nose had stopped bleeding on its own, or if his blood had frozen when the cold air hit it.

Does blood freeze, he wondered? Strange, what people think about at times like these.

He hadn't limped but a few yards when he saw a campus utility truck coming slowly toward him. The driver had already noticed the lone young man limping along the sidewalk and was carefully pulling the truck over to the curb when Mike lifted his arm to wave him over.

"Need help, son?" the driver shouted, rolling down his window.

"Yeah, sure do," Mike answered. "Had a little accident, and I really need a lift. Which way are you going?"

"Anywhere you need me to take you," the friendly man responded. "By the looks of your face, I think I should take you to the emergency room."

"Nah. I'm okay...I think. My nose has stopped bleeding, and I don't think anything is broken because I can walk, although my knee hurts pretty badly. If you could take me to my apartment just off Franklin Street, I sure would appreciate it."

"Sure, son," the man replied. "You just tell me where to let you off, and I'll be glad to take you home. And, son, take it from someone who has nursed a lot of old war injuries—you had better put an ice pack on that knee just as soon as you get home and be sure and keep it raised."

"Thanks, I'll do that. Sure am glad you came along. I was beginning to wonder if I would make it back before next semester."

"Name's Sam...name's Sam." The man reached out to shake Mike's hand.

"Glad to meet you, Sam—very glad," said Mike, cringing with the pain his smile caused. "I'm Mike Kramer."

Sam drove the yellow four-wheel-drive truck slowly through the icy streets, every now and then turning to look at Mike's face to see if he had started bleeding again. He was sure the young fellow would be shocked to see the abrasions on his face when he got home and looked in the mirror. Mike thought all the blood was coming from his nose, but Sam could see that his face had been bleeding in more than one place.

"It's a mite dangerous to be running in this kind of weather, isn't it, Mike?" Sam asked with a big smile.

Mike could feel his already pink face turning red. He smiled sheepishly and answered, "I think that's an understatement, Sam."

The two men laughed together as Sam continued to drive carefully through the snow-covered campus toward Franklin Street. He concentrated on his driving in silence for a few minutes, then asked again, "You all right, son?"

"Yeah. I think so...just sore. I guess my pride's hurt more than anything. It's really embarrassing to fall flat on your face, even if I did slip on the ice. Thank goodness no one was watching me."

"I understand, I surely do," Sam replied. "My pride's been hurt plenty of times, but you know, I'm a better man for it."

"What do you mean?" asked Mike, his entire body aching more by the minute.

"Well, son, I learned a long time ago that pride is my enemy. Pride builds walls between people. Pride means everything in life is about *me*. It means I think of me first, middle and last. It means I care more about me and what people think of me than the other person. I guess you already know the Bible says, 'Pride goeth before a fall'?" Sam couldn't help but grin as he came to the end of the timely proverb.

"Man, you're just full of jokes, aren't you, Sam?" Mike chuckled, embarrassed again.

"That one was pretty good, huh?" Sam laughed at his own joke. "But it's true. The Bible has a lot to say about the sin of pride."

Chapter Two

"Yeah, well, I've sure made a mess of things lately. I guess you could say I've had quite a few falls. Does that mean I'm proud?"

"We're all full of pride, son," Sam said, "but God loves us enough to let us fall so that we can wake up and accept the changes He wants to make in our souls."

"Oh, God..., God again," Mike groaned. "I've never even been sure God exists, yet I can't seem to keep from bumping into Him lately."

"Yeah," Sam smiled mischievously. "He does that."

They rode in silence the last few blocks to Mike's apartment building. The aching young man glanced at his new friend as Sam pulled the truck over to the curb, thinking he would have to remember to connect with him sometime soon, just to thank him again if nothing else. There was something about the old guy, something comfortable and restful.

"I sure am grateful to you, Sam. You came along at just the right time to keep me from freezing to death. I owe you one, man."

"No, no. You don't owe me a thing, son. Just take care of that knee and think about our little conversation from time to time." Sam walked around the truck to help Mike get out.

His swollen knee was throbbing painfully as he limped to the door. "Thanks again!" Mike shouted through clinched teeth as he opened the apartment house door and turned to wave good-bye to Sam. But the yellow utility truck was nowhere to be seen.

Huh? That's strange, thought Mike, glancing up and down the street. *Sam was driving too slow and careful to get away that fast. Hmm...he must have turned down an alley or something. I'll find him through the campus offices in a week or so.*

Chapter Three

"D o you have the tickets, Isaac?" Rachel Kramer asked her husband as she shut the back door of their home and turned the knob one more time to make sure it was locked.

Isaac reached out to help steady his wife's descent down the snow-covered steps. The sun had finally come out after two full days of snow and ice, and although the temperature was still hovering around forty-five, it was a beautiful December day to begin a journey.

"Yes, yes, I have the tickets, my love. We have everything we need. The luggage is all loaded in the trunk, our passports and papers are inside my coat pocket, you have the traveler's checks, and we're on our way to Romania!" Isaac answered, opening the car door for his anxious wife.

"Are you sure Annie will be happy with Sarah and David while we're gone, Isaac? We've never left her for any length of time, and she's only three years old."

"Yes, Rachel. For the last time, Annie will be fine. David and Sarah will keep her so busy during Chanukah she won't have time to miss us until we're home again. And don't forget, she'll have her Mikey with her all during the holidays. Now, stop worrying. This is the journey we've been waiting for all our lives!"

"All right, Isaac," Rachel responded, settling into the passenger seat. "You're right. I'm ready now." She buckled her seat belt and let out a long sigh of relief.

The Gentile and the Jew: A Divine Romance

As Isaac said, they were about to embark on the journey of a lifetime. Throughout all the years of their marriage, they had talked about what it would be like to go to Romania, searching for the family Rachel never knew, hopefully finding strategic pieces to fit the puzzle of the past.

This is unreal, Rachel thought, thinking how strange it would be to celebrate Chanukah in another country. But the winter holiday was the best time for Isaac to be away from his export business, so the plans had been made, and now they were on their way.

For nearly thirty years, Rachel had studied the history of the Jewish people, particularly the era of the Holocaust, but more specifically, her own family history and Isaac's. She truly was *ready* now, ready to face the people and places she hoped would finally put the mysterious puzzle pieces together. She wasn't exactly sure what the picture would look like, but hopefully, it would be clear and it would be complete.

The Kramers' flight left Raleigh-Durham Airport at 8:30 a.m. on Tuesday morning. By the time they went through customs and security in Montreal and boarded their nonstop flight to Frankfurt where they would take the last leg to Bucharest, Rachel was just beginning to grasp the reality of her dream-come-true. The pilot welcomed everyone aboard Air Canada flight 772, and the flight attendants went through the ritual of their safety instructions as Rachel and Isaac buckled their seat belts and adjusted the air vents overhead. Rachel never ceased to be amazed that an airplane could actually leave the ground and fly thousands of feet above the earth, traveling at a speed that enables human beings to move forward and backward in time and space. She always closed her eyes and prayed during take off, clutching Isaac's hand and gripping the arm of her seat with her other hand. But this time, Isaac reached out to place his arm around her shoulders, whispering in her ear, "Don't worry, my love, everything will be all right."

From your mouth to God's ear, she thought. But Rachel opened her eyes to see her husband smiling lovingly at her. He was still so handsome. Isaac kissed the hand he held in his. She loved to gaze into Isaac's dark brown eyes. Like in pools of still water, she could see her own reflection in those loving eyes, and she felt safe there—safe in her husband's eyes.

Catherine and Tom Jernigan were packing the last load of boxes into Tom's four-wheel-drive pickup truck he had insisted on driving because of snow and ice on the mountain roads. Tom was always prepared for everything, especially emergencies, so everything known to men in general could be found in his Chevy truck. "Be prepared" was his motto as well as the Boy Scouts'.

"Come on, Catherine, let's go!" shouted Tom, blowing the horn one more time. "What are you doing? You can't take anything else; the camper shell is full of stuff!"

"I'm coming! I'm coming! Oh, wait! Wait a second, Tom, I want to be sure I haven't left anything."

"You have definitely not left a thing," said Tom impatiently. "Everything we own is in the back of this truck."

Pulling herself up into the high cab, Catherine was mentally running through her long list of everything from decorations to presents to cooking supplies, thinking about each grandchild from the oldest to the youngest and the fun they would have together over the holidays. She absolutely loved being a grandmother.

Their first grandchild had arrived in Catherine's forty-fourth year. A few months later, she had become so ill she was admitted to the hospital. She stayed there twenty-three days. Catherine would always believe that period of three weeks and two days was one of the major turning points of her life. She was tired. She was sick. And she was disappointed. Her faith was being tested as never before. Catherine had come face to face with the harsh reality that people of faith have to face sometime in their lives—many of her prayers had not been answered, at least not that she could tell. In fact, the specific situations she prayed about the most had either stayed the same or had progressed toward an even more negative outcome than when she had begun to pray.

Her second great disappointment was in herself, although she would have turned the two disappointments the other way around. Catherine's deep sense of right and wrong sometimes led to conclusions that were too much for anyone to bear. She believed that if one of her children went down the wrong path, it was surely because either she or Tom had not parented them correctly, and since she had always seen Tom as a good father, the only conclusion left was that she had failed as a mother. The sickness that was already working in her body just added another check mark to her predetermined guilty verdict. So she became sicker...and sicker.

Tom didn't know what to do. He just knew that his beloved wife of twenty-one years was getting worse daily, and he couldn't seem to do anything about it. He had always prided himself on hard work and practicality, his own father having taught him to, "Do what you have to do and do it well." He had told Catherine many times that his own philosophy of life could be summed up in one sentence, "Work hard and use the brain God gave you." During that paradoxical year of joy and sorrow, Tom Jernigan felt that he, too, was being tested, and along with Catherine, he questioned everything.

He took her to see the rhododendron blooming along the Blue Ridge Parkway for their twenty-third anniversary in June of that year, just one month after their first grandchild was born. He saw then that his beloved wife was not getting better as they had hoped but was growing weaker and more somber as the days went by. She *oohed* and *aahed* over the pink and purple flowers covering the shoulders of the Parkway from Boone to Ashville, smiling at the right times and laughing when Tom said something funny. But he could tell that Catherine's spirit just wasn't there…and he didn't know where to find her.

In early September, following doctor's orders, Tom admitted Catherine to the hospital, leaving her trying desperately not to cry and worrying that she was causing her family so much trouble and heartache. As Tom walked out of the room, tears forming in his own weary eyes, a white uniformed nurse strolled in, introducing himself as "John." That was the last straw. Catherine had always hated hospitals since her father had died in one when she was a little girl, but that day, weak and sick beyond comprehension, she had to endure the embarrassment a male nurse was sure to bring. She began to sob, recognizing the onset of a migraine and knowing that if she didn't stop crying, the headache would be unbearable within minutes. But she couldn't stop the tears, and when poor John leaned over her to ask what was wrong, she couldn't bring herself to hurt his feelings by telling him the truth, so she just bellowed, "I used to be such a strong person!"

Bless John's heart, he replied, "I guess someone up there wants you to know whose strength you're leaning on."

Catherine would never forget that sentence as long as she lived.

There was another major lesson to learn soon to follow. She had been placed in an area of the hospital where patients with chronic illnesses were taught how to deal with their symptoms on a day-to-day basis. Pain management, group therapy and classes on assertive behavior filled their days, along with physical therapy and meals taken together in a small dining room. Once or twice a week, a recreational therapist would ask the patients on the hall to meet in the dining room for a little fun which, of course, was supposed to cheer everyone up. One evening near the end of her second week, Catherine joined the group in the dining room. The therapist had discovered that Elizabeth, another patient around sixty-years-old, was originally from England, so thinking it would make a delightful evening for Elizabeth to tell the patients about jolly old England, hopefully diverting their minds from their sorrowful predicaments, the therapist invited her to speak to the group.

Chapter Three

To tell the truth, the only reason Catherine agreed to go was her love of travel and geography in general, so you can imagine her surprise, and that of the therapist, when in her charming British accent, Elizabeth began her story with a tale of woe—the first night of the German bombing of England when she was a young girl. Before the therapist could shake herself out of her shock, Elizabeth had told the group that her home had been destroyed the first night of the Blitz and she and her family had to live from house-to-house and in bomb shelters throughout the entire war.

Finally, the therapist regained her composure and interrupted Elizabeth, "All right, dear. Now, what about Buckingham Palace? Have you ever been to Buckingham Palace?"

"Yes, I have," Elizabeth replied. "Buckingham Palace was bombed as well. Did you know that? That was the night our neighbors were killed in the Blitz. It was horrible! Sirens going off all night long—not just for an hour or two as usual, but all night…."

The therapist interrupted for the second and too-many-to-count-other times that surprising evening, "Could you tell us a little about the Tower of London, Elizabeth? I'm sure everyone would be interested."

"Oh, the Tower was almost destroyed, too," Elizabeth continued her train of thought, "but it's still standing. That night I met my husband-to-be, an American who had joined the RAF to help us fight the Germans. We were married near the end of the war when his plane was shot down and he was sent to a hospital in London. Being then an American soldier's wife, I was sent to the states on a ship, knowing no one and pregnant with our first child. I was only nineteen years old, violently sick the entire voyage—whether seasick or morning sick, I couldn't tell you."

The anxious therapist stared at Elizabeth as she innocently resumed her story. "When I finally touched American soil, my husband's family was nowhere to be seen. It took weeks to find them, but I finally arrived on their doorstep, exhausted, sick and almost ready to deliver my baby. When the RAF finally sent my husband home, he had entered into a reactionary depression that today would be called post traumatic syndrome, but all we knew then was that he never regained his prewar personality. Yes, he was never the same again, but in some ways, that was a blessing because he was never truly impacted when our son was murdered by a drugged burglar when he was twenty-three, and our other son lost his leg due to a rare bone disease."

While Elizabeth took a breath, the therapist gathered up her notes, stood up and tearfully said, "Thank you, Elizabeth. It's getting rather late so maybe we should end our evening now."

"Oh, my, you're very welcome," said Elizabeth. "I'll be happy to tell you more about England anytime." She never seemed to notice the tears streaming down the faces of every person in the room or the look of sheer grief in Catherine's tear-filled eyes.

Her room was just across the hall, and it didn't take her two seconds to get inside and quickly shut the door before the tears gushed out with a loud wail she muted by clamping her hand over her mouth. Just as quickly as it slammed shut, the door flew open, and a new nurse who had seen Catherine rush back to her room, walked in.

"What happened?" she asked. "What hit you so hard?"

"Elizabeth's painful life!" Catherine stammered. "That woman has endured tragedy after tragedy, and now here she is with this terrible disease. I can't believe she was so calm about it all. And she just kept on smiling through the whole story!"

"But that isn't why you are so distraught, is it?" the nurse asked.

"No! I'm upset because I feel absolutely ridiculous and guilty that I've complained about anything in my entire life. Compared to Elizabeth's, my life has been perfect. I feel just horrible, and I want to go home!"

The unknown nurse stared into her eyes and said, "You have a lesson to learn in this, Catherine. You cannot measure pain and sorrow. Elizabeth's pain is her pain. Your pain is your pain. They cannot be compared or measured; otherwise, there would be no comfort for anyone."

She would never forget that lesson as well.

But all that was a long time ago, and I'm a better woman for it, Catherine thought now as she turned to make sure she hadn't forgotten anything. Yes, this trip to the mountains would be wonderful.

Sunday morning had become Mike's favorite time of the week. He usually managed to sleep late, at least until 8:30 a.m. if the dog in the apartment down the hall didn't start barking earlier. His routine was fairly lightweight—piddling around the kitchen making coffee, flipping the TV on to watch *Meet the Press* and taking a shower. If he met all three goals by ten or eleven, he was fairly well pleased with himself. By that time, he was ready to bundle up for the short walk from his apartment to the long row of newspaper vendors on Franklin Street, dropping his six quarters in the slot and pulling out the *Raleigh News and Observer*. Scanning the headlines and trying not to bump into anyone, he continued on down the street to the Corner Cafe, waving to Charlie as he entered the door, craning his neck to see if the back booth by the porthole window was available. By the time he spread his paper out on the table, Charlie or one of the servers was there with his cup of strong Brazilian coffee and *voila!* Mike was a happy fellow.

With almost the entire student body having gone somewhere for the holiday season, Franklin Street was about deserted this Sunday morning, leaving the little town like a large motel with a vacant sign out front. Mike had left his apartment earlier than usual this particular Sunday morning because the dog sounded as if he had cornered a fox around 7:30. *The owner must have died during the night*, Mike growled, gulping his second cup of coffee and finishing the last bite of his western omelet. Newspaper read thoroughly and stomach satisfied, he dropped the tip on the table, grabbed his coat and headed out the door, yelling "see you later" to Charlie as the door closed behind him and the cold wind hit him in the face.

He stuffed both hands in his pockets, took a deep breath of ice cold air and decided to walk a little further on down the street just for the heck of it. He had plenty of time before he needed to head out for the airport between Raleigh and Durham. Sarah and David had taken Annie up to Connecticut a few days early so David could attend a couple of important business meetings for The Kramer Company. Mike was to fly up to meet them and celebrate Chanukah with the Klein family. They planned to leave the rental car in Connecticut and fly back together.

Mike ambled past the closed shops and half-empty restaurants, glancing in store windows from time to time, his thoughts focused on the confusing mess he seemed to be making of his life lately. Even his grades were not up to par in the last few weeks. The chat with the guy in the utility truck seemed to help a little. *What was his name? Sam! Yeah, that was it—good ol' Sam.*

"Hey, man! Watch where you're going!" A teenage boy carrying a boom box on his shoulder yelled at Mike.

"Sorry, man!" he yelled back, stopping dead in his tracks to avoid the booming guy and an oncoming bicycle. Taking that opportunity to look around and see how far he had walked in his reverie, Mike found himself standing in front of an old stone gothic chapel, the large double oak doors opening in and out as parishioners entered the sanctuary for the Sunday morning worship service. Strange. He must have walked past the chapel hundreds of times during the past six years, never really noticing it until today. The chapel was designed like a miniature cathedral, its magnificent stained-glass windows catching the rays of the morning sun, almost blinding Mike's eyes as he stood gazing at the striking building, its bell tower rising high into the clear blue sky. He couldn't

The Gentile and the Jew: A Divine Romance

have explained why he did such an unusual thing, but before he had time to think it through, he quickly climbed the steps and entered the sanctuary.

Mike was awed by the majestic beauty of the interior, the sound of his steps reverberating throughout the sanctuary as he walked across the polished stone floor and the famous pipe organ swelled to Bach's great anthem, "Joyful, Joyful, We Adore Thee!" He searched for an aisle seat at the back, planning to escape quickly if things got too heavy, finally wedging in beside two elderly ladies just opening their hymnbooks. They smiled sweetly, and Mike smiled back at them, thankful to be sitting beside such nice people and not some old grouch or religious nut. By the time the scriptures were read, another hymn was sung and the minister rose to speak, Mike felt fairly comfortable, deciding that he might actually stay until the end of the service.

The minister was an average-looking man with graying hair and clean-cut features, dressed in an ecclesiastical black robe embroidered with the emblem of the university. He began to tell a story, a true story about something he had experienced not long ago.

The minister told the sparse, but attentive congregation that a friend of his, a professor at the University, had discovered he had cancer the year before. Even though the disease was somewhat advanced, the minister and his friend were not deeply concerned because the professor lived and worked in one of the most prominent universities in the country, well known for its medical school and research facilities. It never crossed either of their minds that the professor would die. Why, he was in the best place he could possibly be in his situation, wasn't he?

A few months later, the minister was sitting beside his friend on the cancer floor of that same world-famous hospital. His friend was dying, and there was nothing anyone could do about it. As he sat beside the hospital bed, sometimes holding his friend's hand, sometimes praying quietly, the minister had a lot of time to think about life and death. In those sad but precious moments, he came to the conclusion that life is made up of a series of choices.

In the beginning of our lives on earth, we don't get to choose the date or time of our birth, our families, our economic status in life, our body make-up or our looks. Those decisions and more are made by someone infinitely wiser than us. But, at a very young age, we suddenly have the option to choose. Will we obey our parents, or will we yell an emphatic, "No!" Will we learn to tie our shoes or walk around the rest of our lives tripping over our dangling shoe strings? Those first choices seem simple to us when we are older, but they are the foundational choices on which we build our lives and are just as important or more so as the choices we are offered later in life.

Chapter Three

If our parents are wise, the minister continued, they teach and train us well, praying that we will continue to make the best choices as they prepare us for life outside their daily care. Then they just keep on praying and hoping and watching and praying and hoping, just as our heavenly Father does for each of His own children, knowing that the day will come again, as it had for the professor, when we will not be given a choice. If by then we have not made the right choices, death will come as the greatest enemy of our souls.

One night as the minister visited his friend, continuing to ponder his anxious thoughts, he saw that his friend was dramatically weaker. The professor's wife had whispered the updated prognosis upon his arrival in the hospital room. The doctors did not expect his friend to live until morning. During that long night, minutes seemed like hours and hours seemed like days, giving the minister time to realize that he had entered into a strange relationship with death during the months his friend had suffered. It had grown into what might be called a hate affair in which the most recognizable emotion was fear.

He had begun to picture death as a tangible being, the faceless grim reaper in his long, black hooded robe, reigning terror in all his victims as he ravished hospitals, homes, city streets and highways alike. He had even updated the grim reaper version of death with a specter that looked more like Darth Vader from the Star Wars movies. But the most agonizing issue for the minister was that his faith seemed to be failing him in deference to his fear, and now his greatest concern was that he would fail his friend in his hour of greatest need. But as he sat praying with his dying friend that night, a surprising thing happened that changed the minister forever.

The professor's breathing had begun to change, the air slowly flowing in and out of his open mouth, slower and slower. He was struggling to breathe and too weak from the battle to openly gasp for air. But, another battle was raging in the room surrounding the bed. The minister was waging war with his own fear of death. In his mind's eye, he could see the death specter leave its patient watch in the doorway and move deliberately toward his friend lying on the bed. In that instant, terror struck the minister's heart, adrenaline rushed to his legs and feet, panic coursed through his body from head to toe as his eyes darted from Death to his treasured friend. He almost cried out a warning, "Stop! Leave him alone!" when to his amazement, an invisible force suddenly attacked Death, something that seemed to zap the death specter like a heavenly laser beam. Instantly, Death's entire being was replaced so that by the time his dear friend exhaled his last breath, only Rest and Peace engulfed him.

The sting and terror of death was destroyed because early in life, the professor had made the right choice. He had decided to follow after God and trust Him with his very life so that when his life progressed to the point that choosing was once again taken from him, the choices he had made throughout life had gained him the victory.

Mike Kramer sat perfectly still as the minister ended his story with a challenge to the students to make the right choices. Suddenly, Mike couldn't sit still another second. Excusing himself to the two ladies next to him, he tripped over their feet and clomped his way out of the echoing sanctuary into the vestibule and out into the cold winter wind.

Mike was convinced. Life is all about choices, and it was time he made some wise ones.

Franklin Street was nearly empty by the time Carrie packed her bags for her trip to the mountains to be with her family for Christmas. The bustling college town had become just a small, quiet village once again. She gazed out her upstairs window down at the charming street, all covered in a blanket of white snow and twinkling lights, thinking once again of her mother's miniature Christmas village she had loved to play with as a child. Many villages like hers were collectors' items, very expensive, but Catherine Jernigan wanted her children and grandchildren to enjoy the village and its colorful citizens, so she had collected reasonably priced pieces through the years. Year after year, the children and then the grandchildren would help their grandmother organize the little shops and houses and trees into a delightful little town, happily moving the little people around in their world of make believe.

But I can't move the people around anymore, thought Carrie. *The world outside this window looks almost the same as Mama's little village, but I can't control everything in this real world like I could in that pretend world. Our little villagers were always happy, always singing Christmas carols and shopping and decorating, sledding and playing in the snow.... Oh, well*, she sighed, *time to grow up and face reality as Daddy always says.*

"Dit dit dit DA! Dit dit dit DA!"

Before she had time to think, Carrie had put the phone to her ear and answered, "Hello!"

"Carrie, it's me, Mike. Please don't hang up!"

Her heart began to pulsate wildly. She closed her eyes, trying to calm herself before answering, "Hello, Mike."

Chapter Three

"Carrie? Carrie, can we please get together? I could come over, or we could meet somewhere. We really need to talk before we leave town for the holidays. Please?"

"I'm sorry, Mike, but I'm packing and getting ready to leave within the next hour or so, and I really don't have time to talk now," answered Carrie.

Don't cry! Don't cry! She silently ordered herself.

"We have to talk, Carrie. It's been a month, and it's just not right for us to go on like this. I've had a lot of time to think things over, and I feel as if I have some perspective now. I'm sure you do, too. What do you say? Could you just give me an hour? Half an hour?"

"Well…all right. I guess."

Mike quickly suggested they bundle up and meet at their favorite park bench in the town square. Carrie reluctantly agreed, still thinking this wasn't such a good idea.

Ten minutes later, they were slowly walking toward each other under the glow of the street lights in the midst of an incredible winter wonderland. Mike's breath formed white smoke in the frigid air as he greeted her with a soft hello.

"Mike! What happened to your face?"

The wonderful smile Carrie loved so much spread across his countenance as he gazed down into her eyes for the first time in nearly a month.

"Oh, it's nothing. I just had a little tumble on the ice," he replied. She looked up at him with tender eyes the color of ocean waves sparkling in the afternoon sun.

"You look beautiful," Mike said softly, smiling at the snowflake landing on Carrie's upturned nose.

Neither of them could think of anything else to say, so they just kept staring into each other's eyes as the cold wind whipped around them and snow from the trees overhead danced in the soft glow of the streetlights. Time seemed to stop; the two young people were wrapped in the love they had almost lost, both longing to run into the other's arms but afraid to break the magic of the moment.

Suddenly, a frigid gust of wind almost knocked them down, bursting their protective bubble and forcing them back to reality. They were both embarrassed, quickly recalling the life-changing events of the past month and the unhealed wounds in their hearts.

"Mike, I'm not sure this is a good idea. I have to leave soon, and we really don't have time to iron any of this out now. Why don't we just go and be with our families for the holidays and then get together when we return after New Year's?"

Mike grimaced. "No, Carrie. We need to talk now."

"Everything can't always go your way, Mike."

Surprised by the spark of fire in her beautiful eyes, he wondered for a second if Carrie had changed or if he just hadn't seen that before. But, true to her recent assessment of his character, Mike ignored the obvious and continued with his plan for their conversation.

"But, you don't understand. For one thing, I'm not going home. Mom and Dad left today on a trip to Europe they've been planning for years, and Sarah and David are taking Annie to David's home in Connecticut for Chanukah. They invited me to come along, and I've decided to go with them."

"That's nice. I hope you enjoy the holidays." Carrie's normally pleasant voice seemed as sharp and cold as the winter wind.

"But, wait, let me explain why I'm going, other than to be with my family. David's Dad is a rabbi, a really great guy, and I think it would be good for me to spend some time with him. One thing for sure I've learned from this confusing mess is that it's about time I learn what it means to be a Jew. Mom and Dad would probably cringe to hear me say that, considering all the years they spent teaching me these things, but I realize now that I simply wasn't listening. In one way, I took that part of our lives for granted, but in another way, I just didn't care. My heritage has never meant anything to me, but since Thanksgiving, I realize I can't keep that attitude forever. There comes a point in life when we have to make decisions and choices about everything. Lately, I've come to the conclusion that life is simply a series of choices, and it's past time for me to make a few good ones."

Carrie stared at him, wondering if he had really changed that much or if he had just figured out a new tactic to get his way. She quickly decided not to take the chance.

"I've had time to think things through, too, Mike, but I'm just not ready to talk about it yet. I need more time to process my thoughts and feelings, and like you, I need time to think about my own faith. You probably won't believe this, but I've *almost* decided that Emma and John aren't so weird after all. They have something I don't have, and I think I want it. I just have to find out what it is first."

Mike thought he glimpsed a faint smile finally beginning to form in her solemn face. "Well, I don't know about that, but I do know religion is a great deal more important than I thought it was, and I'm going to take some time to try and figure this thing out."

Chapter Three

"And I'm not sure that *figuring* is the way to do it, but I guess you have to follow your way, and I have to follow mine. This confusing mess as you called it has helped me see more clearly, too, Mike. I was always too quick to accept your way in everything. You said Emma was weird, and I thought Emma was weird. You said the differences in our religions didn't matter, and I believed the differences didn't matter."

"But, I…"

"No, no. I didn't mean that was your fault. You didn't dictate your opinions to me. But, I realize now that I must not think very much of myself to have placed such high value on how you see everything and never to have taken time to decide what I believe." Tears were forming in her eyes as she continued, "I want you to know that I'm truly sorry, Mike," she said. "I was angry with you at first, but I want you to know that I realize I'm as responsible for this mess as you are."

Carrie's apologetic words warmed Mike's heart, and he found himself desperate to touch her upturned face, her soft skin pink and glowing, framed by the furry white toboggan on her head. As the silent snow continued to fall about them, he reached out….

"Oh, no!" Carrie quickly glanced at the clock tower in front of the city library across the street. "I'm going to be late for my ride!" She was shouting as she turned to rush back through the snowy streets to her apartment. "They're supposed to pick me up at 5:30, and I'm not even packed!"

"Carrie, wait!" Mike shouted into the wind. "Don't go yet!"

His plea was lost in the bitter wind. Sadly, he watched her jog carefully through the snow and ice, her face turned away, and hands stuffed deep in the pockets of her long red coat.

Chapter Four

Christmas in the Blue Ridge Mountains—had she been offered this wonderful opportunity any other year, Catherine Jernigan would have been beside herself with excitement. She would have been happily making lists for gift shopping, groceries and hundreds of things to do, including putting together a little holiday itinerary since her big family would all be under one roof—not that she wasn't doing all that to a great extent. If there was one thing she prided herself on, it was her gift for organizing and coordinating. She really did it well, and what's more, she loved every minute she spent making long lists and checking off her accomplishments.

But Catherine's heart was heavy this morning as she attempted to go about her holiday preparations as usual. She was more than a little concerned about her youngest daughter. None of the family had heard from her since Thanksgiving, and even though she was an independent, twenty-three year old young woman, it just wasn't like Carrie to be so out of touch.

Catherine's concern accelerated as she pulled the little village pieces out of their tediously wrapped packing. She had painstakingly packed all the little boxes in big ones and asked her husband to load them in the truck, her grandmother's heart nearly breaking at even the thought of her grandchildren not having the village to play with during Christmas.

"I can't believe you brought all this stuff!" Tom Jernigan growled teasingly as he had when they loaded it into the truck before they left home. "I thought we agreed that you would actually get to relax this year? On top of that, where in the world are you going to put all this?"

"It's all right, Tom," Catherine calmly said. "I will get to relax more this year, but we have to remember that traditions are very important for the children. Each year we're creating precious memories they will never forget."

"Tradition! Tradition!" Tom sang the familiar tune from *Fiddler on the Roof* as he compliantly lifted the treasure boxes out of the back of the truck and carried them inside to lay them one-by-one on the floor at his wife's feet. Chuckling to himself, he couldn't resist the temptation to take his teasing one step further, "Tradition may be good, Catherine, but as old Tevy said, 'On the other hand....'"

Catherine laughed at Tom's silly rendition; her husband's sense of humor was one of the characteristics she loved best about him.

"Seriously, Catherine, tradition can become empty ritual and hard work, and that wouldn't be good for the children either."

"I know, Tom, I know. I'll try not to go overboard." Catherine smiled, continuing to unwrap the villagers. "Just please help me get it all out before the others arrive so the children can help place the pieces tonight."

Catherine had finished setting all the village pieces out and taking inventory when her mind wandered to another serious concern. One of the young girls she was counseling in her church was considering an abortion, and the thought of the little person within 18-year-old Melanie O'Brien never having the chance to live was literally making Catherine sick. What's more, she couldn't understand why nothing she had said to the girl had made any impact. She had talked with Melanie for hours, reading Bible passages about the sanctity of life and sharing heart-wrenching stories about other girls Catherine had counseled who had endured unbearable grief following their abortions. She had held Melanie in her arms as the suffering girl cried mountains of tears over the shame of her predicament and the loss of the little one within her body. But there was no relenting. Melanie would have the abortion, and Catherine couldn't do anything about it, neither could she comprehend the girl's reasoning.

The bottom line in the final decision was that Melanie believed her parents would never forgive her for getting pregnant before she had made something of her life. She knew they were not so concerned over the moral values she had lost—most girls had sexual relations nowadays and her parents were very open-minded—but, ironically, they would be devastated if the plans they had for her future were to be aborted. Melanie just could not handle the rejection she knew would come if she told them about her plight, and since she was

Chapter Four

eighteen, the church counselors and pastors had to respect her wishes not to inform her parents of the pregnancy.

Oh, God, Catherine silently prayed, *please get through to Melanie somehow. Please don't let her take the life of this baby and do irreversible damage to her own soul as well. Send an angel, Lord! Do something! I don't know what else to do.*

BEEP! BEEP!

"Here they are, Catherine!" yelled Tom as he opened the screened door and hurried out to greet the first arrivals coming up the steep driveway.

Startled from her thoughts, Catherine placed the family recipe book she was blankly staring at back on the kitchen counter, smiled deliberately and rushed out the door to welcome her son, John, and his wife, Claire. The two children had been asleep in the back seat during the last few miles of the drive and were slowly waking up to realize they were finally "there." Sleepy little faces smiled up at Catherine and Tom as they opened the door to take the children out and carry them up the steps to see the enchanting log cabin they had been looking forward to for weeks on end.

"Oh my, the view is breathtaking!" Claire exclaimed, standing on the porch looking out over the snow-covered panorama. "I can hardly believe my eyes!"

"I know. It's as if we've entered a gate into a fairy tale, isn't it?" Catherine responded excitedly. "I knew you would particularly love it, Claire. You have always shared your love of the mountains with us."

"Well, who wouldn't like this?" asked John facetiously, throwing his arms around his mother. "Winter Wonderland is an understatement!"

"Come on in and warm by the fire," said Tom. "You won't believe the size of this fireplace, John. Sure am glad you and Ron are going to help me keep the wood chopped and the fire going. Who said we were going to have a restful holiday?"

John laughed with his Dad as they carried the luggage up the steps and into the cabin.

Michele's family was next to arrive. Nana sat beside little Luke in the middle seat, and Papa was safely tucked in beside Blair in the back of the spacious SUV. The grandparents had tried to beg out of this family occasion, saying they would just add to the work, but the entire family unanimously agreed that the Jernigan clan could not celebrate Christmas without the patriarch and matriarch of the family. It just wouldn't be the same. So Nana and Papa were here, a little stiff and sore from the long ride, but happy to be with their children, grandchildren and great grandchildren once again.

The Gentile and the Jew: A Divine Romance

"Nana! Papa! Welcome to the Jernigan compound! Not quite the Kennedy compound, but even more wonderful to us. How was the trip? Are you all right?" Catherine asked all at one time.

"We're fine, Catty," Papa answered, hugging his fifty-three-year-old daughter-in-law, addressing her by the name only he ever called her. Catherine hugged him tightly, always grateful for this dear man who filled the void in her heart and life left by the early death of her own father.

"Come on in, Papa," said Catherine. "There's a chair by the fire with your name on it."

The remainder of the afternoon was filled with lots of hustle and bustle as everyone unpacked suitcases and boxes of gifts, getting everything "in order" as Catherine liked to say. The brothers-in-law helped Tom split the gigantic logs into the right size to fit the huge fireplace, stacking the wood in a pile on the wide front porch. All the children—Nick, Blair, Matthew, and even the smallest, Abigail and Luke—placed their clothes neatly into drawers and helped put away kitchen supplies before they ventured outside to explore. There was a little problem when Claire and Michele insisted that Abigail and Luke were a bit too young to roam around outside in the snow without one of the adults, but the two youngest finally gave in and were soon busy building log cabins for the villagers in front of the roaring fire.

By sundown, Catherine's organizing and her family's willingness to comply had proved successful. Everyone had unpacked, the supplies were all in order, the house was simply but beautifully decorated, and the village was ready for the children's own organizational skills to come into play after an early supper. The men had the firewood split and piled on the porch where it could be easily accessed, and the fire was roaring. Everything was perfect except for one thing—Carrie hadn't arrived.

"When did you say Carrie was leaving, Catherine? And, who did you say she was riding with?" Tom asked for the second time.

"I told you, Tom. She was to leave her apartment after work at 5:30, and that should have put her here at about 7:30 or 8:00, even in the snow. She said she was riding with a classmate whose family lives in Boone. Oh my, I should have asked for their phone numbers, but I just didn't think about it," Catherine said, trying not to sound worried.

"Let's not jump to conclusions," Papa said. "I'm sure Carrie's just fine. You know how it is—most things take longer than we plan."

"Papa's right, Mama," Michele agreed, "let's wait dinner another half hour. If Carrie isn't here by then, Ron will make some calls. In the meantime, let's see how the children have set up the village, and try not to worry." Michele had inherited a few organizational skills herself.

All eyes were turned toward the mantle clock as the big hand moved slowly up to twelve. They were waiting to hear the clock chime nine when little Abigail exclaimed excitedly from the window where she had been watching for her favorite aunt, "Carrie! Carrie!"

All of the adults seemed frozen for a second until Abigail's announcement sank in, but in an instant, they all jumped up and ran to the door only to find themselves blocking the doorway while Carrie struggled to get in with her luggage.

"Oh, Carrie! We're so glad you're here! We were so worried," Claire proclaimed.

"Are you all right, honey?" Tom asked his youngest daughter.

"I'm fine. I'm fine! We had a flat tire on that really curvy section of Highway 421 before you get to Boone—you know, where the highway climbs the mountain and your ears close up? We girls had to wait until someone stopped to help us since none of us was proficient at changing tires—even in good weather! Finally, a really nice Highway Patrolman stopped to help us and got us on our way again. His name was Baker, I think. I'm sorry I didn't call. I forgot the charger to my cell phone, as usual, and the battery was low, so I thought I'd better save my phone in case there was a real emergency."

"If anything like that ever happens again, you call us—no matter how low your battery is, young lady! At least we would know you were safe," Carrie's father reprimanded her.

Little Abigail and the other children were standing close by, watching to see if their favorite aunt was going to get a spanking, but when all the adults started hugging her, they began to jump up and down, squealing in exuberant relief. Then off they ran to put the finishing touches on the village project, asking Papa to help them get the train going so all would be complete for Carrie to see when she finished unpacking.

Michele and Claire set about getting dinner on the long pine table while Catherine showed Carrie to her room. She had immediately taken notice of her daughter's weight loss and the weariness in her ordinarily bright eyes the minute Carrie walked in the door. She watched her normally energetic daughter moving as if in slow motion, hanging her clothes in the closet and placing her books on the table by the bed.

"Come here, sugar, and sit beside me a few minutes," Catherine said, patting the place by her on the bed.

"Not now, Mama," Carrie replied, tears forming in her tired eyes. "I know you sense something's wrong, but if I start talking now, I'm afraid I'll go all to pieces and won't be able to play with the children tonight. I just can't bear to disappoint them, too, Mama."

Catherine instantly caught the meaning of her daughter's words even though she couldn't imagine how her Carrie could possibly be a disappointment to anyone, but she wisely decided to keep her thoughts to herself for now and let Carrie choose the right time to open her heart.

"All right, sugar, come on then." Catherine said soothingly. "Let's see what the children have done with our village, but remember, they need to go to bed and you need to eat something and get to bed early yourself. We made your favorites—country style steak, mashed potatoes and gravy. You could use a little meat on your bones, you know!"

Carrie did rest. She slept until nine the next morning. The children were kept at bay by the concerned adults who had stayed up late sharing their shock at Carrie's thin body and downcast countenance. In the family's eyes, she would always be the baby, and it's a known fact that the baby is adored in any family. Although the attention had not spoiled Carrie in the least, she did feel special and was always grateful for her attentive family, never feeling they were prying when expressing concern for her well being. But this morning as their baby snuggled under the warm quilts, she hoped they wouldn't ask too many questions. She really wanted to stop thinking for a few days and do normal family things like play in the snow with the children and help her Mama cook their traditional Christmas dishes. And she wanted to pray, really pray, perhaps for the first time in her life.

"Carrie," whispered Tom, opening her door just a crack in case she was still asleep.

"Daddy! Come on in," she answered with a weak smile, stacking the pillows so she could lean back against the thick pine headboard.

Tom closed the door and sat down on the edge of the bed, taking his youngest daughter's slender hand in his big one and giving her a big kiss on the cheek.

"How's my baby?" he asked, smiling deeply into Carrie's sleepy eyes.

"I'm okay, Daddy," she softly replied, slowly wrapping both arms around his neck, resting her head on his shoulder.

In Tom's eyes, she was his little girl, always and forever. One night when Carrie was a small child, he had held her in his arms as he watched the nightly news from his recliner.

"I love you, Carrie," he said, squeezing her in his arms.

"I love you, Daddy," she whispered back.

"But I love you four," Tom teased his little girl.

"I love you ten," she answered with a giggle.

"But I love you a hundred."

"I love you a million," Carrie exclaimed, trying to out-love her Daddy.

"I love you a zillion!" shouted Tom.

He thought he had her then. The room was still and silent a few moments as his tiny daughter tried to think of a number larger than a zillion to measure her love for her Daddy.

Then softly, the little girl looked up into her Daddy's eyes and whispered,

"I love you to the last number."

Tom Jernigan's eyes filled with tears, knowing that his little girl had expressed the largest amount of love she could possibly imagine. Neither of them ever forgot that treasured conversation and during all the years of their lives together, at appropriate moments and inappropriate moments, one would say to the other, "I love you to the last number."

Twenty years later, Carrie was still Tom's little girl, hugging him tightly as he whispered in a quavering voice, "I love you to the last number, honey."

The Jernigan family's first day together in the large, but cozy log cabin was filled with last minute preparations for the big dinner and celebration to take place on Christmas Eve. The women took time in the midst of all the tasks on Catherine's list to make Christmas cookies and chocolate fudge with the children as Catherine's mother had before them, using the guarded recipes which had been handed down generation after generation. By the time the little ones licked the last of the mixer beaters, scraped the fudge pot with their fingers and sprinkled red and green sugar on the last of the cookies, they didn't have to be told twice to go to bed. Exhausted little people lifted droopy faces to be kissed by mamas and daddies, grandmas and grandpas, and then toddled off to bed with stuffed animals and blankets lovingly in tow.

"Goodnight, bitsey ones," Carrie called as the last pair of little feet pattered off to a bedroom. "I'm going to turn in, too, everybody. It's been a wonderful day but a long one, and I want to be rested up for tomorrow. I'll probably dream about Mama's list and wake up exhausted!"

"Carrie, I didn't know you resented my list-making!" her mother said, pretending to frown.

The Gentile and the Jew: A Divine Romance

"Oh, Mama! You know we appreciate your lists! We'd never get anything accomplished without them. I just wish I were more inclined to be as organized as you are. Maybe when I grow up, I'll make lists, too!" Carrie said, hugging her mother tightly.

"You just be who you are," Catherine said reassuringly, smiling into her daughter's downcast face. Seeing the sorrow in Carrie's eyes, Catherine couldn't speak again but hugged her baby girl and turned her toward her bedroom.

"Sleep tight," she finally whispered.

Chapter Five

Her heart pounding so wildly she wondered if passersby could see her coat moving in and out, Rachel Kramer walked arm-in-arm with her husband, Isaac, down the narrow cobblestone street near the center of Bucharest, Romania. The two pilgrims were anxiously searching for an old building they hoped was still standing, the building that had once housed Rachel's parents' bakery in the years before the Holocaust. There had been moments on this journey when Rachel was almost sorry she had begun this search—moments when knowing the truth seemed too much to bear and when not knowing would have made life much easier.

Shortly after they arrived in Bucharest, they discovered the Jewish cemetery where her Liebowitz grandparents had been buried just a year before the massacres in Romania had begun. Standing beside their graves feeling a valid part of the past for the first time in her life, Rachel had actually experienced some measure of peace for the first time since they had begun their journey nearly five days ago. As Isaac cleared the old gravestones and the dates of her grandparents' births and deaths emerged through the dirt and grime, Rachel saw that they had died before the suffering of the Romanian Jews escalated into the Holocaust. That wonderful feeling of relief had been the fuel she needed to keep going, to see this thing through to the end no matter what the outcome might be.

"Just one more block, I think," Isaac said, squeezing his wife's gloved hand.

The Gentile and the Jew: A Divine Romance

Their directions were written in Romanian, but in preparation for this pilgrimage, they had taken time to learn enough phrases from one of those quick-study travelers' pamphlets to find the places they were searching for. Much to their surprise and great relief, their childhood knowledge of Yiddish, a conglomerate language combining Hebrew, German and other eastern European phrases, also helped a great deal.

"Here it is, Rachel!" Isaac almost shouted. "I can't believe the building is still here, and it's actually occupied by some type of business."

"Oh, Isaac, I feel as if I might faint!" Rachel replied weakly. "Let me stand here a few minutes and catch my breath before we go inside."

Very carefully, Rachel pressed both palms against the cold stones that made up the outside walls of the building, caressing each one as she moved her hands slowly from right to left and back, again and again. These precious stones had encompassed her living family for many, many years, protecting them from the elements and guarding them from harm. During those rare moments when Jacob and Golda Liebowitz were able to skip over the unspeakable years of their lives and remember the good times in Bucharest before the war, they often spoke of the days they worked in the little bakery on the busy *strasse*. Rachel remembered how she used to picture herself there with them as they recalled those early years of their marriage—mixing and kneading the bread by hand, laughing and talking with Jacob's brother, Joseph, and his wife, visiting with their customers and friends in the close knit old Jewish community. Oh, how she wished these stones could talk! What stories they could tell.

Her parents had shared very little, but during rare and random acts of remembrance, Rachel had sometimes thought she could actually smell the bread baking, and now leaning against the walls that held those coveted memories, she sensed that fragrant aroma still lingering in the cold air.

Her eyes closed tightly, Rachel spoke anxiously, "Oh, no, I must be losing my mind, Isaac! I can smell the bread baking!"

Peering through the building's one front window, Isaac laughed and said, "No, love, your mind is perfectly in tact so far. No one would believe this in a million years, but the building houses a bakery! You actually smell bread baking!"

"What?" Rachel turned around so fast she almost tripped on the uneven cobblestones, but Isaac reached out to steady his wife and show her the window through which he could see shelves of freshly baked bread of numerous varieties and shapes. They were so excited by that time that the sophisticated couple forgot their usual dignity and decorum and peeked like two giddy school children through the timeworn window into the tiny shop. Spying an elderly

Chapter Five

couple, a rotund little man and a tall skinny woman, both wrapped in white aprons, staring back at them, Isaac and Rachel jumped back from the window, breathed deeply, and walked through the door that would later be remembered as a gate to the past and, surprisingly, to the future.

"Shabbat Shalom!" The woman greeted them in Yiddish.

Once more Rachel felt as if she were going to faint, partly in reaction to the baker's greeting which meant they had to be Jewish, and partly because for the first time in her life she had forgotten it was Friday morning and almost time to close the stores in preparation for Shabbat.

"Shabbat Shalom," Isaac weakly replied.

"Could we help you?" the woman asked suspiciously, again in Yiddish mixed with Romanian.

Isaac understood that sentence. It was in the guidebook.

"Da," Isaac replied. "Do either of you speak English?"

"Nu, nu," the woman answered, both shaking their heads from side to side and wiping their floured hands on their aprons.

"Oh, Isaac, what do we do now?"

The disappointment in Rachel's voice was heart-wrenching. Isaac watched the tears forming in his wife's beautiful green eyes, but he didn't know what to do. They both stood there in the middle of the little bakery in the center of old Bucharest just looking at each other, the baker and his wife staring at the strange American couple who had entered their world on the eve of Shabbat on the seventh day of Chanukah in the year 2002.

"I speak English!" A deep male voice with a heavy Romanian accent came from somewhere within the small bakery, resonating throughout the little room thick with the aroma of freshly baked bread.

Startled, Isaac and Rachel simultaneously turned toward the voice and found themselves gazing at a very distinguished elderly man sitting at a small table in the back corner of the little bakery's outer room. The man was obviously Jewish by the *kippa* on his head and the long white beard he wore so well. Rachel noted the fringes of his *tallit* hanging from underneath the hem of his coat and the many books that were spread before him on the table.

"Da?" the voice resonated again.

"I beg your pardon, sir," Isaac said, "we didn't realize there was anyone else here, and on top of that, we're surprised to hear anyone speak English so well. Thank you for speaking to us."

"I assume you are not here to buy *challah* for Shabbat?" The man posed the statement as a question.

The Gentile and the Jew: A Divine Romance

"No..., no, we're not," Isaac replied. "We would like to ask you a few questions about the history of this area if you don't mind."

"Of course. Move my books from the chairs and sit at the table with me. Please...," the old man said, inviting them with his hand motion as well.

"Thank you, sir," Rachel said in a low voice, feeling as if she were being shown a new room in a dream she had been having most of her life. Astounded that the building was still there after over sixty years—the one building in the entire world she knew existed in her parents' hidden past—she was understandably having difficulty getting a grip on reality.

"Come...sit," the old man invited them again. "Ernst would be happy to serve hot tea, wouldn't you, Ernst?" He quickly repeated the sentence in Romanian, and the baker immediately began to nod his head affirmatively. He hurried into the back room to brew a pot of tea for his unexpected guests.

The elderly gentleman was silent as Isaac and Rachel took off their coats and settled themselves at the small table. They sat quietly for a few moments, each one wondering who should speak first. Finally, Isaac spoke up, "Thank you again for taking time to talk with us. Why don't we begin by introducing ourselves. My name is Isaac Kramer, and this is my wife, Rachel Liebowitz Kramer. We have embarked on a rather odd journey of sorts. I guess you could say we're on a Chanukah holiday and a family search mission, if you can imagine such a strange combination."

When the old man kept silent as if he hadn't heard a word that was said, Isaac followed his gaze, realizing the man hadn't taken his eyes off Rachel since he introduced her. She returned his stare and it seemed to Isaac that the old man and his cherished wife were locked in a time warp that for some incomprehensible reason, he was not eligible to enter.

The silence was becoming extremely uncomfortable for Isaac when Ernst, the baker, barged into the room with a large tray in his hands, his thin wife following closely behind carrying a smaller tray of cakes and cookies. Their noisy entrance jolted Rachel and her new acquaintance out of their strange time warp and zapped them back into Isaac's presence, somewhat alleviating his growing concern for the time being. The bustling baker's wife and the old man spoke so fast in their mixture of Yiddish and Romanian that the Kramers couldn't catch even the few words they usually recognized, but by the time the conversation quieted down, the little table was complete with tablecloth, teapot, cups, the plate of sweets and even a flower in a lovely cut glass vase.

Rachel was delighted. As she looked up at Ernst and his smiling wife, she could see that the joy on her face was expressing all the thanks the kind

Chapter Five

couple needed. Their faces beamed even more when she spoke the only word she could think of that meant "thank you," *"Danke, danke!"*

"Wrong language, love, it's *multumesc*," said Isaac.

"They know what I mean," said Rachel, still smiling at the happy couple.

It's amazing how the smallest acts of kindness can affect someone, Isaac mused, reveling in the sight of his wife's glowing face. A little flower in a glass vase, a hot cup of tea—it's the little things that matter most, and it's the little things we forget too often. He made a point to remember this when they returned to their normal lives.

The old man was again gazing at Rachel as well, watching her every move as she chose which cake she preferred while stirring a little lump of sugar into her tea. Finally, he spoke, "I am Abraham Wasserman. My family has lived in this area of the world for thousands of years. I tell you, I am not joking—as you Americans say. The Jewish people have a very ancient history in this land, and I am very familiar with most of it. Hopefully, I can answer your questions. Please tell me your story, my new friends."

For more than an hour, Rachel and Isaac shared what little they knew of her family history with Abraham Wasserman. They tried to keep the story as short as possible because they knew the distinguished gentleman and the gracious bakers wanted to close the shop by early afternoon to be at home with their families for Shabbat and to light the Chanukah candles in their menorahs once again. Abraham Wasserman proved himself to be a good listener and seemed extremely interested in every detail of their saga, interrupting with pertinent questions from time to time.

"We're not sure where they lived, and we don't even know the names of relatives other than Papa's father and mother whose graves we found in the Jewish cemetery," Rachel was saying as the story came to a close. "I do know Papa had a brother named Joseph who helped him operate the bakery, and Mama mentioned a sister named Sarah whom she loved dearly...but she could hardly bear to speak of her. I'm sure Sarah died in the Holocaust as did all of Mama's and Papa's families. That's what makes it impossible to find links to the past. There was never anyone but Mama, Papa and me—*never*." Rachel's voice had faded to a whisper, her eyes brimming with tears.

Isaac thought he saw a tear on Abraham Wasserman's cheek as the old man reached over to pat Rachel's hand, speaking gently.

"Do not be sad, daughter. Like Rachel of old, you are weeping for the children who never were, and you are allowing that sorrow to consume your life. Many of our people have done the same and have wasted precious years living in the horror and sadness of the past. We all lost. We lost six million

The Gentile and the Jew: A Divine Romance

family members in a sense. We can't understand the *Shoah* any more than we can understand thousands of years of *pogroms* and massacres in our history, but we have the present and the future—and we have our faith. We cannot lose our faith in the God of Abraham, Isaac and Jacob, my daughter. We cannot." Gazing intently into Rachel's bright green eyes, he continued, "Our prophet Jeremiah proclaimed,

> *"A voice is heard in Ramah, mourning and great weeping,*
> *Rachel weeping for her children and refusing to be comforted,*
> *Because her children are no more.*
> *This is what Adonai says,*
> *'Restrain your voice from weeping and your eyes from tears,*
> *For your work will be rewarded, declares Adonai.*
> *They will return from the land of the enemy,*
> *So there is hope for your future, declares Adonai.*
> *Your children will return to their own land.'"*[2]

Again, Rachel couldn't speak. She was stunned, wondering how this strange man they had stumbled upon in a foreign country could speak the words of the prophet in such a way that Rachel felt as if God Himself were speaking to her. Slowly, she turned to look into her husband's face and saw that he, too, was at a loss for words. Neither of them spoke again until Abraham Wasserman suggested, "Why don't we meet the day after Shabbat, my friends. I understand you want answers to your questions, but I think it would be good for the two of you to celebrate a day of rest together in the land of your forefathers. Read *Tanach* together, particularly the words we just shared from the Book of Jeremiah. I think you will be ready for our next session by the first day of the week."

"Yes.... Yes, that's a good idea, Mr. Wasserman," Isaac said, watching Rachel nod her head in agreement. "Would you like to meet us at our hotel on Sunday?"

"Nu, I have a better venue in mind. Here is the address where you can find me at ten o'clock Sunday morning," he replied, writing down the information before handing the paper to Isaac.

"Thank you so much, Mr. Wasserman," Rachel said. "Even if we couldn't see you again, our morning together has meant the world to me. I'll be forever grateful to you for taking time to speak with us today."

Chapter Five

"You are very welcome, daughter of Abraham. It was my privilege to listen to your story. I know it was difficult to share it with a total stranger," the old man assured her, peering deeply into Rachel's brilliant green eyes once more.

"Please tell Ernst and his wife that we thank them profusely for their kindness and hospitality," Isaac interrupted. "I'll leave some money on the counter to pay for the tea and cakes."

"Nu, nu! We are your hosts, and we are happy to welcome you to our country and our city. Go in peace," Abraham said in blessing.

"Shabbat Shalom!" Isaac and Rachel chorused, stepping out of the warm, fragrant bakery into the cold streets of old Bucharest. In unified silence, they slowly walked along the cobblestone *strasse* back to the train that would take them within a block of their hotel.

Suddenly, Rachel grabbed Isaac's arm and laughingly said, "We forgot the bakery! We sat there for two hours and never once asked about the bakery. We didn't ask how Ernst and his wife came to operate it and if they knew any of my family! Can you believe that, Isaac?"

At the delightful sound of his wife's laughter and the sight of the happiness in her lovely face, all Isaac could do was throw his arms around Rachel and hug her as tight as he could short of breaking her ribs. He kept one arm around her shoulders as they walked, and she forgot the bitter cold in the warmth of her husband's love.

Mike Kramer sat alone in the midst of the sprawling family his sister had recently married into. Her husband, David Klein, was the perfect host, introducing Mike to each family member and all the old friends who came by the house to visit during the Chanukah holiday. Mike had met many of them at Sarah and David's wedding in October, but that seemed like a foggy dream now. Annie was playing the traditional *dreidel* games with the other children when David's father, Solomon Klein, drew a chair close to Mike and sat down, giving his young guest a friendly pat on the back.

Mike liked the old man. Even though he donned a beard and insisted on wearing his *kippa* most of the time, Rabbi Klein didn't act very religious—at least not what Mike considered religious. David's father laughed a lot and loved to tell ridiculous jokes which Mike hardly ever understood, but he laughed anyway as did the rabbi's family and friends, primarily because it was fun to watch the old guy laugh at his own jokes. He sometimes reminded Mike of the old Red Skelton reruns he watched with his grandparents when he visited

The Gentile and the Jew: A Divine Romance

their home as a child. The silly comedian always laughed hilariously before he made it to the end of his jokes.

The Kleins were orthodox Jews whose family had migrated to America from Germany in 1938. Many times throughout his youth, David had listened to his Dad explain how his own father had discerned what was happening in Germany and how he had worked for years to buy his family passage to America, narrowly escaping Hitler's final solution. The older David Klein was a well-respected professor of engineering at the university in Cologne when he was given a copy of *Mien Kampf*. He could never understand why so many of his fellow countrymen were blind to what was written in black and white—Hitler believed the Jewish people were an inferior race, and he purposed to annihilate them all, even in the 1920's. But the world of reason paid him no mind.

Even before he heard those stories from David, Mike had already noticed that Rabbi Klein had inherited the gift of wisdom from somewhere, and he hoped some of that great wisdom would rub off on him while he was visiting in the Klein home for Chanukah. He was starting out on a new path—the path of right choices—and Mike decided that seeking wisdom like Solomon Klein's was an extremely good choice. He had even shared his hope with David.

"Do you know what wisdom is, Mike?" asked the rabbi, looking his guest straight in the eye.

"Uh oh," Mike stuttered. "David squealed on me, right?"

"Don't be embarrassed, son," the rabbi said. "You have asked for a precious gift—one that our forefathers, David and Solomon, considered the most treasured of all gifts. They both had much to say about the subject. Their words are recorded primarily in the books of Psalms and Proverbs. Maybe that's where you need to begin your search, Mike. I think you'll find our King David very easy to relate to—very down-to-earth, as it were."

"How did you know I'm beginning a search?"

"Anyone who desires wisdom is searching, Mike. You wouldn't realize your need of wisdom if you were not searching. It's like the old adage about the chicken and the egg, I think, don't you?"

Mike nodded in agreement, amazed at the rabbi's ability to answer questions before they were asked. The old guy was definitely worth listening to.

"Mike, if you don't mind, I'd like to share my father's definition of wisdom as a preamble to your journey. I well remember the first time he spoke to me about wisdom. I can see him even now, slowly stroking his long beard, leaning way back in his chair and carefully speaking these words in his thick German accent, 'Vat is visdom, mien son?'

"'I don't know, Papa,' I answered truthfully.

Chapter Five

"'Visdom, my son, is knowing vat to do vith vat you haf,' he said.

"Pretty simple, eh, Mike?" the rabbi quietly asked.

"To tell you the truth, I was thinking that your father's definition is deeply profound," Mike answered.

"Yes, it is. Simple, yet profound. Life is full of paradox, isn't it?"

"Yeah…but, put words like simple and profound together and you get 'difficult,'" Mike concluded, a quizzical frown forming in his face.

The older man patted the younger on the shoulder, saying with a chuckle, "You see, Mike, you're becoming wiser by the moment."

Mike laughed, turning just in time to catch Annie as she ran up to jump on his lap.

"Hello, my Mikey!" Annie greeted her brother as always.

"Hello, my Annie. What big eyes you have!"

"The better to see you with, my Mikey!" giggled little Annie.

After their usual nose-rubbing ritual, Annie cuddled up in Mike's arms, holding her constant companion, Teddy, close to her tired little face. The wise rabbi watched the loving interaction between the two, amazed that the tension Mike had exhibited since he arrived seemed to just melt away as he held Annie in his arms and gazed into her angelic little face.

How odd, he mused, recalling that David had told him Mike was in college when his parents adopted the little girl, yet their unusually close relationship was very obvious, especially considering the age difference.

The rabbi continued to study the pair as Mike's loving eyes finally gave up his watch over Annie and he leaned his head back to rest on her soft, curly brown locks. By this time, Annie and Teddy were in dreamland, and Rabbi Klein knew it wouldn't be long before Mike joined them. He wondered if he should speak so that Mike could take Annie to bed and turn in himself, but he couldn't bring himself to disturb the tender picture painted before him.

On the other side of the room, David Klein was looking at the same picture, but with a much broader perspective that included his father's curious gaze at the young man and the small child dozing in the big wing chair. David stood motionless, watching his wise father's facial expression change from one of curiosity to understanding and acceptance.

Carrie leaned heavily against the porch post and rubbed her eyes, making sure she was awake enough to experience the full effect of the magnificent sunrise being produced on the distant horizon. Zipping the blue ski jacket that made her blue-green eyes look almost turquoise, and pulling her furry white toboggan tightly around her head, Carrie carefully climbed down the snow-covered cabin steps and over to the edge of the yard where the mountain began its descent into the valley below. At that perfect spot, the owner of the log cabin had placed a heavy wrought iron park bench and cemented its legs into the ground. Carrie took the ice scraper and the towel she had taken from the linen closet and cleared the snow from the bench, making herself a little roost on which to watch the re-creation of a new day. This was the special time she had been waiting for since she arrived at the mountain refuge.

"Oh, God," Carrie prayed, "please keep everyone in bed so we can watch this sunrise together, just you and me. And, God, if You don't mind, I really need to have a long, long talk with You."

As the sky began to turn varied shades of blue and white and crimson, a golden globe too bright for human eyes suddenly appeared over the distant purple mountains, enveloping Carrie in a sanctuary more glorious than any cathedral built by human hands.

Catherine was up soon after sunrise, her mind quickly running down her mental list while she rummaged through her handbag for the paper one. She had dressed quickly and put on a big pot of coffee so she could highlight today's priorities while she drank her first cup of the day. Looking out the kitchen window to scan the sky for signs of more snow, Catherine spotted Carrie still sitting on the bench all wrapped in coat and blankets, the bright sky clear and incredibly blue around her scenic watchtower on the snow-covered mountainside.

Carrie looked so peaceful...almost happy, actually. *Something has changed*, she mused. She couldn't help but throw on her heavy coat, pour a cup of coffee for Carrie and set out to meet her daughter through the crunching snow with two cups of steaming coffee in her gloved hands. Carrie smelled the coffee and looked around just in time to welcome her mother with a warm smile and outstretched hands. Reaching for her cup, she lifted the blanket for Catherine to snuggle next to her on the bench overlooking the incredible snow-covered valley below.

Mother and daughter sat in comfortable silence, sipping their coffee and enjoying one another's company as only mothers and daughters can. Neither felt she had to say anything. Words were not needed, but each knew they would be welcomed when they came.

Catherine softly sang the lilting melody she had learned from her grandmother when she was a little girl.

Chapter Five

"Down in the valley, valley so low,
Hang your head over, hear the wind blow.
Hear the wind blow, dear, hear the wind blow
Hang your head over, hear the wind blow."

The song was one of the more widely known ballads passed down from generation to generation in the families of early Scot-Irish immigrants to America. There was a perpetual joke among the Jernigan clan that, along with her file cabinet full of lists, Catherine could produce a song for any occasion. Carrie's brother, John, always said he would be willing to bet that if his mother was with him when he had a flat tire, she would surely belt out a flat tire song, sure as shootin'. On this special cold, clear morning, the wind seemed to accompany her mother's song like a symphony of woodwinds, carrying the haunting melody down into the valley and up to the mountains beyond. Carrie laid her head on Catherine's shoulder, closing her eyes as her mother softly sang the remaining verses of the old ballad of unrequited love.

"You know, Carrie, the farm where your grandfather was born isn't far from here. It's been such a long time since we've been there...in fact, you were probably a little girl the last time we went. Do you remember the farm?"

"A little," Carrie answered. "I remember going to a family reunion there when I was around eight or nine, I think. And I remember climbing with all the other children up to a big rock that overlooked the farm. That's about it."

"Hm, I remember that reunion, too. For many years, even before my father was born, the area was called Hanging Rock after that particular rock formation. In fact, one of the family stories was that my father's older brother and some neighborhood boys used to swing him and his younger brother over the edge of that rock. They were terrified!"

"Oh, now I remember more. We ate fresh cherries right off the trees."

"Uh, huh. There were cherry trees, briar berries, apple trees and gardens full of fresh vegetables. There was even a trout stream that flowed right past the house and down the mountain. We children used to love to go down into the underground spring house on hot summer days and drink the cool milk that was stored there.

"Oh, that farm was entirely sufficient for all the family needs, but the story goes that when my father was a young boy, he felt something was greatly lacking on the farm—candy! Problem was, the farm met their needs, but they had no money to speak of. So, one Saturday afternoon after chores were done, Daddy went through with his well thought out plan. Earlier in the day, he had saved some chicken feed, so he filled his overalls' pocket with the feed, and because of a good-sized hole in the pocket, the feed sort of drizzled down his leg onto the ground as he walked toward the gate that led to the road to Banner Elk. Of course, the chickens followed the feed path he was making, and once he was out of sight, he grabbed one of the hens and off to market he went, trading the hen for a sack full of candy."

"I'll bet he was a happy fellow," replied Carrie, smiling at the picture her mother had painted.

"For about a day, at least, until his mother figured out a hen was missing and caught him sucking a stick of peppermint."

Carrie laughed, snuggling closer to her mother for warmth.

"Oh, these mountains are full of stories, sugar," Catherine continued. "I've always thought it rather interesting that your Daddy's family came from the early Scot-Irish who settled the coastal plain of North Carolina, and my family descended from those who settled the Blue Ridge. Of course, there was a little Welsh and English mixed in here and there." She laughed softly, sparks of remembrance in her smiling eyes. "My grandfather never could understand why a good Scotsman could live in such flat land. I just assumed the call of the sea was stronger in some than the longing for the highlands. In Scotland and Ireland, our ancestors had the sea and the mountains together, but here in America, they had to choose one or the other. Anyway, your father and I came from the same tough stock, and that means you're tough, too." Catherine chuckled, squeezing her daughter's hand.

"I haven't felt very tough lately," Carried quietly replied, her blue-green eyes sparkling with tears, her lips beginning to tremble.

"I know, sugar," her mother softly said. Catherine could tell her youngest daughter was almost ready to share what was laying so heavily on her heart, so she waited patiently and began to softly sing,

"Listen well and I will tell
A tale you'll ne'er believe.
It started way back long ago
On a cold, dark Christmas Eve.

The cabin swept and donned with green
And all the children were clean,
But none had seen the eldest child,
The beautiful Kathleen.

Chapter Five

Her papa searched both high and low
She was nowhere to be seen,
But then he found her high on the hill
Looking out o'er the sea of green.

My bonnie daughter, why are ye so sad
And why do ye stand here alone?
Yer mither is cryin' and worried sick
And the children be wantin' ye home.

Oh, Papa, I tell ye there's comin' soon
A mate God's sendin' to me.
And he'll have all that I will need
To make me one with he.

Then early one mornin' when spring came nigh,
Kathleen went off to the sea.
She kept her watch 'til the settin' sun
Was lowerin' itself in the sea.

O'er the horizon she eyed a sail
On the red and gold paintin' the sea.
She said to herself and all who could hear
'My mate is comin' for me.'

She followed the sail down to the dock
To see who he would be.
And as he lifted his face to the sky
His Kathleen he did see.

Ne'er was a lad so fitted to a maid
As Kathleen and Isaac would prove
For their Messiah had brought them nigh,
The Gentile and the Jew."

"Mama!" Carrie shouted, jumping up from the bench, blankets tumbling into the deep white snow, coffee spilling everywhere. "Where did you get that song? Did you make it up?"

The Gentile and the Jew: A Divine Romance

"No, sugar, I didn't make it up," Catherine replied, surprised by her daughter's sudden outburst. She wiped the black coffee off her hands and quickly reached for the blanket, shaking the snow off, hoping it wasn't too wet to keep them warm. "My grandmother used to sing that ballad when I was a little girl, but to tell you the truth, I haven't thought of it in years."

"But, I've never heard of such a thing, Mama!" Carrie exclaimed. "A Scot-Irish ballad about a Gentile and a Jew? That can't be. Someone just made it up. Right?"

"Well, I don't remember that I ever knew the answer to that question. But ballads are based on real life, at least some level of truth." Her mother was thoughtful as she continued. "Our Gaelic ancestors sang about the important events of their lives whether wars, love affairs, even scandals. The ballads were handed down generation to generation the same as if they were written accounts. Don't you remember Nana telling you children about the *song catcher*—the person in each clan who had the gift not only to sing well, but to remember all the words to the ballads so the stories could be passed down to the following generation? There was certainly room for error, but basically, ballads are based on true events, so I assume *The Gentile and the Jew* must be true, too. Hm.... I'm sure there were more verses to that song, but I can't recall them right now. Oh well, maybe the words will come to me later."

"That is so weird," Carrie stated matter-of-factly. She sat deep in thought for a few minutes, then looked deeply into her mother's eyes and said, "Mama, I have something to tell you."

"I'm all ears. Tell me."

"Mike and I have been going through a rough time since we were with you at Thanksgiving."

"I thought as much."

"Well, it isn't exactly a lovers' quarrel or anything like that. It's more complicated. You see, Mama..., Mike is Jewish."

"Well, that's not surprising," Catherine replied, "considering that Kramer is a very common Jewish name."

"You knew it then? And it doesn't matter to you that he's Jewish?" Carrie asked.

"Mike's being a Jew doesn't change the fact that your father and I think he's a very fine person. We were only with him a few hours during Thanksgiving, but we could tell that he's a very intelligent, well-mannered, ambitious young man. He seems to have many of the qualities we would want in a man who might marry our daughter someday. But, Carrie, you must realize that your religious beliefs are very different."

Chapter Five

"But, Mama, our beliefs are based on the Old Testament, the Jews' Bible, right?"

"Yes. The Jewish scriptures form the foundation for our faith," replied Catherine.

"And nearly all the people in the Bible were Jews, even in the New Testament—even Jesus!" Carrie grinned.

Catherine laughed, too, drawing the blanket tighter around her shivering shoulders, thrilled to finally see a smile on her daughter's face. "Yes, that's true, but most all Jewish people don't believe that Jesus is the Son of God or that He's the Messiah as do we. Mike doesn't believe that, does he?"

"No, I guess he doesn't. Actually, I think we have subconsciously avoided that question, but I'm sure the answer would be *no*. Oh, Mama, this is such a mess! But...oh, I don't know...after this morning out here on the mountain, I feel at peace somehow. Nothing's actually changed—except maybe *me*—but I know it's going to be all right."

Carrie turned her gaze to the ancient blue ridge of the snow-covered mountains beyond. "You want to hear the whole story, Mama?"

"If you're ready to tell me, sugar. But let's walk and talk before we freeze into an ice sculpture on the side of this mountain!"

Chapter Six

Isaac and Rachel Kramer did exactly as Abraham Wasserman had suggested, beginning the weekend with a private dinner in their hotel suite. Rachel lit the candles to welcome Shabbat, and Isaac blessed the bread and wine as they had done each Friday evening for over twenty-five years. For Rachel, the night was almost like Passover, different from all the rest, as she and her husband celebrated Shabbat in the country where her mother and father were born and began their married life together. This Shabbat seemed to her an especially holy time—set apart from all others. She thought of the Hebrew word for holy—*kodosh*—remembering that her father always used the Hebrew translation as if the word itself was too holy to speak in any other language.

Most of the day Saturday, Rachel sat with an open *Tanach* in her lap, reading again and again the words of Jeremiah that Abraham Wasserman had recited to her the day before. She continued to ponder the meaning of the prophecy while she and Isaac looked out their tenth-floor window at the age-old city of Bucharest below. Its striking onion-shaped domes from years of Russian occupation mixed with elaborate old European-flavored buildings and the cold plain architecture of the mid-twentieth century.

The rabbis had taught Rachel to read *Tanach* literally. What was written to the nation of Israel was to the nation of Israel and that was that. But, they also taught her that many times God has underlying meanings in His Book and that He can speak to each of us personally through the written word. Rachel couldn't help but wonder if the Almighty was speaking to her through this passage of scripture, wanting her to know that He was going to answer her prayers and bring her children home to their faith in Him. *Oh, God, let it be,* she silently prayed.

Rachel was up bright and early Sunday morning. She had showered, dressed and made coffee before Isaac rolled over to see why the alarm clock hadn't gone off.

"Rachel? Where are you?"

"Get up lazy bones," she laughingly commanded her husband as she came through the door.

"Wow! You look fabulous, my love." Isaac stared at his fashionably dressed wife, thinking she had never looked more beautiful. "All ready for the next step in our little adventure?"

"Yes! Da! Whatever, I'm ready," answered Rachel, pushing Isaac toward the bathroom. "You have exactly forty-five minutes, my dear. Now, get moving!"

Isaac mulled over the events of the past few days as the hot water pounded his tired body. The difference in Rachel's demeanor since they entered the little bakery Friday morning was remarkable. How he loved to hear her laugh and to see that radiant smile sparkle in her amazing green eyes. He hadn't realized how much he had missed that in the last few months or...had it been a year or more? Perhaps it had.

Like Rachel, Isaac, too, was concerned about Mike's growing political and cultural viewpoints, more especially, his total lack of interest in becoming a part of the family business. Sometimes he thought his only son was deliberately rebelling against his Dad about anything in general. During Mike's undergraduate years, Isaac had pretty much racked it all up to his "college thing," assuring Rachel he would surely come around in the end.

"It's just a stage," he would say, trying to encourage her. "Don't you remember, love? My mother always said everything is just a stage with children—they'll get over it eventually." But finally, now that Mike was beginning his last semester of graduate school, Isaac thought he could see at least a glimmer of the change he had hoped for.

Rachel wasn't convinced. She was one of those mothers who seem to be intuitively connected to their children to the point of knowing when something was wrong before she was told. *I guess it's the old Jewish Mother Syndrome,* thought Isaac, picturing little Annie in the window of his mind. *Oh, well, one more still to go.*

Chapter Six

"Make sure you take your overcoat and gloves, Isaac," Rachel called from the other room. "I'm watching the weather channel on TV, and even though I can't understand what he's saying, I can tell by the little icons that we're going to have an extremely cold day for our meeting."

"I'm ahead of you for once," Isaac answered, coming out of the bedroom with coat and gloves in hand.

"My, you're a handsome man, Isaac Kramer!" Rachel said admiringly, giving her husband the radiant smile he loved so much.

Isaac kissed her cheek. "And you, my love, are a very beautiful woman. Ready to roll?"

Rachel's hopes were soaring when she and Isaac left their hotel to take the train to the station nearest the address Abraham Wasserman had given them Friday morning. Judging by their wanderings in old Bucharest during the past week, they supposed the venue was not far from the bakery where they had met the old man. Rachel wasn't quite as anxious today as she had been Friday morning, but of course, she knew so much more now than she had then—or at least she knew someone who knew, and that gave her more peace than she could have possibly imagined.

The train ride was fairly short, and once again, Isaac and Rachel found themselves tramping down narrow cobblestone streets searching for pieces of the past. And again, Isaac glanced back and forth from the paper in his hand to the numbers on the old buildings, trying to find the correct address while Rachel stood shivering in the cold wind. Looking up and down the street one more time, Isaac said, "Most of these old buildings don't even have numbers, but if I've estimated correctly, it has to be that small synagogue across the street. I wonder why Mr. Wasserman didn't tell us we are meeting in a synagogue? It certainly would have been easier to find if we had known."

"It's almost hidden, Isaac. I wouldn't have noticed it being a synagogue if we were just passing by."

He took Rachel's arm and led her across the narrow street to the massive oak doors that seemed much too large for the building. Each of them touched the mezuzah on the door post, then their lips, entering the ancient door under the sign that read, Beit Emeth—House of Truth.

The anteroom was bare except for an old sideboard piled with papers written in Romanian and Hebrew. Isaac made a mental note to take some of the information to read when they left. They were standing in the middle of the room wondering which way to go when a door just in front of the couple opened and Abraham Wasserman walked into the room. Although the elderly gentleman was leaning heavily on his cane, he manifested authority and dignity on a level totally unfamiliar to the American couple, and finding him here in this ancient synagogue made him even more mysterious than he had seemed in the little bakery on Friday.

"Boker Tov!" The old man greeted the couple warmly, leaning on his cane with one hand and extending the other to Isaac and then to Rachel.

"Boker Tov!" they chorused, returning the Hebrew greeting.

"I hope it was not too difficult to find our meeting place," said Abraham.

"Actually, it wasn't as complicated as finding the bakery, but of course, we didn't have an address for that building," answered Isaac.

"Would you like to see more of the synagogue before we begin our conversation?" Abraham asked.

"Yes, thank you, we would appreciate a tour of the building. I can't tell you how much we have enjoyed studying the interesting architecture in Bucharest." Rachel reached out to take Isaac's hand.

Together, they followed the old man down the hallway and in and out of various rooms used for teaching Hebrew classes and preparing young men for their Bar Mitzvahs. One fairly small room was set with a large round oak table where Abraham Wasserman met with other scholars for hours on end, pouring over passages in Torah and Talmud, particularly searching for understanding of the coming of Messiah. There was even a large room built onto the back of the older building that served as a modern day Jewish community building. Rachel and Isaac were enjoying the little tour, asking a question or two from time to time as they strolled slowly through the rooms and hallways. Then the old man opened the large oak doors leading into the sanctuary.

"Oh!" Rachel gasped audibly as Abraham Wasserman stepped aside to allow her full view of the long, rectangular room. She and Isaac were instantly overwhelmed. Set as a window in the outside wall of one end of the room, a huge, stained-glass Star of David caught the rays of the winter sun and sent the light bouncing off every object in the room. It was as if they were looking through a kaleidoscope of light and color, all originating in the gigantic blue star. Isaac stood mesmerized at the sight of the splendid window while Rachel slowly turned to look toward the other end of the room.

She gasped again and stared with her mouth wide open, but she could find no utterance within herself to express what she felt at that moment. Rows of benches were arranged in a semicircle facing a high platform that held a large oak podium. Between the two sections of benches, a red carpet runner led up to the platform. In the wall behind the podium was the Aron Kodesh, the intricately carved holy ark which held the treasured Torah scrolls. The beautiful birch doors of the ark looked as if they had been hidden away in this synagogue since time began. Oh, how Rachel hoped she would be allowed to see them. She would have to remember to ask Mr. Wasserman. Or was it Rabbi Wasserman?

Rachel could almost hear the cantor singing the scriptures and the rabbi speaking the Aaronic blessing over the people...and she could see her beloved father, young and handsome in his *kippa* and *tallit*, sitting with the other men of the community, her dear mother smiling at him from her place with the women.

Tears were streaming down Rachel's cheeks, and for the first time in years, she had no thought of holding them back. Neither did her husband nor Abraham Wasserman. Then, in the midst of her wondrous vision and uncontrollable tears, the vibrant voice she had begun to hold dear began to proclaim,

"Barukh atah Adonai, Elohaynu, melekh ha-olam
she-hecheeyanu v'keey'manu v'heegeeyanu la-z'man ha-zeh.
Blessed are you, O Lord, our God, King of the universe
Who has kept us alive, sustained us, and enabled us to reach this season.
Amein."[3]

Chapter Seven

Rabbi Klein stood behind the podium in the large community synagogue gazing out at the sea of faces he had grown to love so dearly during the last thirty years of his life. Many were old, old friends whose children had grown up along with his own brood of five, one boy and four girls. Solomon Klein had trained their sons and now their grandsons for their Bar Mitzvahs. He had married their children and circumcised their babies. With each family, he had experienced their joys and their sorrows, and he knew them, really knew them, and because he knew them, he loved them—even the most cantankerous soul like Ida Goldstein, Solomon thought, catching sight of her glowering countenance. The Almighty always sends special agents to keep us humble, the rabbi concluded, deliberately smiling back at Ida's scowling face.

Studying his father's visage from his vantage point on the front pew, David Klein could almost hear Solomon Klein's conversation with himself as he followed his father's smile to Ida's section of the pew. *Good ol' Ida*, David thought with a chuckle. *Dad needs someone to keep him on his toes.*

In that moment, father and son locked eyes, looking deeply into the windows of each other's souls and admiring what they saw there. Solomon Klein was proud of his son. He had followed the instructions of King Solomon of old, to "train up a child in the way he should go," and David had not departed from that way as the Proverb promised. Many of Solomon's peers thought he should be terribly disappointed that David had not followed in his footsteps and entered rabbinical school after college. But Solomon Klein was a very wise man as Mike Kramer had noted earlier in the week, and he couldn't have been more pleased that his only son had followed his heart and worked hard to become a corporate lawyer. To the rabbi, his son still seemed an extension of himself, but with different talents and abilities.

His eyes roamed to Sarah, David's lovely new bride, sitting close to her husband and squeezing his arm from time to time. *I couldn't have asked for a more delightful daughter*, Solomon thought. *Sarah and David make a perfect couple, and I know we'll see great good from this marriage. The old matchmakers couldn't have done better.*

Solomon's eyes continued to roam across the rows of attentive faces—the sheep he cherished as his own family. There were Leah and Jonathan Beckman whose grief he had shared as if it were his own when their little Daniel was killed by a hit-and-run driver four years ago. They were healing as time went by, but he noticed that even during the service, Leah's eyes were more often than not riveted on her remaining two children as if she were afraid she might lose them any minute.

Help them, God, he silently cried.

Solomon's gaze rested on the wrinkled old face of Joseph Perle, the most eccentric character he had ever encountered. Joseph was half hermit and half gregarious socialite, his personality jumping erratically from pole to pole. But most people liked old Joseph, even if they didn't understand him, and Solomon not only liked him, he admired him and particularly enjoyed the rather strange and rambling conversations they had on occasion. You could never tell where old Joseph was going and that's what made him so interesting, thought Solomon, his searching eyes moving on down the pew.

Next to Joseph sat Mike Kramer with his arm around his little sister, Annie. It was good to meet new people—new lives, new challenges. He hoped he would be able to help Mike in his quest to understand his inherited Judaism, but more than that, Solomon hoped he could help Mike find the peace that seemed to elude the young man even as he joined the family in synagogue this morning. He sensed that religion wasn't the only issue Mike was dealing with.

Shalom, mused the rabbi, *is the word of the day*.

Once again, Abraham Wasserman sat with Isaac and Rachel Kramer at the small oak table in the back of the little bakery, having left the old synagogue to begin another one of their treasure-digging conversations. Already, it seemed a lifetime had passed since they arrived in Bucharest, and Rachel was eager to

Chapter Seven

ask the questions that were jamming her mind like an overloaded computer. As if they were old friends, Ernst and his wife happily brought them tea and something like scones to munch on while they talked.

Watching the cold rain coming down in sheets outside the old windows, Isaac again had the feeling they had been caught in a time warp, like that phrase that popped up on his computer screen now and then as he searched the Internet—*unknown zone*. He hoped it wouldn't be too much longer before they were zapped forward into the time zone he was familiar with and could function in. This whole adventure was getting to be a little too weird for his pragmatic disposition.

"Isaac!" Rachel called. "Where are you?"

"I'm sorry," Isaac replied. "I was lost in thought. What were you saying?"

"I was asking the rabbi if he had ever known any people named *Liebowitz* or *Liebovici* here in Bucharest. Our family name was sometimes spelled either way with the 'z' being added in America, I believe," Rachel responded, turning back to Abraham Wasserman.

The strange old man looked deeply into Rachel's eyes as he had the first time they sat at the table together. Isaac was about to jump up and yell, "Okay, let's go home!" when that deep, resonant voice finally spoke,

"Da, my daughter, I did know the Liebovici family. I knew your Uncle Josef and his dear wife, Sura Liebovici."

Rachel's heart was pounding so hard she could feel it in her throat and temples, sounding as if a drum were beating in accompaniment to the rabbi's shocking announcement. She thought she might be having a heart attack, but quickly decided it didn't matter if she passed out. She was determined to get to the end of this conversation. But when she opened her mouth, nothing came out. For the second time today, Rachel was speechless. She turned to her husband, her sparkling green eyes imploring his help.

"Are you sure, Rabbi?" Isaac quietly asked. "You knew Rachel's uncle and his wife who helped run this bakery?"

"Da, I did know them. I knew them very well," Abraham Wasserman replied. "I will tell you the story now, da?"

"Please tell us," Rachel whispered loudly, trying her best to remain calm in her excitement.

Looking the perfect picture of a Hebrew patriarch, Abraham began his story.

"Before the war, my family lived for thousands of years in Kishinev, a town in Moldova which was a portion of Romania before the Soviet Union took it over in 1940. Ah! You think I am exaggerating about the number of years, do you not?" Abraham smiled, not really expecting an answer. "I am not exaggerating, my friends. There were Jews in this area of the world as early as the year 101. This entire region was called *Dacia* in ancient times...."

Suddenly, the old man hushed, seeing the "Oh, no!" expression on Rachel's face, realizing she was afraid he'd never get to her family if he began his story in the second century.

"Ah, the curse of being a lover of history! I will have to skip a few hundred years," Abraham chuckled, continuing the story in his thick Romanian accent.

Rachel smiled sheepishly, blushing from embarrassment, but glad the old man was going to get on with the story.

"Although the Jews of Moldova had experienced a great deal of freedom and success during the years of independence, and to some extent under Romanian rule, the majority of Kishinev Jews were very poor as were most Eastern European Jews in 1941. But, we were home, my friends. Kishinev was our home the same as it was for many other ethnic peoples—Russians, Romanians, Poles, and others—even Gypsies. Jews were allowed to seek higher education, to own small businesses, to go to synagogue and keep Jewish tradition and culture alive, generation after generation. That is, they were allowed these freedoms in the intervening years between anti-Semitic uprisings. Before the war, approximately 65,000 Jews lived in the city of Kishinev."

Abraham leaned heavily on the table as if to glean its support. "It sorrows me greatly to tell you that around 53,000 of those Jews are believed to have perished in the Shoah—the Holocaust."

"Oh, my God!" Isaac exclaimed. "I had no idea that many people from one city were killed."

Rabbi Wasserman nodded, tears quickly forming in his aged eyes. "Da, it is true. But, our story goes back long before Hitler rose to power and the Nazi armies ate up Eastern Europe with the ease of little children playing a game."

He looked up at Rachel. "I am sorry, daughter. You must think I am rambling again, but I must explain for you to understand."

"Don't worry, Rabbi," she said, reaching over to pat his hand. "We didn't come this far for a five-minute summary. Tell us everything we need to know."

"Da, da. I will do that," he said, leaning back in his chair once more. "Da, it seems that the nineteenth century was a time of dramatic change in our area of the world. Romania revolted against the Ottoman Empire in 1821, followed by the Romanian revolt against Russia in 1848. Then came the total upheaval

Chapter Seven

of the Bolshevik Revolution in 1917. Moldova was like the rope in a children's game of Tug of War, continually pulled back and forth between Russia and Romania. The Jewish people had suffered terribly under many of the Czars, the depth of which rose and fell according to which leaders hated the Jews the most, blaming them for whatever problems the empire was experiencing at the time. Even when Romania won independence from the Turks in 1821, the Greek soldiers fighting with the Romanian army marched through the region, slaughtering Jews as they went."

"But, why?" asked Rachel, confusion written all over her beautiful face. "I don't understand. Why would the Greeks want to kill Jews when they were fighting the Turks? Why Jews?"

"That is the question of the ages, daughter, but no one has ever been able to come up with an answer. I can only say that, in my personal opinion, there is an evil greater than nations or Czars or Nazis behind it all." Abraham glanced at the worn *Tanach* resting on top of the pile of books beside the table, reaching over to touch it reverently as he continued his story.

"The persecution of the Jews in Russia and eastern Europe arose in the form of anything from burning homes and synagogues to the massacres of entire villages. I'm sure you know that these series of terrible persecution came to be called *pogroms*. In 1941, my friends, the *pogroms* were coming closer and closer to Kishinev."

The old man's voice began to falter. He sighed deeply as if he were exhausted just to be telling the sixty-year-old horror story. Taking a deep breath, he lifted his shoulders and began again.

"I was fifteen years old in 1941 when my father came home one evening and began to rush from room to room, stuffing anything of value into a feed sack, talking in hushed tones to my mother at the same time. My two younger sisters and I were curious as to what was wrong with my father, so we followed him around the house like little puppies, trying to listen to the conversation. All we could understand was that we were leaving our home and we were leaving quickly. We were never to see our aunts, uncles, cousins and most of our friends again.

"Later, during our clandestine escape to Bucharest, my grandfather, a Torah scholar in Kishinev, told me that my father had stayed awake many nights trying to persuade him and my grandmother to leave their home and go to Romania with us. But it was very difficult for them to grasp the danger we were in, even though they had lived through terrible *pogroms* under the rule of Czar Nicholas II."

The Gentile and the Jew: A Divine Romance

"Yes, I've read about that," said Rachel. "Most people romanticize that era, relating Nicholas's reign to the mystery surrounding Princess Anastasia. But, it must have been a terrible time for our people."

"Da. Rumors were rampant in the early forties, but my father had been told by someone in the Jewish underground that there were Jewish agencies in Romania that would help Jews escape to Palestine. That was true, but he also believed anti-Semitism in Romania had not reached the heights our people were experiencing in the Soviet Union. Of course, that rumor was quickly proven incorrect.

"I am sorry, my friends," the rabbi said in a weary voice. "It is very hard to summarize this story because it happened over many long years, but I will try to 'wind it up' as you Americans say."

"Oh, no, Rabbi," Rachel protested. "I want to know everything. I have to understand."

"Of course, but I will try not to bore you with so many details. You want to know about your family, da?" he asked.

"Yes. I've been on a long, long journey, and I feel as if I'm coming to the end at last. Please...please, continue. Tell us everything," begged Rachel.

"Da. After many nights traveling secretly through forests and fields from Kishinev through Moldova into the eastern section of Romania, my family reached a small village just south of the town of Jassy near the Moldavian border. We found the Jews there to be very afraid and very suspicious of anyone they did not know, so my father struggled to find a Jewish family willing to let us stay the night in their barn. Finally, a man named Avram and his wife, Riga, welcomed us warmly into their home. I remember them even now as if it were yesterday...."

The venerable old man smiled as his voice drifted away with his memories.

"Rabbi?" prodded Isaac, gently.

"Ah, yes. During that long night while we children slept soundly, Avram and Riga revealed to my parents and grandparents the dreadful basis for their fear. Jassy was a city with a population of 100,000 at the outbreak of the war. Fifty thousand of the inhabitants were Jewish. Can you believe that, my friends? We Jews were not the minority in that city, therefore, we have asked for sixty years, 'How could such a thing have happened in a place where half the population was Jewish?' I do not know. No one knows." The old man paused, closing his eyes for a brief moment of rest.

"What happened in Jassy, Rabbi?" asked Isaac, quietly.

Chapter Seven

Abraham shook his head from side to side. Taking a deep breath, he answered, "Unbeknownst to my father, secret anti-Semitic measures had been initiated in Romania even before the revolt against the Soviet Union that began on June 22, 1941. Avram and Riga told my parents and grandparents that between June 20 and 26, the Jews of Jassy were forced to dig two large mass graves in the Pacurari Jewish Cemetery. During the morning of June 29, 1941, Jewish men, women and children were marched in ranks to police headquarters where German and Romanian soldiers surrounded them in the courtyard. About two o'clock in the afternoon, they began to fire into the crowd of Jews with rifles and machine guns."

"Oh, my God," whispered Rachel, her voice tremulous, her hands shaking. She covered her eyes as though she could block the ghastly pictures from her mind.

"The massacre continued erratically until six o'clock in the evening. Can you imagine the horror? Little children standing for hours, everyone screaming in absolute terror all around as the guns exploded continuously for four hours, friends and family falling to the ground in pools of their own blood. My friends," Abraham tearfully said, "it took four trucks and twenty-four carts two days to transport the corpses to the mass graves the Jews had dug for themselves the week before."

Rachel couldn't sit still another second. Sobbing openly, tears flooding her cheeks, she quickly pushed her chair back and stumbled around the table to wrap her arms around the rabbi who seemed to have aged considerably since he began his story only a little while ago. He reached up to grasp her hands, his strong voice finally breaking at the outpouring of love and compassion from the American strangers. Rachel's dignified businessman was weeping openly, not knowing what to do for Abraham Wasserman or Rachel, himself, or the millions of Jews whose blood was crying out from the ground even as Abel's had when his own brother murdered him in the beginning of human history.

Abraham slowly reached into his coat pocket for a handkerchief and wiped his tearful eyes. Finally, he began to speak again. "There is more, dear friends. The twenty-five hundred Jews who survived were herded to the train station. Around four o'clock the next morning, nineteen hundred more Jassy Jews were rounded up and taken to police headquarters. At four fifteen in the morning, the first two trains departed. It was June 30, 1941. The first twenty-five hundred who survived the courtyard massacre were forced into around thirty-four sealed freight cars. When the train was emptied, there were only one thousand seventy-six Jews left alive. Around six o'clock, the second roundup consisting of nineteen hundred and two Jews was loaded into another train of eighteen cars. Eleven hundred and ninety-four of them died."

The old man paused and sighed before he softly spoke the final judgment sentence.

"At the end of the day, over eight thousand Jewish men, women and children were dead."[4]

Ernst came through the swinging door with another pot of hot tea to find the three new friends sitting limply at the small table in total silence. Isaac's shoulders were drooping, as tired as if he had dug ditches all day. Rachel was staring down at the table through glazed eyes, her mouth slightly open, breathing slowly. Abraham Wasserman's elbows rested on the table, his head held in his hands. No one said a word. The baker stepped back, then slowly turned and silently left the room with the teapot still in his hands.

After what seemed like hours, Abraham continued, almost whispering. "When we finally arrived in Bucharest, my father was told that massacres of the Jews had already taken place in January of that year. The Romanian rebels, joined by the mobs, vandalized Jewish properties and destroyed many buildings, including the High Sephardic Synagogue. Then, a group of Fascist legionnaires called The Iron Guard rounded up one hundred twenty-seven Jews, loaded them into trucks and murdered them in the forest on the outskirts of Bucharest. The evil people even took photographs—the naked bodies lying frozen on the snow-covered ground, looking from a distance as if one hundred and twenty-seven leafless trees had been toppled and laid in long, neat rows."[5]

Abraham leaned back in his chair, sighing deeply, his old eyes staring at the table as if he could still see the horrible photographs.

"Did you know any of those people?" Rachel asked gently, wiping her eyes and fumbling in her purse for more tissues.

The old rabbi spoke slowly, almost in a monotone, his voice much lower than usual. "Nu. As I said, it happened just before we fled Moldova, believing Bucharest was a safe haven." His eyes seemed to be drilling holes in the old oak table. When he spoke again, Rachel had to lean forward to understand his thickly accented words.

"But, I know someone who knew them.... Ernst was there," he whispered. "In...in the forest. He saw it all. They said he must have followed the truck trying to get to his papa who had been taken away. Just a small child, he was, maybe six or seven years old. He was running down the road when someone found him. Just running and running and running, with a look of sheer terror on his little face. Never again did he speak. Never."

Chapter Seven

Isaac and Rachel were stunned. Neither of them moved until Rachel suddenly cried out, her hand covering her mouth to quiet her wail, "Ernst, oh Ernst!" She wept uncontrollably, Isaac holding her hand and gulping back his own tears.

"He does not remember that day or the dark months that followed. His dear mother, God rest her soul, not only had to endure the grief of her husband's horrible death and his loss, but the agonizing day-after-day care for her terrorized child. They said he would sit for hours looking out the window, then suddenly jump up and run out into the *strasse*, running and running until someone found him and brought him home." Abraham sighed deeply, ripping his eyes from the horror of the past to stare at the door to the kitchen where the sixty-eight-year-old little boy could be heard banging pans and scurrying around as he and his wife cleaned the utensils they had used to prepare and bake the fresh bread earlier in the day.

"No human should have to see such a thing. Certainly not a child," Isaac said softly, shaking his head from side-to-side. "We Americans can't imagine such horror. The only experience we have had that would even begin to compare to just one pogrom was the terrorist attack on September 11 when three thousand people were murdered in an hour's time. But the United States is a big country, and I'm sorry to say that we forget too easily if the horror doesn't affect us personally. We tend to have an 'eat, drink and be busy' attitude."

"Rabbi, did your family have to hide when you arrived in Bucharest?" asked Rachel, trying to stop her tears with one tissue after another.

"Not at first, daughter," Abraham replied, "but we had to be very careful. Bucharest was a large city even then, and as Isaac said, we humans tend to walk around with blinders on, even when evil surrounds us on every side. But in retrospect, I must say that most good people in the entire world had blinders on in the thirties and early forties.

"So, my friends," the old man continued, straightening his shoulders once again, "my father found a small house in the oldest section of Bucharest where the synagogue is today. All seven of us moved into that little three-room house where our mother and father taught us to be grateful for the blessings of the Almighty, whether great or small. My distinguished father found a job working in the sewers, making just enough money to keep us from starving. Since I was fifteen, it seemed reasonable to me that I should get a job, also, and help with the family's expenses. One day soon after we moved into the cramped little house, I asked my father to allow me to go out and get a job. Ah, it is as if it were yesterday." The old man smiled at the sweet remembrance.

The Gentile and the Jew: A Divine Romance

"'Nu, my son!'" he shouted. "'You must finish your education. You must study hard and become a rabbi like your great grandfather, the Rebbe.'

"'But, Abba,' I said, 'Jewish children are not allowed to go to school anymore. Where will I learn?'

"My father answered, 'I will find you a tutor, my son. The Almighty will supply.'

"I will have to admit that I thought the trauma of our flight from Kishinev and the strenuous labor in his new life had affected my father's mind, but I knew to say nothing. My father had spoken. Days went by, then a week or maybe three, I cannot recall, but one day my father came home all filthy and stinking and announced, 'My son, tomorrow you will begin to study under the tutelage of an old friend from Kishinev, Aron Liebovici.'"

Rachel's body jerked with a start, an involuntary cry leaking from her wide-opened mouth. "I'm sorry, Rabbi. Go on. Who was he?" she urged, her hands trembling once again.

"I will tell you, my daughter. During the days and months which followed that welcomed announcement, I learned that Aron Liebovici was a friend of my grandfather when he was a boy in Kishinev. Even though they had parted ways on some of their religious beliefs, the two men had remained friends and were joyfully reunited in Bucharest. Aron Liebovici had been a student and disciple of a renown man named Josef Rabinowitz.[6,7] Have you ever heard of him?" Abraham asked.

Shaking her head and looking to Isaac, Rachel replied, "No..., have you, Isaac?"

"I don't think so. Who was he?" asked Isaac.

"A very interesting man, but we will talk about that another time," Abraham answered. "I'm sure Rachel is getting anxious to find out about Aron Liebovici, da?"

"Yes, yes!" Rachel exclaimed. "I can't stop trembling!"

"Aron Liebovici was your great uncle, daughter," Abraham proclaimed, his voice gaining strength now that they had entered a brighter chapter of his story. "He was your grandfather's brother, the man who opened this little bakery in order to provide for his family while he studied Torah and the writings of the sages. He was one of those very rare Jewish men who could live in the world of books and the practical world of family and work at the same time. Da, he had the wisdom of Solomon, that man, and with that wisdom, he had a profound effect upon my life and the lives of all the Jews in our community. But that is another story for another day."

Chapter Seven

Then, pulling his torso up to his full height and looking straight into Rachel's eyes, the old rabbi boldly pronounced, "Now, I must tell you, Rachel Liebovici, that I also knew your father, Jakob!"

Rachel jumped to her feet, both hands flying up to cover her gaping mouth and just as quickly reaching down to clutch her heaving stomach. She slowly walked over to the counter in front of the shelves of freshly baked bread, gazing at every inch of the room as if she could now see the family she had lost even before she was born. Loosening her hold on her stomach with one hand to touch the clumps of flour spilled on the counter, she slowly rubbed the white softness between her slender fingers. Even the flour seemed to be hers now, a treasure in time. She had a real family. She finally had a family.

In two giant strides, Isaac was across the room with his arms wrapped around his wife, squeezing her over and over again. He couldn't think of a word to say, so he said nothing, hugging Rachel to his heart's content.

"Oh, Isaac..., Rabbi...I can't believe this!" Rachel cried. "My lost treasure is found—my family! They were real people who truly existed! And, you knew them, Rabbi? You spoke to them and touched their hands and saw their faces?"

"Da, my daughter," Abraham answered with a smile. "Your father and his brother, Josef, were about seven to ten years older than me, but we were often together on our *strasse* and in the synagogue. I guess I knew your family best by coming to this bakery every day to get bread for our family."

Abraham chuckled. "Sometimes I dreaded coming here because I knew the days Aron Liebovici would be here and I also knew he would ask me a question regarding my studies that I might or might not be able to answer. By the time I rushed out the door with the hot bread wrapped in a bundle, my hands were so sweaty I had to wipe them on my trousers."

"But, I always thought my father ran the bakery with my Uncle Josef. You're saying the bakery belonged to his uncle, Aron Liebovici, right?" Rachel asked.

"In the beginning, child," Abraham replied. "Your grandfather, Aron Liebovici's brother, was older than he and very poor as we all were, so he was not able to help his children get a start in life. He and your great grandmother also died fairly young, I believe. I never knew them."

"Yes, they died before your family fled to Bucharest," replied Isaac, recalling the dates on the tombstones.

"Da. Because Aron Liebovici never married and had no children, he taught Jakob and Josef the bakery trade and planned to eventually turn the business over to them as he would have for his own sons."

The Gentile and the Jew: A Divine Romance

"I see," said Rachel. "Go on, Rabbi."

"But the Jewish situation in Romania intensified during that year and the Liebovici family spent countless candlelit nights at a table in this very bakery, discussing the plight of our people and the alternative paths of escape. Your father always wanted to go to America, but his brother, Josef, was bent on seeking passage to Palestine. They argued over this for many months, both of them desperate to keep the family together, pleading with Aron Liebovici to go with them wherever they went. He was a very stubborn old man by that time, much like myself," Abraham said, smiling, "and he would not budge from his determination to stay in Bucharest, his home. I can remember Josef telling me what he always said during those arguments,

"'Nu, my children, I will not flee from the enemy again. We left Russia to find peace and safety in Romania. There is no peace and safety in Romania. There is no peace and safety for Jews anywhere outside the arms of Messiah. You must go. Perhaps the Almighty will have mercy on you in a new land, but I am too old. I will remain.'"

"What happened to him?" Rachel quietly asked.

"I am thankful to tell you he died peacefully in his sleep in the summer of 1943, an old and faithful servant of God. By that time, Jakob and Josef were long gone, so my family and our neighbors laid his body to rest in the Jewish Cemetery where your grandparents are buried."

"I wish I could have known him," said Rachel sadly.

"Da, you would have admired your uncle and loved him as we all did."

"Did you say Papa and Uncle Josef were gone when Aron Liebovici died?" Rachel asked. "I know, of course, that my father and mother eventually made it to America after the camps were liberated, but what about Uncle Josef? What happened to him and Aunt Sura?"

"Da, I will tell you," Abraham answered, "but first...Ernst! Could we please have some tea and maybe some bread and that delicious butter you make? This old man is starving, and I'm sure our guests are hungry, too." He spoke first in Romanian and then in English for the sake of his guests.

Happily, Ernst burst through the door and waved to the rabbi. Wiping his floured hands on his apron, he hurried to the kitchen to prepare food and drink for his visitors. He was back in no time with a large tray loaded with teapot, cups, sugar and milk. His faithful wife followed as usual with a large platter of hot braided bread, the top cooked to a shiny golden brown, its fragrance permeating the warm little room. The baker's wife set the plate in the middle of the table as Ernst placed the tea tray on a low sideboard close by. Taking a long bread knife, he quickly sliced the hot loaf into individual pieces and just as quickly lathered the rich butter over the slices, the butter melting instantly as it touched the hot bread.

Rachel watched every move Ernst made, tears again running down her cheeks until Isaac patted her knee under the table, warning his tenderhearted wife that she was going to embarrass the dear man if she didn't stop staring at him. Isaac thought he had never seen nor smelled a better lunch than this, and along with the rabbi, he and Rachel grabbed bread and teacups and began to devour the tantalizing meal, laying aside for a few delightful moments the heavy topic at hand.

"Absolutely delicious!" Isaac proclaimed loud enough for the baker and his wife to hear in the kitchen.

Wiping her buttery mouth as delicately as possible, Rachel smiled in agreement, "Yes! I have never tasted better food in my entire life! Who would have ever thought that simple bread and butter could taste like this? Thank you so much, Ernst. Thank you, Sarah!"

As the rabbi translated, the baker and his wife came into the room grinning from ear to ear, their faces beaming at their guests' abundant compliments.

"Da, da," said Sarah. "Velcome...tank you," she repeated the English words she had learned in honor of their new friends.

"Yay!" Rachel exclaimed, clapping her hands cheerfully. "That's very good! But, it's we who need to thank you a thousand times over for your wonderful hospitality. You have treated us like royalty, and we are forever grateful."

Ernst and his wife backed out of the room, their faces glowing, heads nodding as Abraham again translated Rachel's compliments for them.

Thanking God for the food after the meal as is the custom of many orthodox Jews, Abraham Wasserman raised his eyes to heaven and spoke the Hebrew words that always caused chill bumps to pop out on Rachel's skin, even in the overly warm bakery. She had heard rabbinical blessings in Hebrew every Sabbath since she was a baby, and she and Isaac faithfully spoke Shabbat blessings and special feast day prayers in Hebrew in their home, but there was just something unequaled about the way Abraham Wasserman proclaimed the ancient words. Watching his face, Rachel couldn't help but think of Moses whose face glowed when he was in the presence of Jehovah.

That's it, she thought in awe. *He isn't just saying a prayer out of tradition. It's as if he's really speaking to God.* Rachel stared at the rabbi in wonderment, feeling privileged to be in the presence of such a man.

Watching Isaac's smiling face and Rachel's intense countenance, Rabbi Wasserman patted his stomach and said, "Are you ready for another chapter of our story?"

The Gentile and the Jew: A Divine Romance

"Oh, yes. Continue your saga, Rabbi," urged Rachel as the bakers scurried about clearing the table.

"Da. After many months, Jakob and Golda made their final decision to go to America, the only country on the face of the earth where Jews could find freedom and safety. Of course, Josef and Sura were just as determined that Palestine was the only answer, and they set about to secure passage on a ship that was to go from Constanta, the Black Sea port of Romania, through Istanbul to the port of Haifa in Israel. All this time, your father was saving every penny, hoping to be able to pay his and Golda's way through the underground to America.

"Josef and Sura left Bucharest first along with another family who lived on our *strasse*. I can still remember the sadness that consumed our neighborhood like a dark cloud. It was terribly hard for them to leave their families and friends of a lifetime to make the dangerous journey through occupied Romania into Turkey and wait there in unknown circumstances for a ship to Palestine, a place that was only a daydream for more than nine million European Jews."

"Oh," Rachel moaned, "I can hardly bear to think about it. Hundreds—no, thousands—of families being ripped apart, never knowing if they would ever see each other again."

"Most of them didn't, two-thirds of the nine million," Isaac responded quietly, staring into space, remembering his own grandparents who had disappeared into that unparalleled darkness and never returned.

"Da, dear friends, it was so," the rabbi stated. "Josef and Sura left Bucharest during the night in early December, 1941, just six months after my family arrived from Kishinev. They had paid all the money they had in the world for passage on a Greek boat called the *Struma*.[8] Many months later, after no word from Josef, Aron Liebovici discovered the fate of the vessel.

"Seven hundred and sixty-nine Jews boarded an old dilapidated cattle boat with one bathroom and no kitchen. They reached Istanbul in three days, but the Turks would not allow the passengers to go ashore. The boat was quarantined in the bay while vain attempts were made to repair the worn-out motor.

"It was during this time that the passengers aboard the *Struma* learned they had no immigration certificates for Palestine. Those who had arranged the passage had lied to them in order to receive exorbitant prices for the tickets, and now the Jews found they would be attempting to make illegal entry into Palestine. But by this time, the nearly 800 passengers had no fresh water and no provisions. For ten weeks, they existed in the little boat off the shore of Istanbul, starving and dying because of the horrid conditions. The Turkish government would not allow them to come ashore, the Romanian government would not allow them back in Romania, and the British government would not allow them to go on to Palestine. The passengers and the Jewish groups who were desperate to find a solution begged the Turks to at least allow the children to go ashore, but the request for mercy was denied. The children stayed aboard.

The old man's voice began to tremble. "On the night of February 23, 1942, the *Struma* and its passengers were towed approximately six miles from the coast and left there. No food, no water. The motor was still not repaired, but even if it had been, there was no fuel. The boat with its doomed cargo drifted for about two hours, then...it exploded."

"Oh, my God!" Isaac cried.

Rachel was stunned. She had thought the rabbi's story was finally headed toward a positive outcome with hope of finding some of her uncle's descendants still alive. Now, she stared at Abraham, her mouth open, awaiting the inevitable end to the story of Josef and Sura Liebovici.

"Most people believe a Soviet torpedo hit the *Struma*," Abraham quietly said. "The last chapter of the horror story is that the Turks did not send out rescue boats until the next morning. Except for one man, those who survived the explosion died during the night in the freezing waters of the Black Sea."

Watching Rachel's dazed expression, Isaac reached for her hand. Holding it tightly, he turned to Abraham and asked quietly, "So Josef and Sura died in the explosion?"

"My daughter," the rabbi began, "for many, many years we thought that your uncle and his wife died with the passengers of that ill-fated boat. You yourself told me that your father died just in the last few years believing that his brother and Sura perished along with the other 767 passengers on the *Struma*, da?"

"Yes. He believed his brother was dead, but of course, he never told me what happened to Uncle Josef. He never mentioned the boat or anything about their deaths. Neither did my mother," Rachel answered.

"Da," said the rabbi, "the survivors of the *Shoah* very seldom speak of the horrors they faced or the family they lost. It is as if they are cursed with a mixture of traumatic grief and unbearable false guilt. If they think of their loved ones, they are forever faced with the unanswerable question, 'Why did they die and I survive?'"

"Yes, my mother and father were like that," Rachel replied. "As long as they could hide the past in some hidden compartment in their hearts, they could live in the present. That's why I could never ask them the questions I longed to have answered. I knew my questions would open that secret compartment and the locked up grief and guilt would overtake them again. Oh, Isaac!" Rachel cried. "I've lost them all again!"

The Gentile and the Jew: A Divine Romance

"Nu, nu, daughter!" Abraham cried. "My story is not complete. Listen carefully. Your Uncle Josef and Sura were not on board the *Struma*."

"What? Are you saying they lived? They made it to Palestine?" cried Rachel, rubbing her temples, trying to ease the headache developing in her anxiety.

"Da, my daughter. Josef and Sura lived. For some reason that we can only guess, they did not wait for the *Struma* to embark, but set out with others to make the arduous and dangerous journey to Palestine by land, aided by the Jewish underground and a few righteous Gentiles. The journey took them more than a year, and by that time, your father and mother had disappeared. Your parents had departed Bucharest believing that Josef and Sura were dead and that they had no family except Aron Liebovici. I am sure they tried to contact him after the war, but by that time, their dearly beloved uncle had died, and they believed there was no family left alive."

Rachel's heart was breaking for her mother and father again, the same heartbreak she had experienced throughout her life—the heartbreak that had become entrenched in her soul since she saw the numbers cut into her father's arm on her wedding day. Sitting there at the table in little bakery where she had been introduced to the family she never knew, she wondered if it would ever end. It seemed only right to mourn for them again even as she asked the question foremost in her mind, "What happened to them? What happened to Josef and Sura?"

"It has only been in the last five years that I myself discovered they did not perish with the *Struma*. For many years after the war, Jewish agencies were set up to help survivors find lost loved ones, but when six million are dead, it is very hard to find a few survivors. Many of our people could not bear to discover the details of their loved ones' deaths. Sometimes it is easier to live not knowing that your mother and father were herded into gas chambers and thrown into blazing furnaces, or that your child was thrown into a mass grave alive after being ripped from your wife's arms. Very seldom is not knowing preferable to knowing, but sometimes…da, sometimes it is better not to know.

"Da, we did not know what happened to hundreds of Jews in our Bucharest community in those first years after the war, including your parents and Josef and Sura. My family and I were blessed to find hiding places during the times of imminent danger, and because of righteous Gentiles who were willing to hide us, most of us survived. We praised the Almighty for this miracle all the days of our lives, and I continue to praise Him, though I am now the last of our family."

Abraham leaned across the table and took Rachel's hand in his. "Rachel Liebovici, five years ago, I had a visit from a young man from Israel. Like you,

108

he was also inquiring about the Liebovici family, giving his name as Aron Safran. He was on a journey much like yours, my daughter, a pilgrimage into the past to find his family and his spiritual heritage. He told me he was the grandson of Josef Liebovici. He was named in honor of Josef's uncle, Aron Liebovici."

That was the last straw for Rachel. Isaac held her in his arms as she turned her head and wept tears of joy into his designer shirt and tie, her lithe body heaving with sobs that couldn't be quenched. She felt that she had been tossed back and forth from sorrow to joy, coming out bruised and exhausted at the end of the battle. But it was worth it all. She had someone, someone whose veins flowed with the same blood as hers, someone who shared the same sorrows and the same history, maybe even someone in whose face she could see something of her father. And maybe, just maybe, even something of herself.

Kissing his wife's hair and forehead over and over, Isaac grasped her head in both his hands and turning her face up to his, he gazed deeply into her teary green eyes and tenderly said, "Next year in Jerusalem, my love?"

Abraham Wasserman rose slowly from his chair and stretched, looking something like a white-haired lion king extremely pleased with his pride. "Before you embark for Eretz Israel, my friends, I would like to invite you to attend our Shabbat services at the Synagogue Saturday morning. Could you come?"

"Certainly, Rabbi!" Rachel replied, dabbing her eyes once again. "We would love to, wouldn't we, Isaac?"

"Yes, we would, Rabbi," Isaac gladly concurred. "We'll see you Saturday morning."

Chapter Eight

You always seem so happy, Nana. Well, I don't know...perhaps that isn't exactly the correct description. Maybe *content* would be a better word," Carrie said, chatting with her grandmother as they sat all cuddled up in the love seat by the fire. "I'm always watching you, you know, this week in particular. I guess it's because I'm wising up." Carrie smiled at the grandmother she adored.

"Yes, I can tell you're wising up, my precious darlin'," her grandmother teased in her soft, Southern drawl.

The rest of the family had gone to do last minute shopping in Boone where they were all to rendezvous at the Daniel Boone Restaurant for dinner at six. Nana begged out of the excursion, saying that her arthritis was acting up a little, but secretly pleading for a little peace and quiet in the midst of the wonderfully hectic family holiday.

Papa had given her a hug just before he walked out the door, whispering as quietly as he could, "You stay here and rest, and I'll find myself a little corner in a quiet coffee shop to read Tim Russert's new book about his old Dad. Glad someone thinks we old men are still worthwhile."

Nana had hugged him back and pushed him out the door with the same words she had sent him off with for nearly fifty-five years, "Be careful! I love you!"

The Gentile and the Jew: A Divine Romance

Carrie had fought a fairly short skirmish with all five children, little Abigail almost in tears at the thought of her favorite young aunt not being there to make the shopping trip more fun. But Carrie finally won the much-coveted prize of resting in the cabin with her grandmother for a few peaceful hours.

"You and Papa still look at each other as if you have just fallen in love even though you must have been married over fifty years now," Carrie said.

"Fifty-five come June," Nana responded.

"But it isn't just that...." Carrie looked up at her grandmother with a quizzical expression on her face. "You seem to be at peace with yourself and everything around you. You amaze me, Nana, and you make me jealous for whatever it is you have. Oh, I do love you so!" Carrie hugged her grandmother for the umpteenth time.

"I know you do, darlin'," Nana replied, cuddling Carrie in her ample lap as she had done from the time her granddaughter was first placed in her arms minutes after her birth. She squeezed her tightly and smiled down into Carrie's adoring face.

"Yes, I know I am loved, my precious darlin'," Nana stated assuredly.

"I guess that's what I'm trying to say. That's what I meant when I said you're at peace. You're never trying to impress people, or trying to fit in, or make yourself heard. You've always been this way."

"No, darlin', I wasn't always at peace," Nana softly replied. She was quiet in thought for a few moments, gazing into the blazing fire. "Do you remember your favorite story when you were younger? *The Velveteen Rabbit?*"

"Of course I do," Carrie laughed. "It's still my favorite story and always will be."

"Do you remember when the little rabbit asked the Skin Horse how one becomes real? I guess he must have thought that it happens in a split second by someone saying some magic words or something. But, the wise Skin Horse told the Rabbit that one becomes real over a long period of being loved, really loved, and that by the time you become real, your fur is all worn and your eyes pop out and you're ready for the trash pile. Well, that's me, darlin'." Nana chuckled softly, her eyes reflecting the blazing fire.

"No, Nana! Don't be silly. You're a long, long way from the trash pile!" Carrie laughed, teasing her grandmother. In her eyes, Nana never changed. It seemed to Carrie that she looked exactly as she always had.

"The Velveteen Rabbit becomes real through the love of a little boy, but Love is God so, we become real by the Love of God—sometimes through other human beings and sometimes not. God used your grandfather more than any other person to love me into becoming real, but He used the hard knocks, too," said Nana.

Chapter Eight

"Yeah, well...I don't think I like the process of becoming real," said Carrie.

"You are definitely wising up, my darlin'," replied Nana, smiling down at Carrie. "As I have listened to hurting people throughout my seventy-seven years, I have come to one conclusion concerning the depth of every person's pain: not one of us is able to grasp how much we are loved. That's the reason Jesus came into this world—to prove to us that we are completely and unconditionally loved. I am totally convinced that God will do everything in His power to get that truth through to each of us, no matter our place in this world, our culture or our race. And, my darlin', I'm also convinced He passes that task, or privilege as it were, on to each of us who has discovered and received His love. That's the basic meaning of bearing fruit, to pass that love on to those around us. This is the simple Gospel that we have complicated so terribly, even to the extent that Christians have often become hindrances to those who are hurting instead of being carriers of His unconditional love."

Carrie reflected on Nana's words for a while, still wrapped in her grandmother's loving arms as if she were a toddler just picked up from play. She knew that if she stayed there long enough, Nana would begin to hum one of the old hymns of her childhood and her big baby would go to sleep if she wasn't careful. That's how they were when the phone rang, Tom calling to find out why Carrie hadn't met them for the smorgasbord in Boone. The grandmother and her twenty-three-year-old granddaughter were wrapped in each others' arms, Carrie fast asleep, Nana nodding and humming contentedly while the flames crackled in accompaniment to her song.

"Shabbat Shalom, my friends!"

"Shabbat Shalom," the congregation answered.

Abraham Wasserman spoke in a mixture of Romanian, Hebrew, and Yiddish, an English interpreter standing close by. Looking around to see if there were other foreigners in the congregation, Isaac surmised the thoughtful old man had brought an interpreter in just for his and Rachel's benefit. He would have to remember to thank him.

"Today, I would like to speak to you from Torah, the book of Leviticus, chapters four through seven," the rabbi began his sermon. "These chapters record the instructions God told Moses to give to our people concerning sin and guilt offerings. Beginning in chapter four, the instructions are first for the priests, then the leaders and then the entire congregation of Israel. Our God is very wise. He does not want priests and leaders who are not accountable for their sins first of all. The essence of the message in Leviticus is this: whether we sin intentionally or unintentionally, we are guilty before God.

"The scriptures take us through a very simple process in dealing with our guilt. First, we must recognize our sin and guilt. Secondly, we are to make restitution if possible. Thirdly, we are to bring an offering to God in our confession. And fourthly, we are forgiven. You could call these steps four foundational pillars upon which our lives are to be built and lived. As in building a house, if the structure is not built upon the foundational pillars, our lives are destined to crumble and fall. Does the house not built on a sure foundation fall because God cursed it? Nu, of course not. It falls because the builder did not follow the right, eternal principles of building.

"Each little sin is a wrong committed against one's self or someone else—ultimately, against God, our creator. For example, any bodily exposure to anything unclean is a sin against my own body. God is good. God is Love. God is *right*. This is why we say God is righteous. He is full of right. He cannot be wrong because He is fully right. We have skewed this word to describe what *we* think, what *we* know, or what *we* do. I am right. You are wrong. This is incorrect thinking, my friends. Only God is right. Only His ways are right. Therefore, *right* is first of all a way of being, not doing."

Rachel listened intently, surprisingly comfortable, feeling very much at home in the old synagogue her family had attended over sixty years ago. Holding Isaac's warm, safe hand, she felt again as if she had been allowed the privilege to step back in time, getting to know the family she had longed for with all her heart. She tried to concentrate on the rabbi's message, but her eyes kept wandering around the old sanctuary filled with memories she could only imagine.

"My friends," said the rabbi, "when I was a young man, I was certain God set up laws and principles for us to follow so He could say, 'Do this. Don't do that,' thinking His ultimate purpose was for us to 'do right.' But as I searched the scriptures and sought to know the ways of God, I understood that He didn't have to set up anything—He IS! He only had to reveal His Name and His righteousness to Moses to enable him to set God's inherent righteousness into place as Torah—the Law. My friends, people of the covenant, this written law kept our people for fifteen hundred years until the fullness of time had arrived."

Chapter Eight

The fullness of time? Isaac glanced at Rachel to see if she was understanding the rabbi's words, but she looked more confused than he was. Where was Wasserman going with this?

"In the fulness of time, God sent His Son, the perfect, righteous Lamb, to be slain for our sin and guilt once and for all," the rabbi continued. "As the prophet, Ezekiel, had foretold, in that perfect act of Love which instituted a New Covenant, the Law, God's righteousness, would be written on our hearts as it is in God's heart. In other words, the Law, which is 'right' would become part of our DNA, inherited from the Firstborn of the New Creation. God was bringing forth a new species of human beings.

"God's Law is simply what is *right*. When we do not live rightly, by commission or omission, we experience the repercussions. It is the ancient principle of sowing and reaping. Now, my friends, we know that Messiah lived righteously—whole, perfect, mature, right, good. Therefore, only He could be the sacrifice for us all. He was and is the only *right* human ever to live on this earth. In Him, we are righteous—only in Him. All my sin and guilt offerings are slain in Him. The writer to the Hebrews said, 'And having been made perfect, He became to all those who obey Him the source of eternal salvation.'

"This brings us back to our four pillars: realization of sin and guilt, first of all; secondly, restitution. Messiah fulfilled this principle when He said, 'If therefore, you are presenting your offering at the altar, and there remember that your brother has something against you, leave your offering there before the altar and go your way; first be reconciled to your brother, and then come and present your offering.'[9]

"The third pillar is this: we must confess our sin with an offering...but I have no offering. I can only complete the foundation in Messiah. He is my offering, my Passover lamb. And fourthly, we receive forgiveness from the Almighty.

"My friends, I have nothing to offer God. The temple is gone. I have no bulls, no rams, nor even turtle doves. What can I do with my sin? The Law says there must be a blood sacrifice. It cannot be coincidence that forty years after Messiah prophesied the destruction of the temple, forty years after He gave His life as the ultimate sacrifice, the Roman armies totally destroyed the temple of the Jewish people. For two thousand years, we have not been able to make sacrifices for our sin.

"My friends, I don't know about you, but I need a Savior, one who can stand before God because He is righteous, because He has made the sacrifice, but more than that because He *is* the sacrifice. I must bring my slain Lamb before God as I confess my sin and guilt, and I must ask forgiveness in His Name. Then, God will forgive my sin.

The Gentile and the Jew: A Divine Romance

"So, my dear friends, along with the writer to the Hebrews, I say to you, "Therefore, holy brethren, partakers of a heavenly calling, consider Yeshua!"[10]

Isaac and Rachel sat stunned, motionless. Neither looked at the other, but stared straight ahead into oblivion as Rabbi Abraham Wasserman chanted the ancient Aaronic blessing over the children of Israel,

Y'varekha Adonai v'yishmerekha.
Ya'er Adonai panav eleikha vichunekka.
Yissa Adonai panav eleikha v'yasem l'kha shalom.
May the Lord bless you and keep you.
May the Lord make His face to shine on you and show you His favor.
May the Lord lift up His face toward you and give you peace.[11]

Chapter Nine

S trange not to be home on Christmas Eve, thought Catherine as she peeked in at the little ones one more time before she could allow herself to relax. *When your family is all together, you are home,* she decided, quietly closing the last bedroom door.

Their large, boisterous family had enjoyed an early supper of chicken salad and roast beef sandwiches before they gathered around the fireplace to experience the once-a-year chaos called "opening presents." Catherine tackled what she considered a serious problem every year trying to come up with the perfect organizational plan for opening presents. Each grandchild somehow managed to know exactly where his gifts were under the tree and, after quickly collecting them all, would rip into them before anyone could see who the giver was. This process left the parents yelling, "Who gave you that?" at the same time all six grandchildren were yelling, "Wow!" and "Just what I wanted!" and "Can I play with that?" In the end everyone was happy, but it just seemed terribly chaotic and unorganized to Catherine.

Last year she thought she had contrived the perfect plan. Somehow, she managed to have all five grandchildren seated on the floor with the nine adults appointed to couches and chairs as Carrie and her Daddy handed out the presents. Then Catherine instructed each member of the family to begin opening gifts as his or her turn came—like an orderly relay, she thought. Everyone would be able to see what each person received and could "ooh" and "ahh" over each gift in turn. But although it seemed like a good idea, after about fifteen of the longest minutes of their entire short little lives, the children flew into their presents full force and bedlam reigned once again in the Jernigan household.

She courageously faced one more annual problem. A few days after Christmas, Tom would inevitably proclaim, "Catherine, we spend too much money for Christmas. We have to cut back."

And each year, she tried. And failed. But tonight, as they had laid all the presents aside and snuggled close together to listen to Tom read the story of the birth of Jesus from the Gospel of Luke, Catherine was assured that her brood knew the true meaning of Christmas and would go to bed with His name in their hearts and minds.

As Tom finished reading the last verse, Carrie began to softly sing,

> *"Oh, come let us adore Him,*
> *Oh, come let us adore Him,*
> *Oh, come let us adore Him,*
> *Christ, the Lord!*
> *For He alone is worthy*
> *For He alone is worthy*
> *For He alone is worthy*
> *Christ, the Lord!"*[12]

Everyone joined in quiet reverence, Carrie's high, clear voice carrying the melody with Claire and Michele while Catherine sang alto and Tom filled in the tenor and Ron and John sang whatever. Of course the children's little voices were the most precious, rising in and out of the worship song between wide yawns. The beautiful harmony seemed to rise through the log beams into the clear, starry night sky as Catherine gazed out the wide bay window and back again to the room full of people. She loved watching her family at times like this. The children's yawns grew more frequent and bigger as they struggled to form the words to the song, signaling Catherine that it wouldn't be long before John would be carrying little Abigail to bed, the other children following soon after. Tom realized they were losing half their choir, too, so he led his family in a prayer, thanking God for sending His Son into the world to redeem us, to reveal His perfect Love.

Children and grandchildren and mother and father soon hugged Catherine and Tom goodnight and drifted off to bed, and now she had the couch and the fire, the twinkling lights and the window all to herself for her own special time alone before turning off all the lights and turning in for the night. Tom had fallen asleep in the recliner as usual, but she cherished his nearness on this special night of the year, even if he was snoring away.

Curled up on the couch in front of the fire that had been blazing earlier but was now lowering itself for the night, Catherine opened her Bible to read more of the Christmas story, but her thoughts began to wander back to other Christmases when her own children were the little ones and there were just five Jernigans by the fire on Christmas Eve. Nana and Papa would have been in their own home then, preparing a big Christmas dinner for their entire family for the next day while taking time out to go to the Christmas Eve services at their little Baptist church.

Catherine thought about the many Christians who are now questioning the celebration of Christmas, bringing up issues like the date of Jesus' birth being set on a Roman winter solstice holiday, there being no mention of celebrating His birth in the Bible and, of course, the greedy commercialization of the holiday. She hadn't shrugged off these issues. She had thought about them a great deal and had prayed about them, too, finally coming to the conclusion that there was nothing wrong with Christians all over the world taking time once each year to celebrate the birth of their Savior. In spite of the horrible commercialization, drunken parties and the like, there were thousands of people who turned their hearts and lives toward God at this time of the year. What's more, it was a time to celebrate family, God's first institution on earth. It was a time of forgiveness, a time of giving, and Catherine loved every minute of it.

She could almost see each of her own three children by the fire just as if those long ago Christmases were yesterday. Being the baby of the family, Carrie was usually the most excited as they wound up the evening with the Christmas story and prayer. But, it wasn't just the presents and candy and fun that excited her youngest daughter. Catherine always knew her little heart was in the right place when, just before she began to yawn uncontrollably, Carrie would want to sing birthday songs to Jesus. *And, oh, that child could sing*, Catherine thought now, remembering her baby girl sitting on her daddy's knee, her face turned up to heaven singing, "Happy birthday, dear Jesus. Happy birthday to you!"

Since the precious moments with Carrie on the snow-covered mountainside early this morning, Catherine had been at peace about her youngest daughter's relationship with Mike Kramer. Anyway, she wasn't going to worry about anything tonight. Her baby and all the children and grandchildren were asleep just a few yards from their Mama and all was well. Tonight, she was beside herself with happiness. Yes, they were all home even though home was in a mountain cabin, two hundred miles from their house. Her children, her entire family, safe and sound in one house, under one roof. *They're all home,* she whispered to the fire, sighing in relief.

Then, in the glow of the dying embers and the twinkling lights of the Christmas tree, Catherine heard her heavenly Father speak deep in her heart, *"Now you know the joy I will have when all my children come home."*

"Would you like to get something to eat?" Isaac asked Rachel as they slowly walked from the Synagogue back to the train. Rachel walked mechanically, almost like a robot, seeming totally oblivious to the cold damp wind whipping buildings and people alike through the narrow city street. A misty rain joined the wind that seemed to fight them, but Isaac held his wife's arm securely as always. He was as dazed as Rachel, having to force himself to keep his mind on where they were going.

I'll have to think about this later, he thought. Yes, that's what they would do—eat lunch, walk back to the hotel and go over Rabbi Wasserman's sermon together. Maybe he missed something or misunderstood his meaning, or maybe the interpreter made a mistake. He was sure that's what happened—it had to be.

"Rachel, I asked if you wanted to get something to eat. Are you hungry?"

"Hm? Oh, I'm sorry, Isaac. I was...somewhere else...not sure where. I'm not sure about anything right now," Rachel sighed. "Yes, let's find a nice little cafe close to the hotel. I suddenly feel terribly weary, and I'd like to go back and rest after we have lunch."

"Sounds good to me. I'm wiped out, too, although from what I don't know," Isaac replied in an uncharacteristically cynical tone of voice.

The train ride was quick, and they soon found themselves turning onto the Hristo Botev Boulevard as it enters Rosetti Square. The wind seemed to calm down a bit in this area of the city, but it was probably due to the taller buildings. Isaac and Rachel walked hastily up the sidewalk toward their hotel, Isaac glancing from one side of the street to the other, searching for a good place to eat lunch. In this section of Bucharest, old Eastern European buildings stood alongside modern skyscrapers as if to say, "We're not giving up our place! You can come in, but you can't take over." Rachel thought the striking architectural mixture of different historical eras was strangely comparable to the feeling she hadn't been able to shake since she arrived in Bucharest—an eerie, confusing feeling like she existed in two different worlds at the same time.

Chapter Nine

The beautiful old Romanian architecture in this area of the city usually absorbed their attention, but today they walked in silence, each one pondering the old Romanian's words, or at least, what they thought he said. It was just too strange to take in— unbelievable! Here was this distinguished Jewish rabbi, descended from generations of Eastern European Jews, a scholar in Torah, Talmud and Mishnah—this man, this rabbi even, was preaching to his congregation that the Jesus of the Christian faith is the Jewish Messiah!

Isaac was miserable, wishing he had verbalized his "Let's go home" thought Monday at the bakery when he had the chance.

"Here, Rachel...," he said, tugging on her arm. "Here's a little deli. Why don't we just order a couple of sandwiches and take them back to the hotel? I doubt either of us feels like eating in public right now. What do you say?" asked Isaac.

"All right, this is fine," Rachel muttered, pushing the door as she spoke. "Just get me anything. I don't care."

"Two corned beef on rye with mustard," Isaac told the clerk, hoping with all his heart the guy could understand English. The blank look on the man's face shot that hope all to pieces, and it was all Isaac could do to muster the energy to point at all the right ingredients. Rachel continued to stare into space until she found herself back in their hotel room, hardly remembering the two-block walk from the deli.

The phone was ringing in their room when Isaac turned the key in the lock.

"*Buna ziua*," Isaac answered the phone in his limited Romanian vocabulary.

"Isaac, my friend, I missed greeting you and your dear wife after the service. Are you all right?" Abraham Wasserman asked.

"Yes, Rabbi, we're fine—just a little confused. Actually, that's incorrect. To tell you the truth, we're very confused," Isaac replied.

"Da. I understand, Isaac," the rabbi said. "I am here to answer any questions you may have as always. Just give me a call when you are ready."

"Yes...yes, we will," Isaac responded weakly. "Good-bye, Rabbi."

Rachel spread their lunch out on the bistro table near the doors to the balcony as he hung up the phone. Any amount of light was welcome on this cloudy day. Isaac looked at his beloved wife, remembering how happy she had been just a few days earlier as their adventure had neared its climax.

Was today the climax, he wondered? If so, he didn't understand what happened, much less where they were headed. He reached out to pull his wife close and fold her in his arms, but she gently pushed him away, saying, "No, no...don't, Isaac. If you protect me too much now, I'll never muster the courage to see this thing through. I have to think. I can't afford to let my emotions rule the day. I have to figure this thing out," Rachel stated adamantly, speaking as much to herself as to Isaac.

"I'm as confused as you are, love," Isaac answered despondently, "and I don't know what to do. I've always been able to protect you, but now I feel useless. When we began this journey, I believed we would either find some family member yet alive, or we would discover there's no one left and put the past to rest, but I never counted on coming face to face with something like this."

"It's all right, Isaac," Rachel responded gently, moving her soft fingers over his face. "You are certainly not useless. You can't always keep me in the protective glass bubble you want for me, but...Isaac, you are my very life. Don't you know that? Without you, I could never have begun this journey, much less hope to finish it. And we will do that, Isaac—we will finish this mission together."

"Yes, we will." He gazed into her flashing eyes, wondering what was happening to his beloved wife. "You seem different, Rachel, stronger somehow."

"I hope so, my darling. I truly hope so."

Chapter Ten

The spacious log cabin was filled with pandemonium from early morning to the minute the Jernigan family gathered around the long pine table for Christmas dinner. The children immediately quieted down then, knowing they wouldn't get to eat the delicious turkey and dressing, creamed corn, mashed potatoes, green beans, collards and, more importantly, chocolate pie if they didn't hush long enough for their granddaddy to thank God for the food and all their blessings. The second after Tom said, "Amen," five little mouths started chattering again, joined by mamas and daddies saying things like, "Nick, you have to eat something green even if you think the collards stink," and "Matthew, if you don't eat your vegetables, you can't have chocolate pie for dessert."

Carrie couldn't help but recall the peace and quiet of the Kramers' elegant guest room as she smiled at her jabbering family seated around the long table. But today, she was enjoying all the noise and excitement a big family brings, playing with the children while the older women cooked and prepared the Southern feast, being the gopher when needed, and just having a good old time.

Each holiday when the family came together, Carrie wondered when she would ever learn to cook. Being the baby of the adults made her the one the children related to most, seeing Carrie as one of their own, expecting her to play with them when she was around. It was only when she was home with just Catherine and Tom that she got to help her mother in the kitchen, trying to glean some of the cooking secrets and techniques Catherine had learned from her own mother.

Maybe I'll be able to afford a cook when I get married, Carrie thought, giggling under her breath. *Sure, girl. Dream on!*

Seated at the end of the table closest to the kitchen so she could jump up and down when the need arose, Catherine kept her mother hen watch over her noisy brood, pleased to note the contentment on Carrie's thin face as she dipped her second mound of mashed potatoes. Another crisis on its way to victory, she silently rejoiced as Melanie O'Brien's face popped into her mind.

Oh, God, please intervene in her life and bring victory in that situation, too, Catherine prayed, passing the hot pepper vinegar to Ron so he could pass it on to Tom at the other end of the long table.

"Catherine, I don't know why you never put but one bottle of hot pepper vinegar on the table." Tom said. "Collards aren't worth five cents without it."

"Don't worry, Tom, there's plenty more where that came from. Aunt Verdie made it for us every year before she passed away, and I still have a few bottles stored away. I guess I'm just being stingy with my little stash." Catherine smiled all the way down the table at her husband.

"Well, this is the best food I've ever eaten, wife! You might be a good cook in a few more years," Tom teased his wife, giving her a big grin. There was agreement all around the table as children and adults alike enjoyed the delicious food and family fellowship.

I haven't been with them enough this year, thought Carrie, clearly seeing her sister, Michele, for the first time in a long while. Time passes faster than we expect, and before we know it, we've neglected those we love in the "busyness" of everyday life. Her relationship with Mike wasn't the only one she needed to work on.

"Michele, I've missed you," Carrie declared, quickly deciding there was no time like the present to begin rebuilding relationships.

Startled by her sister's sudden declaration, Michele didn't know what to say for a second. Then she swallowed the corn bread in her mouth and quietly replied, "I've missed you, too, Carrie."

"Hey! I have a great idea! Why don't you come up to see me soon after Christmas? We can meet in Crabtree Valley Mall and shop the after-Christmas sales. Then we could have dinner at the Olive Garden you like so much and go back to my apartment and have a pajama party?" Carrie beamed at her sister like a little girl inviting a friend to come out and play.

Chapter Ten

"That sounds wonderful, Carrie," Michele replied, surprise written all over her face. "I'd love to get away after the hustle and bustle of the holidays! Ron, could you handle the kids?"

Catherine could see the excitement building in both her daughters' eyes as Ron thought about his schedule for the next couple of weeks, so she decided it was time for Grandma to intervene.

"I'll help, Ron. I'd love to keep Blair and Luke so the girls can be together. You can eat dinner with us after work and be there to tuck the children in for the night if you'd like."

"Thank you, Catherine." Ron gave his mother-in-law a grateful smile. "I may be able to get off early that Saturday afternoon and take the kids to play putt-putt or something if the weather is good. You're a jewel, Grandma!"

Ron turned back to the task at hand, consuming a plateful of the finest home cooking in the South, while Michele continued to steal quick glances at her younger sister, wondering what had come over her all of a sudden. Carrie had arrived only three days earlier looking depressed and almost anorexic in her baggy jeans and braided hair. Now, she was glowing like a lightening bug in June, eating two helpings of mashed potatoes, and inviting her sister for a fun weekend in the Triangle. *I guess miracles never cease*, Michele concluded, turning to wash the chocolate pie off Luke's face and hands, calling him a little monkey and kissing the little monkey's nose.

"I'm not a monkey, Mommie!" he giggled.

"Yes, you are! You're Mommie's little monkey," Michele teased, hugging Luke once more as she lifted him from the booster seat and stood him on the floor, his little feet already moving to scurry back to his Thomas the Tank Engine train set up in front of the stone fireplace.

"Come on, Abby!" he yelled. "You're going to be Percy, the green engine, and I'm going to be Thomas!"

Little Abigail got so excited she forgot she was half finished eating her little slice of pie. Turning to look at Claire with big, blueberry eyes, her tiny mouth all covered in chocolate and meringue, she solemnly asked,

"Down, pease?"

No one could have refused the polite little request, so in just seconds, Luke and Abby were choo-chooing away on the island of Sodor with Percy and Thomas, Sir Topham Hat and Harold the Helicopter. The older children soon finished their dinner, too, leaving the table all at one time, eager to get back to the games they had planned for the afternoon.

The adult Jernigans were now in place for Carrie's favorite family event— gathering around the dining table after a big dinner, drinking coffee or hot tea, laughing and talking about anything that came to their minds—funny things the little ones had said, how Ron was liking his new job, a joke someone had just heard. How she enjoyed the simple, relaxed conversation among people who truly loved and accepted one another.

This is what it's all about, Carrie mused, watching Papa's eyes growing heavy, his head nodding as he struggled to stay awake just a little longer. *Yep, this is what it's all about.*

"Are you ready, Rachel?" Isaac asked. "Rabbi Wasserman would like us to meet him at the synagogue if that's all right with you."

"Yes, darling. I'll be right there." Rachel pulled black leather gloves over her well-manicured hands. There was something drastically important to her about looking nice no matter what the circumstances or immediate crisis. Of course, it was fairly easy for her to look nice because she was naturally beautiful—unusually beautiful. Her eyes were her most stunning feature. Deeply set in her perfect oval face surrounded by thick, auburn hair, one would think they would have been dark and somber, but Rachel's green eyes were unusually brilliant, flashing excitement when she was joyful and judgment when she was angry. Even in her tears, her eyes were bright and beaming.

"I'm ready," she answered, "for whatever surprises the day brings. Considering our track record for almost two weeks now, I'm sure there's a surprise awaiting us around some little corner today."

The dark clouds and misty rain had moved on the day after the Shabbat service, and for two lovely winter days, Rachel and Isaac had toured the sights of old Bucharest, visiting museums and historical sites, even enjoying the magnificent symphony one night. Ah, music! God's gift to the world. Surely, there must be angels of music who minister to us in our hours of greatest need.

They had experienced the excellent cuisine of modern Romania, discussing Rachel's family and the rabbi's infamous sermon over thick stews and luscious desserts. They then walked off the calories exploring beautiful parks and little hidden cobblestone streets in the eastern European city once called Little Paris. Of course, unique boutiques and shops called out as they passed, luring Rachel inside, Isaac reluctantly following close behind, wondering how buying gifts for their children could possibly be exciting enough to get Rachel's mind off the more weighty matters at hand. They also spent a great deal of time on the Internet, researching many of the issues Abraham Wasserman had covered in previous conversations and in his sermon. By the time they called the rabbi on Sunday, they were ready to continue their discussions.

"Well, my love, I have a feeling we had better take a deep breath and gird up our loins before we enter the doors to the synagogue. But even though we're not entirely clear on all the issues, we've done our homework, and we can at least discuss them with some degree of knowledge." Isaac locked the door and took Rachel's hand as they walked out of the hotel into the winter sunshine.

As they walked briskly to the train, Rachel turned to Isaac. "My thoughts keep going back to that very first day in the bakery when the rabbi recited that scripture in Jeremiah to me. It was about Rachel, weeping for her children. Do you remember, Isaac?"

"Of course, I remember," Isaac answered. "That's when this venture began to take on such a strange atmosphere. For a few minutes there, I thought the old guy might actually *be* Jeremiah! Then I looked at your face and thought, 'Oh, no! She thinks he's Jeremiah, too!' It was just too weird for me, love. Still is, for that matter."

"This journey has certainly been strange." Rachel's lovely skin was pulled taut as she thought about what Isaac said. "Weird...hm, I guess that's as good a word as any to describe this exciting adventure."

"You know I'm not a deeply religious Jew, Rachel. I just believe the basics and leave everything else to the scholars and weirdoes."

"I know, darling, but I believe you're deeper than you realize." Rachel squeezed her husband's arm a little tighter, stuffing her right hand deep into the pocket of his overcoat as they hurried to the train, heads bent low to block the piercing wind.

Isaac and Rachel entered the massive oak doors of the synagogue just as Abraham Wasserman came into the foyer to greet them, a loving smile flooding his aged face, his hand extended to grasp each of theirs in a tight embrace.

"Shalom, my friends, shalom," the rabbi welcomed them.

"Shalom," they echoed, truly happy to see their new friend even though a bit anxious about the impending conversation.

"Come," Abraham invited, leading the way. "Come into the room you have not as yet seen—the small world where I live when I am not out with the sheep or tutoring or preaching."

How odd, Rachel mused. As home-oriented as she was, she hadn't thought about the rabbi's having a home, but now it seemed only right that he would live in the synagogue. Her eyes caught sight of a large banner in the foyer she hadn't noticed before. It read: *"Messiah is the end of the Law."*

The Gentile and the Jew: A Divine Romance

Abraham led them to a room at the end of the long hallway. Opening the door, he stepped aside for Isaac and Rachel to enter the room. "Welcome to my home, my friends."

The couple walked through the door into a large, comfortable room filled with furniture Westerners would consider valuable antiques, but eastern Europeans regard strictly as family heirlooms. The room was fairly large for a bedroom, but it wasn't just a bedroom, it was the rabbi's home—sitting room, bedroom, study, even tiny kitchen, consisting of a hot plate and kettle. An ornate iron bed was placed near one wall, a bed table close beside it covered with a crocheted scarf and loaded with a stack of books and a Victorian lamp. A large oak desk surprisingly stood in the center of the room. Abraham liked to see everything around him while he worked—the world outside the window, the warmth of the fire and the family pictures on the walls. As her eyes hastily scanned the neatly hung pictures, Rachel couldn't help but think of the towering walls in the Holocaust memorial in Washington, DC, filled with photographs of millions of murdered Jews.

Near a large, curtained window on the other side of the room was an oversized brown leather wing chair placed to the side of a camel-colored love seat. Along with a padded oak rocker, the seating faced an old stone fireplace blazing with the hot, crackling fire Abraham Wasserman had built for his guests.

"Come...sit, my friends," the rabbi offered, taking his place in the rocker, not the wing chair as Rachel would have guessed. She sat in the middle on the love seat while Isaac took the chair. Rachel's anxiety began to diminish as she snuggled into the worn, plump cushions and rested her head on the back of the couch, gazing at the leaping flames in the blazing fire. Isaac, too, slowly relaxed in the warm, cozy room. He was thinking that even though he and Rachel had many questions, the kind old man would remain their friend no matter what the outcome of today's conversation.

Turning to look at the rabbi, Isaac noticed for the first time that their friend was very old...and very tired. During the two weeks of their acquaintance, Abraham Wasserman had seemed to be ageless, always strong and vigorous. Yet, even though he seemed older and fatigued, the rabbi had an aura of peace about him, the contentment only those who have lived a full life with a good conscience can afford.

"The sound of silence among friends," Abraham said, smiling at Rachel and Isaac, "is the most precious sound on earth."

They both smiled back in perfect agreement. Words were not needed.

Chapter Ten

His vibrant voice quieted by the soothing atmosphere in the room, the rabbi slowly opened the conversation. "Joseph Rabinowitz, my friends. His name was Joseph ben David Rabinowitz."

Rachel and Isaac glanced at each other, remembering that Abraham had mentioned this man in relation to her uncle, Aron Liebovici, during an earlier conversation in the bakery.

"Joseph Rabinowitz was a Chasidic Jew, a lawyer in Kishinev, my family's home in Moldova. My grandfather said he was close in age to his own father, my great grandfather whom I never knew. Many of Rabinowitz's writings are still in print and also many articles about him. I have read them all, including an old copy of his autobiography written in Hebrew; so you see, I know the facts concerning this man's life. But what I know of his heart and spirit, I learned from Aron Liebovici and others whose lives were transformed through the faith of this great man. Are you comfortable, my friends?"

"Oh, yes," said Rachel. "Your home is incredibly warm and inviting. It's just lovely."

"Ah, I am sorry. You will have to forgive an old man's manners. I forgot to offer you tea!" He chuckled at his forgetfulness, placing both hands on the arms of his chair to push himself up to make tea for his guests.

"Don't worry, Rabbi. We're fine. Maybe we could have tea later, after you've solved a few more mysteries for us," Isaac replied with a smile.

"I will try, my friend." Abraham turned to Rachel. "Do you remember me telling you that Aron Liebovici, your great uncle, was my tutor, da?"

"Yes, I remember," Rachel answered. "I've thought of little else in the last few days."

The rabbi continued, "My father sent me to Aron Liebovici for three hours every morning except Shabbat. He taught me everything he knew, or I should say, he tried to teach me everything he knew." Abraham chuckled again, recalling those bygone days as if they were yesterday. "I was a young boy full of energy and mischief, but I knew that in the presence of Rabbi Liebovici I must listen and I must learn. He was a kind man, but he demanded rapt attention at all times. He would never endure silliness or the waste of time. After all, I was two years beyond my Bar Mitzvah; therefore, I was a man, and I should act as a man.

"But, I must tell you my friends, that Aron Liebovici not only taught me Hebrew, mathematics, Torah and the Prophets, he also taught me what Joseph Rabinowitz had taught him and so many others—that Yeshua, our Brother, is the solution for the Jewish people. Now, I will tell you how Joseph Rabinowitz came to know this truth. Are you sure you would not like some tea?" the rabbi asked again.

"No, no. We're fine," Rachel answered, impatient for the old man to continue his story.

"Even though Rabinowitz was born into the Chasidic branch of Judaism, he was a voracious reader from an early age and had sought higher education. He attained a law degree, and became a fairly successful man for the era and region in which he lived. He greatly admired and studied the French Revolution and by an early age had become a new type of Jew—an enlightened one. For Rabinowitz, *enlightenment* meant that a Jewish man could live in God's will by learning all he could about the world in which he lived, including avenues of philosophy other than the Chasidic way. There were a great many enlightened Jews in those days and Rabinowitz had contact with many of them in Germany and Eastern Europe.

"No one is exactly sure when Joseph Rabinowitz received his first Hebrew New Testament, but most scholars, including Aron Liebovici, believed it was given to him by his future brother-in-law, a good friend who was also seeking enlightenment. But no one knows whether Rabinowitz had studied the Testament to any extent when he embarked on a journey to Palestine in the year 1882."

"Palestine?" Isaac questioned. "I had no idea Jews were even thinking about going to Palestine in those days."

"Oh, yes, my friend," Abraham responded. "The Zionist movement had gained momentum, and Theodore Herzl's followers and comrades were scattered all over Eastern Europe. Jews were going home, my friend. That particular year, 1882, became known as the beginning of the first *Aliyah*. But, back to my story.

"Because of the death of the good Czar Alexander II in 1881 and the horrible *pogroms* that swept through southwest Russia afterward, Rabinowitz had long been agonizing over the "Jewish question" as many called it in those days and since. He had finally come to the conclusion that the only answer for the Jews in those perilous regions was to emigrate to Palestine. With that plan in mind, he left on a pilgrimage to the Holy Land in the spring of 1882, hoping to pave a way for the Jews of Kishinev and the region to form a colony in Palestine.

"A few years after Aron Liebovici told me this story, I read in Rabinowitz's autobiography that his tour of Palestine discouraged him terribly. The entire land was desolate from hundreds of years of neglect and endless warfare. At the end of the tour, he climbed the Mount of Olives. Just before sunset that evening, he sat down on the slope by Gethsemane that descends into the Kidron Valley, pondering his disappointment and the hopelessness of his people. The view from his post encompassed all of Jerusalem, ravaged by hundreds of years of conquering armies led by those who believe the Jew has no right to any home in the earth. All of a sudden, a phrase from the New Testament that he had read fifteen years earlier entered his thoughts, 'If the Son shall make you free, you shall be free indeed.'[13] He immediately went back to his lodging and began to read the gospel of John. Another phrase leapt out, 'Without Me, you can do nothing.'[14] Suddenly, he knew the truth, that Yeshua is Messiah and that He alone is the answer to the Jewish question. He alone could save Israel.

"Rabinowitz went back to Kishinev armed with one solution to the Jewish dilemma, much different than he had previously believed, 'The key to the Holy Land lies in the hands of our brother, Jesus.'

"From that specific journey and that one life-changing moment on the Mount of Olives, a move of God swept through southwest Russia, a move of the Ruach Ha'Kodesh which opened Jewish eyes to see the Messiah, their brother, the Jew—Yeshua."

"What happened to him? Joseph Rabinowitz?" asked Isaac.

"Rabinowitz spent the remaining seventeen years of his life proclaiming his revelation to the Jews of Moldova and Romania. The congregation that formed from the believers came to be called, 'The Assembly of the Israelites of the New Covenant.'

"Was it like a regular synagogue?" asked Rachel.

"Da, my daughter. The believing Jews kept Shabbat, circumcised their sons, obeyed kosher laws, kept all the feast days. They were the same as Peter and Andrew, James and John—the first disciples of Yeshua—all living Jewish lives in their Jewish world. They were simply Russian Jews who believed that Messiah has already come once and will come again."

"But, didn't they convert to Christianity?" Isaac was still confused by the semantics involved.

"Isaac, I'm sure you know of many Jewish sects throughout the centuries who believed their leader was the Messiah, even in this day and age. You know of the Lubavitchers, da?"

"The old guy in New York?"

"Da, the old guy in New York, a Hassidim named Menachem Schneerson whose followers believe him to be the Messiah. He died just a few years ago, 1994, I believe."

"Hmm, I see where you're going. So what's the difference in these crazy sects? Why couldn't Schneerson have been Messiah just as easily as Yeshua?"

The Gentile and the Jew: A Divine Romance

"Yeshua rose from the dead after three days just as He said He would. Lubavitch is still dead even though his followers truly expected him to come back to life. That's reason number one."

"Strong point, Rabbi," a smile began to form on Isaac's sober countenance.

"My friends, there were many other Jews who recognized Yeshua throughout the centuries, but the movement led by Rabinowitz was the first since the early disciples that allowed Jews who believed in Yeshua to remain Jews—worship on Shabbat, circumcise their sons, and hold services in Yiddish and Hebrew. They maintained the feasts of Israel and the High Holy Days. Rabinowitz and his followers used the Hebrew name, Yeshua, understanding the full significance of His Name for the Jewish people. It was a new thing that was never to happen again on such a corporate scale for nearly a hundred years until the 1960's when your American Jewish hippies began to recognize their brother, Yeshua. Since then, hundreds of thousands of Jews have reclaimed their Messiah. Of course, you already know that it was Aron Liebovici who brought the message to our community in Romania."

Abraham slowly rose to place a log on the fire and stir the hot coals with the iron poker. Standing with his hands warming by the blazing fire, he said, "I know you are tired, my friends, and possibly overwhelmed. This is a great deal to take in. Would you like to talk more at another time?"

"Rabbi," Isaac began, "I apologize for taking so much of your time. You must be exhausted. Why don't you have dinner with us this evening? You could finish your story and maybe answer a few questions we've jotted down since Shabbat."

"I would be honored, Isaac," the rabbi replied, genuinely surprised and pleased.

"Then why don't we meet at the Green Forum Hotel. We heard they have a great kosher restaurant. Would you like to meet us there at seven?" Isaac asked.

"Da, da. You have made a good choice. The Green Forum was the first kosher restaurant in Bucharest. I will meet you there at seven o'clock." Abraham led the couple back down the corridor to the massive oak doors, this time leaning heavily on his cane.

Once again, Rachel spied the long banner in the anteroom, reading it more slowly this time—*Messiah is the end of the Law*. She paused for a moment, letting the words sink in, saving them in her memory for future reference. Leaning closer, she noticed an inscription in the lower right hand corner—*Joseph Rabinowitz*.

Chapter Ten

"Come on, Rachel. It's getting late." Isaac shook the rabbi's hand warmly as she hurried to the door. Suddenly, she turned and stood on tiptoe to give Abraham a quick kiss on the cheek, surprising him so much he blushed and almost stumbled backward, tears filling his eyes as he patted her on the head and turned back into the synagogue.

"Shalom!" they shouted as they stepped down to the street, Rachel clinging to Isaac's arm as they huddled close to stay warm on the now familiar walk back to the train.

When Isaac and Rachel entered the charming restaurant, Abraham Wasserman was already seated at the table, looking as dignified as ever, deeply engrossed in thought. The Kramers wound their way through the lovely tables covered in sienna cloths and candles lit for the evening meal. They were already standing by the table when the rabbi suddenly realized they had arrived. Rising quickly from his seat, he said, "My dear friends! I did not see you come in. I must have been in another world!"

Isaac couldn't help but laugh under his breath, thinking, *As usual!*

Abraham shook Isaac's hand and kissed Rachel's while Isaac pulled out a chair for his beautiful wife. Easing into their seats, they gave their drink order to the waiter standing nearby as diners all around gazed at the patriarchal figure and the extremely attractive American couple. Abraham Wasserman was dressed as always in a dark suit and white shirt, the fringes on his *tallit* hanging from beneath his coat. His magnificent mane of white hair and beard was capped off with a black *kippa*, embroidered on the edges with white stars of David. Even if he had not exuded such a profound spiritual presence, he would still have made an impact in any crowd by his powerful physical bearing.

Rachel looked radiant, her auburn hair pulled back from her lovely face in a simple french braid, small diamond earrings sparkling as they caught the soft light from the chandeliers. Her lovely face glowed in the candlelight. The flashing green eyes Isaac loved so much danced joyfully as a smile spread across her face.

"My, oh my. I am a privileged lady to be dining with two such handsome men this evening. I've always known I have the best looking man in the world, and now I have two!"

Isaac could have fit the proverbial "tall, dark and handsome" picture of almost any woman in the room, but there was something matchless about him in Rachel's eyes. He always dressed well, and because of continual business appointments, he was usually attired in suit and tie as he was this evening. But he wasn't a slick, neat freak. There was a roughness about Isaac—a roughness that in some paradoxical way expressed itself in gentleness, especially with Rachel. His eyes were as dark and deep as hers were bright and exciting, and now in the light of the candles, Rachel thought she might drown in her husband's eyes and be happy that she did.

Abraham sipped his wine and watched the love passing from man to woman and back again, pleased to know a couple who loved each other like that after twenty-seven years of marriage. He leaned back in his chair and commented, "This was a very good idea, Isaac. It is good to have a meal with good friends, to break bread together. And that reminds me. I am very hungry. Could we order now?"

"Yes, Rabbi," Isaac chuckled. "We're hungry, too! Rachel's hardly eaten enough to stay alive these past two weeks—too excited to eat."

"Except for that delicious bread and butter meal at the bakery!" Rachel exclaimed, scanning the elegant menu. "Tonight's dinner can't be any better than that."

"Hm...Stufat with lamb! I'm ready to order," Isaac proclaimed.

"I'll have the Weiner Schnitzel," Rachel said to Abraham so he could translate the order to the Romanian-speaking waiter. "And I want dessert later with coffee since this is a very special night. We must celebrate our new friendship and the joy you have given me, Rabbi—the blessing of a past and a future. Thank you. Thank you. Thank you!" Rachel beamed at Abraham Wasserman, raising her glass for a toast.

"Yes, Rabbi—to you!" Isaac simply proclaimed.

"Da, my friends, but the thanksgiving and the credit for finding your family must not go to me, an old and forgetful man. We must thank the Almighty for sending the Ruach Ha'Kodesh to lead you on your way."

As the three friends paused and the old rabbi uttered a Hebrew prayer of thanksgiving, the diners close by again had reason to stare at the unique group around the table. But Isaac and Rachel didn't notice them at all. They were just agreeing with Abraham's ancient prayer, "Blessed art Thou, O Lord God, King of the Universe, Who has saved us, sustained us and brought us to this place in time."

"Can't you eat just a bite of this scrumptious cherry cake, Isaac?" Rachel asked, lifting her second cup of coffee to her lips.

"Nooo, no. I can't believe I let you talk me into this apple pie!" Isaac replied, patting his stomach. "It's the best I've ever eaten, but I'm stuffed!"

Chapter Ten

"Talk you into it? No way, Isaac Kramer!" Rachel cried. "You know homemade apple pie is your favorite, and you wanted it, didn't you?"

"Guilty, my love. Shoot me in my misery!" Isaac laughed, turning to Abraham. "You're the only wise one at the table, Rabbi," Isaac acknowledged. "Temperance in all things, eh?"

"Da, Isaac. Temperance is a virtue, but I can only admit that this old man fears heartburn more than anything these days, even to the point of giving up good apple pie," Abraham replied with a chuckle.

The waiter collected the dessert plates and poured more steaming coffee into their cups as Isaac and Rachel tried to remember more questions they wanted to ask the rabbi. But Abraham Wasserman asked the next question of the evening,

"What happened, my friends? You were very anxious after the Shabbat service and to some extent this afternoon as you entered my home. But, tonight, you are full of joy, da?"

"Actually, nothing really happened, rabbi," Rachel responded softly. "We just have this surprising peace. We noticed it when we were walking back to the hotel today, and we talked about it then, but later we both realized the peace came when we first sat down by your warm fire. Suddenly, we just knew everything would be all right. We realized we don't have to have all the answers to everything right now."

"Rabbi," Isaac interjected, "you've given us so much—the family Rachel has longed for all her life and answers to many other questions as well. But, the things you spoke about in your sermon on Shabbat...well, let's just say that we don't understand those things as yet; nevertheless, we won't forget them. Being the good Jews that we are, we will study hard, dear friend." Isaac laughed, patting the rabbi's hand.

"*Bun*, good!" Abraham agreed. "I will be here when you need me. For a while. I do not believe the Almighty is ready to take me home quite yet."

"You had better stick around, dear Rabbi," Rachel adamantly proclaimed. "I have more questions than you could answer in twenty years! And, speaking of questions, this is my last one for this evening. You told us that it's only been since the sixties that great numbers of Jews have come to believe that Yeshua is Messiah. What about all those years between the expulsion of the Jews from the church in the first century to the days of Joseph Rabinowitz? And then from Rabinowitz to the sixties? Were there Jewish believers during those years?"

"Da, my daughter, there were many Jewish believers throughout the centuries—perhaps thousands. Did you know that Theodore Herzl's son believed that Yeshua of Nazareth is the Messiah?"

The Gentile and the Jew: A Divine Romance

"No!" Isaac exclaimed. "I had no idea."

"Neither did I," said Rachel, surprise written all over her face.

"Da, it is true. Then there was Benjamin Disraeli, the prime minister of Great Britain. Paul Levertoff was another Hassidic Jew who lived in Belarus and died in 1954. He had much the same vision as Rabinowitz, hoping to establish a Jewish congregation of worshiping believers. Levertoff aided refugees from Nazi Germany and Austria also, and this is how I know that Herzl's son, Hans, was a believer. Paul Levertoff helped him after the war.

"Then, there was Rabbi Isaac Lichtenstein in Hungary who preached Yeshua as Messiah to his Jewish congregation in Tapio-Szele in the midst of persecution for many years. He was known to say, 'I shall most willingly retract if you can convince me that I am wrong.' But, no one convinced him otherwise, my friends. He was a witness until his death in 1909.[15]

"Ah, daughter," the rabbi continued, pushing away from the table. "There are so many. I have studied the lives of all whose records I could find. One, you will recognize immediately, Felix Mendelssohn, the great composer. He was a believer and also the son of a Jewish believer."

"I didn't know that!" Rachel exclaimed.

"Da, many, many Jews who believe their brother Yeshua was and is the Jewish Messiah. I recall another rabbi who was a student of the famous Rebbe of Ger. He was thrown out of the synagogue in Paris in 1920 because of his belief in Yeshua. He said, 'I have not become a goy, but am a true, completed Jew.'[15] One of the most famous Jewish believers was John Cournos, an orthodox Jew born in Czarist Russia who became a famous novelist and playwright. He wrote an open letter to Christians and Jews. I brought a copy with me tonight because I thought it might interest you."

Abraham reached inside his coat pocket and brought out a yellowed piece of paper. He read, "'Jesus was not only a Jew. He was the apex and the acme of Jewish teaching, which began with Moses and ran the entire evolving gamut of kings, teachers, prophets, rabbis—David and Isaiah and Daniel and Hillel—until their pith and essence was crystallized in this greatest of all Jews....'

"Listen to this, my friends, 'For a Jew, therefore, to forget that Jesus was a Jew, and to deny him, is to forget and to deny all the Jewish teaching that was before Jesus; it is to reject the Jewish heritage, to betray what was best in Israel.... To be a true Jew is to be a Messianic Jew. To be a true Christian is to recognize the Jewishness of Christianity. The fate of Judaism and Christianity hangs together.... I know a number of Jews who believe as I do, who believe that it is time that we Jews reclaimed Jesus, and that it is desirable that we do so.'[16]

Chapter Ten

"And that is exactly what is happening, my friends," the rabbi continued. "Jews all over the world are reclaiming Yeshua, our brother—the Jew."

Isaac was listening attentively but still not sure the rabbi's historical rambling was of any present consequence. "That's all very interesting, Rabbi. But, my question is this: why would a Jew want to be part of a religion that has persecuted our people for two thousand years? All the blood libels, the *pogroms*, the Inquisition, the Crusades and even the Holocaust—all promoted by Christians, Rabbi! Even the few times Christians didn't initiate the persecution, they perpetuated it by closing their eyes as if we did not exist. I'm not one of those crazies who blame every Christian, but facts are facts. What about that, Rabbi?"

"Da, it is true, my son. The Christian Church has worn blinders as well as the rest of the world. But you must understand that in the beginning, in the days of Yeshua and many years afterward, there was only one group of people who followed Yeshua, and they were Jews. This Jewish sect was sometimes called *The Way*, consisting entirely of Jews. Gradually, Gentiles came to believe in Him, primarily through the teachings of a Pharisee from the tribe of Benjamin, a student of Hillel named Saul. He and the first disciples came to understand that Yeshua had come to be the Savior of all men, not just Jews, and they began to travel all around the Mediterranean preaching this good news. Later, thousands of Jewish and Gentile believers were murdered by Rome because of their faith—ripped to pieces by wild animals for the Romans' sporting events or burned at the stake—horrible torture leading to martyrdom, my friends."

Rachel and Isaac listened attentively, sipping their coffee and asking questions from time to time as the rabbi continued his explanation. "A very strange thing happened around three hundred years after Yeshua's life on earth, my friends, something that caused a paradigm shift in the history of the Christian Church. More than that, this event changed the history of the world almost overnight. The Roman emperor, Constantine, supposedly became a believer through his mother's conversion. Suddenly, this religion, as you call it, became not just legal but the religion of the empire. I'm sure you understand what that meant, da? Every person in the empire, millions of subjects, were ordered to lay aside Roman gods and every conceivable type of paganism and convert to Christianity overnight. Do you think they all became true believers, following after the Jewish Messiah's teaching and trusting in his sacrifice? Nu, my friends. Only because the emperor gave the order, thousands adopted this new religion, calling themselves Christian just the same as if they had truly converted."

The Gentile and the Jew: A Divine Romance

"I see," said Isaac. "I knew about Constantine's dramatic conversion from history courses in college, but I've never thought about it like that. On a smaller scale, I guess it would be like the Israeli government ordering all Jews to adhere to ultra-orthodox Judaism, wouldn't it? Those who don't believe certainly wouldn't truly convert just because the government ordered them to."

"Da, my son, you are right. By that time, what was once a small Jewish sect was no longer Jewish, and all remnants of Yeshua's Jewishness were eradicated from the church to be replaced by Roman tradition and culture and the traditions of Roman conquered lands. I guess you could say that as far as most leaders in the church were concerned, Jesus had converted to Christianity and if any Jews wanted to believe, they would have to do likewise, laying aside all Jewish tradition and culture, actually becoming Roman in a sense. The blinders the church had embraced kept the leaders from remembering and understanding that we Jews were given the message first. We don't have to join a new religion. He is *our* Messiah!

"Within the last fifty years, the church's rejection of the Jewish people became known as Replacement Theology, but it has permeated the church for nearly two thousand years as you said, Isaac. But, many church leaders' eyes are being opened by the Ruach Ha'Kodesh in these days as was true of such Christians as Franz Delitzch, friend of Josef Rabinowitz, and the great preacher and scholar, Charles Spurgeon. Now, even as thousands of Jews are coming to faith in Yeshua, many church leaders are also accepting the Jewish roots of their faith and welcoming their elder brother into their fellowship. Does this help you, Isaac?" Abraham asked.

"Well, as Rachel said, we don't understand it all, and I don't know that we ever will. So, I'll have to ask that we can agree to disagree on some issues. But more than anything, Rabbi, we want you to know that we are very grateful for all you've done for us—the many hours you've sacrificed for us as if we were your own family, your gracious hospitality, and most of all, your loving kindness. We will remember you always."

Rachel gently reached for the rabbi's gnarled hand. "I will miss you, Abraham Wasserman. We haven't told you, but our return flight leaves Bucharest tomorrow morning at eight o'clock. We wanted to have this special time with you before we go home."

Tears filled the old man's eyes once again as he took Rachel's slender hand in his and held it tightly. "Da, I will miss you, too, daughter of Jakob Liebovici, niece of Aron Liebovici. You have a prodigious heritage, my dear Rachel. You must remember that always."

Chapter Ten

"Yes...yes, I will, dear Rabbi. I will remember. And, my sons and daughters will remember and their descendants after them. And I will weep no more, for my children are coming home." Rachel clutched the patriarch's strong hand, her green eyes stinging with tears of sadness and joy.

"Come on, Rachel," Isaac said, holding her coat. "Time has slipped by as usual when we are with our new friend, and it's getting very late. We need to get back to the hotel and pack if we're to leave in the morning."

"You don't seem like a new friend, Rabbi," Rachel acknowledged quietly. "Since that first day in the bakery, it seems I've known you forever."

"That is the way of the Almighty with those whose hearts He would knit closely together, daughter. We will meet again, Rachel Liebovici. We will meet again."

"Shalom, Rabbi!" Isaac called as he gently pushed Rachel towards the door.

"Shalom, my friends, shalom."

Chapter Eleven

Someone was knocking on Mike's bedroom door as he came out of the bathroom drying his dark hair with a big white towel. Half-expecting Annie to yell "Hello Mikey!" he opened the door, surprised to find David Klein standing with his right hand raised, ready to knock one more time.

"Hey, man!" Mike greeted his new brother-in-law.

"Good morning, Mike," David responded. "Sleep well?"

"Sure did. Can't help but sleep well in that bed. I thought feather beds were a thing of the past."

David laughed. "Mother's elderly aunt who still lives in Holland sends her stuff like that. She's convinced we're cold here in America where no one has ducks in their backyard."

Mike's face broke into a grin. "Come on in, David."

"No thanks, I don't have time. I'm on my way to an appointment your father set up with a business acquaintance, but I was wondering if you'd like to have lunch with me and a good friend after my business meeting. It's someone I would especially like you to meet. We'll be in Greenwich at the Boxing Cat Grill on Putman Avenue at noon. What do you say, Mike? Can you come?"

"Sure, David...that is, if Sarah doesn't need me to look after Annie today," Mike answered. "But I'd better check with her first."

"Oh, I forgot to tell you. Sarah said she and Mother will take Annie shopping and then down to the park on the Sound if she isn't too exhausted. They'll go to some fun place that she will like for lunch," David explained.

The Gentile and the Jew: A Divine Romance

"That's great. I think Annie's getting a little homesick for Mom and Dad. An active day with Sarah and your Mother will do her good. Okay, sure. I'll be there."

"Good. I'll see you at the Grill at noon," David said, reaching for the door to pull it shut. "Just call a cab, and you can ride back to the house with me after lunch."

Mike hurried back to the bathroom to comb his hair before it dried sticking straight up, thinking that if David introduced him to one more friend, he was going to wring his neck. He had a lot of friends, but it seemed as if David had a Volkswagon Beatle like the ones at the circus, the ones clowns never stop coming out of. Mike grinned at his punk hairdo in the mirror.

"Hope I like this new clown," he laughingly said to his reflection.

By the time Mike dressed, drank a cup of coffee and saw Annie off for her day of shopping, it was almost eleven. He decided he had better call the cab since he didn't know how long it would take to get to the restaurant in nearby Greenwich. If he arrived early, he would just browse around town a bit. *Better take my overcoat*, Mike thought as he headed out the door. *North Carolina cold is nothing compared to this!*

Mike entered the doors of the Boxing Cat Grill just in time to meet David and his friend in the entryway. David's back was turned when Mike walked up and tapped him on the shoulder, expecting to meet the guy David had brought to lunch. But much to his surprise, the friend was not a guy—definitely not a guy, Mike concluded. A beautiful young woman with blonde hair cropped very short, stood before him dressed in a white blouse, open at the neck, and a short black leather jacket. Her rather tight black pants revealed unusually long slender legs and at that point, Mike decided he had better stop staring.

"Hi, Mike, didn't see you come in," David said. "I'd like you to meet a good friend of mine, Rebecca Brody. Becca, this is my brother-in-law, Mike Kramer."

"Hello, Mike," Becca smiled, reaching out to shake his extended hand. "I'm happy to finally meet you. David has told me a great deal about his new brother."

"I hope he told you a few good stories along with the bad," Mike replied with a big smile. "I'm happy to meet you, too, Becca, but I'll have to admit David told me absolutely nothing about you."

They all laughed as the maitre d' led them across the polished wood floor to their table in the back corner by a tall window. The seating areas were designed in varying floor levels separated by wood railings, giving an illusion of privacy in each section, but their table was actually in a cozy little corner. Mike was glad.

Chapter Eleven

He had a feeling this was going to be a very private conversation. David held a chair for Becca as Mike took her coat and his and gave them to their host.

"This is nice," Mike commented, looking around at the popular restaurant and the evergreens in the snow outside the window. "How's the food?"

"Good," David answered, "but if you're hungry, let me suggest something for you. They're rather skimpy with some of their dishes."

"I need skimpy," Becca said with a smile. "A girl must watch her weight, you know."

David smiled back at his old friend. "I've watched your weight for years, Becca, and it's very lovely, eh Mike?"

Becca looked as if she could have kicked David under the table, and Mike had to admit he was a little embarrassed himself. *What's going on here*, he wondered? *Me thinks this is a set up, and I can't believe I didn't see it coming. I should have wrung his neck this morning.* Mike cast a furtive glance at the brother-in-law he had been thankful for up until now.

But the luncheon didn't prove to be the set up he suspected. After the waiter took their order, David began to explain that he and Becca's husband, Sam Brody, had been friends since childhood, attending grade school and high school together, even graduating from Princeton the same year. David had gone on to law school at Carolina while Sam earned a Master's in Journalism at Georgetown.

"That's where we met," Becca interjected, smiling at the memories reeling in her mind.

"Yeah, it was love at first sight, wasn't it, Bec?" David teased.

"No, you loon!" Becca replied laughing. "You know it wasn't love at first sight or second or third, either! I thought Sam Brody was overbearing and extremely irritating when we first met. Never in a million years would I have thought I would fall in love with that crazy guy. He was great, David. He was really great."

Innocently missing the past tense of their words, Mike studied the two friends as their laughter quickly ebbed, the smiles on their faces fading as the waiter appeared with their food. Everyone was silent at the corner table as the plates were placed before them and the waiter asked if they needed anything else. David didn't seem to hear him, so Mike answered the impatient young man, "Thank you, no. This is fine, thank you."

The three diners ate their lunch with little conversation, asking polite questions from time to time and filling in the blanks with the appropriate answers. Mike decided he was going to keep his mouth shut since he couldn't figure out what was going on anyway. If he waited long enough, maybe someone would drop a clue as to why they were having this mysterious little luncheon.

After the waiter poured the coffee all three had ordered in place of dessert, David asked, "I guess you're wondering why we're here, right Mike?"

"You could say that," he replied. "I've certainly enjoyed your company, and yours, Becca, but I'll have to admit it feels as if I'm in the dark. What's going on?"

Becca spoke up before David could answer, "Mike, let me give you some background first. Sam and I married right after we finished graduate school four and a half years ago. He was immediately offered a fantastic job with a major news magazine. I think they hired me as an incentive to get him." Becca smiled at the thought and continued, "But, Sam wasn't satisfied. He felt guilty that so many young Israelis had to serve their time in the IDF and here he was, footloose and fancy free in America. You see, Mike, unlike most young Jews in the States, Sam believed he owed something to Eretz Israel, even if he never made it his permanent home. He and I talked it over almost daily for nearly a year and finally made a decision. He would make Aliyah, knowing that he would immediately be drafted into the IDF where he would serve two years and then come back to his career in journalism—and me."

"What about you, Becca?" Mike questioned.

"That's my biggest regret in hindsight. Sam didn't want me to make Aliyah because I would have had to serve my two years in the army, too, and he just couldn't handle that. It was one thing for him to join up, but he couldn't bear the thought of me being in such a perilous situation."

"I can understand that," said Mike, thinking how much lucky ol' Sam must adore this ravishingly exciting woman.

"Although we knew that being separated nearly all the time for two years would be awful, we kept telling ourselves that we were young and we had our entire lives before us. We would have two years apart but at least sixty together, maybe seventy if we were blessed with good health. Yeah, we had every detail planned...." Becca's gaze drifted to the blood-red cardinals chattering in the snow-covered spruce outside the window. David gently reached over to lay his hand on hers.

"Oh, I'm sorry. Where was I?" She took a deep breath and continued her story.

"So, Sam went through the Aliyah process quickly, and before we knew it, he had finished training and was assigned to a patrol near the Lebanese border. I continued to work for the magazine, asking for foreign assignments so I would be too busy to miss my husband more than I could bear."

Chapter Eleven

Becca again turned her eyes to the soft white snow falling gently outside the big window, her slender hand almost clutching her throat. She whispered, "Two months after he was assigned to duty, Sam was killed by a suicide bomber while on a weekend pass in Tel Aviv. My gorgeous young husband was blown to bits by a young boy who was told he would earn a few virgins in paradise if he would wipe a few Jews off the face of the earth. Can you believe that? I can't. I still can't believe it."

Mike was shocked, staring at her stricken face. He didn't know what to say, so he wisely said nothing. What could he say? David was gazing into his coffee while his friend continued to stare blankly out the window. Mike had always judged David as being a little stiff, too dignified for a guy his age, but Mike was seeing a different side of David today, a tenderhearted man who experienced pain like everyone else. He felt almost as much sympathy for David as for his friend, Becca, as he finally said the only words he could think of,

"I'm so sorry, Becca...David."

"Yes...yes, I know," she responded. "Everyone's sorry. But, no one can do anything about it. Sam's gone and that's it."

Was she being cynical, Mike wondered? She hadn't seemed like that type of person, but who wouldn't be cynical after going through something like that?

At that moment the young widow caught sight of Mike's questioning eyes and quickly asked his forgiveness, "I'm sorry, Mike. I don't want to be bitter. It's just that it's still so unbelievable!" She took a deep breath and leaned back in her chair. "I constantly find myself saying all kinds of crazy things I don't really mean. David and I knew it would be hard to get through this part of our visit with you, but we also knew we had to give you some background before we get to the reason for our meeting."

"Mike," David began, lifting his eyes for the first time since Becca started telling her story, "we have a proposition for you."

"What do you mean—a proposition?" Mike asked curiously. "What in the world are you talking about, David?"

"A job." Becca quickly answered his question. "My editor would like to offer you a job with our magazine as my partner in a new assignment."

"You guys are crazy," Mike responded, his dark eyes darting from one to the other, thinking they must be pulling some weird joke on him. "I won't even have my master's until the end of May. That's five more months. Anyway, why would your editor want to offer me a job? He doesn't even know me."

"I told Becca that you have another semester to go in graduate school," said David. "But we were wondering if you could work it out to put that on hold for about six months? This job would launch your career like a rocket and gain you all the experience you'll ever need. You can still finish your master's program next fall, or anytime, for that matter. Are you interested?"

"Not yet, man. You said I would be your partner in a new assignment," Mike said, turning to Becca. "What assignment?"

"With the Associated Press in Israel," she stated matter-of-factly, staring straight into Mike's dark eyes.

"Whoa!" Mike pushed his chair back from the table. "I thought I was being set up from the moment I entered this place, and now I know it!" Mike laughed as he stood up. "I've always wanted to lead an exciting life, David, but not that exciting."

David and Becca were not surprised at Mike's reaction, but they were not about to give up on him either. David said, "You two grab your coats, and I'll get the check. Maybe if we get some fresh air, we can clear our heads and talk about this some more."

"Yeah, man. Maybe that frigid wind will knock some sense into you guys," Mike agreed with a chuckle, shaking his head. "Let's get outta here."

Mike helped Becca with her coat while David placed his money in the black leather folder and left it on the table. He met his friends at the entrance where the maitre-d thanked them for coming, "Good day, Mr. Klein. Please come again."

"Thank you, Richard." David responded. "We'll see you next time."

The arctic air hit them full force as they opened the door and walked out onto the sidewalk. Turning right toward the parking lot, Mike couldn't help but walk faster than David and Becca, reaching the car well before the two silent friends. He was so wound up he could have walked all the way to the Klein home in the neighboring town if the temperature hadn't been hovering around freezing—even lower with the wind chill.

"We'll take Becca to her hotel and then talk some more, okay, Mike?" asked David. "It would be good if the three of us could meet again before we leave for Wilmington day after tomorrow."

"All right, brother-in-law. I was hoping to let this sink in a little, but I guess I do need a bit more information before I throw the idea out the door."

He was seated in the back seat by then and couldn't see the smile on Rebecca Brody's beautiful face as she thought, *Yes!*

Chapter Eleven

Mike and David almost ran into one another at the top of the stairs as they were coming down to join David's family for breakfast the following morning. They had dropped Rebecca Brody off at her hotel after their curious lunch at the Boxing Cat Grill the day before. They had driven back to the Klein's home where they talked at least two more hours. David divulged more details about Becca's new assignment, giving his brother-in-law a better understanding of what would be required of him if he were to accept the job offer.

Yesterday's meeting was as weird as the name of the restaurant, Mike had thought as he lay in bed last night. He rehearsed the disturbing conversation he had had at lunch and the following discussion over coffee at the Klein's kitchen table. His imagination went wild, envisioning crazy cats in a boxing ring half the night. But this morning, the sunlight beaming through his bedroom window seemed to bring a little ray of light into his mind as well. Having slept soundly until seven when the clock alarmed, Mike hit the snooze button quickly, not yet fully awake, and dropped back to that level of sleep where he began to dream. He dreamed about Carrie and the memory hadn't faded a bit as he showered and dressed for the day.

It was almost as if he saw a portrait of Carrie, he remembered now, going down the stairs in front of David, skipping every other step in his newfound excitement. He didn't know why he felt so good. Carrie didn't speak in the dream, but she was smiling and laughing, looking as beautiful as she used to during the months they were so happy together. Mike wasn't really into dream interpretation and the like, but seeing Carrie glowing like that had certainly made him feel better—like everything was going to be all right. Maybe this surprising job offer wasn't so crazy after all.

Sarah was helping Mrs. Klein place the last of the breakfast dishes on the table when Mike and David entered the sunny kitchen, the aroma of freshly brewed coffee filling the air.

"Good morning, Mike! Morning, David!" Rabbi Klein greeted them jovially from behind his wide-opened newspaper.

David sat down beside his father, jerking the paper down to say, "Good morning, Dad! What's happening in the world this fine morning?"

"Well son, I'm sorry to say there's a lot of news, but not much good news," Solomon Klein answered, raising the newspaper to eye level again.

"Put that paper down and let's eat, Sol," said David's mother, Rose. "I don't know why you always read about the terrible things that are going on in the world before breakfast. It's a wonder you don't have ulcers. You should just relax at breakfast, not take on the weight of the world before your day even begins!" Rose continued to fuss at her phlegmatic husband.

The Gentile and the Jew: A Divine Romance

Mike smiled, watching the good-natured bantering between the two aging lovebirds. Rose glanced over the table to see if anything was missing and quickly sat down beside Sarah. Everyone was ready to eat when Mike suddenly realized something really was missing—someone, that is.

"Where's Annie, Sarah?" he asked.

"That precious child is exhausted," Rose interrupted before Sarah had a chance to answer. "I told Sarah to let her sleep late this morning so she will be rested up for the long ride back to North Carolina. How long is it, David? Twelve hours, did you say?"

"Just about, Mother," David answered, taking a gulp of his coffee and bracing for her next sentence.

"That's too far for a little girl to ride all shut up in a car," Rose declared. "Next time you bring little Annie, you must fly, David."

"Mother! You wouldn't mind us flying? I thought you'd be worried sick if we put Annie on an airplane to come here."

Since their arrival, David had been trying to decide whether to tell his anxious mother that he would be releasing the rental car he had driven up to Connecticut to fly back to Raleigh with Sarah, Mike and Annie, or if he should just conveniently forget to tell her and hope she didn't ask.

"Of course I would be worried, David. You know I would be worried. Why not a train, then? In a train, you won't be four thousand feet in the heavens where only the Almighty should be and Annie will be able to get up and walk around. Yes, the train would be better. Now eat your breakfast, David." Conversation ended.

David rolled his eyes at Sarah's knowing smile and turned back to his father. "Dad, if you're not too busy this morning, could Mike and I visit with you in your study?"

"Of course, son," Solomon replied. "I was hoping for more time with both of you before you go home."

"Oh, my. I can't get used to North Carolina being your home, David," Rose interjected again. "It's a lovely place, and I'm sure the people are very nice, certainly Sarah's family, but it's so far away! We hardly ever get to see you, and when the grandchildren come—*oy vey*! We will never get to see our precious little grandchildren!" David's mother was almost in tears, but just as quickly as she had jumped into her little tirade, she suddenly ended it when she saw everyone was ready for more coffee. Rose Klein's priorities were definitely in order.

David let out a long sigh, glancing quickly at his new bride, his eyes imploring her help.

Chapter Eleven

"Mother Klein, I promise you will get to see your grandchildren when they arrive. In fact, there's no reason you couldn't come down and stay with us a few days or weeks, even before the grandchildren arrive," Sarah said. "We'll have a guest room in our new house, and I would be delighted to have you with us whenever you can come."

"Days? Weeks? Oh, no, Sarah, my dear. Solomon Klein doesn't know how to turn on the stove or how to put his dirty clothes in the washing machine. He would starve before I got back and worse than that, he would smell!"

Sarah smiled at David again and shrugged her shoulders as if to say, "Well, I tried."

Soon after breakfast, Rabbi Klein led the two young men to his study, added on to their home many years after the historical house was built in the mid-nineteenth century. An enclosed hallway had been added much later to connect the study to the rest of the house for modern heating purposes. Solomon liked his hideaway away from the activity of his bustling household. Rose was constantly involved in the lives of the members of the congregation and each of their own four daughters, cooking and counseling and trying to help everybody, keeping up communication with David and Sarah and what relatives she had left in the world. His wife was a good woman, and his daughters were a great blessing, but oh, how Solomon Klein loved to enter the doors of his own private sanctuary.

"This is great, Rabbi!" Mike proclaimed. "Your own little world, huh?"

Solomon chuckled. "Yes, yes, Mike. Everyone needs their own...hm, how do they say it these days...their own *space*?"

"That's right, Dad," David agreed, "and, man, do you need yours!"

The three men laughed together, enjoying the easy male camaraderie.

"You have a door to the outside, too," Mike noted, ambling over to scan the bookshelves filled with everything from the Talmud to John Grisham novels. "I should have browsed your library earlier in the week, Rabbi."

"Take anything you see that looks interesting, Mike. You have a few more hours you could use to read. I'll let you hide in my space if you'd like." David's father grinned from ear to ear, his eyes twinkling with merriment.

"I might do that. I just might," Mike responded, his eyes still scanning the hundreds of books placed neatly on the many shelves that reached to the ceiling.

The room was a little dark for Mike's preference, but the old wood-paneled walls and brown leather furniture made for a cozy retreat. A worn, multicolored oriental rug covered the wide planked floor and gas logs burned brightly in the small fireplace. The rabbi said a wood fire took too much time and effort these

The Gentile and the Jew: A Divine Romance

days, and he was perfectly happy with the warmth and glow of the instant gas logs. There was a nice, familiar fragrance in the room that Mike couldn't quite place until he suddenly remembered his grandfather Liebowitz's old curved tobacco pipe. *That's what it is*, he thought—*cherry pipe tobacco!*

Rabbi Klein was watching intently as Mike closed his eyes and took a deep breath, savoring the memory of his grandfather's presence. Smiling sheepishly, the rabbi confessed, "You're right, son. It's a cherry-blend pipe tobacco. I'm so glad I didn't know it would kill me years ago when I smoked. It gives the room a really nice fragrance, don't you think?"

"It sure does," Mike laughed and said. "My Grandfather Liebowitz smoked this blend of tobacco in an old curved pipe he brought to America with him from somewhere in Eastern Europe. You know, the kind of pipe you see in old Sherlock Holmes movies? It was one of the few possessions that made it through the years it took for him and my grandmother to arrive safely on Ellis Island." Mike leaned his head back on the soft leather couch, clasping his hands behind his head.

"Yeah, to Sarah and me, that old pipe was enshrouded in mystery. Dad said it was impossible for him to have kept it with him in the camps, so we surmised that someone very special gave it to him after the liberation. In my memories of him, he always seemed to have that pipe close by, either in his hand or on the table next to his chair."

Solomon was listening empathetically. "The pipe was probably his only connection with the family and friends he lost, Mike. My own mother had a lace scarf she treated as if it were one of the holy vessels from the first Temple. She laid it in a special place in our home, and all during the day, she would go over and touch that scarf, recalling memories we children could only imagine and she would never share."

"Yeah, it's hard to understand what that generation went through, especially when you're the third generation. My mother has always been much closer to it. In fact, I don't know if David told you or not, but my parents are in Romania right now, trying to put together some of the pieces of the past for my mother. I have to admit, Rabbi, I've always thought she was a little obsessed with the whole deal—you know, the Holocaust and all. But, if she needs to know more to be able to put the past to rest and find peace, then so be it. I just hope she finds her answers."

David and his father exchanged knowing looks as Mike came to the end of his sentence. After a moment, David said, "Dad, Mike had lunch with Becca Brody and me yesterday, and we told him about Sam and the assignment in Israel. Of course, he was surprised as we expected, but he's been mulling it over and wants to know what you think about it. I told him that Becca's editor is a close friend of yours and that you knew about the proposition before we did. That's about it."

"Rabbi," Mike added, "you and I have talked a great deal about wisdom since I came to visit, so I know you'll understand the question I'm about to ask. Laying aside the physical dangers of this assignment for a moment, do you think it would be wise for me to drop out of graduate school now, this being my final semester? I don't want to do something foolish."

"I understand your question, Mike, and I believe that, in most cases, it would be very foolish to discontinue your education just when you're about to complete your degree." Rabbi Klein sat quietly for a moment, then continued, "Maybe it will help if I explain how David and I came to know about this opportunity. I've spent many hours here in this room listening to my old friend, Daniel Silverman, explain the situation. Daniel is Becca's editor, you see. That's how I got involved."

Mike nodded, thinking this whole thing sounded like an amazing set of coincidences—too amazing to be true, actually. But he quickly concluded that even if Sarah and David were engaged in a bit of loving manipulation, the old rabbi surely wasn't. He didn't even know Mike very well.

"Mike, you have to understand that David and Sam were the best of friends from the time they were little tikes playing ball in our backyard to the day Sam was killed. Since then, my David makes it a point to communicate regularly with Becca just to make sure she's all right. She's almost like one of his sisters, and it's my understanding that Becca and Sarah have become good friends as well. Right, David?"

"They have, Dad. They've become very good friends." David smiled and said, "When I see them together, I think of the odd couple. Becca's wild and adventurous and crazy, and my Sarah is gentle and sweet and practical—just what I need." David blushed slightly, realizing he had gotten more personal than he'd intended.

Solomon smiled at his son and continued, "When Becca was offered this assignment, she phoned David, and they discussed all the pros and cons to great lengths, finally coming to the conclusion that it would be good for Becca to somehow help fulfill Sam's mission, as it were, and of course, to bring some closure to her grief. Right, David?"

"Yes, well, after that decision was made, Becca began to share more details about the assignment, including the need for a partner—more of an assistant, I guess—for the journey. When she began to describe the type of person needed for the job—a young male in top physical condition who could take over in situations where raw manpower is needed; a journalist or someone with a degree in journalism; a person she could trust and feel safe with; and, preferably, Jewish—well Mike, I couldn't help but think of you right off the bat. At that point, we brought Sarah into the discussion, and she agreed that you should at least be given the opportunity." David looked back at his father, waiting for him to take up the story.

"After that lengthy phone conversation, Becca went to Daniel Silverman with the recommendation that you be offered the job, Mike. Day before yesterday, when my old friend and I met for our weekly schmoozing, he told me that Becca wanted him to offer you the job and asked me what I thought. Of course, I told him that you and I hadn't had much time to get to know each other very well in the two years we've been acquainted, but in the time I've known you, particularly this past week as you and I have enjoyed long conversations in my home, I would proudly recommend you for the job."

Profoundly touched by the affirmation, Mike said, "Thank you, Rabbi Klein. You'll never know how much your trust means to me." Surprised to find himself fighting back tears, he leaned forward on the leather couch, his forearms on his knees, fingers loosely intertwined, and asked, "But, other than recommending me because of whatever good character you see in me, and because of the job requirements that David feels I meet, why do you think I should take this offer? In other words, why me?"

The rabbi paused for a second, gazing intently into his young friend's dark eyes. Mike wondered if the older man could actually see into the depths of his soul.

"Because you're searching, son, and when a man is searching, he needs to have every opportunity to find what he is searching for, even if he doesn't know what it is. You have told me that one factor in your quest is to understand what it means to be a Jew. What better venue than Israel to find the answers?"

"I see," said Mike.

"Why don't you go out with David and Sarah this afternoon and enjoy yourself," the rabbi suggested. "Or, better yet, stay here in my study and read if you'd like. I have an appointment with a family in our congregation, so I'll be out all afternoon. Get everything off your mind for a few hours, son. I'm sure you will have your answer by morning."

As the door to the study slowly opened and a tiny little face peeked in, Mike Kramer was heard to quietly say, "I have my answer now, Rabbi Klein... David. My answer is, 'Yes.'"

Chapter Twelve

It was New Year's Eve, and the airport was packed with holiday travelers, some weary and impatient to get home, others excited and revved up for the biggest party night of the year. Sarah drilled Mike not to put Annie down for a second, and Mike kept telling his sister not to worry, he wasn't about to put her down in this mob.

They ended up spending about three hours in La Guardia, but the flight back to Raleigh didn't take much more than an hour, giving Mike very little time to talk to David and Sarah about how they should present his shocking news to their Mom and Dad. It really wouldn't have mattered if there had been more time because Annie jabbered a mile a minute, excited to be going home to see her parents after what seemed to her a very long holiday. By some remarkable coincidence, the Kramers' flight from Montreal would get into Raleigh-Durham just an hour before their children's flight from New York, and both parties were filled with anxious anticipation to be together once again.

The winter sun was high overhead, and the sky clear as the Boeing 747 skidded down the runway, Annie squealing with delight at the "fun ride" and Sarah taking a long, deep breath. She wondered if she could have inherited her mother-in-law's aversion to flying.

"We're back, Annie!" Mike said. "Hold on a minute until I get my bag down, and I'll carry you into the terminal to find Mom and Dad."

"Hurry, Mikey, hurry!" said Annie, giggling and bouncing up and down in her seat.

The Gentile and the Jew: A Divine Romance

"Here, Mike, I'll get your bag," David offered. "You just grab Annie, and let's get out of this mob as quickly as possible."

"Gotcha!" Mike said, lifting Annie as she made her next bounce. "Come on, Tigger!"

"Yay! I'm Tigger, and you're Christopher Robin, Mikey," squealed Annie. "Let's bounce some more, Christopher Robin!"

"Christopher Robin doesn't bounce, honey, just Tigger," Mike assured the merry little girl, weaving in and out of the crowd as they headed down the connecting ramp and into the gate area, David and Sarah following close behind.

"Mommy! Daddy!" Annie yelled, almost jumping out of Mike's stronghold. He put her down a few yards before they got to Rachel and Isaac so she could have the joy of running into her parents' arms once again. He stood silently by, watching the joyful reunion between his parents and their little girl, his mouth set in a stoney smile. David greeted the Kramers quickly and then hurried off to the baggage claim area, shouting to Sarah that he would meet them at the main terminal doors in just a few minutes. But Sarah didn't answer. She was watching her brother's face, and she was the only one who caught a glimpse of the deep sadness in his dark eyes.

Isaac had already taken the shuttle to the long-term parking lot and had driven his wife's mini van back to the lot just across from the terminal. Jiggling Annie in his arms, Isaac handed the keys to Mike, asking his son to go get the van and pick them up at the main terminal entrance. When they finally retrieved all the baggage for both groups, Mike and David loaded all the luggage in the carrier on top, and the entire Kramer family loaded up for the two and a half hour drive to Wilmington. Buckled in her child's seat in the middle beside Rachel, Annie fell asleep before they turned off Aviation Parkway onto Interstate 40. Too tired to get into any lengthy conversation, the weary European travelers nodded in and out of dreamland as Mike drove and Sarah and David dozed in the back seat.

Eastbound Interstate 40 ends at the city limits to Wilmington, North Carolina. Actually, the highway itself doesn't end there, but becomes Michael Jordan Freeway, then College Road, continuing on south through the city of Wilmington and New Hanover County until it merges with Highway 421 at Monkey Junction. From there it becomes Carolina Beach Road, turning into Lake Park Boulevard, then into Fort Fisher Boulevard the last few miles to the end of the peninsula. So many name changes could be confusing to visitors in the area, but the most interesting thing about the highway in Mike's view, even from the time he was a young boy, was a green information sign that was erected close to the spot where Michael Jordan Freeway becomes I-40 on the westbound side of the road. The sign reads, "Barstow, California 2,547 miles."

Mike hardly remembered a time in his life that he hadn't noticed that sign as he was heading out of Wilmington, and whether he was traveling just a few miles or a few hundred miles, he could always feel the excitement rising in his spirit. Sometimes, he even noted the back of the sign driving into Wilmington as he did today. By the time Mike was about twelve, the interstate had been completed and he had traced the coast to coast highway on every road map of the United States he could find, believing that one day he would take off driving down that highway and end up in Barstow, California, and points beyond.

Even though they could certainly afford long trips, Kramer family vacations were few and far between. Of course, Isaac flew to New York and other major cities on business trips fairly often, Rachel joining him only when her children left home for college. He had been a workaholic as long as Mike could remember, always stressing hard work and responsibility as priority to everything else in life. He knew his Dad's motives were good. He was right about hard work and sacrifice to a degree, but today, as Mike drove past his sign once again, he wondered if his father's rigid workaholism was one of the reasons he had always wanted to break away and do something crazy and adventurous. Holding the wheel with his right hand and leaning his head on his left, he drove over the Market Street overpass, whispering only to himself, "I guess I have my chance."

Annie was still asleep when they pulled into the winding driveway leading up to the Kramer home. Surprisingly, she was still asleep when Isaac carried her into the house and started to take her to her room.

"Wait, Isaac," whispered Rachel, "just lay her on the sofa in the den so if she wakes up, she'll find us close by. I can't stand for that baby to be away from me another minute, and I don't want her to wake up and find us not there."

Isaac obeyed his wife's orders and laid Annie on the plump cushions, covering her tiny body with a soft velvety throw that was lying on the end of the sofa. Leaning over to kiss her tired little face for no telling how many times since they hugged in the airport, Isaac began to stretch his arms and pull at his tie. He then slowly ambled into the master suite off the little den to help Rachel unpack their two-week supply of clothing.

Rachel was flitting about the room, already busy at the tedious job of unpacking and reorganizing after a long journey, hoping Leah remembered she was expecting her help tomorrow. She automatically glanced at Isaac as he walked into the bedroom looking as if he was about to pass out from exhaustion. Immediately, she stopped what she was doing and just stood there, suddenly realizing that she and Isaac had experienced the most incredibly amazing two weeks of their entire lives, only to fall right back into their same old routines, forgetting each other in the busyness of everyday life.

She walked across the plush carpet to her husband. Reaching up to touch his face and gaze into his dark eyes once more, she softly said, "Isaac, why don't we lie down and rest for a while? I can get this done later, or tomorrow for that matter. And, Isaac?"

"Hm?" he answered, delighted to find that the wife he had rediscovered in Romania was still with him.

"Thank you. Thank you for everything."

Mike had dropped David and Sarah off at their condo in Mayfaire Village. They planned to unpack and rest a bit and then to drive out to the Kramer home for a simple New Year's Eve celebration. Too tired for anything more and wanting to talk to their parents about Mike's job offer, the younger Kramers had suggested pizza and popcorn to bring in this already peculiar New Year. The kids thought the parents didn't know just how different the coming year was going to be, and the parents thought the same thing about their children.

Since he was driving back to the University the next day, Mike decided there was no reason for him to unpack, so he threw his bag on the floor and collapsed on his familiar old bed. *What did Thomas Wolfe know*, he thought? *Of course, you can go home again.*

Mike had almost dozed off when he remembered he had promised Jordan he would call just as soon as he returned from Connecticut. Leaning on one elbow, he grabbed the phone beside the bed and quickly dialed Jordan's number. "Hey, man! I'm back!"

"Hi, Mike. Welcome home."

"Man, you just don't know how good it is to be here. We don't even know what winter is here in the south, even if we are northern south," said Mike, laughing.

Chapter Twelve

"I'm glad you're back. What about your parents? Are they home?" asked Jordan.

"They are. Amazingly enough, their flight landed at RDU about an hour before ours. We all rode back to Wilmington together."

"That's good. Glad everyone's home safe and sound. What time do you want me to pick you up tonight?" Jordan asked the dreaded question.

"I think I'm going to pass on the party tonight, man. With my parents just getting back from Europe, this will be the only chance we'll have to hear about their trip and talk over some things that have come up. Everyone's exhausted, too, so we're just going to hang out here and order pizza," Mike replied, fully expecting an argument from the other end of the line.

But there was no argument, just silence as Mike again wondered what was with Jordan. A ten-day vacation hadn't helped the attitude his friend had developed long before the holidays. He had expected Jordan to be disappointed and even a bit perturbed that Mike wouldn't be going to the New Year's Eve party tonight, but he certainly hadn't expected the silent treatment. Jordan was never silent about anything.

"You there, man?" asked Mike.

"Yeah, I'm here," Jordan said. Silence again.

Mike quickly decided an apology was in order and might possibly help the situation. He *had* told Jordan he would go. "I'm sorry, man. I just can't go out tonight. Some pretty awesome situations have come up, and we really need to have a family meeting of sorts." Mike explained a little more in detail, hoping that would help Jordan accept his decision.

"Does this have anything to do with Carrie?" Jordan asked, his tone still sharp.

"No, not really. But in the long run, certainly anything that affects me will affect her. I'm going to see her just as soon as she gets back from the mountains. I've really missed her."

"Sure, you have," quipped Jordan.

Mike had an inkling why his best friend was reacting this way, but he was too tired to get into another argument about the past, so he very calmly said, "Why don't we meet at Riverboat Landing for lunch tomorrow? We can't ride back to Chapel Hill together because we both have our cars, but this will give us a chance to talk before we get back into the grind. What do you say?"

"Sure. See you tomorrow," Jordan replied, not sounding too thrilled about it.

After hanging up the phone, Mike rolled over onto his back and placed both hands under his head, wishing Jordan would just get off his back. But, he couldn't worry about that—he just had to sleep. He didn't move a muscle until Annie bounced on his bed two hours later, blowing the New Year's horn he had bought her in the airport.

The next day Mike packed his belongings in the Mazda, hugged Rachel and Annie good-bye three or four times, and pulled out of the long driveway onto the lane that led to Market Street. He headed down the beautiful old tree-lined avenue to the river front.

For over two hundred years, giant oaks dripping with Spanish Moss had grown along the straight avenue that led from the Cape Fear River to Highway 17, formerly the King's Highway and before that, the ancient Indian trail along the east coast. A few of the streets closer to the River were still paved in the same brick that horses and buggies had traveled on for over two centuries. The lovely old town still kept its antebellum flavor and beauty after raging fires, wars and more destructive hurricanes than old timers could count, even up to Bertha, Fran and Floyd in the late 1990's. Mighty Fran surprisingly had ripped up many of the ancient oaks along with thousands of longleaf pines as she took an unexpected turn into the mouth of the Cape Fear River, roaring up the River Basin as far as Raleigh and on into the rolling Piedmont countryside. The southeastern part of the state had never looked the same since, thousands of North Carolina pines felled to the ground by the mighty raging winds and pounding rain.

Mike drove across one brick street and then another as the Cape Fear River suddenly came into view, looking as if it met the city head on at the bottom of Market Street. It was actually the beginning of Market Street and not the bottom as most natives said, but when the River first came into view, it looked as if the street descended straight down into the winding waters once called the Rio Jordan by early Spanish explorers.

Mike parked the car at the tree-lined median close to Water Street, the old brick lane perpendicular to Market. It seemed to hug the deep blue River as it wound its way past the oldest section of Wilmington. There was nothing but a board walk between Water Street and the Cape Fear River at this spot, and it was here that Mike had asked his old friend to meet him.

Had anyone asked Tom Jernigan if he was glad to be home, he would have said that was the understatement of the century. Having cast an affirmative vote along with the entire family to celebrate Christmas in Banner Elk this year, he had honestly enjoyed the week immensely, much more than he had expected.

Chapter Twelve

But Tom secretly hoped he would never have to spend another Christmas on earth anywhere other than in his own home, by his own fire and in his own chair. He was born a homebody, and he would die a homebody, he declared to no one but himself as he helped Catherine bring the last load of bags and boxes into the house.

"Where are we going to put all this stuff?" he asked his wife. "And how come we ended up bringing more stuff home than we took up there?"

"Don't worry, Tom. Some things are ours, the village boxes and most of the decorations, but most of this belongs to the children," Catherine replied.

"Then why didn't they take it home with them?" asked Tom.

"They didn't have enough room in their vehicles, Tom, not with all the children and the luggage, your mother and father, and Luke and Abby's new puppies. Oh, my goodness, can't you still see the look on those two little faces when they took the tops off those baskets at the same time? That one moment was worth all the work and preparation for the entire week," said Catherine, smiling at the precious memory they had made.

"I'm not so sure it was worth listening to those puppies yapping all night," Tom complained, heading upstairs to take the last box to the attic to await next year's holiday season.

"Oh, you'll get over it, sugar," assured Catherine with a smile. "Tonight, you can sit back in your own leather chair with all the indention in the right places and flip your remote controls to your heart's content. You can turn on the television, the stereo and the radio all at the same time, and I won't say a word, my very best husband in the whole wide world."

She then blocked her husband of thirty-three years as he was coming into the den and threw her arms around his neck, reaching up to give him a big kiss and whisper, "I know you didn't really want to have Christmas in the mountains, sugar, but you went along with it for my sake and I want to thank you and tell you that you're the best, the very best."

"Am I that transparent?" Tom asked, leaning down to give her a return kiss and a big hug.

"Only to me, sugar, only to me," Catherine replied, closing her eyes as she rested her head against her husband's chest. "Oh, it's so good to be home."

After putting everything away and filling the washer with the dirty laundry, Catherine looked around to note where to begin her day when she got up in the morning. Even though it would be New Year's Day, Tom would go to his office to make sure everything had run smoothly while he was gone and to catch up on the pile of mail that had come in.

The Gentile and the Jew: A Divine Romance

Hm, thought Catherine, *tomorrow will be a good time to check on Melanie O'Brien. I just can't get that girl off my mind.* She made a mental note to call Melanie in the morning right after she read her Bible and prayed. *Better pray first—before I talk to that child*, she thought.

"Catherine! Come sit down with me," Tom called from the den, reclining in his own dearly beloved chair. "The ball's going to fall in Time Square, and it will be 2003 before you know it."

"Oh, I don't care about that old ball, Tom, and all those drunken people in Time Square! But, I do want to bring in another new year with you." Catherine smiled at her husband as he got up to sit with her on the couch, flipping the TV off with one hand and the stereo on with the other, just like his favorite gunslingers in the old westerns.

By the time this year became last year and the new year became this year, man and wife were asleep in each other's arms, their home filled with the music they had danced to and loved to for over thirty years,

> *"Kiss me each morning for a million years.*
> *Hold me each evening by your side.*
> *Tell me you love me for a million years,*
> *Then if it don't work out,*
> *Then if it don't work out,*
> *Then you can tell me good-bye."*[17]

Carrie's friend turned her car onto Franklin Street from the bypass at Eastgate Shopping Center. Only small white patches of snow and ice remained along the lovely street as it wound its way to the center of town. Happy to be the passenger and not the driver, Carrie enjoyed the pleasant Sunday afternoon drive past the beautiful old homes along the main street of the university town. Being away for a while made her appreciate the beauty of the quaint little village, cottages hidden in little ravines all along the street, others built on hills so high you'd have to stick your head out the window of the car to see their roofs.

Jana, her friend from Boone, stopped the car in front of Carrie's apartment house and left the motor running as she started to jump out to help Carrie with her luggage.

"Don't bother with that, Jana!" Carrie called out. "It's only one suitcase and a bag, and I can get it easily. Let me know how much I owe you for gas, okay?"

Chapter Twelve

"I will, but remember, we're not splitting it evenly. Vivian and I were going to Boone anyway, and we were glad to have you along for the ride—especially when we had that flat tire," Jana said with a laugh.

"Well, I'm glad we didn't have one on the way back. Vivian would have never made it back to Greensboro in time for the concert tonight," Carrie replied. "See you tomorrow! Thanks for the ride!"

Thank goodness for luggage on rollers, Carrie thought, the big suitcase bumping from step to step as she climbed to her second-floor apartment in the newly renovated old building. She could have found a place further out of town in one of the new apartment buildings with elevators, but Carrie loved the older sections of town the best—especially downtown—plus her apartment was within walking distance to the campus and the Corner Cafe.

Unpacking is a bore, Carrie thought, dumping her belongings out on her bed to separate the clean clothes from the dirty ones. She couldn't help but laugh out loud as she thought what a fit her mother would have to see her do something so disorganized.

"Carrie," she could hear her mother say, "take a laundry bag with you to put your dirty clothes in. If you put the clean clothes in with the dirty ones, the clean ones will be dirty, too!" And "Carrie, unpack your suitcase one item at a time and put it immediately in its drawer or closet space. Then, you won't have a mess all over everywhere."

Oh, Mama, Carrie thought now, *I love you so much*.

She was trying to decide where to put the clothes to take to the cleaners when the house phone and her cell phone began ringing at the same time. Not remembering where she put the cell phone as usual, she ran back to the bedroom and grabbed the other one, "Hello?" she answered, almost out of breath.

"Welcome back!" Mike's cheery greeting came as a big surprise, her heart pounding the second she heard his voice.

She took a deep breath and replied, "Hello, Mike. Welcome back to you, too. How was your trip?"

"Great. It was a very good trip. We really enjoyed being with David's family. His Dad is a great guy, and his Mom is...well...interesting. You'd like her. I want to tell you all about it, but...Carrie...I can't tell you how much I've missed you. I've really missed you."

I've missed you, too, Carrie thought, not saying a word.

Mike wasn't sure what her silence meant, so he tried again, "I dreamed about you the other night."

"You did? What did you dream?"

The Gentile and the Jew: A Divine Romance

"I dreamed I saw you looking at me as if you were in a portrait, except you were real, moving and laughing and smiling at me. You looked beautiful, honey, beautiful and happy." Mike's voice was loving and tender.

"Hm...interesting. I am happy, Mike. I enjoyed the holidays with my family, but I'm happy to be back, and...*very* happy to hear your voice," she quietly said, a shy smile slowly spreading across her face.

There was a pause on the line for a few seconds, Mike trying to analyze the tone of Carrie's voice, hoping he had heard her correctly and wondering how she looked at that exact moment. Then he remembered the dream. *She looks just like she did in the dream!*

"You're beautiful," Mike whispered, "just like you were in my dream— beautiful and wonderful, and...I love you, Carrie...and I don't want to lose you. Can you forgive me for failing you and give us another chance?"

"Um...maybe," Carrie teased, blushing from head to toe.

"Maybe? That's not the right answer, girl!" Mike cried.

"Mike?"

"Yeah?"

"Why are we talking on the phone?"

"I dunno. I didn't think you would want to see me, I guess," replied Mike.

"Why don't you come on over?" Carrie softly asked.

"YES!" Mike yelled into the phone. "I'll be right there!"

"Bye, Mike."

Carrie floated about the apartment, smiling at her dirty clothes, at the suitcase she put away in the back of the closet, at the coffee filter she took out of the drawer to make a pot of freshly ground coffee for Mike. She just kept floating and smiling until all of a sudden, she screamed, "Oh, no! I must look a sight!"

Hurrying to the bathroom mirror to see how bad she looked, Carrie grabbed the ringing cell phone that had fallen on the floor when she threw her handbag on the couch.

"Yes? Hello?" she answered.

"Carrie? It's me, Emma. Are you back in town, yet?"

"Hey, Emma! Good to hear from you! Yes, I've been here around an hour or so. What about you, are you back?" asked Carrie.

"No, I'm still in Nashville," Emma replied, "and I have a problem."

"What? What's wrong, Emma?"

Chapter Twelve

"It's my mother. She's very sick, much sicker than I thought when I told you she was having some health problems in November. She became worse, and...Carrie...," whispered Emma, "my mother is dying."

"Oh, no!" Carrie shouted into the phone. "I can't believe it, Emma! Oh, I'm so sorry."

The love and sympathy in Carrie's voice was the last straw for Emma who had tried for days to be a tower of strength for her family. She began to sob, saying over and over, "...and I don't know what to do for her! I just don't know what to do."

Carrie cried with her friend, the two girls five hundred miles apart, but as close as if they were standing side by side, as close as when they had sat together on Carrie's couch before the holidays, talking about the pain of Carrie's broken relationship with Mike, sharing their lives and their dreams.

"Emma," said Carrie gently, "can you tell me what happened?"

As Emma's sobs began to wane, she replied, her voice broken and weak, "You remember Mom was getting good reports since she had breast cancer two years ago?"

"Yes, I remember," Carrie answered.

"Well, in November she began feeling bad, tired and sluggish, even dizzy sometimes. The doctor had some tests done, but nothing showed up—at least not right then. But just before Christmas, Mom was feeling even worse and having bad headaches, so my sister, Beth, took her back to her doctor right away. Mom was sitting at the doctor's desk with her hand on her head when he asked her if that was the area of her head that was hurting. When she said it was, Beth said he walked around the desk and examined Mom's head, saying that he wanted to do an MRI that very day. Two days later, he told Mom and my sister that Mom has an inoperable brain tumor."

"I just can't believe it. Your mom is so young! Oh, Emma, I'm so sorry."

"We're all in shock," Emma replied tearfully, "even Mom. She feels like she's having a nightmare and can't wake up. That's how I feel, too, but I...oh..., Carrie, I have to go. I have to go now. Beth is calling me. She and I are going to cook dinner and stay with Mom tonight. After dinner, John is coming over to talk. I don't know what to do about school. Pray, please pray."

"I will, Emma, I promise. I'll call you tomorrow. I love you, Emma," said Carrie, her eyes filling with tears once more.

"I love you, too. Bye now."

Before the receiver hit the cradle, the doorbell started ringing and wouldn't stop. Outside her door, Mike Kramer stood ringing the doorbell with an almost silly grin on his happy face. He could hardly wait just to look at Carrie and, hopefully, hold her in his arms once again.

Standing on one foot and then the other, Mike was about to start pounding when the door slowly opened and Carrie came into view. He gazed at her tearstained face, her eyes staring blankly back at him until it finally registered in her mind that someone was there for her, someone who loved her very much, and when Mike reached out for her, Carrie fell into his arms, sobbing uncontrollably.

Minutes later, still standing in the doorway holding Carrie in his arms, Mike could not imagine what could have happened in the fifteen minutes it had taken him to get from his apartment to hers that could have affected her so terribly. He waited until her crying eased and she pulled away from him to find the tissue box to say anything, hoping with all his heart that whatever he said, it would be the right thing. But Carrie spoke first, blowing her red nose, then pushing her long brown hair behind her ears, totally forgetting she had planned to freshen up and put some makeup on before Mike arrived.

Between sniffles, Carrie said, "Emma called right after you did. She's still in Nashville with her family and…. Oh, Mike, Emma's mom has cancer, and she's dying!"

Mike was stunned, but being the young male he was, he had no idea what to say, so he sat down beside Carrie on the couch and took her hand in his, hoping he could be of some comfort to the beautiful young woman he loved so much.

Carrie leaned her head on his shoulder and began to explain what Emma had told her on the phone just minutes earlier, tearing up from time to time and wiping her eyes with the tissues.

"That's all I know," she said. "I told Emma I would call her tomorrow and find out what she and John decide is best for her to do right now, whether she will head back here to start classes Monday or drop out for this next semester to be with her mom."

"I'm sure it will be a hard decision either way," Mike replied, putting his arm around Carrie's shoulders and resting his head on the back of the couch.

"She's so young, Mike! As long as I've known her, Emma's mom has been busy and energetic, always moving and doing and helping everybody. I can't imagine her sick and helpless. It's just unreal!"

They sat quietly for a while, the clock on the end table ticking away, the sounds of the traffic from the crowded street below muffled through the closed windows of her apartment.

Chapter Twelve

Mike didn't know how long they sat there like that, him leaning on the back of the couch and Carrie leaning on him, but it gave him opportunity to reflect on the events of the past few days, time to decide it definitely wasn't the right moment to tell Carrie about Rebecca Brody and the assignment in Israel. He would wait until this shock settled in before hitting her with another one.

What rotten timing, he thought to himself.

Chapter Thirteen

arrie had pre-registered, so there wasn't much to do Monday morning except try to get to class on time and fall back into her regular routine—half a bagel and fruit with grapefruit juice for breakfast, steaming hot coffee, of course, then the rush over to the nearby campus for her first class at eight o'clock. This semester, her classes were more spread out over the day than usual, allowing more time to study and work on reports in between. This being her last semester in graduate school, Carrie knew she would need more hours than usual to work on the research papers and reports her courses would require, so she had worked it out with Charlie to work the evening shift at the Cafe three nights a week and every other weekend. She hoped to have more time with Mike, too, rebuilding their relationship—or maybe building a new one. She wasn't sure which would be better at this point.

After last night, Carrie had begun once again to believe in a future for the two of them. She loved him. She knew that now. He seemed like Mike again, only more serious and mature. Not that he was ever a clown like his friend, Jordan, but...well, Mike had certainly been more into *doing* rather than *being*. He was always planning something adventurous for the future or playing devil's advocate in heated political discussions, even with his professors to Carrie's dismay, coming out with a better grade than hers in the end because they liked his gumption and his multi-sided arguments. But, last night Carrie had seen something new and different in him, something deep and kind and good, and she wanted to get to know this new side of Mike. Since they would have more

The Gentile and the Jew: A Divine Romance

time to be together, she was already planning activities they liked to do, things they held in common—a night at the North Carolina Symphony, a romantic evening at Cappers in Raleigh, their favorite restaurant, and maybe even a stroll through one of the art museums in the Triangle area.

Walking across campus to her first class, Carrie smiled as she thought about last night—Mike's deep concern for Emma and her mother and the tenderness he expressed trying to comfort her were real. She had thought she loved him before with all her heart, but after last night, she knew she loved this improved Mike even better than the old one, and she could hardly wait to tell him.

Checking her watch to see how much time she had before class began, Carrie sat down on a bench under one of the giant campus oaks to call Emma. She was about to hit "send" when she remembered Nashville was one time zone behind North Carolina and she might be waking Emma if she called this early. *I'd better wait until after my first class*, she decided, grabbing her bag and heading for one of the oldest buildings on campus.

There was still a lump in her throat this morning as she accelerated her walk along the sidewalk, thinking about Emma's mom and what the whole family must be going through. Carrie knew most of Emma's family well, the two friends having visited one another's homes many times since they were roommates in their freshman dorm. She was feeling a little guilty to be so happy about her reunion with Mike when her best friend was going through such hell, but she knew Emma would be happy for her. *I don't know what I would do if it were my Mama*, she thought, pushing the heavy door of the old building. But she couldn't bear to think about that.

After a morning of classes that seemed more like days, Carrie hastened toward Franklin Street to meet Mike in a little downtown deli for lunch as they had planned. Later, they would walk back to their mutual afternoon class together. Mike arrived first, ordered their drinks, and was watching the door for her when he spotted her through the window, her chestnut brown hair loose and flowing over her red wool coat, smiling at everyone she met. *I'm a lucky guy, or at least, I hope I'm a lucky guy*, he thought, relishing Carrie's warm reception last night and hoping it wasn't just because she was vulnerable in her grief over Emma's mom.

But, he was sure it wasn't just that, he thought now, still watching out the window. She was definitely happy to hear from him when he called, even before she knew about Emma's mom. She had invited Mike over to her apartment, hadn't she? But, he wondered how she would feel about him after he told her about Israel.

Chapter Thirteen

Carrie caught sight of him just before Mike raised his hand to get her attention. Her face breaking out into a big smile, she never took her eyes from his as she wound her way through the tables and chairs to where he stood waiting. Just before she touched the chair he held for her, Carrie looked straight into his dark eyes and declared, "I love you, Mike Kramer."

He just stood there beside her chair, gazing into those eyes the color of the ocean and wondering why on earth she had picked such a public place as this to tell him what he had been longing to hear. He wanted to hug her and kiss her and shout his happiness to the top of his lungs, but here they were in this little deli packed with students beginning the new semester.

"Well, aren't you going to say anything?" asked Carrie, smiling even more and blushing, too.

Standing there as if glued to the floor, Mike quickly made a major decision—a choice as it were, he would remember later. He laid his self-consciousness aside, took both her hands in his and declared, "I love you, too, Carrie Jernigan."

"Whooooeeee! Yeah! Yeah! Yeah!" the kids at the next table cheered, clapping wildly.

This time Mike blushed right along with Carrie, but he was overjoyed at being able to express what was in his heart and not just what was in his head, even if the whole world heard him. He loved this beautiful young woman standing so close to him he could smell the faint fragrance of her perfume, and he didn't care who knew it. He loved her thick brown hair that swung back and forth when she walked down the street. He loved her blue-green eyes and upturned nose, the way her mouth always seemed to be smiling even when she was sad, and he loved her heart, always full of kindness and forgiveness.

"Mike," Carrie said quietly, still gazing into his dark brown eyes, "I'm not hungry anymore, are you?"

"Nope. Let's get outta here," he replied, grabbing his coat from the back of the chair and throwing some money on the table for the drinks he had ordered.

They walked and talked for the next hour and a half, every now and then stopping just to look at each other, drinking in the cherished features they had missed so much over the past six weeks apart. When they came to one of the campus benches, they sat a while, Mike with one arm around Carrie and one clutching her gloved hand. Carrie shared random acts of remembrance from her holiday with her family, painting Mike a better picture of her loved ones and the life she had with them than she ever had before. She told him about Christmas dinner and how she had suddenly realized how much she loved

169

her family and how much she had neglected them during her past two years in grad school.

"I invited Michele up for a fun weekend real soon," Carrie said. "We're going to shop and eat and rent some tear-jerker movies and just have a good time together like we used to before we got too busy for one another. I don't have to work at the Cafe a week from Saturday, so I thought that would be a good time for her to come. Maybe you could have brunch with us on Sunday before she drives back to Wilmington." Carrie happily chattered away as they walked hand-in-hand across the campus to their first afternoon class.

Mike was glad she hadn't noticed his lack of response in the midst of her excitement about her sister's visit, but her invitation to Sunday brunch reminded him that he only had two days to drop his classes and cancel his tuition for this semester in order to have his money refunded. Then there was only one week to prepare for the journey to Israel—boning up on all the information Becca had given him to read, flying up to New York to meet with Daniel Silverman and Becca to officially accept the job, shopping for the things he would need to live in Israel for six months—all that and more. Of course, he wanted to spend some time with his family, too, and that would mean little time with Carrie in the next nine days before flying back to New York to join Becca for the flight to Tel Aviv.

By the time they walked up the steps of their building, Mike's anxiety level was rising like the needle of a thermometer in the dog days of August. He glanced at his watch to see how much time they had before class was to begin. Only ten minutes, he thought, not enough time to get into this now. He was beginning to feel guilty that he hadn't as yet brought up the subject, but he assured himself there hadn't been an opportunity since they had been back in town. So, he laid the weighty matter aside once more and asked Carrie, "Have you heard from Emma today?"

"Yes, I have. I called her after my first class. She said that she and John begged her mom to approve of her dropping out this semester so she could stay in Nashville to help out. Of course, Emma doesn't want to leave for her own sake, too, but her mom wouldn't hear of it. She wants Emma to finish her last semester of graduate school now while she's into it. She's afraid that if Emma drops out now, something might happen to keep her from getting her master's."

My parents said the same thing, thought Mike, remembering the New Year's Eve discussion that had gone on into the wee hours of the morning. But, oddly enough, after hours of debating the details of each alternative with Mike and Sarah and David, the Kramers had agreed to give their blessing to this surprising

Chapter Thirteen

new turn in their son's life. Probably reacting out of mother's intuition, Rachel couldn't help but wonder if this job opportunity had any connection to her own proposed journey to Israel, the journey that would have to wait until Isaac was able to take more time off from his business. But she kept that theory to herself for the time being. Interestingly enough, Isaac and Rachel never got around to sharing much about their own exciting journey that night. That story would have to be put on hold for a while in lieu of their son's imminent plans.

Mike's greatest desire during that long New Year's Eve was for his father's approval. Isaac Kramer had never hidden his disappointment in Mike's decision to seek a career in journalism instead of working towards an MBA and joining him in the family business, and now he was learning that his only son wanted to drop out of graduate school and go on some crazy hiatus to terror-ridden Israel for six months. But his Dad had been strangely quiet and calm about the whole thing. Mike wasn't sure what was going on, but whatever it was, it seemed to be in his favor.

Although she seemed far away during much of the long discussion, Rachel had been the one to ask most of the questions. But even she wasn't as upset as Mike had expected, and in the end, his parents agreed that he should officially accept the offer.

"Mike," Carrie was saying as he came to the end of his train of thought, "you haven't told me anything about your holiday."

Watching his eyebrows rise quickly, she laughed and said, "Hey, now, don't say anything! I know I've done all the talking, and you couldn't get a word in edgewise, as Nana says!"

Mike's smile spread into that big grin she loved so much. His hand reached out to touch her soft cheek, his eyes trying to memorize every detail of the face he held so dear.

Six months, he thought. *Six long months.*

At some point in the middle of the ninety-minute class, Mike suddenly realized it was ridiculous for him to be sitting in on a class he was going to drop tomorrow morning just because he hadn't yet had an opportunity to tell Carrie about the job. *What a weird chain of events*, he thought, glancing out the corner of his eye at Carrie who was still smiling at anything and everything, even the grouchy professor. Just when he was beginning to get his life straight and things were working out between him and the woman he loved, it turned out he was headed thirty-five hundred miles away from her, having absolutely no idea what he was getting into. Nothing seemed to make any sense, yet even though he was overly anxious about how to tell Carrie about the job, he still knew in his heart it was the right thing to do.

The Gentile and the Jew: A Divine Romance

Throwing his arm around her shoulders as they headed out of the classroom, Mike asked, "If you don't have to work tonight, would you like to have dinner with me? Maybe we could drive over to Cappers in Raleigh, have a nice, relaxing dinner and just talk. What do you say?"

"That sounds wonderful, Mike. What time?" asked Carrie, smiling happily.

"I'll pick you up at seven, okay?"

She smiled up at him, trying hard to hold on to some measure of sophistication in the midst of the school-girl giddiness she was feeling, "Great. I'll see you at seven." All of a sudden, she decided to throw timidity and restraint out the window, quickly wrapping her arms around his neck, surprising Mike with a big kiss right in the mouth, standing there on the steps of the crowded classroom building.

"Hey! I could get used to this!" he responded, reaching out to pull her into his arms.

But before he could grab her, she flitted away like a little bee, laughing happily as she ran down the steps and through the trees lining the sidewalks of the enchanted, snow-dotted campus.

They arrived at Cappers around 7:30, just in time to get a nice booth close to the piano where they knew a good Jazz or Blues combo would be tuning up around eight. The elegant but comfortable restaurant with its beautiful stained glass ceiling had been their favorite place for romantic dinners since they started going out four months earlier. They often enjoyed the relaxed atmosphere, the good music and, of course, the delicious food the little restaurant served, sitting for hours with their elbows on the table, hands under their chins, smiling into each other's eyes.

Tonight is even better than ever, thought Carrie, as Mike walked over to whisper something to the pianist. *What is he up to*, she wondered? *You had better not embarrass me, Mike Kramer!*

Carrie ordered her favorite, filet mignon with crab meat and béarnaise sauce, and Mike ordered the filet topped with oysters. They laughed and talked quietly through their salads and by the time the band started playing, the server brought their entrees and left them with a friendly, "Enjoy!"

And enjoy they did—the delicious dinner, the romantic ambiance, the talented band that seemed to make music just for the two of them. But, most of all, they enjoyed each other. The lovers were in a world of their own—that is, until Mike realized it was growing late and he'd better get to the issue at hand or he'd be sitting in on a class he wasn't taking again tomorrow.

"Carrie," he began hesitantly, "there's something I've been wanting to talk to you about since we came back from the holidays, but with Emma's crisis last night and classes today, there just hasn't been time to bring it up."

"Sounds serious," teased Carrie, her smiling eyes twinkling.

"It is serious," Mike paused to take a deep breath, hoping his words would come out right.

"What, Mike? What is it?" The constant smile on her face was beginning to fade, and she felt as if a little butterfly had begun to flap its wings in her stomach. "Tell me what's wrong. Something's wrong, isn't it?"

"Not wrong, exactly," he answered. "It's just that something pretty amazing happened while I was in Connecticut with David's family, and I want to tell you about it." Mike paused again, trying his darndest to think of the best way to tell this angelic creature sitting before him that he was going to leave her for the next six months.

"Go on. Tell me." She was growing more anxious by the minute.

By the worried look on her face, Mike knew he hadn't got off to a good start, but it was too late now, so he decided he had no choice but to go ahead and jump in over his head.

"A couple of days before we left Connecticut, David asked me to have lunch with him and a friend, and since he's always introducing me to his unlimited supply of friends and acquaintances, I thought 'what the heck, one more introduction won't kill me,' so I obliged my new brother-in-law and met David and his friend for lunch that day."

"Go on," Carrie quietly said.

"Well, to make a long story short," continued Mike, "I was offered a job."

"A job?" asked Carrie, confusion written all over her face. "I don't understand. You haven't completed your master's, Mike. How could you get a job now? Why would you want to take a job now?"

"It isn't just any job. Let me back up just a bit." Mike was trying hard to explain something he didn't fully understand himself. "Do you remember the night we came back from Wilmington after Thanksgiving? We hadn't said a word to each other during the entire two-hour drive, and when I drove up to your apartment, you jumped out of the car and wouldn't talk to me for weeks. Remember?"

The Gentile and the Jew: A Divine Romance

"How could I forget?" whispered Carrie, looking down at her cup of coffee. "But Mike, I thought we had forgiven each other and put all that behind us? I thought we were starting over. Why are you bringing it up now?"

"Oh, honey, I'm not bringing it up to hurt you! I'm sorry if it sounded that way. I just want you to know that, when you jumped out of the car that night and slammed the door behind you, it felt as if the light went out of my life. I didn't realize it until much later, but in that very moment, when the door banged shut, I began to change. At least, I began to want to change. It was as if I'd been zooming along in life like the old cartoon Roadrunner and suddenly rammed into a brick wall. But, Carrie, I've had a lot of time on my hands, not only to realize how I've treated you, but to think about the haphazard way I was living my life. I'm finally recognizing the character flaws in myself that need to change. In my own blind selfishness, I see now that I had just assumed I could do whatever I pleased and sweet little Carrie would always be there when I needed you. But, I discovered that all my grandiose dreams were just that without you—just dreams, silly dreams. Do you understand what I'm saying?"

"I think so," she softly replied.

"I tried to explain what was happening that evening in the snow before you left for the mountains, remember?" asked Mike.

"Yes, I remember," she responded, her features softening now as her heart began to understand what Mike was trying to say.

"But, you had to hurry back to your place to meet your ride, and there wasn't time to talk it over. You said we needed more time apart, and you were right. But honey, so much has happened since then that I want you to understand," Mike said tenderly, smiling into her tearful eyes and reaching across the table for her hand.

"You've changed, Mike," she said, studying his face, trying to see deeper into the heart of this man she was only now really getting to know. "I'm astonished at the changes I've seen in you just during the past twenty-four hours." Carrie squeezed his hand and said, as if surprised by her sudden realization, "I love you now more than ever."

"You can't imagine how happy that makes me, honey." He kissed her hands and held them tightly.

"I want to hear about everything," Carrie gently assured him, "but please tell me what this job thing is all about first. You're scaring me."

"Honey, I truly believe the job offer has something to do with the root issues that caused us both to take a good look at our relationship—the issues we've successfully avoided for the past two days," said Mike.

Chapter Thirteen

"Our religious differences," she stated matter-of-factly, nodding her head in agreement.

"Yes," said Mike. "That evening in the snow, I also told you that it's time I find out what it means to be a Jew, remember?"

Carrie nodded again.

"Well, after listening to David explain the details of this job for hours, and later talking the whole thing over with his Dad, the rabbi, I'm convinced this job is the key to solving that dilemma," Mike explained.

"Just tell me, Mike," Carrie whispered.

"David's friend is a journalist with a major news magazine, and I've been offered a job as her assistant on a six-month assignment in Israel," blurted Mike, squeezing Carrie's hand in fear that she might pull it away any second.

But she just sat there staring at him, three of his spoken phrases blinking like neon signs in her mind's eye: *six months—Israel—*and*...her.* When she regained some composure, the one that came out of her mouth was, "*Her?*"

Instantly, reality hit hard. Seeing the stunned expression on Carrie's face and catching the negative sound accompanying that little one-word question, Mike suddenly realized how naive and just plain stupid he had been not to expect the girl he loved to be concerned about his traveling with another woman for six months. Mike had obviously expected Carrie to be extremely worried about the dangers of living in Israel and their being separated for half a year, but...*how dumb can I be*, he wondered, thinking this would be a good time for the Coyote to come along and hit the Roadrunner in the head.

So, for the next hour or so, Mike told Carrie about David's friends, Sam and Rebecca Brody and how this whole thing had come about, assuring her that Becca Brody was still a grieving widow and not the least bit interested in getting romantically involved with him or anyone else. He told her about Rabbi Klein's wise counsel, how he seemed to see into Mike's soul that day in his study and how the rabbi's affirmation had seemed like some type of spiritual blessing he had been subconsciously waiting for all his life.

She responded with a little nod every now and then even though her two-day smile had dissolved a while back, leaving her countenance grim, her eyes downcast and filled with tears as Mike ended his explanation.

"Carrie, I can hardly bear to even think about being away from you for six long months, but I know I *have* to do this. I'm not asking you to understand what I don't even understand myself. I'm just asking you to trust me. Can you trust me? Will you try?"

She tried hard to smile, feeling as if her heart was going to break for the second time in only two months. Then she sighed deeply and said, "You've

175

talked a great deal about choices lately, Mike, and I'll have to admit that I don't fully comprehend all that you're saying, but.... Well, I guess this is as good a time as any for me to begin making better choices, too. Yes, I choose to trust you, Mike. I do. I trust you."

Mike reached out to touch her cheek, her soft skin quivering as she tried hard not to cry. Clutching his hand to her face as if she would never let him go, the held-back tears burst the dam and flowed silently down her glowing cheeks. For the second time that day, Mike thought he must be the luckiest man in the world.

They didn't see the piano player gazing curiously at the young lovers just before he gave a nod and the band began to softly play:

At the end of the rainbow, you'll find a pot of gold.
At the end of the story, you'll find the truth's been told.
Tell me you love me and I'll be satisfied,
And our love will go on 'til the end of time.[18]

Chapter Fourteen

Ten days later, around 10:00 a.m. Israel time, Mike Kramer found himself waking up in a room on the tenth floor of the King David Hotel in downtown Jerusalem. *Downtown Jerusalem? That can't be correct phraseology,* he thought, throwing off the covers and walking over to the window to pull the drapes back so he could see the city and get a feel for where he was. Their flight had arrived late the evening before, and by the time he and Becca Brody had collected their baggage and hailed a *shiroot* to take them to Jerusalem, jet lag overcame Mike with a vengeance. Conked out for the entire thirty-minute ride from Ben Gurion Airport to Jerusalem, he hardly remembered checking in at the hotel desk, much less taking the elevator to his room and getting undressed for bed.

Whish! Blinding light burst into the dark room as the drapes flew apart. Mike's eyes slammed shut. After a couple of tries, he was able to open them wide enough to see the astonishing panorama outside the wide window. *Maybe downtown Jerusalem is correct,* he thought, gazing at the phenomenal mixture of international vehicles, crowded buildings and scurrying people, cell phones to their ears as if they were in Raleigh, North Carolina, or even New York City. Definitely not what the young American Jew expected to see in his first view of the Holy City.

"Ooo-kay," Mike said to no one in particular. "Here I am."

The Gentile and the Jew: A Divine Romance

The phone was ringing off the hook when Mike stepped out of the mosaic tiled shower. He threw a huge bath towel around his waist, drip-drying as he hurried to the desk to grab the phone.

"Shalom, Mike!" Becca Brody's excited voice sounded as if she had taken a seven-minute ride in a taxi instead of a seven-hour flight forward in time.

"Shalom to you! You sound incredibly chipper this morning, considering the normal effects of jet lag." Mike smiled, thinking it was just like Becca's inherent energy to enable her to skip the awful malady.

"Isn't it wonderful? My friends are always jealous of my gift. Are you jealous, Mike?"

He knew she was grinning, relishing every opportunity to tease him or anyone else for that matter. "Of course, I'm jealous, but I'd rather talk about breakfast...or lunch, or whatever meal is available at the present. My stomach feels like I haven't eaten in two days. How about you?"

Becca was laughing before he finished his sentence. She had a curious, melodious laugh, sounding as if she not only thought something was hilariously funny, but that the joke had made her day as well.

I definitely won't be bored for the next six months, Mike thought.

"I'm starving! We may as well enjoy the excellent cuisine in our luxury hotel since we won't be staying here for long. The magazine wants us to live inside the Old City while we're in Jerusalem, and that means no luxury hotels. The powers-that-be think we'll get a better feel for the different people groups, particularly Arab and Jew."

"Sounds like fun," said Mike, wryly.

"Loads of fun," Becca replied, laughing again. "I'll meet you down in the restaurant in fifteen minutes, okay?"

"Sure. See you then."

"So, what's the plan?" Mike asked as they finished the appetizing Israeli brunch, beautifully presented on various buffet tables scattered among the palms and other green plants decorating the lovely restaurant beside the courtyard. He had never seen such fruit—huge oranges, mangos, kiwi, pineapple and wide slices of the reddest, sweetest watermelon he had ever eaten. Breakfast in Israel was evidently an artistic as well as culinary event.

Chapter Fourteen

"The plan is this, Mr. Kramer," Becca teased. "I'm going to find the rooms Daniel reserved for us to sort of set up camp in the Old City. Then I'll make a list of what we're going to need. Those rooms will be my little home away from home plus office, and you'll stay in a hostel close by. Told you we'd better make the most of this luxury while it lasted."

"How long do we have?" asked Mike, glancing around their impressive surroundings. "I've never been much into roughing it."

Becca laughed at the thought of the immaculately groomed young man trekking through the desert with nothing but a lame camel and a canteen. "I'd say about two more nights. We should have our rooms well organized by then. We won't need much since the place is already furnished, but we'll have to purchase a few basic office supplies—paper, pens, maps, dark room chemicals and paper—things like that. The office has already shipped our computers and printers, and we have our camera equipment with us."

"So, what's my assignment for today?" asked Mike, leaning back to fold his arms across his chest.

"Your assignment, Mr. Kramer, is to become acclimated to Jerusalem. Go exploring, Old City first. Don't even take your camera this go around. You need to see the regular tourist sites, so you'll understand why people of all faiths come to this holiest of all cities on earth. But I want you to go deeper than that. Find the hidden paths and get to know them well. Watch the people. Get to know them, too. It will take time. They probably won't trust you, but we have to earn their trust. That's why this assignment will take six months, not six weeks."

Becca looked more sober than Mike had seen her since she talked about Sam back in Connecticut. He could see this assignment wasn't fun and games to her. It was a very serious matter. It was for him, too, although he had to admit, if only to himself, that he just wasn't into this "promised land" thing yet. *I guess it takes a while*, he thought, watching Becca check her notebook to see if there was anything else she needed to tell Mike before they parted company for the day.

"You definitely won't have time to cover all of the Old City in detail today, but you can finish up tomorrow and the day after. Then start exploring out from the Old City into the new. Well, newer, I guess I should say. There are some unique little ultra orthodox Jewish communities just outside the walls like Yemin Moshe and Mea Shearim. You may not be allowed to visit some of them just yet. And remember Mike, our assignment is not just to understand the heart of the Jewish woman in Israel; it's to understand the Israeli woman, no matter her ethnic identity."

The Gentile and the Jew: A Divine Romance

"I understand, boss," he answered with a grin and a mock salute. Inwardly, he was thinking how ironic it was that he had been sent thousands of miles from home not only to understand what it means to be a Jew, but to understand women as well. *Man, I might need to write a book when I get home—maybe two—What it Means to be a Jew and How to Understand a Woman No Matter Her Ethnicity. Sounds like one of Jordan's get-rich-quick plans.* Mike almost laughed aloud as he thought about his comical friend, pleasantly recalling that Jordan had finally shed the chip on his shoulder during their New Year's Day conversation when he was finally able to hammer into his head that he truly loved Carrie and didn't want to hurt her.

"Oh, Mike," said Becca, wondering what was so funny but in too much of a hurry to ask. "Just in case we don't have time to chat later in the day, you need to know we'll be meeting a guy named Salim for dinner tonight. He'll be helping us from time to time—sort of a guide, chauffeur, helper person." Noting the concern in his expression, she quickly said, "Don't worry, Mike! You'll like him."

"Is he Muslim?" He was already more concerned than Becca could have imagined.

"Nope. He's Christian, an Arab Christian. Isn't that interesting?" Becca jumped up and bee-bopped out of the dining room, throwing her backpack over one shoulder and waving good bye with her other hand.

Mike ambled down the corridor to his room, still wondering how Becca could have so much energy after flying a quarter of the way around the world. He hurried as fast as his tired body could move, brushed his teeth and grabbed his jacket and backpack, remembering Becca had warned him to drink plenty of bottled water in Israel even though they had arrived in the dead of winter. He was almost back to the elevator when he spied a large window at the end of the corridor. Pressing the down button as he walked by, Mike continued on down the hallway to look out the window while he waited.

"Whoa!" he blurted out loud. He couldn't believe his eyes. There before him in spectacular panorama was ancient Jerusalem, her walls shimmering in that color known to artists as Jerusalem Gold. Mike didn't know it yet, but as twilight settled over the holy city this evening, those walls of stone would take on an iridescent glow that for ages had inspired poets and songwriters to name the city, *Jerusalem of Gold*.

He had no idea how long he stood there gazing out at the Old City, deceivingly safe in the embrace of its magnificent golden walls. The western gate was wide open, pointing travelers to the seaport town of Jaffa, or Joppa, just as it had for thousands of years. Just beyond the gate, the Tower of David

180

Chapter Fourteen

rose into the clear blue sky, giving those who entered there the feeling they were being safely guarded by the ancient watchtower.

Mike's eyes followed the curve of the wall to the right as it wound its way over modern day Mount Zion and on to the most ancient sections of the Old City, David's Zion and Abraham's Mount Moriah—since Solomon's day, the Temple Mount. But, there was no Jewish temple standing as there had been for a thousand years. And there was no mistaking the Islamic mosque known to the world as the Dome of the Rock. *No one can say the structure isn't extraordinary*, Mike thought, its golden dome and blue mosaic tiles reflecting the midmorning sun as if it were beaming signals around the world.

Lifting his eyes from the Temple Mount, he could see the top ridges of the Mount of Olives east of the Old City, still riveting though crowded with cemeteries, ancient tombs and Catholic shrines—even capped with a hotel on top. Mike couldn't see the Kidron Valley, but having studied the maps Becca had given him, he knew it was there, separating Zion and Moriah from the Mount of Olives. Scanning the horizon to the north, he could see the tower of the Hebrew University perched atop Mount Scopus, rising high above the golden city.

"Hey!" Suddenly startled by a bell hop carrying a tray of clinking glasses to a room near by, Mike thought, *I can't stand here all day!* As he left his post by the window, the last view he saw was the winding road up to Jaffa Gate. He had always wondered why the psalms spoke of going "up to Jerusalem." Now he knew, and the concept would become more deeper ingrained in the days ahead.

Minutes later, he was climbing the steep road up to the western gate, passing crowds of busy pedestrians of varying people groups and nationalities. Becca had said the crowds he would see were nothing compared to the population of Jerusalem before the latest *intifada* began in 2000, supposedly with Ariel Sharon's visit to the Temple Mount. Of course, since it was January, the scarcity of tourists wouldn't make as much difference as in the high tourist season.

Arriving at the top of the ramp-like road, Mike turned sharply to the right to walk the last few yards to Jaffa Gate. He tried not to stare impolitely, but he couldn't keep his eyes off the incredible assortment of humanity everywhere he turned. About three yards in front of him walked a group of eight, four men and four women, looking as if they had just stepped out of Red Square around 1918. The tall, slender men wore long black or white garments tied at the waist and black fur hats on their heads. The women following them looked like peasants from *Fiddler on the Roof*. He made a mental note to remind Becca to interview these women. They would surely have an amazing story to tell.

The Gentile and the Jew: A Divine Romance

Quickly passing Mike on his left, two ultra-orthodox Jewish men, complete with black hats, black clothing and side locks, kept their eyes on the sidewalk to avoid seeing the Russian women as they walked past the group. Another Chasidic man walked by and then another. Mike turned around to see where they were coming from and was surprised to see a stream of ultra-orthodox men coming from a bus that was still unloading at the curb.

I wonder where they're going in such a hurry, he thought. Stepping up his gait a bit, he reached Jaffa Gate quickly, hoping to see where the men were headed. But as he walked through the thick arched gate into the Old City, Mike's attention was quickly drawn from the Hassidim to the throngs of scurrying people, mysterious shops and aromatic restaurants just inside the second busiest gate into old Jerusalem. For a few moments, he stood perfectly still, mesmerized by the hordes of humanity hurrying around him like a river rushing to the sea. He felt as if he had instantly been cast as a character in the Arabian Nights or a Cecile B. DeMille production of the life of King David.

Just ahead on his left a large sign caught his attention—*Money Changer*. Mike walked over to the booth beneath the sign and handed the man a hundred dollars. The money changer gave him a handful of shekels in paper bills and coins in return. *I hope he's honest*, thought Mike, stuffing the money in his pocket. *Now, where to go from here?*

The way straight ahead seemed to be a street lined with small shops; the narrow passageway filled with tables full of merchants' wares, anything from clothing to jewelry to house wares as far as Mike could see. To his right was another street, not quite so narrow but much less traveled, originating between the Citadel on its right and an Anglican church and courtyard on the left. Listening to the jabbering voices of the bartering merchants and their customers, Mike's first thought was to take the more exciting crowded street, but then he saw that more of the ultra-orthodox Jews were streaming the other way, still looking as if they had a definite goal in mind. Curiosity won the draw. Mike decided the bazaars could wait until another day, and he set off down the timeworn stones of the quieter path feeling like Dorothy on the yellow brick road.

After walking a few yards, he realized he was in the Armenian Quarter of the Old City, passing by a restaurant releasing warm, tantalizing aromas into the cold winter air. A book store, a little gift shop and the beautiful old St. James Cathedral drew his attention, but even more so, old wooden doors that had no signs, emitting an aura of mystery he found fascinating. *What I wouldn't give to go through some of these doors*, he thought, following the winding street to the left, passing by the Armenian Museum. He'd have to save that for another

Chapter Fourteen

day, too. Becca said to see the Old City today. Anyway, he didn't want to take the chance of losing the guys in the black hats.

Minutes later, Mike was browsing the streets in the Jewish Quarter, glancing in the doorways of elegant little shops filled with fabulous watercolors and canvas art, glass cases of unique silver jewelry, all kinds of perfumes and fragrant oils and menorahs upon menorahs. There were tee shirt shops and tourist paraphernalia, too, but most all the shops emitted a quiet dignity, a peaceful air compared to the bazaars he had passed earlier. He looked for the name of the street, planning to come back here to do some shopping for Carrie and his family when there was time. The sign read, "The Cardo."

Rambling onto an extremely narrow street, he saw the Sephardic Synagogue on his right. Making a mental note to explore this area in more detail later on, Mike suddenly realized he wasn't sure what Sephardic meant. *Man, I must be an ignorant Jew! I have a lot more to learn than I thought.*

Then he spied a place he had read about, The Temple Institute, where a group of orthodox Jews were planning the equipping of the third temple. But, he decided a visit there would take the greater part of a day, so he saved it for later, too, and walked on.

Wafts of a more familiar aroma were passing under Mike's nostrils as he continued on his way through the narrow streets. Falafals! *Got to eat a falafel my first day in Jerusalem*, he thought, arriving at a little stand with tables inside and outside on a pretty terrace surrounded by stone buildings and alleyways. Ignoring the cold, he decided to sit on the terrace and watch the people milling about while he ate his authentic Israeli lunch.

Mike was quickly acquiring a new hobby he had never even considered—people watching. *Carrie was always the people person*, he thought now, eyeing two Israeli soldiers leaning on the balustrade across the terrace. They seemed to him a contradiction in terms. The huge guns slung casually over their shoulders along with their camouflage uniforms spoke of trained experts in the ways of war, but their faces revealed tender young men no more than eighteen years old, just out of high school. An even younger looking female soldier walked up to them, her gun gigantic in proportion to her petite body and girlish face. A doll would have seemed more natural in her slender arms than the frightening Uzi.

Mike thought of Sam Brody and wondered if his death had any redeeming value. More than that, he wondered what Sam Brody was made of, what he understood about this ancient land that Mike didn't and why the nation of Israel never crossed his own mind, much less the thought of joining the Israeli army. He continued to study the three soldiers as he finished his falafal. He then picked up his backpack to resume his exploration of old Jerusalem.

He turned east, walking down uneven stone steps to a little landing where he lifted his eyes to get his bearings and decide where to wander next. Mike stopped perfectly still, not moving a muscle as if he were suddenly glued to the ancient stones. He had heard about this ancient holy place all his life, but he certainly hadn't anticipated the powerful effect it was having on him now. Feeling as if a low current of electricity was coursing just along the surface of his skin, even his hair was tingling. He stood dumbfounded, staring at the Western Wall.

The sacred Wall was spread before him across an open plaza that seemed even wider than it actually was in comparison to the narrow streets and alleyways Mike had meandered through for at least an hour. Hundreds of people were gathered in the plaza, but he couldn't take his eyes off the Wall that had been the most holy place in the world for the Jewish people since the destruction of the Temple in 70 CE. The gigantic stones that were proven to have been the western wall of Solomon's Temple were topped with the lesser stones of the Second Temple, all crying out the prayers of the Jewish people throughout their three-thousand-year history in the great city on a hill.

In his reverie, Mike recalled an audio tape his parents had played for him and Sarah one time when they were trying to spur some interest in their family's Jewish heritage. It was a recording of the voices of Jewish soldiers as they charged through the nearly destroyed Old City in 1948, suddenly arriving at the base of the Temple Mount, directly facing the Western Wall. Hardened soldiers, most of them much older than the youth Mike had watched on the terrace, were openly weeping as their hands and faces touched the stones of the Wall, their only physical place of prayer for two thousand years. Even from this distance, Mike could see the large cracks between the gigantic stones stuffed with hundreds of little white pieces of paper, the deepest, heartfelt prayers of Jews from all over the world, faithfully tucked into the very heart of God.

Mike started, jolted by a group of pilgrims rushing down the steps, his eyes finally seeing something other than the sacred Wall itself.

"Hey," he said aloud, "so that's where those guys were going!"

Carrie stared at the clock, anxiously anticipating the phone call she and Mike had set up via e-mail. She had made sure he believed her when she told him not to be concerned about calling the first few days after he arrived in

Chapter Fourteen

Israel, knowing he would be exhausted from traveling and busy settling into life in a strange country. But, now...well, suffice it to say, she was ready to hear Mike's voice.

Two o'clock here, add seven...yes, she had it right. Mike said nine o'clock Israel time....

Rrrrrrnngggg!

Carrie nearly jumped off the couch, almost dropping the phone she was clutching in her lap before she could pick up the receiver and yell, "Hello, Mike?"

"Hey, honey."

Those two tender words were all that was needed to start the tears flowing. Carrie couldn't believe she was going to sob throughout this long-awaited conversation, but she couldn't catch her breath.

"Carrie? Are you there?"

"I'm so sorry, Mike. You must think I'm nothing but a crybaby," she answered, her voice broken and trembling.

"You did cry a lot that last week before I left," he said, hoping his smile traveled long distance.

"I know. I can't help it. I guess you'll just have to accept that I have leaky valves in my eyes."

"I love everything about you, including your tears. They're beautiful, you know. Even your tears are beautiful. I can see them now, flowing out of those ocean-colored eyes. I love you, Carrie."

His voice was so sweet she nearly started blubbering again, but instead she sighed deeply and said, "Oh, Mike, I love you, too, and I miss you so much."

"I know you do. I had no idea it would be this hard, and we've only been apart five days. How will I live through six long months without you?"

"You'll be busy—very busy, I'm sure." Carrie quickly realized she should be the one to encourage Mike, him being a few thousand miles from family and friends. "Tell me about Israel, Mike...and your work. Tell me about everything."

"Well, we've almost finished setting up our office, and we already have some interviews set up for next week. There are at least a dozen highlights I want to give you of my first three days here, but I can tell you all that in an e-mail. I just want to hear your voice tonight. Wish we had those video phones so I could see your beautiful face. But I can see it anyway, you know. Those last days and nights we were together I memorized you, and when I close my eyes, you're here with me. I do that all the time, especially when I visit places I know you would want to see. And sometimes, just before I go to sleep, I see you like I did in the dream I had in Connecticut during Chanukah, remember?"

"I remember. You said I was very happy, smiling and laughing. Maybe that's how I'll look when you get back, Mike."

"Yeah, I know." The voice she loved so dearly grew soft and quiet. She could feel his longing for her. Her yearning for him was no less, her entire body aching to be held in his strong arms. Just to rest her head on his chest and feel his heartbeat once again would be heaven on earth. *Oh, God*, she silently prayed, *I'm not doing a very good job of encouraging my man.*

"Carrie? Are you there?"

"Yes, I'm here...always."

"Hon, I've been concocting a great idea as I've browsed about Jerusalem these last few days. Want to hear it?"

"Of course, crazy man! What wild adventure are you planning now? Don't you have enough excitement in your life?"

"Yes, but I need some more. I need you! Okay, here's the plan. You'll complete your master's by the end of May. I know you've planned to schedule potential job interviews, but why don't you take a break? You've been going to school for eighteen years, and I think you need a vacation. Carrie, come to Israel after graduation...please?"

"What?! I haven't even considered such a thing!"

"Well, think about it now. Think fast, too!" Mike's laughter warmed her heart.

"I just assumed you would be totally engrossed in your work the whole time you're there, and I'd be head over heels into my research papers and finals. Then, there's Emma and her Mom. I'll catch you up on that situation next e-mail. And then, there's the money—rather, no money. Are you serious, Mike?"

"Yes, I'm serious," answered Mike, smiling at her excited chatter. "I'll take care of your ticket. Don't worry about that. When I was considering this job for all of three days, I forgot to ask about the salary. It just didn't seem important at the time. But, it pays fairly well so that by May, I'll have plenty saved to buy your ticket and show you Israel first hand. Our assignment will be well on its way to completion by then, and Becca says I can take some time for myself while she starts wrapping things up in preparation for the last phase. What do you say?"

"Oh, Mike, you know I want to go—more than anything. Let me talk to Mom and Dad and make sure they wouldn't be terrified at the prospect of my going to the Middle East. And, I need to know that Emma will be all right. Her

Chapter Fourteen

Mom is in remission right now, but who knows what will happen in the next few months. Oh, Mike, I'm getting excited just thinking about it!"

"Me, too, honey. I can't wait."

"I know I'll cry when we say good-bye, but I guess we should hang up now. You'll be too broke to buy my ticket at this rate!" Carrie giggled like a little girl, the cherished sound ringing in Mike's heart like bells on his wedding day.

Chapter Fifteen

pring had come to eastern North Carolina. Dressed in khaki capris and a blue denim shirt, sleeves rolled up to her elbows, Rachel Kramer stood on her stone patio with a glass of iced tea in one hand and a letter from Mike in the other, thinking how incredibly beautiful the azaleas were this April. She was grateful the Wilmington area hadn't experienced the late frost that sometimes destroyed the tender buds before they had a chance to bloom. All over the city, various shades of pink, purple and white azaleas created an explosion of glorious color, surrounding homes, schools and businesses alike. The coordinating committee for the city's annual Azalea Festival wouldn't have to wait with their fingers crossed this year, hoping thousands of azaleas throughout the city would bloom in time for the long anticipated weekend of festivities. Even masses of cheerful, multicolored tulips had agreed with the azaleas on their blooming time throughout the bustling Port City.

Rachel smiled at the splattering of dogwoods mingled among the tall pines and azaleas framing the backyard. Sometimes the low flowering dogwoods bloomed later, but this year nature's timing was perfect and clusters of pink and white blossoms watched over the brilliant azaleas and tulips surrounding the expansive green lawn.

Rachel loved springtime—when the whole world suddenly came to life, everything new and green and excited to be alive. She ambled slowly down the step-stone path that edged the lawn, separating the grass from the trees and azaleas banked in fragrant pine straw. Pausing to sit on a shady garden bench to read Mike's surprisingly lengthy letter, she thought what a good son he was to phone his parents regularly and write as often as he could.

"Dear Mom and Dad,

Please hug Annie for me right now before you read another word and tell her how much I miss her. I miss you guys, too. Three months away from home and family is a long time, even for an old guy like me who's been away at school for six years."

Rachel smiled at the thought of her twenty-three-year-old son seeing himself as old.

"Our assignment is moving right along. My first day or two in Jerusalem, I thought I had picked up a new hobby—people watching—but it didn't take long to realize it wasn't to be a hobby for me. People watching is an integral part of my new job, and if I do say so myself, I'm getting pretty good at it! Becca says my interviewing techniques are improving, too, especially for a guy who's never been good at listening—just talking!

"We've met some really great people over here. The Sabras, native Israelis (See, I'm learning more than you thought, huh?) are fantastic. Straightforward. Honest. Hardworking. You'd feel right at home, Dad! They have this hard, tough exterior, and you know right where you stand with them immediately, but they're goodhearted, too, and kind when kindness is called for.

"Rabbi Klein was right on when he said Israel would be the best place on earth to find out what it means to be a Jew, but I had no idea there were so many different types of Jews. I've encountered Israeli Jews, Russian Jews, Ethiopian Jews, Yemenite Jews—every nation you can think of is represented here on this little piece of property measuring only ten thousand square miles. There are secular Jews, orthodox Jews, ultra-orthodox Jews, reformed Jews, unreformed Jews and no telling what else. So, my question for the day is, 'What am I?' Profound, huh?

"Forgot to tell you about the Arabs. The media makes us think all Arabs are Muslim, and I'm sure the great majority is, but I've discovered a group called Druze who live in good relationship with the Jews, even serving in the Israeli army. Then, there are Arab Christians. One works with us quite often. He and I have struck up a good friendship, and he's even invited me to his home on occasion. In fact, last week Becca and I went to his house for dinner (He's married and has a little boy.) and were joined by an Israeli couple about my age. There we were, sitting around a table loaded with the most wonderful lamb kabobs, rice, flat bread and

vegetables you've ever tasted—two American Jews, two Arab Christians and two Israeli Jews. What a combination! But, it was even more amazing than you might think. The Israelis were what they call 'believers.' They believe that Yeshua (Jesus, to Americans) is Messiah. They don't use the term Christian. Guess it has too many negative connotations for Jews. The guy's name is Aron Safran, and his family background is Romanian. Isn't that an amazing coincidence? For some reason, he nearly fell out of his chair when I told him my mother's family was from Romania, and your maiden name was Liebowitz. He wants us to get together soon."

Rachel's heart was pounding faster than in Bucharest, her hands trembling as she tried to hold the paper still enough to finish reading Mike's loving good-bye. *This is unbelievable*, she thought. Totally dazed, she rose slowly from the bench, wishing she had carried her cell phone with her so she could call Isaac immediately.

For the past three months, Rachel and Isaac had discussed when to tell Mike and Sarah about the discoveries they had made in Bucharest in December, especially anxious to share the news with their son since he had incredibly ended up in Israel before they were able to make the trip themselves. And now, miracle of all miracles, her innocent son had unknowingly met the one blood relative she had in the whole world—at least the only one she knew existed. She had to get to a phone. Isaac would know what to do.

Just six more weeks. Mike was counting the days and hours until Carrie would arrive in Israel and he could hold her in his arms once again, winding his fingers through her soft brown hair, watching the laughter dance in her beautiful eyes. He could almost smell the light fragrance of her favorite perfume as he closed his eyes and pictured her there with him on the hillside, his body growing warm at the very thought of her nearness. Oh, how he missed his southern girl, he groaned inwardly.

He was sitting cross-legged on his favorite perch on the western slope of the Mount of Olives, overlooking the Old City across the Kidron Valley. Mike came here in the evening as often as he could, arriving just before sundown to watch the peaceful twilight miracle when the walls of old Jerusalem turned shimmering gold, waiting for the moon to rise to its watch over the Eastern Gate. He was fascinated by the sealed gate, enshrined in mystery from its very foundation. Because Messiah was prophesied to enter Jerusalem through the

The Gentile and the Jew: A Divine Romance

Golden Gate as it is often called, the Muslim officials had barred and sealed it years ago to keep anyone out who might claim to be the Jewish Messiah. They took precaution one step further by creating cemeteries just outside the gate, assured that a priest of Israel would never dare risk becoming unclean by walking through a graveyard.

This peaceful spot was where Mike Kramer took time to ponder the changes that were taking place in his life—facts and revelation he was gleaning about his Jewish heritage, his relationship with Carrie, the incredible job that seemed to have fallen down from heaven—change so drastic it seemed his whole world was shifting on its axis.

The job had proven more fruitful than he could have possibly imagined, beginning with the astounding interviews with Israeli women, often visiting in their homes and getting to know them and their families intimately. Never in a million years would Mike have believed there were so many diverse people and opinions in one tiny country. No one group seemed to agree with anyone else, but after a few weeks, he had begun to understand why the explosive controversies in Israel were so complicated. Most Americans, and certainly other nationalities as well, were at least partially informed about the seemingly irresolvable Arab/Israeli conflict, but Mike had discovered there were scores of other conflicts equally confusing although obviously not as perilous. Even among the over eighty percent Jewish population, there were more opinions than he could possibly count.

During the last few weeks, he had come to the simple conclusion that Israel was still in the making. During the fifties and even into the sixties, many reporters and historians referred to Israel as a "young" and exciting nation. But now, particularly since the nation's fiftieth birthday, they seemed to think the world should recognize Jews as only invaders occupying a land not their own. Of course, most of the world has always been against Israel, but it seemed to Mike that something more malignant had happened. Something evil was going on here, and he was determined to dig until he found its tangled roots.

Interviewing the women had been like gazing through a magnifying glass into the very heart of the land. Though all but the Sabras came from very divergent backgrounds and cultures, the women drew one simple bottom line while their husbands argued over the Palestinian problem, settlement withdrawal, national identity, regulation of holy sites, etcetera, etcetera, etcetera. Mothers in Israel had one concern—their children. What would happen to generations of children if the warfare went on and on? Hadn't the Jewish people worldwide lost nearly an entire generation of children only fifty years ago and more since? They wanted peace. They wanted their children to live.

Chapter Fifteen

Arab mothers drew the same line. When they were convinced no one could hear and they were not being recorded, many of them openly wept with Becca, sharing the gut-wrenching agony each felt the second she heard of another suicide bombing or shooting, hoping beyond hope it wasn't one of her own.

"What a mess," sighed Mike, suddenly remembering he was to meet Aron Safran and his lovely young wife at their flat for dinner. Now, they were a pair! He jumped up and leaped into the old red Jeep he and Becca had leased the week after they arrived in Israel.

"Don't know why I thought we could walk all over this country. It isn't *that* small," she had said in her laughing voice.

Mike jerked the gear shift forward, quickly letting up on the clutch and ramming the gas pedal as he swung the little vehicle around on the graveled overlook. Trying to recall the address Salim had given him, Mike thought about his new friends. Aron Safran didn't look much different than himself. He was a nice looking guy somewhere around Mike's age, fairly dark hair and eyes, but lighter skin compared to most Sabras he had met. He guessed that was the Romanian background.

Aron's wife was another matter altogether. Born of Moroccan parents who had escaped to Israel during the anti-Semitic uprisings in North Africa after the 1948 war, Levana Safran was absolutely gorgeous, dark hair flowing about her shoulders and great big eyes as black as ripe olives. *Whew! I'm glad she's taken,* he thought, laughing aloud.

Speeding down the narrow trail from the Mount of Olives across the Kidron Valley and into the busy streets of west Jerusalem hoping he wouldn't be late for dinner, Mike's thoughts again turned to Carrie, but within minutes, he was pulling the bouncing Jeep over to the curb in front of the Safrans' apartment building. Mike sprinted up the walk and through the front door, taking the steps by leaps and bounds to save time.

Ding dong! The door opened quickly, and Aron Safran greeted Mike with a jolly, "Boker Erev, Mike Kramer!"

"Shalom, Aron. Good to see you again."

Mike wondered why this guy always looked so familiar as the two men shook hands and Aron led his guest into the living room. Levana sauntered into the room looking every bit like a Moroccan princess if there was such a thing. She was wearing a long dress made of some type of rich brown flowing fabric that made her smooth skin look almost copper in tone. The skimpy sandals on her feet and the anklet that jingled as she walked completed her authentic Middle Eastern aura.

The Gentile and the Jew: A Divine Romance

Levana Safran was as friendly as she was beautiful, thought Mike as she grabbed both his hands. "Shalom, Mike! Welcome to our home!"

"Toda Rabah," he answered with a big smile. It had taken three long months, but Mike had finally mastered enough Hebrew to at least greet, thank and say good-bye when he needed to.

"Come sit with Aron and make yourself comfortable. Dinner's almost ready. Hope you're hungry, Mike!" Levana quickly swirled out of the room as gracefully as she had come in.

"You can't have my wife, Mike," Aron said jokingly, watching Mike's eyes follow his gorgeous wife into the kitchen. "She is beautiful, isn't she?"

"I'm sorry, man." Mike blushed easily, turning back to Aron. "I apologize for staring, but you're right, she's stunning. But don't worry, her eyes are only for you, and anyway, I have someone, a beautiful southern belle from North Carolina, USA."

"Great! Are wedding plans in the making?"

"No, not just yet. We haven't progressed quite that far. She's finishing graduate school in May and we're planning for her to come here in about six weeks. I would certainly like for her to meet you guys."

"Wonderful! Let's plan on it. Levana would be thrilled to put together a little dinner party for you two, wouldn't you, darling?" Aron's wife had just burst into the room carrying a steaming platter of couscous and lamb.

"All I heard was dinner party, but that's enough for me." Levana smiled broadly at the two men, placing the dish on the lovely table set for three. She stopped abruptly, placed both hands on her hips, and gazed at the beautifully decorated table, wondering if she had forgotten anything. "Tell me more during dinner," she said, turning back to the kitchen. "Aron, pour the wine while I bring the bread. Everything's ready."

"Mike, what can I get for you," Levana asked. "Would you like more coffee?"

"Yes, please, but no more food! Levana, this is one of the best meals I've had in Israel," said Mike. "You're a fantastic chef."

"Todah! I love to cook. And I love dinner parties, so yes, I would love to throw a party for you and your fiancé. Just tell me when." Levana swept out of the room and was back in seconds with hot Turkish coffee for everyone.

"Carrie's not exactly my fiancée—not yet, anyway," said Mike.

"Well, pop the question, Mike! What's holding you up? Cat got your tongue?" Totally gregarious and Israeli to boot, Levana shot straight to the target.

Chapter Fifteen

"Levana! He may not want to talk about his personal relationships right now," Aron chided his adorable wife. "But, I want to know, too, Mike. What's the problem?" Aron smiled comically at Mike, placing both arms on the table, staring him in the face.

"Okay, I'll spill my guts if that's what you want to see," said Mike with a grin.

"That's us, gut watchers!" Aron laughed heartily at his own joke.

"Actually, you guys may be able to help. Bottom line is...Carrie isn't Jewish."

"Uh oh," the couple chimed.

"Yeah, well...she's about as un-Jewish as you can get, coming from a long line of Scot-Irish Presbyterians turned Baptist."

"You do have a problem. Your parents, right?" asked Aron.

"Yeah. To make a very long story short, Carrie's first—and last—visit with my family was not exactly successful, you might say. And, it was all my fault."

"What do you mean?" asked Aron. "Why do you think it was your fault?"

"My parents did a great job rearing me as a good Jewish boy, but I somehow managed to live in the dark about my heritage—tradition, religion, God—all that stuff. Actually, until this conflict arose, I never thought about any of it. My philosophy of life most definitely did not include a Jewish perspective. Suffice it to say, Carrie was really hurt, and I almost lost her."

"What about your parents? Have you talked it over with them?" asked Levana softly.

"No...no, I haven't. Being away in graduate school was a hindrance, and then Carrie went to the mountains for the holidays while I went to Connecticut for Chanukah and Mom and Dad traveled to Romania."

"Sounds like a circus!" Levana laughed at the chaotic picture Mike had painted.

"Yeah, it was a rather hectic holiday. And then, while we were all separated, this job offer came up, and there was no time for a lengthy conversation with my parents about anything else."

He paused, having noticed Aron's surprised expression at the mention of his parents' journey, but when Aron kept silent, Mike continued his explanation. "Mom is the one who will never give her approval. Dad has his hang-ups, too, but I don't think he would really stand in the way when it comes right down to it. But Mom has this thing about family—Jewish family. Her mother and father were the only family she ever knew. All the others died in the Holocaust. As a result of their suffering, her parents could never talk about what happened, leaving Mom in the dark about everything. Ever since I can remember, Mom has longed for her family, mourned for them. And she worries about our losing our Jewish identity in America, the great melting pot of the world. No, she will never approve of my marrying Carrie."

Mike slowly shook his head. His voice had gradually softened until his hosts could barely hear his last words. His eyes were downcast, his fingers fidgeting with his coffee cup.

"Aron, why don't you and Mike make yourselves comfortable in the living room while I clear the table? I can bring more coffee or maybe a sweet, after dinner wine."

"Oh, no thank you, Levana. I'm overstuffed and wired with enough caffeine to stay up all night." Mike seemed lifted a little by the change of conversation as the two young men rose and walked into the living room.

Settling into the comfortable couch across from Mike, Aron looked as if he couldn't quite decide where to begin the next chapter of the evening's conversation, and because of three months learning to listen, Mike could tell Aron had something to say, so he kept quiet and waited.

"Mike," Aron began, "when we met in Salim's home a few weeks ago, you said your mother was of Romanian descent and her maiden name was Liebowitz, right?"

"Yes...*ken*," Mike answered, quickly switching to Hebrew. "That's right."

"I don't recall you mentioning your parents' journey during that conversation, but tonight you told us they recently traveled to Romania, right?"

"Ken. They flew to Bucharest in December during Chanukah," Mike replied, wondering why Aron was so interested in his parents' travels.

"I assume they were searching for your mother's family or, at least, some knowledge of them. Do you mind my asking what they found in Romania?" Aron seemed very serious all of a sudden.

"To tell you the truth, I don't know. That's something else we haven't had a chance to talk about. Mom and Dad arrived back in North Carolina the same day I got back from Connecticut with the news about this assignment in Israel. Our family discussion that night was entirely focused on the surprising turn of events in my life, and I'm ashamed to say I never even asked them about their trip. Why do you ask?"

Aron was silent. Levana quietly entered the room, only the soft tinkling of her anklet announcing her presence. She curled up beside Aron on the couch and laid her head on his shoulder.

Chapter Fifteen

"Mike, if you remember, I told you that night at Salim's that I was also of Romanian descent."

Mike nodded. That low current of electricity he had felt at the Western Wall his first day in Jerusalem was beginning to tingle over his skin again.

Aron leaned forward, his arms resting on his knees. "I'm not absolutely positive, Mike, but it's certainly possible that you and I are fairly closely related. I think your mother and my mother may be first cousins."

"What?!" Mike almost tripped over his own feet as he quickly moved to the edge of his seat. "Are you sure?"

"No, not one hundred percent, but I can definitely say I'm ninety-five percent sure," replied Aron.

"This is incredible!" Mike stared at the young man who might be his cousin, glimpsing Levana glancing back and forth from him to her husband when, all of a sudden, it came to him. *That's why he looks so familiar. He looks like me!* Mike almost stuttered his next words. "Do you think my Mom knows anything about this?"

"I don't know, Mike. That's what I want to find out. You see, I took a journey to Bucharest much like your mother's about five years ago. My beloved grandfather, Josef Liebovici, died in 1992 here in Israel. His only son, my mother's brother, was killed during the Six Day War in '67. My own father was killed in southern Lebanon in the eighties. Other than the elderly uncle who stayed behind in Bucharest, my grandfather had only mentioned a brother who was to leave Romania soon after his own escape and make contact when, or if, he arrived in America. When he never heard from him, my grandfather assumed the worst. He and my grandmother told us very little about their lives in Romania and their escape in December of 1941, so like your mother, we thought we had no other family. Then I went to Romania and rambled about until I found an interesting old rabbi who knew the family back then. He said it was almost impossible for Jews to find family members after the war. It was like the proverbial needle in a haystack."

Mike was squirming in his seat, gulping as he asked the next question, "Did your grandfather ever mention his brother's name?"

"Ken, his name was Jacob Liebovici."

Mike bolted out of the chair, throwing his arms up in the air. "It's true!" he shouted. "Jacob was my grandfather! Yes! I have a cousin!"

Aron jumped up and threw his arms around Mike, both of them laughing wildly while Levana began dancing around the room, her anklet jingling like crazy as she grabbed each of the men's hands to draw them into her dance. The three of them produced something akin to the *hora*, a Jewish folk dance, laughing and cheering and rejoicing that what was lost had been found. When exhaustion hit the happy threesome, each of them collapsed in the closest chair, out of breath, but still in awe of their amazing discovery.

"Hey! I have to call Mom!" cried Mike. Pulling his cell phone off his belt, he quickly glanced at his watch to see where his parents would be at this hour. "It's just two in the afternoon there, so Mom should be home. Aron, what about your mother? Is she here in Jerusalem?" Mike's thoughts were playing leap frog.

"My mother's name is Sura, after her own mother, and she lives in Netanya up the coast. I'll take you to see her any time you'd like."

"I'm ready, man!" The phone was ringing. And ringing.

"Hello?"

Mike's heart jumped as he heard his mother's mellow voice. "Mom? It's me, Mike."

"Mike! Oh, it's good to hear your voice. I miss you so much."

"I miss you, too, Mom, more than you'll ever know, but Mom, I have something to tell you."

"You sound excited. What is it?"

"Mom, I have a cousin—a live one! I mentioned him in my last letter, but I didn't know who he was then. I'm standing right here in his living room in Jerusalem. Mom, are you there? I said I've found our cousin."

Rachel's answer was so soft Mike struggled to hear her,

"I know, son, I know."

Chapter Sixteen

arrie Jernigan was flying high in every sense of the word. Her Al Italia flight had taken off from its stopover in Rome right on time. The flight was smooth, and the weather was great. Never in her entire life had Carrie been so excited. She had read and reread Mike's e-mail with his instructions about what to do in the airport just in case he and Becca got tied up in an interview. If there was only one thing he had learned about the Middle East, Mike had told her many times, it was that no one in the entire region has ever heard the old saying, "Time is of the essence." Whatever takes five minutes to do in the US of A, might take five hours in Israel or any of the surrounding countries Mike had visited. She placed the instructions in her bag alongside her baggage claim ticket and prayed Mike would be there and nothing would go wrong.

With great trepidation, the entire Jernigan family had escorted Carrie to the airport in Raleigh to see her off. During all the hugs and tears, she had made a mental note to tell Mike that she couldn't help her leaky eye problem—it was definitely hereditary. Everyone in the airport from ticket agents to security guards probably thought Carrie was off to deepest, darkest Africa, never to return. Of course, they hadn't wanted her to go to begin with, but in the end, they hugged her tightly and said they wanted her to do what she thought best and what would make her happy. *Well, this little North Carolina farm girl is one happy camper*, she thought now as she buckled her seat belt and braced herself to ride the aircraft into the land of Israel.

The Gentile and the Jew: A Divine Romance

After what seemed like hours going through customs being questioned and searched, Carrie was pulling her backpack over her shoulders when she heard a voice calling her name. Quickly turning around, she glimpsed Mike across the open room, coming toward her as if he were moving in slow motion. She dropped the large bag she was pulling and started running through the airport thinking she could certainly get to him faster than he would get to her, considering the unusually slow pace he was taking.

All of a sudden, Carrie felt like she had run into a brick wall. Two armed security guards grabbed her, one on each side, spinning her around and escorting her back to her luggage. She wondered why Mike wasn't yelling at them to stop. Where was he, anyway?

The two uniformed men carrying guns spun her around and two more guards, women this time, rushed up and began questioning her all over again. *Why were you running? Why did you leave your luggage? Who is the man you are meeting? What's wrong with you?* Questions were shot at her like a machine gun from every side, and all she could do was stand there dumbfounded, wondering where Mike was all this time and why he hadn't rescued his damsel in distress.

Another hour later, she found out. When the security agents saw her running to Mike, they instantly sent three guards to arrest him and take him into a room for questioning. By the time all the guards had compared their stories of why Carrie was in Israel and she had been searched one more time, the two lovers were finally released into each other's arms.

They stood locked in that deep embrace for a long time. Carrie was exhausted and confused, feeling as if a tornado had engulfed her the minute she stepped foot on Israeli soil. Mike was just relieved, knowing where they could be right now if the guards hadn't believed them—held in custody somewhere awaiting hours of investigation. He was thankful Israel had such tight security, but man, was it scary sometimes!

"You and your exciting adventures," Carrie finally mumbled into his chest.

Mike laughed and Carrie started giggling. She couldn't stop. They laughed so much people started staring at them until Mike looked around and decided he had better get Carrie out of there before they got into more trouble.

"Come on, you crazy girl," he said, giving her a big kiss to save for later. He grabbed her bags and whispered, a big grin spreading across his handsome face, "Don't hurry. Don't be loud. Just act normal."

Chapter Sixteen

It was all Carrie could do to stave off another laughing fit, but she smothered it quickly, and linking her arm in Mike's, she followed him out of the airport and through the parking lot to the little red Jeep.

"Your chariot awaits you, my love!" Mike threw her baggage in the back and lifted Carrie up into the Jeep, giving her a tight squeeze before he let her go and ran around to the other side.

"What fun!" she shouted as they sped off down the highway going up—up to Jerusalem.

The following evening, after she had slept twelve hours straight, Carrie and Mike were sitting at a small table on the terrace of the King David Hotel overlooking the streets of Jerusalem. He had decided Carrie deserved first class accommodations her first trip out of the US, especially considering Becca's place was only an office with a single bed and his was a small cell-like room in a nearby hostel. Because of his salary from the magazine and a carefully controlled trust he had received from his parents when he turned twenty-one, Mike could certainly afford to lavish a little luxury on his beloved, and he was overflowing with secret plans for more of the same. He had a list a mile long of places he wanted to take her, things he knew she would want to see, including his own special sites like the Western Wall and the Mount of Olives.

After quite a few visits with Salim and Aron during the past three months, he had begun to read Tanach fairly regularly, and for some unconscious reason, Mike often ended up in the book of Song of Solomon which, of course, set his thoughts on a rabbit trail leading directly to Carrie. And now, here she was—finally. His voice was soft and tender as he took her hands in his across the candlelit table.

"Arise, my darling, my beautiful one, and come along.
For behold, the winter is past, the rain is over and gone.
The flowers have already appeared in the land.
The time has arrived for pruning the vines,
And the voice of the turtledove has been heard in our land."[19]

Mike's eyes were tender, floating in shimmering pools of love, his gaze so penetrating Carrie felt her heart would surely burst as she answered in the only words she could remember from the ancient song of passionate love,

"My beloved is mine and I am his.
Let him kiss me with the kisses of his mouth
For thy love is better than wine."[20]

The Gentile and the Jew: A Divine Romance

He drew her slender hands to his mouth and held them there, slowly kissing the backs of her hands over and over again. He pressed his face into her palms, drinking in her deepest fragrance as his thirst for her increased by leaps and bounds. Their "I love you's" had almost become obsolete. There were no human words for love so deep.

"Hmph!" The waiter cleared his throat to get their attention.

"Oh, I'm so sorry," Carrie muttered, blushing from head to toe. "I haven't even looked at the menu."

"Neither have I," said Mike, his eyes still gazing into the windows of her soul.

The young waiter gave them a knowing smile, saying, "That's okay. I'll check back in a few minutes."

"Oh, Mike, I still can't believe I'm here. Just think, only three months ago neither of us had ever dreamed of going to Israel, and now, here we are, you and me, eating dinner in the King David Hotel in the middle of Jerusalem, of all places! It's just too much to take in. It's as if we're in a dream."

"Yeah, I know. We must feel a little like the exiled Jews when they returned to Jerusalem after the first Diaspora in Babylon." Mike still held her hand, but turned his gaze toward the lights of Jerusalem.

"What do you mean?" Carrie asked, wondering how he knew so much about the Bible all of a sudden.

"'When the Lord brought back the captives of Zion, we were like those who dream.' It's from the Psalms," said Mike, smiling sheepishly. "I've had a lot of time to read lately."

"I see you have. I'm impressed," she teased.

"Well, don't be. What I've learned in these three months is a drop in the bucket compared to what I need, and want, to learn. But, I think I'm getting a hang on this religion thing. Interestingly enough, I seem to be surrounded on every side by really good, sincere people who are trying to glorify God in their everyday lives the way it was meant to be."

Carrie smiled, amazed at the change in Mike, quickly deciding it would be best to keep her observations to herself. She would just keep watching... and listening.

"Oh, yes! That reminds me of something I've been meaning to tell you," Mike said. "Just before the holidays, I fell on the ice while I was jogging early one morning and.... Hey! You remember! You wondered why I was all scratched and bruised when we met in the snow just before you left town."

"Yes, I remember."

Chapter Sixteen

"Well, this guy in a campus utility truck picked me up and took me back to my apartment. Sam, that's the guy's name, talked about God making it a point to bump into us to get our attention, and he talked about pride in a simple way that made me understand a lot about myself. I'm telling you, Carrie, I didn't realize it right away, but that short, simple conversation had a powerful effect on my life. And by the way, I called the campus offices to thank Sam about a week after my fall, and they said there was no one named Sam on their payroll. I had the girl go down the list of all campus employees, and there was no Sam! What do you think about that?"

"I don't know. Do you think you were having hallucinations? Maybe you hit your head and didn't realize it."

"Nope. I was totally conscious. And somebody definitely drove me back to my apartment. Anyway, what I'm trying to say is that I've been bumping into God continually since I set foot in Israel, or more to the point, He's been bumping into me." The wide grin Carrie loved so much spread all over Mike's handsome face as if he were smiling from deep within.

"Are you ready to order now?" The waiter was again standing by their table, pleasant but more impatient this time. Neither Mike nor Carrie was about to tell him the menu hadn't entered their conversation as yet.

"Shall I order for you?"

"Please!" Carrie scanned the confusing menu thinking she had never eaten anything she couldn't pronounce.

"We'll have Mediterranean salads and the Shashlik with all the trimmings," said Mike.

"Good choice," said the gracious young waiter, pouring bottled water into their glasses.

Later that evening, the young lovers leisurely strolled arm-in-arm down King David Street to a place where Carrie could clearly see the Old City, bathed in its glorious golden light. She was breathless at the awesome sight, again feeling as if she were in a dream, holding tight to the man she wanted to spend the rest of her life with. But in that moment, Carrie Jernigan instantly fell in love for the second time—with the Holy City, Jerusalem of Gold.

Mike had picked Carrie up at the airport on Sunday afternoon and by Thursday evening, they had investigated nearly every nook and corner of the Old City, Carrie's eye valves leaking again and again as she stood in the very places she had read about in her Bible while she was growing up, places where Jesus had taught his followers and prophesied over Jerusalem. As for Mike, it was strange to see the city again through Carrie's eyes. Places that were insignificant to him were precious to Carrie—the Via Dolorosa, the way of sorrows where Jesus had carried his cross on the way to Golgotha, even the Church of the Holy Sepulcher which Mike considered ridiculously ornate. They learned that most Protestants believe Jesus was buried in a little garden just outside the Old City walls near a winepress and in full view of a hill of rock that looks amazingly like a skull. But Carrie's guidebook said there is a strong possibility the Church of the Holy Sepulcher, which was outside the city walls at the time, was actually built over the tomb of Jesus. She wanted to make sure she explored every option.

Mike had to admit to himself that there were moments during those happy jaunts through old Jerusalem when he felt as if Carrie was stealing his city from him. He had been desperate to introduce his beloved to *his* city, the place made holy by God from the foundations of the earth, especially for the Jewish people. Now, she was turning it into a Christian city, and even though he was gaining a greater understanding of who this Jesus was through his discussions with Aron and Salim, Mike couldn't help but feel robbed. But, he was trying to "get over it" as Becca would have said, even taking time to share his feelings with Aron yesterday while Becca and Levana took Carrie on a girls' morning out to a Dead Sea spa.

"Let it go, Mike," Aron had advised him. "Her New Testament is all she knows about our country, and she relates everything she sees here to her Christian upbringing. But, she is a wild olive tree grafted into the cultivated tree, and now that she's seen Jerusalem in relation to her worldview, you must show her Jerusalem in the eyes of a Jew. Don't worry, Mike, she will see it—through your eyes."

Mike had tucked Aron's words away, hoping with all his heart they would prove prophetic. Just this afternoon, he had begun to see the change—or maybe "shift" was a better word. He couldn't have explained the difference, but somehow Carrie was beginning to understand that this city went back much further than two thousand years. The same light he had seen in her eyes watching and listening to his parents light the candles and say the Shabbat blessings at the beginning of that infamous dinner last Thanksgiving was beginning to glow again. He was glad he had taken Aron's advice and kept quiet. *Choices again*, he thought, smiling to himself as he turned to look at her tanned face, her long brown hair blowing in the soft breeze.

After a busy morning working with Becca, choosing pictures for her latest article, Mike had taken Carrie to see the Roman ruins at Caesarea which had

Chapter Sixteen

proved only fairly interesting compared to Jerusalem. But now they were both delighted to walk barefoot along the beach, enjoying the true highlight of the day, the deep blue Mediterranean Sea, spectacular in the afternoon sun. Both having lived near the Atlantic Ocean all their lives, they were thrilled to be near the restorative waters, wading and splashing in the surf, sometimes just standing in the white foam gazing out at the incredibly blue waters. Mike wrapped his arms around Carrie's waist, holding her tightly and wishing they could stay like that forever.

Only one wave of conflict had rolled over them during those blissful days in Jerusalem, and even that was stilled before it incurred any major damage. Mike had led Carrie up to the ramparts of the Old City where they had strolled along the top of the thick walls just as watchmen did in ancient days, the citizens below desperate to hear them shout, "All is well." But all was not well when Mike told Carrie that he had not yet talked to his parents about their relationship. Isaac and Rachel had no idea the two had even resumed their relationship, much less had fallen so deeply in love that Mike had asked her to join him in Israel.

Carrie's sparkling eyes had looked as if they were spitting fire as she pushed him away, glaring at him as if he were an enemy trying to sneak over the wall. But, when he quickly explained to her that he had only visited with his parents one day since Thanksgiving, and at that point, he and Carrie were not even back together, she began to calm down. He reminded her how pushed for time he was the week before he left for Israel. With the research Becca had given him to cram, the trip to New York to accept the job, packing for six months out of the country and spending as many hours with Carrie as possible, Mike never once found time to visit his parents before he left. Surprisingly, they had understood, and for Annie's sake in particular, Isaac and Rachel had taken her to the airport to see him off. But a few minutes in a crowded airport was neither appropriate nor sufficient time to get into that dreaded conversation.

As they climbed down from the ramparts that day, Mike thought, *One hurdle safely crossed. One more to go. But will I make it across the next one?*

"Come on, let's rest on that big rock a few minutes." Mike grasped her elbow as they climbed onto one of the gigantic rocks that seemed to be scattered randomly all along the shore and on out into the Sea. A man and his young son were standing on one of the largest rocks farthest from shore, fishing with the longest fishing poles the young Carolinians had ever seen.

"I wonder what kind of fish they catch with those poles," Mike was saying as they carefully settled down on the flat rock that looked similar to slate. He didn't put his arms around her this time but positioned himself to see her face as they talked.

"Time for a serious conversation, huh?" She beamed him a loving smile, then turned her eyes to the Sea. "Oh, Mike, I wish we had weeks here in Israel together, don't you?"

"I wish we had years here together. And maybe we will, who knows?" He couldn't take his eyes off her as she sat with her knees pulled up to her chin, her arms wrapped around her wet legs, her long brown hair blowing in the breeze coming from the Sea. The reflection of the dark blue water was deepening the blue-green color of her eyes as Mike gazed at the amazing transformation. *Everything's changing,* he thought, *even the color of Carrie's eyes.*

She turned to him with a smile that brought sparkles to those beautiful eyes and said, "Okay, Mike, what's up? I can tell when you have something on your mind."

"Think you know me pretty well, don't you?" he grinned and leaned over to kiss her lightly on her upturned nose. "And, you're right. I do want to talk to you."

Sitting there on that solid rock in the edge of the Mediterranean Sea, Mike brought Carrie up to date on his search for his Jewish identity, sharing things that had seemed too sensitive to write about in e-mails or phone calls. He told her about his Christian Arab friend, Salim, and the deep conversations they had enjoyed over the past three months, how the assignment itself had opened doors for him to know firsthand the hearts of the Jewish people in Israel and how just rambling about the land itself had caused him to feel more a Jew than ever in his life. Then, he told her about Aron and Levana Safran and the astonishing revelation that had given him an amazing sense of family heritage he never knew existed.

"And," said Mike, coming to the end of his chronicle, "not only do Aron and Levana believe Yeshua is Messiah, he told me that his grandfather, my Mom's uncle, was what they call "a believer," even back in Romania before he escaped to Israel."

"That's wonderful, but...well, it seems strange, don't you think?" asked Carrie, as amazed as Mike by the extraordinary sequence of events. "Your own grandfather wasn't a Christian, was he?"

"If he was, my Mom didn't know it, and that wouldn't be likely. But, it isn't as strange as you might think according to the history lesson Aron gave me. It seems Mom had a great uncle, Aron Liebovici, who was a follower of a man named Joseph Rabinowitz, a Chasidic lawyer who had experienced an unusual revelation of Yeshua as Messiah. He made a great impact on the Jews of southwest Russia and even led a congregation of Jewish believers."

"This is incredible," Carrie sighed, reaching out to caress his face, smiling into his dark, somber eyes. "I'm so happy for you, Mike. And selfishly, I'm happy for me, too, because the more you become who you were meant to be, the more I admire you and respect you. And, I must say…the more I love you."

He longed to hold her close and kiss her until the sun went down over the blue waters, but if he kissed her now, he knew they would never make it to the topic at hand, the story he wanted to share with her now.

"When Aron told me all this, I just assumed he believed Yeshua was Messiah because his grandparents did, but he said that was true only up to the time he graduated from high school. Since he had grown up in Israel in a Messianic congregation as they call it now, he had always thought himself as Jewish as anyone else, but when he had to serve his two years in the army, he began to question his sort of "inherited" belief system. He wasn't confused about his Jewish identity as I was, but he questioned his family's belief that Yeshua is Messiah.

"Aron told me that about a year into his quest, I guess you'd call it that, he came home on a weekend pass and found that his grandfather was concerned about him. He had sensed Aron's doubts and unrest. They talked about everything that day. Then, just before Aron went back to his post, his grandfather casually repeated a story Joseph Rabinowitz had passed on to his uncle sometime in the mid 1880's. Aron said the parable changed his life forever."

Carrie was totally engrossed in Mike's story, her head resting now on her knees, her eyes glued to his face as he began to share the parable.

"Rabinowitz said that a number of Jews were traveling in a four-wheeled cart through a little town in Poland. They lost one wheel, but kept on going, the cart wobbling as the horse pulled it on down the road. They saw another carriage driving far out in front of them, going in the same direction, so they sent one of the Jews to run forward up the road and ask if the people in the other carriage had seen a lost wheel on the road. The driver replied, 'You foolish man! You must go back, and not forward, to find your lost wheel.'"

"What does it mean?" asked Carrie.

"Rabinowitz told his people that the four wheels were Abraham, Moses, David and Messiah. The fourth wheel, Messiah, had been lost, and the Jews must go back and find it. When they did, Israel's four-wheeled chariot would run safe and secure."

"Hmm…. It seems so simple, doesn't it? Like something my Nana would say."

The Gentile and the Jew: A Divine Romance

"Yeah, I'm beginning to believe we humans have complicated everything more than God ever intended." Mike rose up and reached for Carrie's hand, pulling her to her feet and helping her step carefully over the slippery rocks to wave good-bye to the Sea. And once again, they went up to Jerusalem.

Like the other visitors coming out of Yad Vashem, the holocaust memorial in West Jerusalem, Mike and Carrie were conspicuously silent. They stood outside in the street for a good while, just taking deep breaths and trying not to stare at the older people emerging from the museum, knowing that many had more than likely personally experienced the horrors the young couple had only glimpsed in the exhibits and movie reels.

Carrie leaned against Mike's shoulder as they ambled slowly down the Avenue of the Righteous Gentiles. Earlier, as they had meandered quietly through the exhibits, Mike had shared with Carrie what little he knew about his family history, the sketchy stories his Kramer grandparents had shared and the very rare glimpses into those terror-filled years his Grandpapa Liebowitz had revealed.

By the time the couple walked from the pervading darkness of the museum out into the sunlight, Carrie felt she knew Mike in a way she had never thought possible. Because of the timing of his birth, he had been exempted from the horrors of what many Jews believe was the scriptural "time of Jacob's trouble," but he was still very much a part of it all. It seemed to Carrie that those years had created a corporate suffering that would forever flow through the veins of everyone related to the six million murdered Jews and the three million who had survived. Of course, that included every Jew who lived and would ever live until the end of time. She felt honored that Mike had waited to visit the Memorial with her, sharing an experience so profound it seemed more intimate than bodily contact. She wanted to know everything about the man, especially the family he loved.

"Mike, tell me about your family at home," she asked gently, lacing her arms into his. "I rambled on and on about mine after the holidays, but you didn't say much about yours. Oh, I know, I know. I didn't give you a chance to tell me anything, chatterbox that I am."

"I love your chattering, my little chipmunk," he said, reaching over to kiss her gently on the forehead.

He knew it was time. He had to tell her and face the consequences. There was no other choice this time, not if they were to have a good life together.

Chapter Sixteen

No, he thought, watching the innocent smile on Carrie's face, *I can't put it off any longer.*

Embarrassed by the quickly formed tears in his eyes, Mike turned from her and said, his voice a little raspy, "Come on, let's find a more private place to talk."

"Uh, oh. Another serious conversation?"

"Sort of," he said.

"I'm not sure I can handle anything heavy today. Our tour of the museum was abysmal enough. Let's just talk about your family. I want to get to know them better—your Mom and Dad, Sarah and David, and little Annie. I know it will be hard for them to accept me, Mike, but I want so much for them to like me. There's bound to be a way to edge my way into their hearts."

"Oh, they like you. I know they do. Who could help but like you?"

How could he make her understand? "I've told you, Carrie. The problem isn't you. Mom just has her heart and soul set on my marrying a Jewish girl, and it's going to take some time for her to get used to the fact that I want to spend the rest of my life with a Gentile. It's like I'm not speaking her language."

Carrie's countenance fell, a tear rolling slowly down her velvety cheek.

"Oh, don't worry," said Mike, pulling her close to his side, squeezing her shoulders. "Here, let's sit awhile." He led her to a bench in the park-like area.

"I'm sorry. I guess the dreadful horrors we've seen over the past several hours have got me down. I don't know how a Jew can stand to see all that."

"Yeah, it's hard, but much worse for those who lived during that era. Unbearable for most. Even my Mom has never been able to get through the memorial in Washington, and she was born after her parents escaped to America."

"I've always thought my ancestors had it tough—generations of dire poverty, their days consumed with excruciating physical labor from dawn to dusk. But their lives were perfect compared to what we've just seen. It's hard to comprehend that six million people were deliberately and systematically murdered, isn't it?"

Mike nodded, pulling her closer to his side. Carrie laid her head on his shoulder once more, closing her eyes for a second, trying to shut out some of the horror she had just seen. He looked down at the face he thought more beautiful than any in the world, and brushing a wisp of hair from her cheek, he turned her face up to his and softly kissed her mouth.

"I love you."

"Mmm. Say it again."

"I love you. I love you. I love you," he whispered in her ear.

"I love you, too," she murmured. "And that's why I want so much for your family to accept me. I know you won't be happy if they don't. It would be as if I'm a wall between you and your parents."

He hugged her tighter but said nothing.

"I feel sure Sarah and David would accept me, don't you, Mike?"

"Of course. I could see that at Thanksgiving. I predict you and Sarah will be very good friends."

"And then there's Annie. She likes me." Carrie smiled through her tears, looking up at Mike with questioning eyes.

Oh, God, help me. "Yes, there's Annie."

He gulped back the stinging tears, hoping audible words would come out when he began to speak.

"That's what I want to talk to you about, Carrie."

"Annie?"

"Yes, Annie…." Mike cleared his throat. "I'm sure she was a great surprise to you."

"Surprise? More like shock, I'd say." Carrie laughed quietly. "But, I really enjoyed being with her. She was probably the only trickle of joy in that miserable weekend. I just couldn't believe you had never told me you had a little sister."

"That's what I want to explain."

"Oh, don't worry about that. You don't have to explain. Since we didn't see each other for weeks after that infamous weekend, I guess I never thought to tell you that your Dad explained her adoption to me before you came into the living room that first night. So, it's all right. I understand." Carrie looked up into his face and smiled, wondering why he looked so grave.

"There's more to it than that."

"What do you mean?"

"Carrie, I love you more than life, and I believe you love me with all your heart, but I want you to know that I'll understand if…if…."

"If what?" She suddenly felt as if the eerie darkness had followed them out of Yad Vashem. "What are you talking about?"

"Annie."

"What about Annie?"

"Annie is…Annie is my child."

She stared at his face, her mouth partially open, looking to Mike as if she were waiting for him to say something that would clarify the incomprehensible words he had just spoken. But there was nothing left to say.

Chapter Sixteen

She whispered slowly, still gazing deeply into his dark eyes. "Annie? Annie's your little girl?"

"Yes..., she is. I know it's a shock, but I want you to understand, Carrie. I want to be totally honest so there's nothing left between us."

She didn't move a muscle. The news she was hearing now was almost as inconceivable as what she had heard and seen in Yad Vashem.

"Are you listening, Carrie?" Mike was getting worried. This was going to be worse than he had imagined.

"Yes," she whispered, still staring incredulously into the dark eyes she loved so much, unconsciously hoping she would see something that would enable her to understand.

"At first, I didn't even think about telling you. You see, when Mom and Dad decided to adopt Annie, we all agreed that when the papers were signed, none of us would ever speak of it again. She was to be my parents' daughter and my sister and that was that. But this past year, when I realized I was falling in love with you, I knew I would have to tell you. It wouldn't have been fair to keep it from you." Mike could see the pain and disappointment in her beautiful eyes, and he could hardly bear to look at her. He realized now there was nothing he could say that would make it any better. What had he done? What could he say? The truth, that was his only choice.

"I'm sorry, Carrie. I'm sorry that I made some really bad mistakes before you came into my life. But, I'm not sorry there's an Annie."

Carrie continued to stare at him even though her eyes didn't seem to see anything. Finally, she nodded her head in resignation and then turned her eyes toward the old man who was weeping silently as he came out of the memorial. Strangely enough, she couldn't take her eyes off the unknown man. The pain stabbing so deep in her heart must be absolutely nothing compared to what that old man must have suffered. Strange, they seemed vitally connected somehow. She wished she had the nerve to walk over and hug him, to do something for him. Maybe she could comfort him in his grief and receive some measure of consolation in her own. Why not? What harm could it do? The worst he could do would be to reject her, and she had certainly learned that rejection doesn't kill, not if you don't let it.

Carrie quickly slid out of Mike's embrace. Caught off guard, he quickly tried to pull her back, thinking she was going to leave him sitting there and run away, but she pushed his hand aside and quickly walked toward the old man standing so conspicuously alone in the narrow street. He pulled a handkerchief from his jacket pocket and wiped his eyes, trying unsuccessfully to control his emotions.

Carrie reached the suffering man in seconds. Placing her hand gently on his arm, she whispered tenderly, "I'm sorry. I'm so very sorry."

Surprised by the unexpected human contact, he started, looking deeply into her eyes thinking to brush her off in his embarrassment. But, the aged survivor immediately knew that the compassion he saw in Carrie's eyes was real. They stood silently for a few moments, eyes locked in subconscious understanding. Then, he grabbed both her hands and answered in a rough, broken voice, "Todah. Baruch Ha Shem." Thank you. Blessed be the Name.

Sighing deeply, he then turned away. Shoving his warmed hands into his jacket pockets, he walked slowly down the narrow street. Carrie watched him until he was out of sight, thankful she hadn't resisted the leading of her heart. She felt better. She could handle this thing. She knew she could, but... not yet.

Turning back to Mike who was watching carefully, she reached out her hand and said, "Come on, let's go."

As they ambled slowly through the streets of West Jerusalem back to the hotel, Carrie asked only for the details she felt she needed to know for her own peace of mind. He answered truthfully, sharing the very short story of his one-night relationship with Annie's birth mother after a carousing fraternity party. He was ashamed to say he hardly even remembered the night and was in a state of shock when the girl tracked him down two months later to tell him she was pregnant with his child. The following weeks were consumed by intense meetings with both sets of parents, debating the alternatives—abortion, adoption or raising the baby. Of course, marriage was never considered. The two college seniors barely remembered one another. Mike's parents were dead set against abortion, but the girls' parents fought hard to win the Kramers over, arguing for their daughter's right to choose. They continually pointed out that Mike was unprepared to be a father, even honestly admitting their daughter was too immature and selfish to be a mother at that point in her life.

Rachel and Isaac had fought hard to give up the baby for adoption, honestly believing that would be best for all concerned. But when Rachel was told the girl was Jewish, all arguments ended. It suddenly dawned on her that this baby would not only be a full-blooded Jew, but would be her Papa's great grandchild as well.

"So that was the end of it. Mom won the day, and she and Dad were there when Annie was born, ready to take her in their arms and claim her as their own. Other than my immediate family, no one ever knew except Jordan. He was angry with me for not telling you early on."

Chapter Sixteen

At least someone thought of me, thought Carrie. But she asked, "Will you ever tell Annie?"

"I don't know. I thought not in the beginning, that it would be best for her to always believe Mom and Dad are her parents. But now, I just don't know."

"Do you still believe it was the right thing to do?" Carrie had asked as they neared the hotel, their shoulders about a foot apart.

"Yes, but it's been difficult. Most of the time, I believe she really is my little sister. But, that's usually when she's far away. When I go home and she jumps into my arms, my heart breaks over and over again. And sometimes when she just says 'Mommy' and 'Daddy' to my parents, I get ridiculously jealous, knowing I have no moral right to feel that way."

Carrie stopped him right in the middle of King David Street, looked him straight in the eyes and said, "I want you to understand that this is hard for me...terribly hard. I guess I'm in shock and I'm not sure exactly how I'll feel when the shock wears off. But I do know that I love you, Mike Kramer. I love you for better or worse, in sickness and in health, for richer or poorer. I love you. I just love you."

He reached out for her, longing to take her in his arms, but she quickly backed away.

"No, Mike. I love you, but I don't like you very much right now. I feel dirty, and I hurt so badly I think I'm going to be sick." Her lips were trembling as the tears began to flow.

He gazed at her for a long time. He didn't try to touch her. Not now.

"I'm sorry," he whispered. "I wouldn't have hurt you for anything in the world."

Carrie could only nod, quickly turning to rush through the hotel doors. She hurried through the lobby, trying to hide the tears she knew she couldn't stop. Never had she wanted so desperately to be alone.

The next day and the next, she adamantly demanded to be alone. She didn't want to see Mike, not even talk with him on the phone. She had to process his shocking confession and settle in her own heart what forgiveness really means. Wasn't the old saying, "Forgive and forget?" How on earth could she forget that Mike had a child out of wedlock with a woman he didn't even know, especially when that child was a part of his family? On the other hand, why should Carrie even need to forgive him? All that had happened three years before she had met him. What did it have to do with her? But if it had nothing to do with her, why was she crying for hours on end, her stomach swimming with nausea, her head throbbing continually?

In the early morning hours of the following day, the phone Carrie had stuffed under the bed rang and rang until it finally woke her from a series of tormenting dreams.

"What? What is it?" she mumbled, still half asleep.

"I'm sorry to wake you, Carrie," the voice said, "but it's an emergency."

"Huh? Who is this?"

"It's John Owens. I'm in Nashville, and I'm afraid I have some bad news."

"What's wrong, John?" Her stomach was suddenly tied in knots.

"It's Emma's mother, Carrie. She's much worse, and the doctors don't expect her to live much longer. Maybe two weeks...more likely a few days. Emma wanted you to know."

"Oh, no! I can't believe it!"

"I know. We're all walking around like zombies in disbelief."

"Oh, John," Carrie mumbled between sobs, "please tell Emma I love her, and I'll be praying for her. And thank you for calling. Thank you so much."

She hung up the receiver and slid the phone back under the bed. She slowly curled up into a fetal position and pulled the covers over her head. Then she cried until there were no more tears, and exhaustion pulled her back into a fitful sleep.

The next day was worse. John's phone call had just propelled her further into the black hole. All the tears were gone, but there was no relief. Darkness rolled in like a black night with not a star in sight. Eating was out of the question. Just thinking about food brought the nausea swimming back to her stomach. So, she slept and slept some more.

After three days, Carrie was finally willing to take long walks with Mike through the streets of the Old City. Quite often, they climbed the ramparts and found a place to sit and silently watch the teeming crowds of people going about their daily business. There didn't seem to be any need for confrontation. What was there to confront? Mike had told her the facts. There were no arguments. Daily, he declared his love for Carrie and how much he wanted her in his life. The script had been written and read, but the finale was mostly up to her now.

From their perch on the walls of the ancient city on a hill, Carrie's gaze often turned toward the south, scanning the Judean hills and the seemingly infinite expanse of desert beyond. For thousands of years, it had been called the Negev, the south country or southland. Abraham had pitched his tents there. Four thousand years later, David Ben Gurion had retired to spend his last days in Sid Boker, a kibbutz he founded right smack in the middle of the arid desert.

What was it about the desert, she wondered, as a bell began to ring faintly in her memory bank. *Ohh..., yes.* She remembered. One Christmas when Carrie was a teenager, Nana had given her a book called *Hinds Feet on High Places*, written by a woman who lived in Israel, Hannah Hurnard. It was an allegory about spiritual growth. The main character, a young girl named Much Afraid, set out to climb the Mountain of Spices, seeking to overcome her weaknesses in the strength of the Good Shepherd she followed. At one point in her journey, she comes to a dry desert, filled with nothing but rocks and sand, the heat and lack of moisture insufferable. But, as Much Afraid trudged across the hot desert, she spied a tiny orange-red flower peeping out from a bed of rocks much like a Crocus in early spring. The young pilgrim was amazed that anything could live there, not even a weed, certainly not a lovely flower. Kneeling down to study the little blossom more closely, Much Afraid knew that it couldn't possibly receive more than a tiny drop of moisture for months at the time, perhaps years. Amazed, she asked the flower its name. For Much Afraid and her modern counterpart, Carrie Jernigan, the answer was life-changing. The lovely flower replied, "My name is *Acceptance-with-Joy*."

During that timely recollection, her heart began to soften, becoming pliable so that healing could take place. Gradually, their silent walks became laced with quiet conversation, just a few words here and there at first, then more as their hearts opened to one another. Trust was slowly building as the hours passed by. By the end of the week, Mike reached for her hand one more time, and she didn't pull it away.

The next day he had to go with Becca to one of the most strategic interviews they had been offered. The Jewish woman was the wife of a Knesset member who had put them off for months. Mike wanted Carrie to go with them, but she had encouraged him to go on without her, assuring him she would enjoy a day in Jerusalem by herself. Actually, she needed to be alone again, and he understood. So after breakfast, he hurried off with Becca, giving Carrie a quick phone call to say, "I love you." He promised to pick her up for dinner early, around 5:30.

"Eat a light lunch," he had said. "You'll need a good appetite tonight."

As Mike drove the red Jeep, jerking the gear shift back and forth as they sped through the jammed streets, Becca chatted away, briefing him with last-minute instructions in preparation for the coveted interview. But Mike was having a hard time keeping his mind on what she was saying. He kept thinking of the cherished moment last night when Carrie had finally let him touch her once again. His eyes had gone over every inch of her beautiful face, the face he had memorized so often he could now see her clearly when she wasn't with him, even in his dreams. Then he cupped her face in his hands, brushing her hair back and leaning forward until his lips were just inches from hers, their noses almost touching as he continued to gaze deeply into her ocean-hued eyes. He still said nothing, but silently he was thanking God, the God he wasn't even sure existed just a few months ago. Then he moved forward, their lips touched, and he kissed her for a long, long time.

Carrie agreed to be ready at 5:30. She hung up the phone and rolled over, quickly falling back to sleep as she snuggled under the warm covers. She slept late that day, still wiped out from the strain of the days since Mike had stunned her with the news that Annie was his child. When she finally awoke around ten o'clock, she felt completely rested, so energized that for the first time in nearly a week, her thoughts didn't go directly to Mike and Annie but to the shopping she wanted to do for her family while she was in Israel. Mike had suggested she browse the intriguing shops on Ben Yehuda Street, but as Carrie pulled back the drapes and viewed the golden walls of the Old City, she knew her day's wanderings would take her into the narrow streets of Old Jerusalem once again.

Savoring the brisk walk up to Jaffa Gate an hour later, her thoughts bounced back and forth from the shopping list her mother would be so proud she had made to the traumas her relationship with Mike had suffered since last Thanksgiving. It seemed more like six months of constant warfare than a love affair, one hard fought battle after the other. She was growing confident, however, that their love for each other was strong enough to overcome any obstacles life might place in their path. This last one was the test of all tests. She prayed it was the final exam.

Strange, she thought, even though Mike's confession was a total shock, their love had deepened and strengthened so much in the months since Christmas that she wasn't nearly as shaken as she had been from Thanksgiving to New Year's when she had wondered daily if he truly loved her. But even with the surety of Mike's love and the obvious strengthening of his character, it was hard to completely forgive. There was still a little *"Why should Mike get off so easily?"* attitude floating around in her mind. Every time her mental VCR replayed his confession that day at Yad Vashem, the old bitterness Carrie had dealt with since childhood rose to the surface and she hated it. But, the bitter voice sounded perfectly logical. At least Annie's biological mother had suffered the pain of childbirth and having to give up her baby. And, of course, Annie herself would suffer deeply when she discovered the truth no matter how or when it was revealed. Mike's parents had certainly suffered even though they obviously loved and cherished Annie and had welcomed the emotional, physical and financial responsibilities required to rear another child in their latter years.

Yes, the voice said. *Mike is getting off way too easily.*

Taking a deep breath of the warm spring air scented with aromatic flavors of Middle-eastern spices and perfumes, Carrie walked quickly through the ancient archway, planning to stroll through the Armenian shops as she made her way to the Jewish Quarter and the Cardo.

My goodness, she thought, *where did all these people come from?* Having arrived in Israel a month after Passover and just after the celebrations surrounding Independence Day, her rambling days in Jerusalem had been fairly crowd-free. But today there were people everywhere. She literally had to wait in line to get out of the plaza and past the Tower of David. *Not the best day to shop,* she thought, turning to the woman erratically bumping against her arm.

"Do you speak English?"

"Yes," the older woman replied, impatiently trying to push her way through the throng.

"What's going on? Why the huge crowd?"

"It's Shavuot," she replied in perfect English.

"Oh."

Noting Carrie's blank expression, the woman explained, "The Feast of Weeks, the Jewish celebration of the spring harvest and first fruits."

"Oh, yes. Thanks. I've been reading about the Feasts, but I started with Rosh Hashanah, and now I'm studying Passover. Guess I haven't gotten to this one yet."

"Are you Christian?" the woman asked, standing on tiptoe to see if there was any chance of getting past the mob anytime soon.

"Yes, I am. Why?"

"Because you're probably more familiar with the term *Pentecost*."

"Oh, of course!" exclaimed Carrie. "Pentecost was fifty days after Passover, right?"

"Right. And we Christians celebrate Shavuot because of the outpouring of the Holy Spirit in the Upper Room as the followers of Jesus waited in Jerusalem as He had told them to do after His resurrection. Pentecost is considered the birthday of the Church."

"But what about...."

The Gentile and the Jew: A Divine Romance

"Hey Bill! Wait for me!" The friendly woman yelled at a man waving at her from the entrance to Christ Church and was gone before Carrie could finish her question.

I can't believe this, thought Carrie. *I'm in Jerusalem on Pentecost!*

Inching her way through the Armenian Quarter, moving only when the mob moved, Carrie tried to recall what she had read about Pentecost, remembering vividly the Bible stories of her childhood. She recalled the mystifying tongues of fire that came from Heaven and sat on the heads of the one hundred and twenty believers in the Upper Room, and she remembered the thousands who came to believe in Jesus that day and the miracles that followed. By the time she got to Zion Gate, she was caught up in the excitement of the large crowd, convinced that her being in Jerusalem on Pentecost was certainly not coincidence.

In an instant, she canceled her plan to spend the day shopping in the Cardo and hurried out the arched Gate, turning back briefly to stare at the ancient passageway riddled with bullet holes from the 1948 war. Stopping only once to ask unneeded directions to the traditional site of the Upper Room, she weaved in and out of the large mass of people, moving more quickly than most, being a lone pilgrim in the midst of large church groups slowly making their way to the building. Up she climbed over rocks where Levana had told her Jesus was sure to have walked, this misnamed western hill of Zion being outside the restored city walls.

Finally, she edged through the masses waiting to enter the large open room that had been built over the tomb of King David and more than likely, the original Upper Room. Aron had told her there had been more than one Messianic congregation on this ground through the centuries. Normally, the jostling crowds would have taken away from any spiritual significance she might have experienced, but Carrie knew in her heart that she was meant to be in this room on this particular day during this two-thousand-year-old celebration. She found a fairly vacant spot in a corner and planted herself there, listening intently to the various Christian leaders reading from the Book of Acts, reminding their congregations of the site's significance in the history of the Church. Her mind wandered from their words to the thoughts and feelings flowing through her mind and heart.

"This room or the one under it is very likely the site of the Passover meal Jesus ate with His disciples the night before He was crucified," the speaker was saying. "This is where He told them He would die, where He explained the New Covenant, where He washed their feet and where He revealed the one who would betray Him."

Chapter Sixteen

Strangely enough in such a packed crowd, silence followed the Pastor's statement, the kind of silence that seems filled with action, movement you can sense but not see or hear. Carrie caught her breath, her eyes filling with tears she didn't even try to explain, not even to herself. She knew that others were weeping, too. She didn't have to see them to know.

Out of the silence someone began to softly sing,

> *Amazing grace, how sweet the sound,*
> *That saved a wretch like me.*

All over the large cathedral-like room, people began to join in, a few at the time, sometimes just one, until the room was filled with the sweet harmony of the cherished profession of faith,

> *I once was lost, but now I'm found.*
> *Was blind, but now I see.*[21]

On and on, the song continued its crescendo until the roof seemed to lift so the simple melody and heartfelt words could ascend into the Heavens to find their place in worship at the very Throne of God. Carrie slid down the cool wall in the corner, her head lifted as she sat on the cold stone floor, softly weeping and joining her voice with the believers assembled there in the Upper Room. Something awesome was happening, and she was wise enough not to analyze it.

There must have been hundreds in the room singing the familiar old hymn, worshiping the Jewish Messiah, King of Kings and Lord of Lords. But there seemed to be another sound more harmonious than anything she had ever heard filling every recess of the room, above the people yet somehow among them, too. *Are the angels joining in?* she wondered as chills coursed through her body. Tears were pouring down Carrie's cheeks, her hands folded under her chin like a child at prayer.

"Oh, Father," she whispered, "you have forgiven me so much. I have no hope on my own. I need a Savior. You sent Your blameless Son into the world as the sacrifice for my sin so that I can live forgiven and free from this bitterness. Even so, I forgive Mike, Father, as You have forgiven me. Thank You, Father! Thank You for Yeshua, my Hope, and the Hope of Israel."

The Gentile and the Jew: A Divine Romance

Around six o'clock that evening, they were walking through Jaffa Gate into the plaza where Mike had stood transfixed his first day in Jerusalem, making their way through the crowds to his favorite restaurant in the Old City, the Armenian Tavern. Mike hadn't asked her what had happened earlier that day, but he could tell something was different. Throughout the week, he had watched her painful struggle, knowing that he had taken a great risk in choosing to tell her about Annie. But, as the healing hours gradually ticked away, he was more amazed than ever at the power of right choices. Somehow, Carrie had come to a place of acceptance and forgiveness. And miraculously, from Mike's right choice and her forgiveness, a deeper love had developed than they had ever known.

He was thrilled to see Carrie smiling once again, but there was something else, something more.... Peace, that's what it was. Peace pervaded her, contrasting drastically with the agony he had watched her endure over the past week. *Who knows? Perhaps if your heart is open when you come to Jerusalem, peace will find you,* Mike reasoned to himself.

He held her arm tightly so as not to lose her in what seemed like biblical multitudes. She had a habit of glimpsing something that caught her attention and just wandering off to look at it, not realizing she could get caught in one of those waves of humanity and end up lost before she knew it.

"Come on, hon, I'm hungry. We can ramble around after dinner."

"Okay, but I still haven't shopped for my family. After dinner, I'd like to browse those little shops across the plaza just past the Money Changer if they're still open."

"Sure. If not tonight, we'll go there tomorrow. You still have a couple more days. I've been there before. Those guys are very friendly, not pushy. They have nice things."

"Mike, why did you want me to skip lunch and have dinner so early?" Carrie asked as he led her down the less traveled path.

"Because I have a surprise for you, and we have to get there before twilight," he answered, smiling mysteriously.

Melodious Armenian music greeted the American couple as they entered the little tavern through its old wooden door, looking down into the seating area from the top of a stairway. The place was packed—men, women and children seated at round and rectangular wooden tables closely placed on the Jerusalem stone floor. All around the room, colorful Armenian mosaics were encased in the brick and stone walls, the ancient Armenian presence in Jerusalem creating a cozy and unique atmosphere for visitors and locals alike.

Chapter Sixteen

"Hmm...smells wonderful!" Carrie exclaimed, delighted at the warmth of the quaint little restaurant.

"You just wait," said Mike, smiling and taking her arm as the waiter led them to their table in a nice cozy corner by one of the splendid mosaics.

"It's a good thing we're doing so much walking," said Carrie, looking over the menu. "After eating all this scrumptious food, I'd be rolling if I were back at the University studying and working at the computer day after day."

"I know what you mean. I haven't ordered anything I didn't like yet."

"That's because you order lamb every time!" Carrie teased. "Hm...this is great, Mike. This menu only offers four entrees, so you won't have to wait all night for me to make up my mind. I'll take the Jerusalem Mixed Grill, this luscious-sounding chicken dish. What are you going to order?"

Mike smiled sheepishly. "Shishlik," he mumbled.

"Oh, you! Lamb again?" Carrie smiled, her bright eyes laughing as she teased him.

"You just can't beat Middle Eastern lamb," said Mike. "Anyhow, there are chicken houses all over eastern North Carolina, dear one. You can get chicken any time."

"Not like this, I'll bet," she answered.

"You have a point."

They had eaten the mouthwatering lamb and chicken entrees and were finishing up with Paklava and coffee when the Armenian music began to slowly liven up, unnoticeable at first but, suddenly, all over the room, diners began to clap their hands. Some even sang with the music, more of a *"lai, lai, lai"* song than real words. But they could have been real words as far as Carrie could tell, Armenian being one of the last languages on earth she would have ever thought her southeastern North Carolina ears would hear.

The cheerful music and joyful zest of the Armenians was contagious. Other diners, along with Carrie and Mike, began to join the merrymaking, clapping and "lai lai-ing" along with the best of them. In no time at all, some of the men, young and old alike, got up from the tables and started dancing around the crowded room, gradually creating a circle as some of the more timid ones joined the lively group. Everyone was laughing and smiling and rejoicing as if something wonderful had just happened. The next thing she knew, Mike was on his feet, grabbing the hand of an elderly Armenian, dancing and singing to the top of his voice.

Talk about changing! Carrie could hardly believe her eyes. Mike had been adventurous, but not like this! He had always exuded an air of sophistication that had revealed itself more clearly when they visited the Kramer home last

The Gentile and the Jew: A Divine Romance

November. Coming from homey, rural America, she had admired his worldly sophistication, often hoping some of it would rub off on her, but now, well...now, she was seeing an altogether different side of the man she loved. She wondered if there were more facets in his character she had yet to discover.

The music finally stopped, according to Mike in his exhausted state. He made his way through the crowded room back to their table to say, "Let's go, hon. I need some air!"

Holding hands as they walked back up the Armenian Patriarchate Road to Jaffa Gate, Carrie asked suspiciously, "Where did you say we're going?"

"I didn't, nosey girl. I want to surprise you."

Quickly tramping from the western gate down what Mike called "The Ramp Road," they found the Jeep, and within minutes, Mike was zooming through the crowded streets so fast Carrie lost track of her newly-gained sense of direction. They were riding the little red Jeep like a bucking bronco, down into the Kidron Valley and up the other side when she finally realized they were headed up the Mount of Olives. All she could think about was that she hadn't yet been to Gethsemane. Surely, Mike wouldn't be taking her there this late in the evening.

He suddenly pulled off the side of the road onto a gravel parking area. "Don't turn around," he said quickly, gazing at whatever it was that he didn't want her to see quite yet. "Just look up the hill or at me for a few more minutes."

"Well, looking at you won't be hard at all, handsome fellow that you are," she said with that familiar twinkle in her sparkling eyes.

"Don't embarrass me, Carrie, this is serious business," teased Mike.

She continued to gaze at him, studying each facial feature as if she had never seen him before, suddenly remembering she would be leaving in just a few more days, not to see him again for another three long months. It seemed that every time their relationship took a giant step in the right direction, they had to part again. Carrie looked somber then, and sad, but before he had time to wonder why, Mike said, "I want you to close your eyes and come with me. Don't open them until I say so, okay?"

"Okay, but how am I going to get out of the Jeep?"

"This way," he said, lifting her in his arms and swinging her over the side. He decided he might as well carry her the rest of the way and not run the risk of her tripping on the rocks with her eyes closed. Furthermore, she felt good in his arms, and he didn't want to put her down.

Eyes still closed, Carrie felt Mike place her on something that felt like a huge rock, still holding her tightly to keep her from falling.

Chapter Sixteen

"Are you cold?" he asked gently. Jerusalem was often cold at night even if the temperature was high during the day.

"A little."

"Here." He took off his lightweight parka and placed it about her shoulders. For a few moments, he forgot what they were doing on the hillside and stared at Carrie's face, tracing his fingers over her forehead, across her closed eyes and down her upturned nose, resting them on her parted lips. He could feel her warm breath, his heart pounding as he leaned forward, his lips finally meeting hers with a hunger that couldn't be quenched.

When he opened his eyes again, twilight had fallen. "Okay, open your eyes," he whispered, gently turning her face toward the west.

"Oh...Mike!" she gasped.

She had no idea how long they sat there on the hillside east of Jerusalem. She sat in front of him on the big boulder locked in his warm embrace, his face touching hers as they watched the twilight miracle. The Holy city began to glow in its golden light. The glow that came now at twilight was something more than flood lights. It seemed as if light came from deep within the ancient stones, or maybe from an altogether deeper realm than that of stones and clay and men.

Mike was happier than he had ever been in his life. He knew Carrie was seeing what he was seeing even if neither of them quite understood what it was. And he was satisfied...satisfied that everything was going to be all right.

"The sages of old believed that Jerusalem is the center of the earth, its navel," he whispered into her ear.

"Maybe it is. I certainly wouldn't be surprised."

"Yeah, I know...Carrie?"

"Hmm?"

"Do you love me?"

"You know I love you," she whispered, squirming a little to sink deeper in his embrace.

"I love you, too."

"I know."

The thick quietness enveloped them, the atmosphere waxing even more surreal as time stopped and love took over.

"Carrie?"

"Hm?"

"Will you marry me?"

The Gentile and the Jew: A Divine Romance

If Mike's arms hadn't been locked around her slender body, Carrie would have fallen down the steep hillside into the Kidron Valley below. Instead, she turned her eyes within inches of his and whispered, "What did you say?"

"I said, 'Will you marry me?'"

She was stunned, her eyes as big as saucers, her mouth wide open. Mike could tell that those beautiful ocean eyes were about to start leaking once again as she continued to gaze into his dark eyes.

"Well? Are you going to give me an answer?" He leaned forward the couple of inches that separated their lips to give her a soft kiss, moving slowly to her ear and then down to the base of her smooth neck. "Your neck is like an ivory tower," he whispered the words from the Song of Songs.

"Ohhh...of course, I will. I mean, I do. Oh, whatever it is you're supposed to say," she moaned.

"What about 'yes'?"

"Oh...YES!" she shouted, loud enough to wake the dead in the zillions of graves on the ancient hillside, her own mind suddenly waking to the reality that she had been proposed to by the man of her dreams in about the most awesome setting in the entire world. As his lips reached hers again for a kiss that seemed to be infinite, she could feel him placing something on the third finger of her left hand. When their lips finally parted, she looked down to see a brilliant emerald-shaped diamond on her slender finger. She gasped loudly, staring at the precious gem, sparkling even in the moonlight as Mike laughed and said, "Didn't you know Jerusalem of Gold is the diamond capital of the world?"

Chapter Seventeen

The flight attendant came down the aisle checking to see if each passenger aboard the El Al flight was ready for landing, seat belts buckled, trays put up and electronic equipment shut down and put away.

"We're preparing to land, Mr. and Mrs. Kramer. Are you all right?"

"Yes, thank you," Rachel replied. "Where are we exactly?"

"We'll start descending now, Mrs. Kramer. We'll be circling Tel Aviv in just a few minutes. You should be able to see the city out your window as we come into Ben Gurion Airport." The attendant smiled and crossed over to her seat to prepare herself for landing.

Rachel leaned over her sleepy husband, wishing now that she had taken the window seat when they boarded the huge aircraft. She was always in a dilemma when she got on an airplane, boarding pass in hand, pulling her carry-on bag through the narrow passageway, and wishing she had packed lighter. Isaac didn't see it as a dilemma, but as the script for a Broadway show that had been playing for years. After studying their passes to see which two seats they were assigned, Isaac would say, "All right, love, which seat do you want—aisle or window?"

He had to admit that if the plane was a big one with five seats in the middle section, and IF they were assigned the middle seats, the situation didn't become quite as complicated. But, most of the time his usually pre-organized wife would answer, "Oh, I don't know, Isaac. If I take the window seat, I can see the lovely countryside when we take off and land, but I can't get out easily

225

to go to the bathroom in an emergency. But, if I take the aisle seat, I can't see out the window very well. But then, what if I were to get really sick and had to throw up but was sitting beside the window all blocked in? I could throw up all over your nice suit, Isaac."

Then, Isaac would say, "Rachel, that's what they have those little bags for—to vomit in if you get motion sickness. They've had them for years and years on every plane we've ever flown in."

"Oh, Isaac, I couldn't throw up in a little bag! What if I missed the bag and had to call the attendant? Oh, it would be so humiliating!"

By this time, Isaac's impatient lines were written in stone, "Rachel, there are people waiting to find their seats. You're blocking traffic and possibly even holding up take-off. Airlines do have schedules you know!"

The play's finale always ended with Rachel's last words, "You decide, Isaac. You know it's too hard for me to choose."

And very quickly, Isaac would inevitably make the wrong choice.

"Isaac, wake up! Look! We're flying over Tel Aviv and the Mediterranean Sea!" Rachel whispered loudly, shaking her drowsy husband's arm.

Isaac lifted his head and looked out the window, Rachel almost in his lap by now, and together, they saw the land of Israel for the first time. The plane was low over the city, giving them a clear view of what could easily have been any modern coastal community in America, the city of Tel Aviv having only been in existence since the fifties. But, this wasn't just any city in America. This was Israel and they were *home* for the first time in their lives.

Isaac and Rachel continued to peer out the small window, the new city and its harbors spreading out into the magnificent Mediterranean, looking as if millions of diamonds were bouncing off its incredible blue waters. Rachel was still leaning on Isaac when the pilot said, "Thank you for flying El Al. We hope you enjoy your stay in Eretz Israel."

Carrie was happily flipping her hand from side-to-side, watching the glittering diamond catch the light coming from the hotel window as she waited impatiently for the overseas operator to connect her to the Jernigan home in eastern North Carolina.

"Mama?"

"Carrie! Oh, sugar, we've been hoping you would call soon. How are you? Is everything all right?"

226

Chapter Seventeen

"Yes, Mama. Being in Israel is unreal, but absolutely wonderful! We're having a great time. Mike has taken me to see most all the places we've read about in the Bible—Jerusalem, the Sea of Galilee, Nazareth, the Jordan River. Can you believe it, Mama? I stood on the Mount of Beatitudes where Jesus fed the multitudes!"

"I'm so happy for you, sugar. Maybe someday your Daddy and I will go. But, be careful, Carrie. I worry about you being there in the middle of all those terrorist attacks."

"Don't worry, Mama, I'm fine. Things have been fairly quiet since I arrived. Mama, I have something very important to tell you. Could you get Daddy on the phone?"

"Of course. He's already standing here waiting to cut in."

"Wait! Wait, Mama! Run to the bedroom and pick up the other phone. I'll talk to Daddy while you get there."

"Hey, baby girl. Seen any camels?"

Tom heard his little girl laughing. "Not only have I seen camels, I've ridden one!"

"No way!"

Catherine interjected from the bedroom. "I'm here, sugar. Go ahead and tell us your news,"

"Mama...Daddy...Mike asked me to marry him last night. I said, 'yes.'"

Silence.

"I'm outrageously happy! Mike proposed on the Mount of Olives. Can you believe it? We were looking at Jerusalem across the valley as the sun went down, and the Old City turned all gold and...."

"Carrie! Hold on a minute! We're shocked, to say the least, honey. You told us that you and Mike were back together in January, and we realized you were getting serious, but we had no idea things were moving quite this fast," said Tom.

"Your Daddy's right, Carrie. Are you sure you aren't rushing this relationship?" asked Catherine. "What about your religious differences? Are they resolved?"

"I understand your concerns. I really do. And I know you think our whole dating experience has been a little unusual—three months falling in love, then six weeks apart, then by the time we got back together, Mike was off to Israel. But from January until now, we have been constantly communicating, talking about everything. And, I mean *everything*! Oh, I'm sure, Mama...Daddy. I love him so much, and now I'm totally convinced that he loves me just as much. I just wish you were here so I could tell you about the past few weeks. But for now, please bless our engagement, you guys. You just have to."

"Well, it won't be easy for you; no marriage ever is. But we trust you've prayed about this long and hard, knowing it's the most important decision of your life. But, don't rush it, sugar. Please. Don't set a date too soon." Catherine was beginning to cry as Tom cut in.

"I'm not sure I can bear to give my little girl away." Carrie could hear his voice breaking.

Tom's little girl's eyes filled with tears as she softly replied, "I'll always love you to the last number, Daddy."

The party was in full swing. Levana Safron looked extraordinarily beautiful tonight, according to her husband. She was doing her thing to her heart's content and doing it well, flowing in and out among her guests with the ease of a ballerina in her prime. Aron greeted their guests at the door and mingled with the interesting accumulation of people crowded into their west Jerusalem flat. Every now and then, he caught Levana as she twirled by, giving her a quick hug and admiring smile. Dressed in a long flowing dress the color of dark purple irises, her bronze skin glowing, Levana moved graciously among her guests serving drinks and passing trays of her tantalizing Middle Eastern cuisine.

"Can't you be still a few minutes?" Aron caught her around the waist this time. "You don't have to work so hard. I'll help you serve."

"I'm having a ball, dear one! Haven't you noticed I can serve, talk, smile and hug all at the same time?"

"Actually, I have noticed that." Aron laughed, giving her a quick kiss as she slipped out of his arms and swept across the room to chat with Mike and Carrie, the guests of honor.

"Levana, the party is absolutely wonderful! Thank you so much for all you've done." Carrie's blue-green eyes sparkled with happiness, her arm linked through her new fiancé's. Everything was wonderful to Carrie tonight, beginning with Mike's obvious admiration of the striking turquoise dress Levana had helped her choose in a delightful little shoppe on Ben Yehuda Street. They had even bought jewelry to match, the turquoise stones and silver looking much like the jewelry Native Americans create so beautifully.

"Yes," agreed Mike, "you and Aron have gone above and beyond the call of duty. The food is incredible as usual and...."

"And you've made everything so beautiful!" Carrie interjected.

Chapter Seventeen

"Todah Rabah," said Levana, thanking them in Hebrew. "Throwing parties is my 'cup of tea' as you Americans say. I particularly enjoy bringing diverse people together. It's so much fun to gather all kinds of people into one room and watch what happens." Levana laughed and whirled off again, her silver anklet jingling as she went.

"I'm amazed you've met so many people in such a short time," Carrie said as Mike offered her a bite of the mysterious morsel he had taken off Levana's tray.

"Mmm...good!" said Carrie, munching the spicy canapé.

"Yeah, you're right, hon. I've met a lot of great people here in Israel. Some have become especially good friends, like the Safrons and Salim Ahmed and his wife and kids."

Mike glanced around the crowded room, quickly spotting Becca Brody talking with Salim's wife, Jerra. He grinned broadly watching Becca, the extrovert, chattering away while quiet little Jerra listened attentively, probably amazed that a woman could say so much at one time.

Other new acquaintances were there as well, among them Ari and Miriam Sadler and Miriam's mother, Rivka, whom he and Becca had befriended while interviewing Israeli women for their assignment. *Man, that Rivka really has a story to tell*, he thought now, almost pushing Carrie across the room to meet his new friends.

"Thank you for coming," said Mike as he shook Ari's hand and smiled at the two women.

"Shalom," said Ari, happy to see his new friend. "I assume this is your lovely betrothed?"

"Yes, this is my Carrie," replied Mike, wrapping his arm around Carrie's shoulders and giving her a quick squeeze. "Honey, these are my friends, Ari, Miriam, and Rivka."

"It's so good to meet you. Mike has told me a little about all of you, and I've looked forward to getting to know you as well. Should I say 'shalom' now?"

Ari laughed and said, "Always. You can say, 'Shalom,' anytime in Israel. We always need shalom." Ari was teasing, but Carrie sensed he was very serious in his plea for peace.

Feeling a tap on his shoulder, Mike turned around, surprised to see Daniel Silverman, editor of the news magazine he and Becca were working for.

"Hey, man!" Mike exclaimed, reaching out to shake Daniel's outstretched hand. "What a surprise! What are you doing here?"

"Oh, I come to Israel fairly often," Daniel replied with a smile, "particularly when I need to check up on our journalists."

The Gentile and the Jew: A Divine Romance

"Uh, oh," said Mike, laughing. "What's Becca done now?"

"What kind of question is that, Mike Kramer? Whose side are you on?" Becca Brody had slipped up behind Mike, overhearing the conversation.

"The boss's side, of course," teased Mike, ruffling her short blonde hair.

"Well, the boss wants to meet your lovely fiancé. Can that be arranged?" asked Daniel.

"Of course! Daniel Silverman, I'm very pleased to present the beautiful love of my life, Carrie Jernigan." Mike's adoring eyes were glued to her radiant face as she smiled and held her hand out to Daniel. He graciously bowed to lightly kiss her hand, tickling her skin with the short beard he wore with such dignity.

"So, you're the villain who sent my guy four thousand miles away from me?"

"Oh, no, my dear. That was Becca." Daniel smiled, quickly raising his arms to block Becca's impending punch.

"What is this, blame Becca day?" she asked, pretending to be furious at Daniel and Mike.

"Now, what would we do without you to tease, my dear Rebecca?" replied her beloved boss. "Actually, if my memory serves me correctly, you're the one usually teasing us!"

"Imagine that," she responded with a sly smile.

"Carrie, my dear, how are you handling this wild woman?" asked Daniel.

"Oh, I'll have to say she's been really great so far, but I'm sure she has a few quirks I'll have to get used to." She smiled at Becca, appreciating the wild woman's gregarity.

Carrie had to admit that Becca Brody had truly gone all out for her since she arrived in Israel nearly two weeks ago, quickly dispelling any floundering worries she had about Mike and Becca working so closely together for six long months. The day Becca and Levana Safron hauled her off to one of the wonderful spas at the Dead Sea had been more fun than she could have imagined. Watching the two strikingly beautiful opposites mopped in black mud from head to toe and laughing hilariously was a sight she would long remember. But the other women in the spa saw three beauties, Carrie's soft brown hair and blue-green eyes contrasting sharply with lively blonde Becca and dark, mysterious Levana. *Yes, Becca and I will get along just fine,* she thought, as Mike led her off to meet more of his new friends.

Chapter Seventeen

"Isaac? Are you awake?" Rachel whispered, hoping her exhausted husband would say something, but trying not to disturb him if he was still asleep.

"I am now," he answered, turning over onto his back to find his lovely wife all dressed and ready to go down to breakfast. "I can't believe you're already up. What time is it?"

"It's eight o'clock. Time to go find Mike. I can't wait to see his face when we surprise him. Come on, lazy bones!"

"Ohhh," groaned Isaac. "We're getting too old for these around-the-world adventures."

"Speak for yourself, dear. I'm not old."

"Certainly not, my love. You just married an old man."

"A very handsome old man, I assure you." Rachel reached up to give her husband a quick kiss and then pushed him into the bathroom.

While Isaac went through his morning routine, Rachel sat in the comfortable chair beside the window overlooking Jerusalem, hardly able to believe she was actually here in the ancient city of her forefathers. They had chosen the King David Hotel just because it was the only one they had heard of and because Rachel loved the name. But, this morning she had discovered it was an excellent venue, considering its close proximity to the Old City and the sights of west Jerusalem as well.

Jerusalem! I can't believe it, she thought, wondering if she should pinch herself to see if she were dreaming. The old synagogue in Bucharest had seemed like home, but not like this. This was truly home.

Yerushalayim, the Hebrew pronunciation rolled over her tongue easily. She felt as if she were Esther or Sarah or maybe Miriam, finally coming home to the city each had only envisioned with a longing heart. What she wouldn't have given for her mother and father to be sitting here with her today. She could almost hear her father speaking in his unique mixture of English, Hebrew, Yiddish and Romanian, "Next year in Jerusalem!"

"Come on, Rachel, let's go!" Isaac's call severed her precious daydream.

"All right. I'm ready. Do you remember how cold it was in Bucharest, darling? At least we'll have nice weather for this adventure."

"How could I forget? I don't think I've ever been so cold, not even when we lived in New York."

Rachel's auburn hair was shining in the light from the window as Isaac took her hand to pull her up and give her a hug to start the day off right. It was a part of his newfound determination to be more attentive and loving since their journey to Romania last December, realizing from their probe into the past that he only had a limited amount of time on earth with this beautiful treasure he

231

called, "wife." Wrapping his arms around her, he pulled her close and gazed into her amazing green eyes.

"I love you, my love," he said softly.

"I love you, too," she replied as his lips met hers.

"Hmm. We'd better get out of here," said Rachel, smiling as she pushed him toward the door.

"All right, all right. I'm going."

Isaac grabbed his wallet and cell phone, and off they went to enjoy the lovely breakfast buffet in the hotel restaurant. Minutes later, they were eating kiwi, pineapple, cucumbers, tomatoes, boiled eggs and fish, seated at a cloth-covered table by a palm tree in the lovely courtyard. The delicious food and steaming coffee were energizing the jet-lagged couple as they made a list of all the places they wanted to visit, hoping Mike could be with them as much as possible. Of course, their main goal was to meet and get to know Aron Safron, the young Israeli *sabra* Mike had discovered to be his cousin, the grandson of Rachel's Romanian uncle, Joseph Liebovici.

Rachel smiled into space, recalling those fascinating days in Bucharest with Abraham Wasserman, particularly the day he told her about Aron. He had given her a ray of hope that at least one member of her lost family was alive and well, living in Israel.

"Isaac, I don't think I can wait to meet Aron until after we've toured Jerusalem. I won't be able to enjoy the Old City thinking about my family being so close by after all these years." Rachel looked up at her husband and laughed. "Did you hear what I said? I said '*my family*'! Can you believe it? After all these years, I can finally say, '*my family*'!"

Isaac smiled at his excited wife, enjoying her newfound happiness. He, too, could hardly wait to meet her young cousin.

"First of all, we need to find Mike and see what his schedule is like. I'm sure he can give us an idea of when it would be best to visit Aron and his family. By the way, did Mike ever say if Aron has a family or not?"

"You don't remember? He said Aron has a gorgeous wife. Levana is her name, I think."

"Oh, yes. I remember, she...."

Rachel sipped her coffee, glancing up at Isaac to see why he stopped speaking in the middle of his sentence. He was staring past Rachel, a quizzical expression plastered on his face.

"What is it, Isaac?"

Chapter Seventeen

"Ah, nothing. I thought that girl looked familiar for a second. Isn't it strange how you can travel thousands of miles and bump into someone you know from home?"

"Yes. I think Romania is the only place we've ever been that we didn't see someone we know. Isaac, what is it? You look as if you've seen a ghost."

"Maybe I have," he answered quietly.

"Whose ghost?" asked Rachel, curiosity gaining ground by the second, especially considering Isaac seldom paid any attention to the people around him when in public.

"You'll never believe this, but I think that's the girl Mike brought home last Thanksgiving. What was her name?"

"Candy? No, Carrie—that's her name. No, it can't be. What would she be doing in Israel?"

Isaac just sat there, mute, gazing at a point somewhere beyond Rachel's shoulder. Finally, he began speaking, very slowly, as if in a daze. "Because Mike's here. Right here in this restaurant. He just walked in, and he's leaning over to kiss her."

"What?" whispered Rachel loudly, her stunning green eyes flashing.

Isaac couldn't answer, still staring at the unbelievable sight. His only son was in Jerusalem, not Chapel Hill, North Carolina, having breakfast with the girl they thought he broke up with at least six months ago. Rachel was stunned, so afraid Isaac might be right that she dared not turn around to see for herself.

"What should we do?" he finally asked.

"Don't ask me," said Rachel, sharply. "I'm so angry I could scream! I thought you said everything would be all right? It was just a stage, you said!"

"Me? You're blaming me for this? I'm as shocked as you are, Rachel. How on earth can you blame me?"

"Oh, Isaac, I'm so sorry," she said quickly, tears beginning to fill her green eyes. "It's just that you're supposed to fix everything. You know I always depend on you to fix everything."

He could see she was about to fall apart, so he reached across the table and took her hand in his. "Everything will be all right, Rachel. I promise."

"What should we do?"

"I'm going to walk right over there and say, 'Hello,' to my son, the deceiver." Isaac took a swig of his coffee as if it were a shot of whiskey in a Wild West movie and quickly stood up.

"Well, wait for me," said Rachel, adjusting the collar of her sage green blouse, then fishing her lipstick out of her purse.

"Rachel, this isn't a beauty contest!" scolded Isaac.

The Gentile and the Jew: A Divine Romance

"Yes, but your mother always said one should look nice no matter the circumstances."

"Yeah, she did say that," recalled Isaac, smiling at the fond memory.

"Okay, I'm as ready as I'm going to be," said Rachel.

Isaac took her arm and quickly propelled her across the courtyard. They were standing by the young couple's table before the lovebirds could take their eyes off each other to notice anyone else.

"No, thank you. We don't need anything," said Mike, thinking the waiter had come back.

"Hmph!" Isaac cleared his throat as quietly as possible, trying not to be conspicuous to the other diners.

Mike looked up as if to say something else, but his mouth fell open, and no words came out. Carrie was still gazing adoringly at her beloved until she suddenly realized something was very wrong. Following his gaze, she looked up into the grim faces of Rachel and Isaac Kramer.

"Hello, Mike," said Isaac, stoically.

"We thought we'd surprise you." Rachel's tone was definitely not surprising.

Her son finally regained his composure, replying weakly, "You sure did."

"Yes, we can see that," she quipped.

"Ahhm.... Do you remember Carrie?"

The expression on Rachel's face read, "Vaguely," but she managed to reply with a polite, but distant, "Of course. How are you, my dear?"

Carrie was in shock. This was worse than the Thanksgiving fiasco, but this time she wasn't going to cower in fear and embarrassment. Confident of Mike's love now, she opened her mouth to answer his mother's question, but stopped short when Rachel gasped loudly, both hands flying to her chest as if she were having a heart attack.

Rachel's flashing green eyes were glued to the sparkling diamond on Carrie's left hand, her own right hand creeping up to clutch her throat. Carrie looked to Mike for help, and Isaac, who hadn't seen the diamond, reached out to steady his trembling wife, wondering why the situation had worsened all of a sudden.

"Mom, are you all right?" Mike stood up and grabbed his mother's arm.

Her voice trembling, Rachel almost whispered, "It seems we get the surprise."

"I'm sorry, Mom. I wanted to be with you when I told you about Carrie and me, but there just hasn't been time to do that."

"Well, here we are!" Rachel snapped.

Chapter Seventeen

Still not understanding that his son and the young woman were already engaged, Isaac had begun to realize people were staring at the agitated little group. "Hush, both of you," he whispered. "We're making a scene. Rachel, we're going back to our suite. Mike, I think it would be a good idea for you to go with us. A little chat is in order, don't you think? I'm sure this young lady would be happy to give us a little time with our son, wouldn't you, my dear?"

Rachel was still glaring at the diamond as if she could somehow make it go away. Carrie was trying hard not to cry. What else could she do?

Smiling down at her, Mike placed his hand on Carrie's shoulder, speaking tenderly, "Mom and Dad, I love this beautiful woman with all my heart. I asked Carrie to marry me a few days ago. We're engaged, Dad."

"What!" Isaac glanced from one to the other and then back to Rachel, desperately hoping someone would tell him he hadn't heard correctly.

"She has a ring, Isaac," whispered Rachel, still glaring at the diamond.

Quickly turning to look at Carrie's hand, he joined his wife's seemingly permanent stare for a second or two and then quietly said, "Well then, I believe it would be appropriate for the young lady to join us as well."

The following two hours in his parents' suite were extremely uncomfortable for everyone but nothing short of miserable for Carrie, even though she could tell Mike thought they might be getting somewhere at last. Recognizing the hurt his parents were feeling aside from their anger, he had sincerely apologized for his lack of communication regarding his relationship with Carrie. During the past few months, he had realized that Carrie was right in her assessment of one of his character flaws. He did avoid conflict at all cost, thinking everything would go his way in the end if he could put off confrontation long enough. He had finally admitted that to Carrie one day on the ramparts of the Old City and had asked her forgiveness, again making a strategic choice to amend his foolish ways.

Rachel and Isaac were beginning to calm down, seeing firsthand the change in Mike they had only glimpsed on New Year's Eve. The more they listened to their son while Carrie sat beside him holding his hand, looking one minute as if she adored Mike and the next as if she wanted to jump up and run out of the room, Rachel was sorry she had reacted so terribly in the restaurant even though she had good reason.

Poor girl, thought Rachel guiltily. *She must think we're ogres right out of some horrible fairy tale.* "Carrie, dear, please know we're not angry with you, and please don't take our reaction as a personal affront. We don't even know you."

"I really do understand, Mrs. Kramer," said Carrie. "We haven't exactly had an opportunity to get to know one another."

"No, and that's my fault," admitted Mike, "but we need to get to the deeper issue right now. There hasn't been time to talk with you, of course, but the bottom line is that, unconsciously, I have avoided discussing our relationship with you because I knew you wouldn't approve of my marrying a Gentile. You proved that at Thanksgiving."

"Mike...."

"No, Mom, please wait until I've finished. There are a lot of things I haven't discussed with you guys, and I'm sorry for that."

"Son, you're a twenty-three-year-old young man. You don't have to tell us everything," replied Isaac. "On the other hand, marriage is the most important step of your life. Certainly, it should be discussed with your family."

"I know, Dad, and again, I apologize. But, in the last few months, along with growing to love this wonderful creature with all my heart, I've also been dealing with questions and issues I've neglected throughout my life. For example, I'm learning what it means to be Jewish. I told you guys during New Year's that was one reason I took this job in Israel, remember?"

"Of course, we do." Rachel suddenly recalled the words of Jeremiah the prophet, spoken so profoundly through Abraham Wasserman in Romania. *"Your children shall return,"* he had said. *Could it be now?*

"I'm overwhelmed with what I've learned during these five months, but I'm finally gaining enough wisdom to realize I've only scratched the surface. As I mentioned in one of my letters, I had no idea there were so many different types of Jews, and trying to find where I fit in has been a genuine dilemma for me."

Noting his mother's raised eyebrows, he quickly answered her unspoken question, "No, I haven't quite found my place yet, but I'm convinced I'm on the right path. David's Dad says that if you're searching for truth, you'll find it."

"Mrs. Kramer, Mr. Kramer, I...."

"My name is Rachel, dear, and I would be pleased for you to call me that." She smiled compassionately at the lovely young woman who had hardly said a word in the past two hours. Her heart seemed to be melting toward the girl, and she didn't know why.

"Thank you...Rachel. That's very kind of you." Carrie returned her sincere smile. "I'm sure by now you have some idea of how much I love your son, but I just want you to know that I have never, and will never, try to take Mike away from his Jewish heritage. I am very grateful that God brought me not only a handsome, intelligent, wonderful man, but that he's Jewish as well. I'm proud that he's Jewish." Carrie turned to look into Mike's dark eyes, squeezing his hand a little tighter. "Since I've been here in Jerusalem with Mike, I've been drawn to one Bible passage over and over, especially the day we went to Bethlehem and the night he proposed." Carrie's eyes filled with tears as she softly spoke the familiar words of Ruth, the Moabitess, "'Whither you go, I will go; and whither you lodge I will lodge. Your people shall be my people and your God, my God.'"[22]

As Mike reached out to caress her face, smiling deeply into her eyes filled with waves of tears, Rachel and Isaac suddenly saw what they had missed up until now but so desperately needed to see. Their son had found true love, and they knew that for this they should be eternally grateful. But the fears of a lifetime were etched in Rachel's face as she turned to her husband, his own eyes brimming with tears as he grasped her hand and began to speak.

"Mi Adir al hakol. Hu y'vareykh et he'khatan v'et ha'kalah. He who is supremely mighty, may He bless the Groom and the Bride." But, it would take a lot longer than two hours for Rachel's blessing to be released.

Chapter Eighteen

Catherine was scurrying about the kitchen preparing for Carrie's home-coming when the phone began to ring. She almost decided not to answer it; she just had too much to do today to waste time chatting on the phone. But something checked her and she hurried over to the counter to grab the phone before it stopped ringing. "Hello?"

All she could hear was someone crying, obviously trying to say something though the breathless sobs.

"Who is this?"

"I...I...I'm...so sorry...Mrs. Jernigan."

"Melanie? Is that you, Melanie?"

"Yes," whispered the distraught girl.

"Where are you, dear? And where have you been? I have been trying to get in touch with you for weeks." Catherine's heart was pounding in her ears. She was anxious to hear from the girl but fearful of what she might learn.

"I...I know. And I'm so sorry. I...."

"Melanie, sugar, tell me what's wrong. Would you like to come over? Carrie will be coming in soon, but we could talk while I cook."

"N-n...no. I can't," she sobbed. "I don't want to see anyone."

Catherine's heart dropped to her stomach. "What's wrong, Melanie?" she asked quietly.

"My...my baby...is...dead. I...killed my...b-a...by." Her sobs wracked her entire body.

239

The Gentile and the Jew: A Divine Romance

Catherine closed her eyes tightly and uttered a frantic silent prayer, *O God, help me!* "Melanie, come to my house. You need to be with someone."

"N-n... no, I can't. I ... I have to get to school. Summer school starts tomorrow...and my parents wanted me to get a good head start in college. I... I'm on my way now."

"Oh, sugar, be careful! You shouldn't be driving in this shape."

"I ... I have to, Mrs. Jernigan. I have to get on with my life...but...but...how?" Melanie broke into sobs once again, causing Catherine's heart to feel as if it were being twisted. She listened as the grieving girl tried to gulp back her tears. "It's been...months now. At first, I ... I just kept on going, finishing up my senior year and all the activities surrounding graduation. I graduated with honors, did you know that?"

"Yes, sugar, I heard." Catherine groaned inwardly, knowing that no amount of acclamation was going to help Melanie. She didn't think congratulations were in order right now so she kept silent.

"I...I was okay until vacation started after graduation, and then...all of a sudden, it felt as if there was a huge black hole inside me somewhere and no matter what I do, nothing fills it up. I can't stand it, Mrs. Jernigan! What am I going to do?"

"Melanie, you have to come and talk with me or perhaps one of the other counselors at church; anybody, just talk to someone. We'll pray together," pleaded Catherine.

"N-n...no, I can't."

"Of course, you can, sugar. We love you and what's more, God loves you."

"Oh, no! That's the worst part! He can't love me anymore. Oh, Mrs. Jernigan, I'm going to hell! I just know it!" Melanie was nearly screaming into the phone between her sobs.

"Sugar, no! Don't you let the old devil destroy you like that!"

"You don't get it, Mrs. Jernigan. I destroyed my own baby and thought I was doing the right thing. Now, I will be destroyed, too! And if God doesn't destroy me, this excruciating pain will!" By this time, Melanie sounded as if she were growing weaker, her tone of voice resigned to her fate.

"Yes, you will be destroyed, Melanie, but only if you allow the accuser to destroy you. God is Love, dear child, and Love is forgiveness. And yes, you have done a terrible wrong, but God is with you. He said He will never leave you nor forsake you, remember?"

"Yeah...but...that's just for people who do right."

Chapter Eighteen

"Oh, no. That promise is for all of us. We have all done wrong in so many ways."

"But not as wrong as this, Mrs. Jernigan. I have committed murder," whispered Melanie as if she were afraid someone else would hear.

Catherine paused, but only for a second. "So have I," she said.

"Wha-a...what do you mean? You've never hurt anyone. I know you haven't. And, you've never had an...an...." She couldn't bring herself to say the word.

"An abortion? No, I haven't. But I have committed murder."

Melanie was finally listening. "How?" she asked cautiously.

"I hated someone in my past; hated him so badly I wanted him dead at times. Of course, I didn't acknowledge that, even to myself. But it was true nevertheless. And then one day when I was a young woman, I was reading my Bible and came across a passage where Jesus says that hate is the same as murder. I can't tell you how shocked I was. Like you, I had no idea I had done something so horrible, so ungodly."

"What did you do?" whispered Melanie, a little hope finally sounding in her voice.

"I faced the truth. I was a murderer and the sentence was death. But I also had an advocate to take my case, sugar. And the marvelous thing was that my advocate had already served my sentence. It's sort of like double jeopardy, I guess. I committed murder. Jesus was served the death sentence and died in my place. Now, I am free. Do you see?"

"I'm not sure." Melanie's breathing was slowing down and her voice was a little stronger. "It doesn't seem fair."

"No, it doesn't," replied Catherine, a smile forming on her face for the first time since she answered the phone. "But it's God's way. It's Love's way and God is Love."

"But...but, this black hole is still in my heart and the fact remains that I'm the one who did this terrible thing and my baby will never have a life on earth because of me." Catherine could hear the sobs again. "Oh, God!" Melanie cried out. "I was the mother and I was supposed to take care of my baby and protect her and I killed her instead! Oh, God...oh, God!"

"You're crying out to the right One, sugar; just keep crying out to Him. And yes, you're right. We will experience the consequences of our wrongs to a point, but not forever. And, too, He will take even this terrible wrong and use it for your good and for His Glory in the world around you. Just wait and see."

Melanie's sobs subsided once more. Her breathing became more regular.

"Melanie?"

"Yes," she whispered.

"Did I hear you say your baby was a *her*, a little girl?"

The answer was almost inaudible. "Yes."

"What is her name?"

"What? What do you mean?"

"Every child needs a name," replied Catherine.

"I never thought about naming the baby. I never even thought much about it being a girl. I guess I assumed it didn't matter now that the baby didn't exist."

"Well, do it, because she does exist. Give her a beautiful name with a good meaning that God Himself will show you. Go out and buy one of those name books at a bookstore, a good one, and ask our Father to show you her name. Go before your Father in heaven and tell Him all the things you have said to me today. Then, receive His forgiveness, Melanie, not because you deserve it, but because He Himself said that if we confess our sins before Him, He will be faithful to forgive us because He loves us unconditionally."

"Well...I don't know, but...okay, if...if you say so. I'll try." Melanie sighed deeply and Catherine sensed it was the first deep breath she had taken in a very long time. Promising to visit Catherine during her first college break and to call once a week, she said good-bye with a very weak but genuine, "Thank you, Mrs. Jernigan."

Catherine hung up the phone and wiped the tears from her eyes. Oh, if she could just hear of a baby who had been saved.

Catherine was watching out the window as Carrie drove her little blue Saturn onto the asphalt driveway and parked beside the sidewalk leading to the front porch of the white framed house. Tom was at work, calling nearly every thirty minutes to find out if she had arrived yet. They didn't know much, certainly no details of what had transpired in Israel before or since Carrie had called to announce her engagement. But, they were concerned from the tone of their daughter's voice when she phoned about three hours ago to let them know she was driving home from the airport. Of course, she was tired. Maybe that's all it was.

The front door was left standing open as Catherine rushed out to greet her youngest child. Carrie opened the door and slowly got out of the car. Tired and overcome from jet lag, she didn't notice her mother waiting on the porch until she had opened the trunk to retrieve her bags, pausing briefly to close her eyes and take a deep breath. The heady scent of gardenias drifted on the early summer breeze. Hit hard with a wave of homecoming nostalgia, she smiled at the thought of the magnolia blossoms already transforming into new growth on the gigantic tree in the backyard, reminding her of the day so long ago when she and Michele and John had lovingly carried the magic red seeds home from Aunt Verdie's and planted them in the ground with great care and excitement. No one except the three little gardeners had believed anything would ever come of that handful of seeds.

Catherine couldn't wait another second, bouncing down the steps and around the little car with arms opened wide. "Welcome home, sugar!"

"Mama!" She dropped her bags and fled into her mother's loving embrace. "Ohhhh, I'm so happy to be home!" She was too tired to cry and too tired to talk, so she just stood there wrapped in her mother's arms, resting her head on her shoulder. Sometimes, she wished she could stay in a safe place like that forever.

Finally, Catherine leaned back and lifted Carrie's face to hers. "Hm hm," she said knowingly. "Just as I thought. You need a long hot bath, some good country food, and about twelve hours sleep. Then we'll talk."

Carrie nodded, amazed as always at her mother's sensitivity to her present state of mind and body. *How does she do that?*

"Leave the heavy luggage for Daddy, sugar. You go on and call him, so he'll know you're safe and sound while I fix you a plate of fresh out-of-the-garden vegetables. We have string beans, squash and cucumbers."

"Mmmm! I was going to say I'm not hungry, but I've changed my mind. Any fried chicken to go with all that?"

"Of course. And rice and gravy, too. Whoops! We're too late. The phone's ringing. Go talk to your Daddy, sugar."

Utterly exhausted, Carrie had literally fallen into her old bed around seven in the evening, barely remembering the tight hug her Daddy gave her when he came home from work. Wondering if it was possible to lie in one position all night without moving, she squinted at the clock, surprised to see that it was only eight in the morning. She felt like she had slept for days.

Propping up on the pillows, her eyes roamed about the cozy bedroom where she and Michele had spent many happy hours in their childhood and teenage years. Carrie smiled and chuckled aloud as the memories paraded before her. Michele was four years older and sometimes not too thrilled to have her baby sister for a roommate, but most of the time they enjoyed one another's company, laughing and carrying on all hours of the night. *Oh, if these walls could talk!*

Before she could manage to push back the covers and swing her legs off the bed, there was a soft rap on the door and then a whisper, "Carrie? Carrie? Are you awake?"

"How do you do that, Mama?" She was wide awake now.

"Do what?" asked Catherine as she pushed the door open with one hand, carrying a hot mug of coffee in the other.

"How do you know the minute I wake up?"

"I hear you."

"No, you don't. I hadn't even turned over but once."

"Well, I heard that."

"Oh, forget it. We've always thought you had some sixth sense anyway."

"Don't you say that, Carrie Jernigan! Why don't we just rack it up to old age?"

"But you're not old!"

"I'm older than you."

"Okay, Mama. I give up. Mmm! Thanks for the coffee."

"You're welcome. Now, what about breakfast?"

"How can you ask me that after the feast I ate last night?"

"That was over twelve hours ago, young lady. You need some nourishment, but I'll have to say you look much improved since Christmas."

"You should have seen me eat in Israel. Every time I turned around we were eating Falafals, kabobs, flat bread, the most delicious watermelon and mangos you've ever tasted, chicken, rice.... Oh! I'm getting hungry just thinking about it."

"Well, get on up and dress while I make you an omelet with toast and grits. Just cheese?"

"Yep. Just cheese."

"Michele called. She's coming by around noon. Can't wait to hear all about Israel."

"I'll bet! She just wants to hear all the intimate details and see my.... Oh, no! I forgot to show you and Daddy my ring!"

Rachel couldn't think of a better word to describe this long-awaited day than *glorious*. Flooded with sunshine and excitement, it was the day she was going to meet the family she had yearned for all the days of her life. She was

Chapter Eighteen

grateful for the hour's ride up the coast, giving her ample time to reflect and prepare for what she expected would be an emotion-packed meeting with Sura Liebowitz Safron and her family. Mike had kept quiet about Sura's existence until yesterday, planning to surprise his mother with more than one relative, a closer one at that. But as the day for their meeting quickly approached, he had begun to worry that the surprise would be too much of a shock, so he had told her. Rachel was well prepared now, as prepared as one could possibly be for something like this.

Rachel had begged Isaac to rent a car for the journey, privately telling him she couldn't possibly handle bouncing in that little red Jeep for over an hour. Now, Isaac and Mike were discussing the morning headlines in the Jerusalem Post while she sat quietly in the back seat enjoying glimpses of the deep blue Mediterranean as they rode by, smiling at the rolling Sea and the beguiling strangers walking the beaches and those fishing from the gigantic flat rocks.

Sura...what a lovely name, thought Rachel. She wondered what it meant— something precious, of course. What would she look like? What would they say to each other? Would they have anything in common? So many questions raced through her mind.

Rachel was well aware that she had lived her entire life reaping the freedom and prosperity only America can offer. Her parents were almost penniless when they arrived in the land of the free, even though she barely remembered the early days in Brooklyn when her mother worked as a maid for a wealthy family, taking her daughter with her to the elegant Brownstone as often as her employer would allow. But her Papa had worked hard building up his bakery business, eventually expanding the small shop to include a kosher delicatessen and news stand. It wasn't long before the successful combination drew in enough business to open another shop a few streets over, enabling her mother to quit working and stay home to take care of Rachel and her baby brother, Joseph.

Oy vey, she exclaimed silently, surprised that she had fallen back into the familiar Yiddish of her childhood. *I can't go there...not today. No, back to Sura.* What kind of life had she led growing up in Israel after the War? Had her mother made her lovely dresses to wear to birthday parties? Had she gone to dances with boys dressed up in Madras, button-down collar shirts and tan pants with Bass loafers shining on their feet?

What silly questions, she chided herself. For half a century, she had dreamed about this day, and now it was here. She thought about pinching herself. What if she was still dreaming and would soon wake up as she had so many times before?

The Gentile and the Jew: A Divine Romance

"Mom...Mom?" Mike glanced in the rearview mirror, wondering if his mother had fallen asleep. She had been so quiet.

"Hmm?"

"I just thought I'd give you a little warning. We're almost there. Maybe a half mile or so."

"All right. I'm ready."

Yes, I'm ready. Hardly a day had gone by in fifty-three years that she hadn't hoped and prayed for this day, and yet she hadn't really believed it would ever come. Rachel inhaled a deep breath, slowly let it out and turned to gather up the photo albums she had brought along to show Sura pictures of her Mama and Papa. One album fell open to a yellowed black and white photograph of Rachel and her parents when she was ten, one of only a few of the three together. She was standing between them in her new white organdy dress, her doting Papa smiling down at her as she and Mama squinted into the camera lens. How well she remembered the special dress Mama had made. She had felt so pretty, all dressed up that day. But more than that, she remembered her Papa's smile and the warmth and security of his unconditional love.

"Oh, Papa," she whispered softly, "I found them. I finally found them."

Mike turned the wheel easily, pulling the white Toyota over to the curb in front of a typical Israeli apartment complex, characterized by flat roofs and that neutral limestone color which seems to be no color at all. Isaac got out of the car and walked around to open the door for Rachel, glancing back to check out the neighborhood. He had noted that in Israel, architecture seemed to be either ancient or fairly new, nothing in between, and Sura obviously lived in one of the newer developments built since 1967. Netanya itself was new for that matter.

Isaac opened the door and reached in to help Rachel from the car, amazed that she seemed to have grown more beautiful since discovering evidence that some of her family was yet alive. There was a glow about her now, an inner beauty released from the happiness and fulfillment deep within. He pulled her close and whispered in her ear, "This is it, love. This is your day. I love you, you know."

"Stay with me, Isaac." Her flashing green eyes smiled into his as she grasped his arm and held it tightly.

"I'm here where I'll always be, right beside you all the way."

"Come on, you two," called Mike, already hurrying toward the building. They followed the walkway around the side and through an open gate into the ground level of the two-story apartment complex.

Chapter Eighteen

"Sura lives on the second floor," said Mike. "We'll have to take the stairs. There are no elevators."

"Lead on, son. We're right behind you," replied Isaac.

Mike took the steps two at a time while Rachel and Isaac followed at a normal pace. About the time they caught up to him on the landing a door creaked loudly and a male voice called out, "Shalom! Welcome! Levana and Ima have been watching out the window for at least an hour; they saw you drive up." Aron walked quickly toward his guests, his arms extended to grab Mike's hand. He was grinning from ear to ear.

"Hey, man, good to see you." Mike shook Aron's hand and threw his other arm around his friend's shoulders. Rachel and Isaac waited, watching the two young men greet as if they had known one another all their lives.

When Mike moved aside, Rachel couldn't believe her eyes. Her son was right. Aron did look like Mike, only a bit shorter and leaner perhaps. They could have easily passed for brothers instead of second generation cousins.

"Mom, Dad, this is Aron Safron—your cousin, Mom."

Rachel couldn't move. She just stood there like a statue as Aron slowly walked toward her and reached for the hand hanging limply by her side. It was only when his fingers touched hers that she seemed to wake up, saying with a tearful smile, "Oh, my dear boy, I've waited a lifetime, and all I get is a handshake?"

Aron smiled into her familiar eyes, and throwing his arms around the beautiful woman, he tenderly responded, "Shalom, Rachel, my dear cousin."

"Ohhhhh," she softly groaned as she returned his warm embrace, touching her Papa's flesh and blood for the first time in her life, repeating his greeting over and over again in her mind—*Shalom, Rachel, my dear cousin. He means me! I'm someone's cousin!*

"Come," Aron said. He took her hand and gently led her down the hallway toward the apartment door which was standing slightly ajar. "Someone is waiting for you."

Levana had opened the door so she could see and hear every scene of the long-awaited reunion. She wasn't about to miss a thing. But as Aron approached, she opened the door wider and stepped aside, knowing she wasn't the one Rachel was desperate to see.

It was as if she was in a dream moving in slow motion. *Where have I heard that before*, she wondered? *Oh, yes, the Psalms. When the exiles returned to Zion, it was as if they were in a dream.*

Aron was speaking tenderly to a person in front of him. "Ima, your cousin Rachel is here. Rachel Liebowitz." He reached down and kissed his mother on the forehead and turned and walked around to stand behind her chair, still clutching her hand in his.

If Rachel was shocked by Aron's close resemblance to her son, she was literally stunned by the sight of the woman sitting regally, yet humbly, before her. Sura Liebowitz Safron slowly rose from her chair, squeezing her son's hand before she turned it loose and stepped forward. Rachel was staring into the brightest pair of green eyes she had ever seen other than her own. She couldn't believe it. Sura was not as tall as Rachel, but her lovely face was framed by the same auburn hair, though cut short with filmy bangs across her forehead. Their mouths were not alike, Rachel's more like her mother's, but the eyes and hair overshadowed all other differences. If Aron and Mike could have passed for brothers, their mothers looked more like twin sisters. It was eerie, but absolutely wonderful.

Rachel didn't think she had taken a step, but obviously she had because the two women were suddenly within inches of each other, staring into one another's eyes in amazement and wonder. Neither spoke as yet, their eyes grasping more than words could possibly express. It was only when Sura suddenly gasped and broke into sobs that Rachel pulled her into her arms and held on as if she would never let her go. *Thank you, God. Thank you, God*, she silently prayed.

Everyone in the room was crying, surrounding the two women like a protective fortress. Aron, Levana, Isaac, even Mike, were wiping tears from their eyes amidst trembling smiles and open sighs. Surreptitiously, tiny chuckles began to creep into the weeping, and suddenly, contagious laughter consumed the entire family. As usual, Levana's excitement emigrated to her feet, and she began to dance around the room, swirling from one to the other in what looked like a Middle Eastern square dance. Her constantly dangling anklets and bracelets jingled merrily, and along with the joyous laughter, they created a sense of celebration unparalleled in any of their lives up until today. Rachel and Sura finally pulled away just enough to look at one another again and like two giddy little girls playing *Peas Porridge Hot*, they clapped hands and giggled and laughed until they were literally exhausted.

"Come, Rachel," said Isaac. "Why don't you and Sura sit down before you collapse?"

"Oh, Isaac, I'm so sorry! I'm monopolizing her. Sura, this is my husband, Isaac Kramer."

Chapter Eighteen

For the first time since Rachel entered the room, Sura took her eyes off her and turned to greet her cousin's husband, offering him her hand and speaking broken English in that unique accent owned by Israeli sabras. "Shalom, Isaac. It is so good to finally meet you."

Isaac brought her slender hand up to his mouth with both of his and kissed it tenderly. "There are no words to express our happiness just in knowing you exist, Sura, and to have the opportunity to meet you is beyond our wildest dreams. You're almost as beautiful as my wife, dear lady."

Sura's wet face glowed, but no more than Rachel's as she stood beaming at her beloved husband and long-lost cousin. Mike kept swiping his eyes with the back of his hand. It had never occurred to him that he might need a handkerchief today. By this time, Levana had whirled into the kitchen and brought back last minute hot dishes for the table, filled the water glasses and prepared the wine and *challah*. All day, she and Sura had prepared for this night, wanting everything to be perfect. They would light the candles and welcome Shabbat together as the Liebowitz family for the first time in sixty-two years. She glided across the room and nuzzled her husband, whispering, "Everything's ready."

"It's almost twilight, everyone," Aron said with a smile. "Do you think we can contain our excitement long enough to gather around the table for the Shabbat blessings?"

They all laughed once again and began moving toward Sura's beautifully decorated table. "Aunt Rachel, why don't you sit next to Ima's place at that end, and Isaac can sit next to you. Mike and Levana on the other side and me at this end."

Sura Liebowitz Safron stood quietly at the head of the family table carefully placing a hand-painted blue silk scarf over her auburn hair. Taking the lighted *shamas* candle from its holder, she waited reverently, her sparkling green eyes drinking in the precious family now gathered for the first time around her table. Each face was a treasure, an overwhelming blessing she knew she didn't deserve. As her gaze moved to Aron at the other end of the table, she marveled at his resemblance to her dear father whom he had loved so much and patterned his life after. Yes, her only son would make a fine patriarch. He was already filling his beloved grandfather's shoes. And now there was another to help carry on the family heritage. Smiling into Mike's dark eyes, she couldn't help but nod her head affirmatively. Slowly, her eyes moved on to Levana, her daughter-in-law's beaming face reminding her that the hour had come. Purposely, she lit the two candles and began to sing,

The Gentile and the Jew: A Divine Romance

"Ba-ruch atah Adonai, Eloh-haynoo melech ha olam,
Asher ki-di-shaynu b'mitz-vo-tov, v' tzi-vaynu l' hi-yoht or l'goy-im,
v'nah-tahn lanu Yeshua Me-shi-khay-nu, ha-or la-oh-lahm."
"Blessed are You, O Lord our God, King of the Universe,
who sanctified us by your commandments and commanded us to be a light
for the nations and gave us Yeshua our Messiah,
the Light of the world."

Once again, tears of joy and thanksgiving were pouring down every face as Sura reached out for Rachel's hand, creating a chain reaction as each family member grasped the hand next in line all around the table. Sura and her son locked eyes for a second, and he instantly understood her meaning. Holding Isaac's and Levana's hands tightly, he began to pray.

"Father in Heaven, we praise You and give you Glory for the miracle You have performed in bringing this family together after being separated for over sixty years. In our hearts, this miracle is as great as when You brought our people out of the land of Egypt and into the Promised Land where we, incredibly, gather this night to welcome Shabbat and share our love for each other. Truly, we have come to a place of rest. We thank You, Almighty God, Ruler of Heaven and Earth. We give you praise. We offer our thanks, our praise and our prayer in the Name of Yeshua, our Messiah."

Aron then raised the *challah* to heaven saying,

"Baruch atah Adonai, Eloheynu Melech haolam,
hamotzi lechem min haaretz.
Blessed are You, Adonai our God, King of the Universe,
Who brings forth bread from the earth."

It seemed to Rachel as if the comforting sounds and aromas of this extraordinary Shabbat were gently lifted into the heavens by the power of familial love and sent backwards in time to the little bakery in Bucharest where Jakob and Joseph Liebowitz sat around a table with their own Mama and Papa, their young faces glowing as the light of the Shabbat candles filled the cozy room. *Yes, this is what it's all about…family…and love.*

When someone dies, the individual's loved ones feel as if time stops, at least until the initial shock begins to fade away. Things that are top priority one

Chapter Eighteen

day suddenly become minor annoyances the next, or so it seemed to Carrie Jernigan as she stood near the grave site of her best friend's mother, her eyes riveted on Emma who was sitting like a statue between her sister, Beth, and her fiancé, John Owens. The pastor was reading the twenty third psalm, his voice blending with the hum of the bumble bees in the thick quietness that seemed to envelope the graveside congregation. The quiet had been just as obvious in the church earlier and had pervaded Emma's home since her mother had died. Everyone spoke in soft tones, even whispers, as if the dead might be disturbed somehow by loud noises. But it was a peaceful quiet, thought Carrie, as she watched the gentle spring breeze ruffle Emma's curly blonde hair and dry the tears she was trying so hard to hold back.

Carrie pulled her eyes away from her friend for a few seconds, glancing around the cemetery that looked more like a beautifully landscaped park than a place for the dead. *Americans must spend millions of dollars each year to pretend death doesn't exist,* she mused. *We're all gathered here to honor the life of a very special woman, and yet most of us are sitting here in this fairy tale land like nothing's wrong. But everything is wrong. Emma doesn't have a mother anymore.*

Even though the family had known Jean Tate was terminally ill for nearly a year, they were still in shock. *Death is unreal,* thought Carrie, silent tears pouring down her cheeks. *It isn't normal. No matter how much someone suffers, we are never prepared for them to leave us. The younger the loved one is, the more life left unfinished, the less we're prepared to let go, the deeper the pain.* Emma's mother was not old enough to die.

Yesterday afternoon, Carrie had finally stolen a few minutes alone with Emma. They sat arm-in-arm in the reclining chaise on the patio overlooking the green hills of Tennessee to the east of Nashville, saying little but listening intently to each other's hearts. Out of the comfortable silence, Emma began to speak softly, "Machete."

"Hm? What did you say?" Carrie turned to look at her friend.

"Machete. It's a machete."

"I don't understand, Em. What's a machete?"

"That huge knife I've been trying to think of for days, the kind that's big and sharp and can slice a person in two with one quick whack."

"Why are you thinking about that?"

"Because that's what's happened. People keep trying to comfort me, especially John, and I know they mean well, and it honestly is a comfort to have them around, but I wish everyone would just give me a hug and keep quiet. No, I wish they'd shut up. They say the stupidest things that just make me feel worse. The dumbest one is, 'How are you?' How on earth do they think I am? What am I supposed to say? *Great?* I can't lie quite that badly, but I usually answer with something just as ridiculous like, 'I'm fine.' That's where the machete comes in. Yesterday afternoon, after more 'How are you's' than I could bear, I began to wonder how I could explain my true feelings if anyone really wanted to know, and that's when I envisioned the huge, sharp knife blade severing the lifeline between my mother and me. In one split second, a huge part of my heart and life was sliced away from me, and it hurts so badly I can hardly breathe for the pain." Emma was almost breathless, her quavering voice reduced to a whisper. "I...I know everyone sees me as the strong one, the daughter whose faith is as strong as her mother's," she sobbed, "and I know God is with me, and He's going to get me through this, but I certainly don't feel strong. I feel so weak that if He doesn't carry me through, I won't make it."

Carrie blinked back a flood of tears and squeezed her friend's arm a little tighter, reaching over to give her a light kiss on the cheek. She couldn't say a word and knew it was better if she didn't.

Now, she watched her friend trying to say good-bye to the person who had given her life. Suddenly, she envisioned the machete, too, and instantly, she realized that our umbilical cords are actually cut twice in our lives—the day we're born and the day our mothers die.

Oh, how she wished Mike were here. She missed him so, now more than ever. Carrie glanced down at the sparkling diamond on her finger, reminding her that the man of her dreams had sealed his love with a promise to love and cherish her forever. But he would never take her Mama's place. Never. No one could.

Back at the house after the funeral, Carrie offered to help the women from Emma's home church prepare lunch for the family and friends who gathered once more in their sorrow. But every time she asked what she could do to help, she was told to run along and that every thing was under control. Or, "You don't want to help, honey. You might ruin your nice dress."

She felt useless and terribly alone. Across the living room, Emma and her sister were talking quietly with the pastor. John Owens and Beth's husband were sitting on the sofa looking as if they were trying to think of something to say to each other, something to pass the time. Other friends and relatives were scattered around the large comfortable living room speaking in hushed tones. *They're probably discussing the service,* Carrie decided.

Suddenly, she couldn't stay there another minute. Slipping through the crowd as unobtrusively as possible, she tiptoed up the stairs to Emma's room and headed straight for the phone.

"Hello? Mama?"

Chapter Eighteen

The answering machine clicked in, and she heard her father's voice asking callers to leave a message.

"I just wanted to tell you how much I love you guys. My flight leaves at three tomorrow afternoon. I'll see you soon. I love you."

Disappointment added to Carrie's grief, pushing her to the brink of uncontrollable tears. She gulped back the sobs and fished the cell phone out of her purse, her hands trembling as she pressed all the right buttons to connect her to Mike.

"Shalom."

"Mike?"

"Yes? Carrie? It's good to hear your voice, honey, but you don't sound like yourself. Things are pretty bad there, huh?"

"Yes, it's terrible. Death is terrible. We got back from the funeral about a half hour ago, and I began to miss you and my family so much I thought I'd die if I couldn't talk to you. The women from the church are preparing lunch, so I sneaked off for a few minutes."

"How is Emma?"

"As good as can be expected. Oh, Mike, I don't know how she and Beth can endure this! I can hardly handle it myself, and I know that what I feel is nothing compared to the agony they're experiencing."

"Well, at least you're there for Emma. I'm sure your being there is a great comfort to her."

"I hope so. Emma and Beth wanted the service to be a celebration of their mother's life and a testimony of her close relationship with God, and it truly was, but...but somehow I just couldn't get into the celebration part. I kept thinking about how horrible death is and how permanent. That sounds silly, doesn't it?"

"Of course not. When we have more time, remind me to tell you about a sermon I heard when you and I were broken up during the holidays last year. It might help. I love you, Carrie."

"I love you, too," she whispered, her lips trembling. "Mike, I just have to get my mind on something else a little while." She wiped her eyes again. "I know. Why don't you tell me about your Mom's reunion with her cousin. With all this going on, we haven't had a chance to talk about it."

"I wish you could have been here, Carrie," said Mike. "It was certainly a once-in-a-lifetime experience, that's for sure. Probably once in a millennium! Mom's still walking around as if she's shell-shocked or something, but with a constant smile etched into her face. She and Aunt Sura talk for hours on end, each one filling in the blank years for the other, even the most painful parts.

The Gentile and the Jew: A Divine Romance

They laugh a while and then cry a while. Sometimes, they just sit on the balcony overlooking the Sea watching the sun go down, holding hands like little girls. Yeah, it's been awesome...just awesome."

"I'm so happy for you and your family, Mike."

"*Your* family," he quickly reminded her.

"Well, my future family, I hope."

"What do you mean, you *hope*?"

"I just mean I hope your Mom will one day come around and accept me as one of the family. I long for that day, Mike."

"I know. I do, too." His voice had changed tone, becoming low and tender. "Mom's always been so unbending in anything she felt strongly about, but particularly the Jewish thing. I understand it better now, but that doesn't make it any easier to deal with."

"Has she always been this way?"

"Oh, yeah! By the time I was a teenager, I had begun to rebel against what I saw as her demanding and controlling ways, but now...well, I realize she was only trying to keep us safe because she lived with so much fear. Of course, she may never give up her little Jewish mother thing, but she is changing. She's softened a lot, I can assure you. Anyway, just remember that I love you with all my heart and soul. At least they know how much we love each other now."

"Yes, I think they do. But your mother still can't accept you marrying me, and I don't know if she ever will. I've tried to understand, Mike. Honestly, I have. I've talked it over with my parents and grandparents for hours since I returned, and they've really been great in helping me see your Mom's point of view. Daddy has always frustrated me to no end playing devil's advocate in all our family debates, but he really got through to me this time. He's helped me understand that it would take a major paradigm shift in your mother's belief system for her to accept our marriage, and I just don't think that's likely to happen, Mike. Not in our lifetime. Short of an earthquake, that is."

"Speaking of earthquakes, I think Mom and Dad may have already been shaken up a bit."

"What do you mean?"

"Well, first there was the excitement of meeting Aron and Levana, then Mom and Dad flew over here to be reunited with her family, but found out about our engagement first. So, there still hasn't been much time for them to share what happened in Romania last December; not with me, anyway. I'm certain Mom and Sura have discussed that journey to great lengths. But I have talked with Dad. He and I have enjoyed quite a bit of time together since the reunion, and he's filled me in with bits and pieces while I've shown him around the country."

"What did he say?"

"Well, to make a very long story short, most of Mom's family have been believers since way back, somewhere around 1883 or so. Do you remember what I told you that day on the rocks at the beach? The story I had heard from Aron?"

"Uh, huh. But I guess I just assumed he meant his line of the Liebowitz family, the ones who emigrated to Israel."

"That's what I thought, too, but no, all of Mom's family in Romania were believers or whatever they called themselves. Before the Holocaust, that is. Dad thinks my grandfather either lost his faith in the Camps like so many others or, at some point, he decided to keep it hidden. But Dad also said that the old rabbi they stumbled upon in Bucharest spent hours with him and Mom explaining the roots of Messianic Judaism, even going back to the first-century Jewish disciples. Then he verbally drew a timeline throughout the centuries up to the present, assuring them that there have been thousands of Jews who believed Jesus was the Messiah and that those people honored their faith without giving up their Jewish identities, neither in culture nor even in religious observance. Dad said the old rabbi himself oversees a Messianic congregation in an ancient synagogue that looks and feels more Jewish than the one we attend in the states. They celebrate Shabbat, the feasts, all the holidays, same as we do."

"Sounds like what the early church must have been like."

"Yeah, I guess so. But, do you understand what I'm saying? Even though Mom and Dad certainly didn't agree with or even comprehend everything the rabbi tried to explain for hours on end, they came away wondering if true Christianity might not be as drastically different from what we believe as Jews as they had once thought. And listening to Dad's short and to the point highlights of their discussions with Abraham Wasserman, I can't help but believe that Mom has to be more open now, even though she didn't seem to be when you were here."

"I hope so, Mike. I hope so."

"Carrie?"

"Yes?"

"You seem to be forgetting something."

"What?"

"You said, 'Yes,' when I asked you to marry me. My recollection is that neither my proposal nor your acceptance was conditional to receiving Mom's blessing; although, of course, we want her blessing. You're hemmed in on all sides, my gorgeous bride-to-be."

She sensed Mike's grin over the thousands of miles that separated them. Laughing softly, she replied, "Oh, I don't know. I'm sure there's a way to weasel out of it if I use my woman's prerogative. I might just change my mind."

"Oh, no. You can't."

"And, pray tell why not?"

"For your information, a Jewish betrothal is just as binding as the wedding. You'd have to obtain a writ of divorcement to get rid of me."

Carrie burst out laughing. "Oh, great! Does that mean you're stuck with me, too?"

"Sure, it does. Are you disappointed?"

"Oh, no. I'm the happiest woman in the world. I love you so."

"And I love you, Carrie."

"Thanks, Mike. I feel better now."

Epilogue

Five months later...

The Jernigan family's eye valves were not just leaking, they were flooding profusely. Even the little ones were beginning to feel the emotions their elders had experienced from the time they had arrived in Israel five days ago, awed to be in the land of the Bible and even more awed that their Carrie was about to be married in Jerusalem, the Holy City they hardly realized existed outside the Bible.

"Tom, let me take one more look at you," said Catherine, straightening his tie for the third time today.

"Leave me alone, woman! I look good enough to eat already, Cat, and I'm not getting married anyway."

"Certainly not, Tom Jernigan. You're taken, that's for sure." She reached up to give him a quick kiss before the ceremony was to begin. "Oh, no, look what I've done, smeared lipstick all over your cheek!"

"Don't worry. I'll tell everyone you've marked me for life!" Tom started to hug his wife but quickly decided against it, knowing she would scold him for wrinkling their wedding clothes.

"Mama, Daddy, we're ready for you," called Michele, coming through the doorway of their room. "We're supposed to be with Carrie for the *Bedekken*."

"The what?" asked Tom.

"The *Bedekken*, Daddy. It's the veiling of the bride," said Michele, reaching up to straighten his tie.

The Gentile and the Jew: A Divine Romance

"Leave my tie alone. Your Mama has fixed it at least ten times."

"And, you look very handsome," said his oldest daughter, smiling slyly.

The three of them walked out together to join Carrie's brother, John, following him to the room where Carrie would wait with her family for the groom to come and veil his bride. Claire and Ron were tending all the children; including little Annie who was thrilled to discover that Mikey's Carrie had come fully equipped with five new playmates.

Catherine and Tom stopped short as they entered the room, astonished at the sight of their youngest child. She was sitting like a queen on her throne in the middle of the large room, dressed in a gorgeous white satin wedding gown adorned with white pearls and appliqués. In her arms were at least a dozen pink rosebuds and white peonies, mixed with soft white freesia. Her lovely long brown hair was shining, simple and flowing as Mike liked it best, a long white veil billowing from the crown of her head.

"You give new meaning to the word *radiant*, my dear sister," said John as Carrie received her family with a glowing smile.

"Oh, sugar, you're so beautiful!" Catherine exclaimed, the tears beginning to flow again. "No, no! I'm going to look terrible," she said, fumbling in her purse for a tissue.

"Listen!" Michele held up her hand to stop the chatter as the sound of the *shofar* increased its crescendo to a long, almost deafening blast, announcing the arrival of the bridegroom.

Suddenly, the double doors flew open.

Mike entered the room. He was accompanied on either side by his mother and father, Sarah and David following close behind. Attired in his wedding garments—a black morning coat, black slacks and the traditional white pleated shirt with black tie—Carrie's betrothed moved slowly but deliberately toward his bride, never taking his eyes from hers as he crossed the open room.

Solomon couldn't have been more handsome, she thought, her face beaming brighter than the light coming through the large windows. She stood regally and held out her hand as he approached her chair, remembering the night he had spoken the ancient love song to her, "*Arise, my darling, my beautiful one, and come away with me, for behold, the winter is past and gone and the sound of the turtledove is heard in the land.*"

He took her hand in his, pure love flowing out from his every pore—body, soul and spirit. She drank that love into every fiber of her being, still locked in his gaze and the gleam of his adoring smile.

There was nothing to say now. Their love said it all. Mike slowly and gently pulled the soft white veil up from behind her head and tenderly lowered it over

Epilogue

her face, identifying the treasured woman underneath as his very own. Then he turned and walked out of the room.

In the lovely garden far behind the seated guests and out of view, Rachel Kramer waited silently beside her handsome son. Isaac stood like a sentinel on his other side looking to Rachel as if he were Mike's older brother, not his father. As much turmoil as their family had been through in the past year—searching for her ancestry and roots in Romania, Mike's move to Israel, the subsequent discovery of family she never knew existed and the long struggle to accept their son's marriage to a Gentile—Rachel was thankful to admit that today she was finally at peace.

Fondly reflecting back to that incredible day in May when Mike introduced her to the Safrons, her eyes rested on Sura Liebowitz who already seemed more like a sister than a first cousin. *Oh, God, Your loving kindness endures forever*, she thought, tears forming at the thought of the miraculous blessing she been given in being reunited with her long-lost family.

The garden surrounding the wedding party and guests was breathtaking as everyone anxiously awaited the sound of the second *shofar*. Huge clusters of bright pink and purple bougainvillea naturally hung all down the walls, surrounding the meadow-like area as if they had been draped by an interior designer. Rachel couldn't have been more pleased with Levana Safron's diligence in coordinating all the preparations for her son's wedding. The delightfully energetic young woman had even catered most of the hors d'oeuvres for the banquet herself.

Scanning the beautifully decorated garden for Aron, her smile broadened when she spotted him blowing a kiss to his gorgeous wife across the heads of the one hundred or so guests. She was still amazed at his striking resemblance to Mike. Rachel laughed. Suddenly, it seemed funny that her tiny Jewish family was becoming so diversified. Mike was marrying a Gentile, her only relatives in the entire world were Messianic Jews, and there were Arabs scattered all through the wedding assembly, including one of the groomsmen, Salim Ahmed. *Who'd believe it? Certainly not Mama and Papa.*

"Ready?" asked Levana, startling Rachel as she came up behind the bridegroom and his parents.

"Yes! Let's get this show on the road!" said Mike, suddenly more nervous than he thought a groom should be.

The Gentile and the Jew: A Divine Romance

Levana laughed and waved to a guy standing near the *chuppa* where Abraham Wasserman waited patiently, as dignified as ever with his blue-striped prayer shawl across his shoulders, his long white beard mingling with its lengthy fringes. Rachel's heart warmed at the sight of the dear old man who had opened the treasure chest of the past, giving her riches far beyond those of this world. Oh, how happy she was that he had come from Romania to officiate the wedding ceremony. She couldn't think of another person in the world who was able to build the bridges needed for her son's marriage to Carrie. Her eyes caught his as she smiled, her mouth silently forming two powerful little words, *Thank you.*

The *shofar* blasted long and loud, announcing the sudden appearance of the bridegroom. Mike and his parents began the processional down the carpeted aisle between the two groups of guests, arriving to stand under the flower-strewn *chuppa* with Abraham Wasserman. Joy and tears abounded as they greeted the beloved old man with grateful smiles.

Following the groom and his parents ambled Mike's best friend, Jordan, all dressed up for the party and grinning happily, the incessant mischievous twinkle in his eyes more evident than ever. Then came Aron Safron followed by Salim Ahmed.

The odd couple, thought Rachel, smiling again.

And then there was David Klein, the son-in-law she and Isaac had accepted as their own son, trusting him explicitly in the Kramer Company and all family affairs. *My, he looks handsome today.*

The excellent quartet transitioned into another arrangement and suddenly, they all heard the most astounding voice begin to sing a tribute to the land in Hebrew,

> *"Yerushalaim, all of gold*
> *Yerushalaim, bronze and light*
> *Within my heart I shall treasure*
> *Your song and sight."*[23]

As the incredible tenor reached the finale's high note, tears and chills were competing all through the gathering of amazingly diversified guests. No one moved. The classical guitarist waited a few moments; then accompanied by the quartet, he began to finger the joyful melody of John Michael Talbot's instrumental, "The Wedding Dance."

Rachel was now in position to see everything, her thoughts wandering back to her own wedding day as she stood under the *chuppa* with Isaac and her

Epilogue

beloved Mama and Papa. She smiled at the precious memory as she watched her son's beautiful bride come into full view at the back of the garden, her mother and father stationed protectively on either side. In the past weeks and months, Rachel had many times thought that if she could see her own heart, it would look like tenderized meat, pounded by the butcher's mallet. Now, as she gazed upon her glowing daughter-in-law, she wondered how she could have ever been so hardhearted toward such a precious girl who obviously loved her son unconditionally. Yes, it would work. She just knew it.

As the jubilant music swelled, Michele, dressed in a soft, tea-length lavender gown, walked gracefully up the aisle, followed by Becca Brody, exuding her own unique beauty in the lavender dress that flowed softly about her long legs as she sauntered toward the *chuppa*. Next came Sarah, the most loving daughter any mother could have asked for, glowing in the pregnancy she and David had announced at the rehearsal dinner last night. Rachel was beginning to wonder if one could literally burst from too much happiness after years living in the valley of the shadow of death.

There were only three bridesmaids for four groomsmen, but Carrie hadn't wanted anyone to take Emma's special place on her wedding day. Her best friend's absence was the only low note of the festive wedding week, but everyone involved sympathized with her decision to stay in school, having dropped out of the spring semester about two months before her mother's death. *They are all good people*, Rachel thought, watching Mike catch sight of his cherished bride as she waited to begin the walk down the aisle to stand beside her beloved forever. Guests and family alike were in an excited, festive mood, the delightful music and the big grin on the groom's face spurring a contagious spirit of joy throughout the lovely garden.

Within seconds, the level of excitement rose even higher as little Annie Kramer came into full view, merrily walking, almost frolicking along the white carpet, happily dropping pink rose petals all along the way. She was adorable in her soft lavender dress, her light brown hair pulled up in a loose clip, bouncing curls flowing out of the ring of baby's breath circling the crown of her head. Finally arriving under the *chuppa*, she delighted everyone again by spinning around two or three times, trying to find the spot Levana had marked for her to stand. Ah! There it was! She placed her little foot on the marker and smiled up at her Mikey, pleased as punch. He mouthed, *What big eyes you have*, sending the little girl into giggles instantly reproduced across the captivated congregation.

The music stopped. The sudden silence was thick with anticipation. Mike pulled his shoulders up even straighter and breathed deeply. He was ready.

261

The Gentile and the Jew: A Divine Romance

A silver trumpet blasted its fanfare into the clear October air, the sound bouncing off the garden walls, reverberating endlessly throughout the shaded garden and over the stone walls throughout old Jerusalem.

And there she was.

The bride stepped forward.

She seemed to float lightly but deliberately through the seated guests, smiling at everyone, but never taking her eyes from her bridegroom's face. Her parents walked just a few paces behind so everyone could clearly see the long-anticipated bride. Though it seemed like hours to Mike, Carrie joined him under the *chuppa* in only a few seconds, softly trembling as she smiled up at him through the sheer white veil.

Rabbi Wasserman's deep voice resounded throughout the enclosed garden. "Who gives this woman to be married?"

Tom answered clearly, "Her mother and I."

He looked down at his daughter and whispered, "I love you to the last number, honey."

Under the white veil, her lips quivered as she softly replied, "I love you, too, Daddy...to the last number." Tom placed her hand in Mike's.

The music swelled once more, and Carrie began to slowly walk around her bridegroom, both mothers following after her. She encircled him seven times, fulfilling the words of Jeremiah the prophet, *"A woman shall encompass a man,"* before she took her stand at his right side.

Abraham began the blessing of the bride and groom in Hebrew and then in English:

"He Who is supremely mighty. He Who is supremely blessed.
He Who is supremely sublime. May He bless the groom and the bride."

As Mike traditionally lifted the veil to make sure the woman underneath was truly his betrothed, the entire assembly of wedding guests broke out in laughter at the sight of the couple's happy faces. But Mike couldn't help but think of the terrible night when Carrie had jumped out of his car, leaving him feeling as if she had taken all the light from his life. And now, even though many happy months had preceded this day, it seemed that in one brief moment, when he lifted back her veil, the light of his life fully returned. He was overjoyed, even more so when Carrie opened her mouth and began to sing her pledge, her clear high voice pure and sweet,

Epilogue

"Whither thou goest, I will go.
And, whither thou lodgest I will lodge.
Thy people shall be my people, my love.
Whither thou goest, I will go."[22]

That did it for Catherine, and most everyone else in the gathering, including a few onlookers who were delighted to have stumbled across a beautiful wedding in old Jerusalem during the Feast of Tabernacles. Throughout the brief message, or *Drashah*, and the repeating of the vows, she desperately tried to hold back a torrent of tears, her heart breaking that her youngest daughter was flying from the nest but, at the same time, so happy she thought her heart would surely burst. Blotting her nose again, she heard the rabbi ask, "Do we have a ring for the bride?"

Mike took the gold band from his father. Smiling down at Carrie, he said, "Behold, thou art consecrated unto me with this ring, according to the Law of Moses and of Israel."

Gently, he placed the ring on the third finger of her left hand.

"Do we have a ring for the groom?"

With tears of joy, Michele received Carrie's bouquet and handed her radiant sister the slender gold ring.

"Behold, thou art consecrated unto me with this ring, according to the Law of Moses and of Israel and of Israel's Messiah, Yeshua." Carrie slipped the wedding band on Mike's finger and held it tightly.

Abraham Wasserman's resonant voiced boomed throughout the small garden:

"O Magnify the Lord with me, and let us exalt His Name forever!"

What a nice Jewish ceremony, Rachel thought, listening to the rabbi give the seven blessings and then present the cup of the covenant to the bride and groom. Her heart was beating wildly as her fatherly friend pronounced, "Beloved guests, family and friends, as witness to the covenant of marriage according to the Law of Moses and the Law of the Messiah of Israel, I introduce to you Mr. and Mrs. Michael Jacob Kramer, husband and wife. You may kiss your bride, Michael."

A terribly unsophisticated "aaahh" echoed throughout the garden as Mike leaned down to meet Carrie's lips, quickly discovering it's very hard to kiss someone while grinning from ear to ear. In the end, the bride and groom laughed and hugged instead as Abraham Wasserman, in his thick Romanian accent, proclaimed the Aaronic Blessing, looking every bit like the High Priest himself. "May the Lord bless you and keep you. The Lord make His face to shine upon you and be gracious unto you. The Lord lift up His countenance upon you and give you peace. Amein!"

Bride and groom happily took a sip from the covenant cup together as husband and wife just before Mike threw the glass on the ground. "Bam!" He stomped it quickly, crushing the glass in the traditional act of remembrance of the destruction of the Holy Temple.

"Mazel Tov! Mazel Tov! Mazel Tov!" The entire assembly rose to its feet, cheering and clapping and yelling congratulations over and over as Mr. and Mrs. Michael Kramer nearly ran down the aisle, laughing and smiling and greeting their loved ones with thanksgiving and blessings. The quartet played joyfully, the tempo increasing by leaps and bounds as the level of rejoicing climbed to greater heights.

Before the attendants and parents could catch up, Luke and Abigail got so excited they jumped up to run after the newlyweds, Matthew, Nick and Blair quickly following the little ones. Annie ran in and out between the older attendants, hurrying to make sure she didn't miss whatever the children were up to.

By the time the wedding party got to the back of the seating area, the merry children were circling the bride and groom, happily singing and clapping and dancing, the delighted couple reveling in the children's loving celebration. Sisters and brothers and friends alike joined in, creating a larger circle around the happy couple. Tom was so moved, he turned to Catherine to give her a big hug, but she wasn't there.

Still standing under the *chuppa*, her motherly eyes taking in the entire panorama of joyous merrymaking, she gazed at her beautiful daughter and her daughter's new husband and began to softly sing,

> *"Ne'er was a lad so fitted to a maid*
> *As Carrie and Michael would prove.*
> *For their Messiah had brought them nigh,*
> *The Gentile and the Jew."*

Endnotes

1. Wesley, Charles, "Amazing Love" (1700s)
2. Jeremiah 31:15-17
3. This blessing is said on the first day of the Feast of Tabernacles, *Sukkot*, and other celebratory times as well. Art Scroll Siddur, "The *Shehecheyanu*"
4. The massacre of Jews in Jassy, Romania, in June of 1941 was only one of many like occurrences throughout Eastern Europe. I found this particular source invaluable. Braham, Randolph L., "The Tragedy of Romanian Jewry" (Columbia University Press, 1994)
5. The photographs published on these websites provided a window of reality into the horrors experienced by the Jewish people in Romania. These sites are excellent resources: www.motlc.wiesenthal.com/gallery and www.heritagefilms.com/ROMANIA, "Jewish History of Romania."
6. I found Kjaer-Hansen's in-depth biography of Joseph Rabinowitz a valuable source of information for this book. Written in 1995, Kjaer-Hansen has collected a treasure chest of resources on the life of Joseph Rabinowitz and merged them into one excellent source. Kjaer-Hansen, Kai, "Joseph Rabinowitz and the Messianic Movement" (Grand Rapids Michigan: William B. Eerdmans Publishing Co., and Edinburgh, Scotland: The Handsel Press Ltd., 1995)
7. This account of the baptism of Joseph Rabinowitz by someone who was there provided wonderful insight into the faith and personality of Rabinowitz. Mead, C. M., "The Baptism in Berlin of Joseph Rabinowitz

(A Russian Jew)" pp. 245-253 in *New Englander and Yale Review*, v. 52, iss. 240, W.L. Kingsley, etc., New Haven, CT, March 1890.

8.   I found many sources for the history of the *Struma,* the boat filled with Romanian Jews that sank off the shores of Istanbul in December, 1941. This website is the source I found to be simply factual and useful: www. history1900s.about.com, "The Boat That Never Made It."

9.   Matthew 6:23-24

10.   Hebrews 3:1

11.   Numbers 6:24, "The Aaronic Blessing"

12.   This song is one of the most well-beloved worship songs ever written, sung not only during the Christmas season but throughout the year. Wade, John, "O Come, All Ye Faithful" (1700's)

13.   John 8:36

14.   John 15:5

15.   I found this website to be a wonderful source of information on Messianic Jews through the centuries: www.israelinprophecy.org, "A Brief List of Some of the Most Famous Jews"

16.   Having studied the lives of many Jews who believed in Jesus as Messiah, I found the life of John Cournos to be of great interest. I used his most famous letter for this source. Cournos, John, "An Open Letter to Jews and Christians" (New York: Oxford University Press, 1938)

17.   This song was made popular by The Casinos. Loudermilk, John D., "Then You Can Tell Me Good Bye" (January, 1962)

18.   This song was made popular by Brook Benton. Grant, Earl, "The End" (1958)

19.   Song of Solomon 2:10-12

20.   Song of Solomon 1:2

21.   This song is perhaps the most beloved hymn of all times. Newton, John, "Amazing Grace" (1779)

22.   Ruth 1:16

23.   Along with *Ha'Tikva*, the national anthem of Israel, this song is held dear in the hearts of Jewish people everywhere. Shemer, Naomi, "Jerusalem of Gold" (1967)

To order additional copies of

Have your credit card ready and call:

1-877-421-READ (7323)

or please visit our web site at
www.pleasantword.com

Also available at:
www.amazon.com
and
www.barnesandnoble.com

CPSIA information can be obtained at www.ICGtesting.com
Printed in the USA
LVOW041630201111

255830LV00002B/34/A

9 781414 105802

mL   12-11